Also by D. M. Pirrone

No Less in Blood

The Hanley & Rivka Mysteries

Shall We Not Revenge

For You Were Strangers

D. M. Pirrone

 ALLIUM PRESS OF CHICAGO

Allium Press of Chicago
Forest Park, IL
www.alliumpress.com

This is a work of fiction. Descriptions and portrayals of real people, events, organizations, or establishments are intended to provide background for the story and are used fictitiously. Other characters and situations are drawn from the author's imagination and are not intended to be real.

Book/cover design and maps by E. C. Victorson

Front cover images:

Unknown woman, ca. 1870: courtesy of the Moorland-Spingarn Research Center, Howard University Archives, Howard University, Washington DC

Henry Mumbower, Tamaroa, Perry County, Illinois, ca. 1870: publisher's private collection

Adaptation of "daguerreotype picture frame" by Craig McCausland/Shutterstock

"vintage background with old paper and letters" by caesart/Shutterstock

ISBN: 978-0-9890535-9-4

Library of Congress Cataloging-in-Publication Data

Pirrone, D. M.
  For you were strangers / D. M. Pirrone.
      pages ; cm
  Summary: "In Chicago, in the spring of 1872, Irish detective Frank Hanley investigates the murder of a prominent Civil War veteran. Meanwhile, Rivka Kelmansky is reunited with her brother, Aaron, who is being pursued by those linked to a Civil War conspiracy"-- Provided by publisher.
  ISBN 978-0-9890535-9-4 (softcover)
  1. Irish Americans--Chicago--Fiction. 2. Jews--Chicago--Fiction. 3. Murder--Investigation--Fiction. 4. United States--History--Civil War, 1861-1865--Veterans--Fiction. 5. Conspiracies--United States--History--19th century--Fiction. I. Title.
  PS3616.I76F67 2015
  813'.6--dc23
                              2015034313

For my sons, Dave and Isaac,
who remind me of why I write in the first place

But the stranger that dwelleth with you
shall be unto you as one born among you,
and thou shalt love him as thyself;
for ye were strangers in the land of Egypt.

Leviticus 19:34

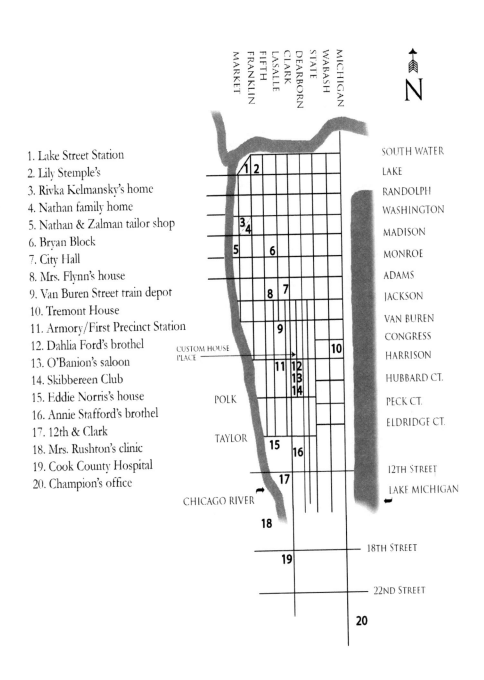

See Following Map For Westside Locations

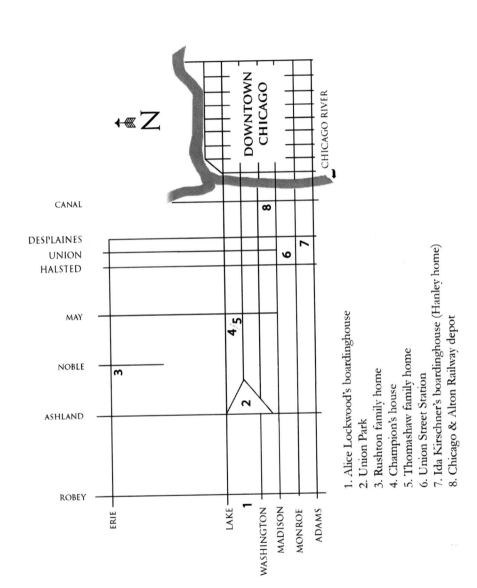

N

DOWNTOWN CHICAGO

CHICAGO RIVER

CANAL

DESPLAINES
UNION
HALSTED

MAY

NOBLE

ASHLAND

ROBEY

ERIE

LAKE
WASHINGTON
MADISON
MONROE
ADAMS

1. Alice Lockwood's boardinghouse
2. Union Park
3. Rushton family home
4. Champion's house
5. Thomashaw family home
6. Union Street Station
7. Ida Kirschner's boardinghouse (Hanley home)
8. Chicago & Alton Railway depot

Westside Locations

For You Were Strangers

ONE

May 1864

The small camp is quiet, the Union soldiers getting their dinner and settling in by their fire. Dorrie can smell frying salt pork and the rich, bitter odor of coffee. Saliva rises in her mouth, and she swallows. It's been a time since she tasted coffee. A time since she ate food she didn't pick or hunt, slept in her own bed, wore a pretty dress. She had so many once. Silk, lace, organdy...All before, all gone.

No time for such thoughts. She shakes her head to knock them loose. Maybe there'll be some coffee left after things are finished here. She grips her rifle. The stock feels hard and slick under her callused hands. The gun is who she is now. The gun makes her strong.

"Spread out," her brother Tom says, his voice barely audible, even though all six of them are standing close: Dorrie, Tom, his friend Jefferson Holt, and three others. None of them but Tom knows she's a girl. A woman, who should've been a bride last winter—but then word came of her fiancé dead at Gettysburg, and days after that the Yankee soldiers on her family's land, in her home. A swarm of them in blue, like the locusts in the Bible. She peers through the darkness toward the light of the camp. The Yankees took everything she knew and loved. Left her nothing. *Made* her nothing. Until Tom came home and showed her how to fight, gave her back her pride, along with the men's clothes on her body and the rifle in her hand.

1

Tom motions for their little band to surround the camp. Not many to deal with. Five men. A foraging party sent out in advance of a larger army, or scouts hunting bushwhackers—the Yankees' name for Dorrie and Tom and others like them who do God's work by night. The irony of that appeals to her—the hunters becoming the hunted, not knowing they've found their prey until the bullets find their mark. She keeps to the thin tree line, moving fast without sound. She's lost track of Tom and the rest in the dark. She moves another few feet, then stops and waits.

A hoot owl's cry breaks the quiet. Rifle fire splits the night. Dorrie watches her target go down—a blue-clad soldier with a long brown beard, thrown forward off the log he was sitting on, her bullet buried in his neck. The other Union soldiers dive for the shadows. Dorrie reloads. Not fast enough. Answering fire spits back, and she hears a familiar voice cry out. She raises her rifle and aims at the nearest patch of shadow. With luck, she'll account for two dead Yankees tonight.

A hand jerks her gun away. Something crashes against her head and darkness engulfs her.

∞

"I should kill you where you sit." The Yankee soldier crouched in front of her wears an officer's bars on his shoulder, just above a pale blue cloth patch shaped like a crescent moon. She can see it, and his face, in the light from the lantern beside him. He has blunt-cut hair, butternut brown; an old knife scar across one sharp cheekbone, just above his full beard and mustache; long, straight nose; hazel eyes, deep set. The eyes burn with hatred and contempt.

"I'm dead anyway. Go ahead and finish the job." She stares past him as she says it, at the two men standing behind him. Farther away, near the campfire, she can hear moaning. Another Yankee? Tom? Terror bolts through her at the thought of Tom, wounded. Or dead. He can't be dead. He promised he'd stay with her. He's all she has left.

The tree trunk feels solid against her back, the rough bark poking through her baggy shirt and the extra strip of linen wrapped tight

2

around her chest. The ropes that bind her wrists behind her and to the tree chafe against her skin. She does her best to ignore the pain. She knows in her bones that Tom and the others are out there, in the dark, waiting for the right moment to shoot this bastard down and get her free. She pulls against the ropes. The tree bark scrapes her hands. Where is Tom? Where are Holt and the rest? Why is she still sitting here on the damp ground, a prisoner of enemy soldiers?

The wounded man moans again. "Billy," the hard-faced Yankee officer says.

"Aye, Captain." The soldier on his left—beardless, black-haired, looking scarcely older than Dorrie's own twenty-two years—nods and moves away to tend the injured. The way he carries himself seems familiar, but only for a moment.

She can see beyond the captain now. Two bodies lie on the ground—one near the fire, the other closer to Dorrie and the soldiers, but still partway inside the circle of firelight. The first body wears blue. A white bandage splotched with red crosses the sleeve high on one arm. The Yankee named Billy squats near him and checks the dressing. He takes a scrap of cloth from his pocket and gently wipes the man's forehead.

She wants to avert her eyes from the second body, but she can't. That blank-eyed face turned toward her, that curling red-gold hair. She fastens her gaze on his fingers, curving upward from the dirt next to his fallen gun, and tries not to look at the gaping wound in his chest. Tom. Suddenly the warm night feels cold as the dead of winter.

"We don't do things that way." The captain sounds like he wants otherwise. "You'll be brought back to the regiment, then to a brig. After that you'll stand trial for treason. In the meantime, you'll tell us what you know of the other bushwhackers hereabouts." His smile belongs on a skull. "If we like what we hear, we'll tell them to kill you fast. One bullet instead of the rope."

"I'm a loyal Confederate citizen." She tears her gaze away from her brother's corpse. "You're the ones committing treason. You and your tyrant Lincoln."

The next heartbeat, there's a blade at her throat. The captain leans close, pressing it against her skin. "A tyrant would kill you here and now." The blade shifts from flat to edge. It bites into her neck, brings a warm trickle of blood. "A tyrant would be your judge, jury, and executioner for what you've done tonight."

Fresh terror sweeps through her. She can't die like this, trussed to a tree while a Yankee slits her throat. Bleeding out like a slaughtered hog, like—

The metal edge presses deeper. His hot breath chokes her. She's shaking as if with an ague, her sight blurred with tears. The hillside, the tree at her back, they're gone. There's only the blade and the face next to hers, the blue uniform, the body heat and odor of the man who holds her life in his hands. Words burst out, torn from deep inside. *"Don't touch me!"*

"Captain." She's barely aware of the soft voice, the figure at the captain's shoulder. Another bluecoat, she can't tell which. "Captain. Ben."

For a moment, no one moves. Then firelight flashes in her eyes as the blade flicks upward. New fire burns an inch below her jawline. She gasps as warm blood seeps downward. Slowly. It takes her a moment to realize what that means, that he hasn't killed her.

The captain wipes his blade on the grass. "Hanging's good enough." He stands and walks away, tossing a few words over his shoulder toward the soldier who spoke his name. "We'll see to Carroll's body in the morning. Billy, take first watch."

"Aye, sir," he says.

Slowly, her breathing returns to normal. Her neck throbs where the Yankee captain cut her. Dully, she watches the soldiers set out their blankets and roll themselves up. The one named Billy fills a tin cup with coffee and drinks it, then douses the fire. In the few moments it takes for her eyes to adjust, she hears him walk over to her and sit down a few feet away.

The chirping of crickets fills her ears. Even the breeze has died. Safely hidden by the dark, she lowers her head and weeps silently for Tom. She strains against the ropes, suddenly enraged that they should keep her from his side, from cleansing that terrible wound and closing his dear eyes. Enraged too that Jefferson Holt is gone, the other bushwhackers are gone, vanished into the night like the cowards they are. Especially Holt. He was Tom's friend. Of them all, he should have stayed. She could pray, but the will to do it won't come. She can't feel God through the anger that burns like lye in her stomach, and the cruel helplessness she swore she'd left behind.

A sound escapes her, a strangled cry hissed through her teeth. She hears the watching soldier stir, sees his outline in the starlight.

"You need water?" His voice is flat, empty.

"No." She wants to scream it, strike like a bullet with her fury, but she also doesn't want to give him the satisfaction.

"You all killed a good man."

"People die in war." But not Tom. Never Tom. He *promised*. She wants to curl up around her anguish and howl it into the earth. Instead, she bites her lip so hard she tastes blood. She will not let this Yankee see her pain. She's betrayed enough weakness tonight.

He moves close, grabs her chin and tilts her face upward, stares at her for a long time. Then his hand falls away. "Dorrie. Dorcas Whittier."

She rubs her chin where his fingers dug into it. This Yankee, this stranger, knows her name. Recognizes her. Impossible. "Who are you?"

The answering silence is so long, she wonders if he'll ever break it. Maybe he'll just walk away, leave her alone. Then he speaks. "Billy. Tom and I gave you rides on our shoulders. Ada did, too. Until your father sold her."

She remembers him now. In his uniform, with these white Northerners, she'd taken him for another of them—but he's Nigger Billy, all right. He's grown to a man, but she can still see in him the thin, high-yellow boy with the wavy black hair. Not quite so big as Tom, but strong enough to swing her high and make her shriek with laughter. The boy whose clever fingers whittled her tiny birds from cedar chips, and whistles they all blew until Billy's mother made them stop. He'd been another brother, slave or no. Then one day, he was gone.

Until she says them, she doesn't know the words are going to come out of her mouth. "We took care of you. And you left us."

He stalks away, toward the remnant of the fire. For a moment she wonders if he'll come back, but then she sees him returning. He stops next to her, bends down, and with a strip of cloth swipes the blood from her neck. A rough touch, as if he'd like to hurt her but won't let himself. Then he drops two objects at her feet. She peers at them. One is a canteen in a leather bag, the other a flat wrapped packet. With her hands bound, she can't reach them.

"You'll heal up," he says, in that empty, hard voice. "Sunrise'll come about seven hours from now. You best be long gone by then."

He walks away again and settles down halfway between her and the sleeping soldiers. Slowly, she turns one wrist until her fingers feel the rope. She explores the thickness of it, the shape of the knot, the ridges in the bark.

She twists her hands in the ropes, back and forth, working to beat the dawn.

TWO

April 24, 1872

The body lay sprawled near the open bedroom door like a discarded rag doll. Except rag dolls don't lie in pools of their own blood, wide and dark and congealed across the floor. The smell of it, and a worse odor, lingered in the air. Detective Frank Hanley swallowed and put a hand to his nose, then moved further into the room. Behind him, Officer Rolf Schmidt swore quietly in German. "*Verdammt.* Poor bastard."

Covering his nose didn't help much. Hanley walked to the nearest window and flung it open. Cool air touched his face and ruffled the thin muslin curtains. The fresh morning breeze mingled with everyday outdoor sounds—a passing horsecar a block away, birdsong, the distant whistle of a train somewhere to the north. The latter noise came often now, with the rail sections rebuilt that the Great Fire had destroyed. Like many Chicagoans, Hanley hadn't realized until the whistle-shrieks returned just how much he'd missed them. Five thousand passenger trains a day, he'd read in a paper somewhere, and a thousand freight. The city was coming back. He stuck his head out the window and breathed deep, then turned to face the murder scene.

The dead man had fallen face down. The reddened blade that killed him stuck up through the back of his shirt. His left hand was half-clenched, his right hand open. He wore no shoes. A pair of black leather boots stood a few feet away from him, one on its side. Apart from the dark pool that had spread from beneath the corpse, Hanley saw no other blood—no drops or smears, or anything that looked like a footprint.

He took out his sketchbook and swiftly drew the body, then beckoned Schmidt over. "Help me turn him."

The limbs stayed rigid as they moved the corpse. Rigor mortis had set in. The victim's shirt was unbuttoned, though not his trousers. Blood had soaked both, most likely as he lay on the floor. A ridged brass hilt as thick as Hanley's two thumbs protruded from the base of the ribcage. The sight of it gave Hanley a cold jolt of recognition.

"Bayonet," he said. "Remington, sixteen-incher. He'd have gone fast if our killer knew what he was doing." He hoped that was the case. One quick thrust, straight up to the heart. Otherwise, a slow and agonizing death as the victim drowned in his own blood. Hanley suppressed a shudder at the thought. He'd seen men die like that in the war. Done for a few himself, the hardest ones to let go of.

Schmidt let out a low whistle. "Somebody sure don't like this guy. We looking for a fellow soldier?"

Grimly, Hanley studied the bayonet. "This could just as easily belong to our victim. He might've brought it home when he mustered out."

The dead man—as they'd learned earlier from his cleaning lady, Mrs. Flynn—was Ebenezer Champion. "Captain Champion, don't you know," she'd said, looking pale but composed when they'd met her on the front steps half an hour earlier. "Served with the Eighty-Second Illinois Infantry. Got through the war just fine, and now to die like this. A fine man. Always gives me extra pay at Christmas, asks after my old Pat and our boys. My Pat's alive today because the captain paid for the doctor when he took a bad chill last winter. What sort of devil'd do the man like that?"

The neighbor who'd come to fetch them—in his late thirties by Hanley's guess, with a crumpled collar and looking as if he rarely got much sleep—had confirmed her account of the body's discovery. Mrs. Flynn came to his house in some agitation, he said, after finding Captain Champion's front door partway open. Fearing a robbery, she'd not wanted to venture inside alone. Upon entering the house together, they'd seen no sign of any disturbance. The smell, however...here, Mr. Thomashaw cleared his throat. He'd grown up on a farm, he said, and helped slaughter pigs as a youngster. He knew the odor of blood.

They'd gone upstairs to the master bedroom—Mrs. Flynn two steps behind him, unwilling to spare her nerves despite his caution to her—and found...well, Detective Hanley and his officer knew what they'd found. Would the detective please excuse him? He was feeling indisposed. If the police wished to talk with him further, he would gladly oblige—but just at the moment...

Seeing the green in his face, Hanley took his proffered calling card and let him go. Mrs. Flynn they had likewise sent home, after her heartfelt promise of further cooperation should it be needed. "It must have been some lunatic," she said before she left. "Though what a person like that would be doing in a fine neighborhood like this, I surely don't know."

Hanley glanced away from the bloodied bayonet and opened his sketchbook. A break from the sight of the thing was welcome. "Look around the room carefully," he told Schmidt. "Note everything down. Anything might be important."

Schmidt nodded. He took a small notebook from his coat pocket as he moved away.

Hanley turned back to the corpse and sketched the bayonet protruding from it, laying down the angle and position in a few swift strokes. Seeing the body and weapon as a pattern of lines on paper kept his instinctive revulsion at bay. Next, he drew the corpse's face—eyes frozen wide in what might have been shock, jutting nose, well-trimmed beard and mustache framing the partly open mouth. A thin scar, as if from an old knife wound, snaked across one cheekbone. The beard and hair were light brown and short, the empty eyes hazel. He looked again at the body position. "Whoever stabbed him must have been near the door. Got him right after he came through it."

"Housebreaker?" Schmidt said, then shook his head. "*Nein.* Guy like that brings his own knife or whatever."

"With his shirt undone and stocking feet, it looks like he was turning in for the night." Hanley glanced toward the bed. The sheets were turned down, but the bed hadn't been slept in.

"Had a woman with him, maybe?" Schmidt scowled at the bayonet. "But what woman stabs a man with a thing like that?"

"A strong one, that's for certain. If it was a woman."

Schmidt continued inspecting the room as Hanley tucked his sketchbook away. Carefully avoiding the blood pool, he knelt by the body, grasped the bayonet and tugged. Pulling it out took effort. He laid it on the floor and studied the wound. No fresh blood welled up. "Been dead awhile. This must've happened sometime last night." That fit with the presence of rigor. Hanley glanced at the left hand. "Could've had ahold of something. I wonder what."

He watched Schmidt bend down by the dresser and pick up a small, square object. Schmidt held it up, and Hanley saw it was a gold cufflink. Its mate sat on the dresser top, bright against the dark wood. "Fell down," Schmidt said. "Or got knocked down." He eyed the dresser's surface. "Hair comb, nail scissors, half-dollar, and some pennies." He set the cufflink next to its twin and returned to his task.

Hanley stood and quickly searched the room. An empty bracket on the wall opposite the bed told him where the bayonet had come from. Interesting that Champion kept it where it would be the last thing he saw before dropping off at night. The nightstand was empty, except for a water glass on top and an oddly shaped key in the drawer. Not a door key, more like one to a strongbox or a safe. He kept an eye out for any such thing as he continued his search. The victim's pocket-watch was laid away in the dresser. He found Champion's service revolver, gleaming with fresh oil, in its case on a shelf in the wardrobe.

"Cufflinks again," Schmidt said. He was standing by a shirt rack. He lifted the sleeve of the dress shirt on it, and Hanley saw a glint of gold. "Thief don't leave those behind."

"No," Hanley agreed. "Looks like this was personal."

C３

After Schmidt went to fetch some men from the nearest police station at Union Street, Hanley wandered back through the house. He went to Champion's study, a comfortable room that looked well used. No safe in sight, unless one was built into the wall. He walked over and lifted the single painting behind which a safe might be concealed, but saw nothing. A plump armchair, its upholstery slightly worn, stood near the front window where it caught the morning light. A slender volume lay on a small, round table nearby. Hanley picked up the book. *Drum-Taps*, by Walt Whitman. A ribbon marked a page, well thumbed from the ease with which the book fell open just there in his hands. He read a few lines.

> *Who are you dusky woman, so ancient hardly human*
> *With your woolly-white and turban'd head, and bare bony feet?*
> *Why rising by the roadside here, do you the colors greet?*

He set the book down and glanced around. Bookshelves covered the far wall, crammed with volumes of varying sizes. A side table held a crystal decanter and glasses. The decanter was half-full of tawny liquid. Hanley walked over and sniffed it. Whiskey. Only one glass had recently been used.

In the middle of the room was a double desk with a chair drawn up on either side. The desktop held an oversized blotter and a capped inkwell, with two pens pointing toward the left-hand chair. The drawers had no locks, and their contents—more pens, stationery, blank paper, and bills, all organized with precision—appeared undisturbed. One item briefly snared Hanley's attention, a handbill advertising a reunion of the Eighty-Second Illinois Infantry at Farwell Hall near Clark Street—but the date was last August, before the terrible fire in October. Kept as a memento, most likely.

A brief trip through the dining room and kitchen showed evidence of company for supper—plates and silverware for two, fry pans with the remnants of scrambled eggs and sliced potatoes fried in bacon fat. A guest, and apparently not a drinker. Who?

The sound of wagon wheels outside told Hanley the patrolmen from Union Street had arrived. He let them in and led them upstairs with orders to take the bayonet as well as the body, then followed them out with their sheet-wrapped load and fell into step beside Schmidt as they all left the house. The breeze outside smelled of lilacs, a welcome change from the odor of blood. Two steps ahead of him on the flagstone walk, Schmidt halted, then scrabbled in the grass. When he straightened, Hanley saw a gold chain with a ring on it dangling from his hand, the bright metal flashing in the sunlight.

"This belong to Champion?" Schmidt asked. "Or someone else?"

Hanley held out a hand. Schmidt gave him the jewelry. The thin chain had snapped near the clasp. The ring itself was a thick gold band edged with twined leaves. In a deep groove down its center were several strands of dark brown hair woven into a narrow braid.

"A mourning ring," Hanley said. Wealthy people often bought them as mementos of the dead. They were made to hold a lock of the departed loved one's hair, enameled or preserved under glass, so the grieving survivor could wear it in memory. He slid the ring off the chain and tried it on. It met slight resistance at the second knuckle. He slipped the ring off again and eyed its underside. Tiny, graceful lines and whorls made a brief inscription, too small for clarity. "I can't read what's here. We'll need a look at it with Will Rushton's viewing contraption."

"More to find out," Schmidt said. He sounded eager for the challenge.

Hanley grinned as he pocketed the ring and chain. "I told Moore you'd make a good detective."

"Soon as a place opens up, *ja*."

They reached the wagon. Hanley swung himself up in the back. He and Schmidt took seats at the rear of the right-hand bench that ran the wagon's length, keeping their distance from the sheet-draped corpse. No bloodstain on the cloth—Champion must have bled out overnight. A twinge of pity ran through him. As Schmidt had said, poor bastard.

"I'll let you know what Rushton tells me," Hanley said. Schmidt's patrol shift started soon, making the long trip to the morgue and back out of the question for him.

Schmidt nodded. "Tell the sergeant thanks for the chance." For a moment, he looked shy. "If I make detective...with the extra money, my Liesel and me can get married. You will come?"

"Happy to. With every man in the *ceilidh* band and as big a bottle of whiskey as I can lay hands on."

Schmidt shook his head in mock dismay. "You Irish," he said, as a grin crept across his broad face. "You don't know yet, nothing beats a good German beer?"

THREE

Rivka sat back on her heels, rubbed an arm across her sweating forehead, and surveyed the wet kitchen floor. The freshly scrubbed boards gleamed in the late morning sunlight. The breeze coming in through the windows would dry them by the time she finished with her girls' English class in the afternoon.

Her arms ached from the past hour's labor, but for once she hardly minded. It felt almost pleasant to see how clean the room was. A wry smile tugged her lips at the notion of taking satisfaction, however slight, in a clean floor. Another new experience since the bitter winter's end. *Mameh would be proud,* she thought as she set down the scrub brush by the bucket of wash water. *Papa, now...*

The thought of her father brought a pang of loneliness, still sharp after nearly three months of grieving. Even the full year of *shneim asar chodesh,* mourning for a parent, hardly seemed like enough. She brushed her hair out of her eyes and stood. It felt good to straighten her legs. She looked around the kitchen. Everything was swept and scrubbed that needed it, everything put away that should be. When Tanta Hannah came over, as she did every day, she would find all in order. *That should sweeten Onkl Jacob.*

She lugged the bucket to the back door and tossed the dirty water out into the yard. Across from the house stood the *shul,* its straw-yellow wood rising from patches of spring green. The harsh winter had weathered it less than she'd expected, the house too. Beyond the shul, between rebuilt houses and storefronts, she caught glimpses of carts and wagons bustling along Franklin Street. Their little riverfront neighborhood was busier now, reviving along with the rest of the city. Onkl Jacob spent more time than ever at his tailor shop, he and Moishe working extra hours every day except Shabbos—or so Tanta Hannah said, with a meaningful look in her eye whenever she spoke Moishe's name.

Rivka set the bucket down. Onkl Jacob hadn't wanted her to stay here after Papa's murder. "Alone? A girl by herself, with no one to look after her? How should you live like this, Rivkaleh?"

"I'm twenty-four. I can look after myself."

"No, Rivka. Such things are not done. You will come to us. There is no more to be said."

"Onkl Jacob." She had tried to be reasonable. "How should I live in your house? There isn't room."

"You can share with the girls."

"Four in one bedroom, when it's crowded with three?" She shook her head. "I am well enough in my own home, with you and Tanta Hannah next door, not even five steps away."

"An unmarried girl does not live on her own." His voice had taken on a stubborn edge. "You will stay with us until your mourning time is over. The house will keep until your brother returns or you can live in it with a husband. That is all I have to say."

We don't know if Aaron will ever return, she'd thought, but knew Jacob would not want to hear it. Ten years earlier, her brother had run off to war and they'd heard no word of him since, not even after the fighting ended and the soldiers came home. Gradually, painfully, she and Papa had learned to accept that Aaron was likely dead, one of countless Union soldiers buried or simply left on a battlefield somewhere in former rebel territory. "I am staying in Papa's house, Onkl Jacob. In *my* house. With my memories of him." *And of Aaron.* Where once she might have raised her voice, she kept it quiet and steady. "You and Tanta Hannah are always welcome. But I will not abandon my home."

Of a husband, she said nothing. She knew Jacob expected Moishe Zalman to speak with him about her. After three years of shy not-quite-courtship, it was high time. With Papa's death, Onkl Jacob was now the closest she had to a father. But until Moishe actually did something, she refused to think about it, Tanta Hannah and her pointed remarks notwithstanding.

Onkl Jacob gave in, as she knew he would. It was either that or have her carried to the Nathans', and he had no wish to go that far. The Nathan girls had backed her up—especially Tamar, for which surprise Rivka felt grateful. Though not such a surprise as all that—Tamar already shared her room with two younger sisters, and would not have welcomed the equivalent of another. Especially not Rivka, her rival for Moishe's affections.

"You're welcome to them," Rivka muttered as she dusted off the top back step and sat. She would need to make dinner soon to share with Tanta Hannah, then change to a clean dress for school, but just for a moment she wanted to sit and feel the sun on her face. Poor Moishe. Growing up with Fray Zalman for a mother would have pressed the spine out of sterner souls than his. Rivka couldn't work out why he wanted *her,* anyway. She wasn't a beauty, she couldn't make a decent loaf of challah, she still mostly hated housekeeping, and she always felt too restless for any place she was in. Except with her students, or in Papa's study, reading and talking. About life, about faith, about things that mattered. Did Moishe talk about such things? He must think about them sometimes. Would he talk about them with her? Could he even imagine doing such a thing with a woman?

A gust of wind brought her the smell of horse. She wrinkled her nose. There must be something the matter with her, that she would wonder such things about a prospective husband. And that she didn't mind being unmarried at her age...much. She should ask Moishe what he thought about spiritual things or something else important sometime, just to see what would happen. He would blink his owl eyes at her and be shocked. The idea made her laugh, which brought a twinge of shame. She shouldn't mock him. He was a good man, kind and considerate. *With a terrible mother,* she thought, and laughed some more. It felt good to laugh again after the awful events of the winter.

She looked across the sun-drenched yard. The mud and snow had given way to young grass and weeds that spread over the soil in a green haze. Here and there, wildflowers made dots of color—blue, purple, yellow, white. Gazing at the bright new growth and the sun-warmed synagogue walls above it, she found herself thinking of Hanley. Of him standing on the boardwalk that last day, looking back toward the house where he'd left her as if he meant never to look away. That day had been sunny, too, the air softer than it had felt in weeks.

Warmth rose in her cheeks. She stood, stretched, and went back inside. She picked her way across drying sections of floor until she reached the stove, still warm from the banked fire, took the dairy fry pan from its iron hook, stirred the coals under the nearest stove lid, and set the pan on it. Butter next, from the icebox—a small lump set to melt while she plucked potatoes and onions from nearby baskets. She took a knife from a drawer and began to slice the onions. Detective Frank Hanley was the last person she should be thinking of. What they had shared—the search for the truth of her father's death, the danger—was over now. He had no part in her daily life. If she were sensible, she should hope he never did.

She blinked away the onion sting, then laid the slices in the melted butter and picked up a potato. A knock at the front door startled her into dropping it. Tanta Hannah was early. She retrieved the potato, moved the fry pan off the heat, and went to answer the door.

Three people stood on the front step. Two were strangers—a tall woman in a blue calico dress, and a boy some twelve or thirteen years old. Both had black wavy hair and skin the golden brown of pulled taffy. The man with them—she drew breath to speak, but couldn't utter a sound.

"*Shalom aleichem*, Rivka," he said. His smile belied the anxiety in his eyes.

"Aaron." His name left her lips without conscious intent. The sound of it in her ears gave it reality. Gave *him* reality, standing here in front of her after a decade's absence. With a mulatto woman and child. *What is he doing here, with these people?*

He glanced at the woman and boy, then looked back at her and spoke in English. "May we come in? I need to see Papa."

The floor seemed to drop from under her feet. She gripped the doorjamb as sudden tears blurred her view of Aaron's worried face.

She said his name again, reached toward him. She couldn't manage more. Couldn't do anything but hold tight to his fingers, warm as they closed over hers, while a distant part of her wondered how to tell him Papa was dead.

FOUR

At the morgue, Hanley found Will Rushton in the empty inquest room, finishing the paperwork on a corpse. "This poor girl was run over at a train crossing," Will said. Sadness deepened the lines of his face. He'd been police surgeon before Hanley first wore copper's blue, yet he still saw in each dead body the living person he or she once was. Hanley respected him for that, as well as for his skill. "Mangled beyond recognition. All we've got to identify her is a silver bracelet she was wearing and a birthmark on her right shoulder. It's going to be hell for the family." He signed the paper and stood. "What've you got for me?"

"Murder," Hanley said as they walked down the short hallway to the examining room. "Ebenezer Champion. A captain in the Eighty-Second Illinois Infantry. Stabbed with a bayonet. Rolf Schmidt and I found it sticking out of him."

Shock crossed Will's face. "Good God." They reached the examining table, and Will laid a hand on the sheet that covered the corpse. After a moment, he drew it back in careful folds. From the spareness of his movements and the tense line of his shoulders, Hanley had a sense he was holding himself in check.

A memory nagged at him, of an evening at a nearby tavern where he, Will, and a few other Lake Street coppers had traded war stories. "Weren't you in the Eighty-Second? I thought you said, once."

Will nodded. "Company A." He took a slow breath. "Captain Champion was my squad commander."

"I'm sorry." Inadequate words, but they were all Hanley had. "Did you keep in touch?"

19

"Not since muster out." Another brief pause. "He was a lawyer. Civil cases, probate and such. My uncle may have worked with him on occasion." He gave a thin smile. "You know how it is...all the lawyers seem to know each other, at least by reputation."

"What was he like?"

Will made a final fold, leaving the top portion of the body exposed, and stared into space. "A good man, though he could be ruthless when he had to. Especially against the Rebs. We knew we could trust him to watch out for us, spend our lives as dearly as if each were his own."

"Well off, I'd guess, from where he was living." Enough to buy his way out of service, probably, yet he hadn't. Hanley thought of the Whitman poem in Champion's study, about the dusky woman greeting the colors. "Was he strictly a Union man, or did he go in for abolition?" Not many of the latter in Hanley's own regiment, the Twenty-Third Illinois Infantry. Most of the men in the Chicago Irish Brigade could have cared less about slavery, and some resented the Negroes for being the cause of the war. They'd fought for the Union, nothing more. Ending slavery just happened to be part of it.

"I can't say. He only spoke of it the once. On a night..." The bleakness of Will's expression deepened. "In the spring, it was. In '64. Our squad lost a man, hunting bushwhackers, and we feared losing another who took a shoulder shot. By the time we could get him back to the regiment and the field hospital, we knew it'd likely be too late to save his arm. Time like that, you get to asking yourself what the hell you're doing, dying and killing and crippling people. So that night, we asked each other."

"And Champion said he'd joined up to free the slaves?"

Will's grip tightened on the sheet. "He said slavery was our besetting sin. That God had sent this war, the way he sent plagues to Pharaoh, until we let his people go." He shook his head slightly. "Whether he was an abolitionist before the war, I can't tell you. Outside of our service, I didn't know him that well."

He went to the sink, where he dampened a small length of cloth, brought it back to the examining table and began swabbing the skin around the ragged hole just beneath Champion's ribs. The cloth turned dark red as he cleaned away the dried blood, revealing the dulled purple blotching of lividity. He set the cloth down. "Show me the weapon."

Hanley unwrapped the bayonet, which lay bundled in a potato-sack next to the corpse. Will took it and eyed the blade, then the body. He swallowed hard and inserted the blade into the wound. The metal slid easily into the mottled flesh. Hanley gripped the table edge. He knew the man was dead, but the sight of the weapon sinking in brought back memories he'd as soon forget. *A gray-clad shape in the cannon smoke, pistol at the ready…a bayonet in Hanley's hand, the jolt of terror and triumph as he plunged it into the Reb's stomach before the man could fire…*

Will looked queasy as he slid the blade out and laid it on its wrappings. "One thrust, I'd guess. I'll know for certain after I open him up. It was likely quick, thank God."

Hanley echoed the sentiment. He forced the nameless Reb out of his mind. "So our killer knew what he was doing. Makes it likelier he was a soldier. Do you recall anyone Champion had trouble with?" Though as he asked, he wondered what quarrel from the war would take seven years or more to resolve through violent death.

"This was his." Will pointed to the bayonet hilt. Hanley saw scratches in the brass at its base: *E. C.* Ebenezer Champion.

"I figured," Hanley said. That Champion had kept it wasn't unusual. Many soldiers from the War of the Rebellion brought such souvenirs home with them. "What about time of death?"

"He was in full rigor when you found him?"

"Yes. Around nine this morning." Hanley described the murder scene, the body position, the turned-down bedclothes. "I'm thinking he was killed last night."

Will pushed himself away from the table. "Rigor starts around four hours after death. It takes another few hours to set in all over. So if he was in full rigor around nine…he must've been dead by one in the morning. Possibly earlier."

"How much earlier?"

Will hesitated. "As much as twelve hours before you found him."

"Could be nine or ten at night, then." The earlier hours fit better with Champion's half-dressed state, unless he'd gone out and come home late. Champion's neighbors, or Mrs. Flynn, might know if he normally retired late or early. They might also have noticed the arrival of his supper guest, whoever it was, and what time—or whether—that person left. "Anything else you can tell me about Champion?"

Will shook his head. "As I said, we lost touch. I'd heard nothing of him since '65." He went to the sink and began washing his hands.

Hanley took the gold ring and chain from his pocket. "Do you remember if he ever wore these?"

Will glanced at them. "I don't recall them." He held out a hand. "May I...?"

Hanley gave him the jewelry. Will examined the ring, ran a finger over the hair-braid, eyed the inside surface. His frown deepened. "Where'd you find this?"

"In the grass outside Champion's house. There's an inscription I can't make out. I wondered if we might look at it through that contraption of yours."

Will handed the jewelry back. "The microscope? Not for a week or so at least. Cracked lens—I ordered a new one, but it'll take a while to get here."

Hanley eyed Champion's corpse. He slipped the ring off the chain, lifted one dead hand and slid the ring onto the third finger. It fit. *Why the chain, then?* he wondered as he took the ring off and tucked the jewelry away.

"You'll let me know how things go?" Will sounded casual, but the look in his eyes said it mattered to him. Hanley wasn't surprised. Will and his dead captain had lived through the hell of the battlefield together—it made a bond, even in the absence of any deeper tie.

"Of course." He clapped Will on the shoulder, thanked him and left, for North May Street and a talk with the neighbors.

FIVE

May 1864

"You fell *asleep*?" Ben Champion keeps his voice low, but there's no mistaking the intensity of that last word. "How could you let that happen?"

"It was only for a few moments, sir. I didn't even know it until—" Billy swallows, stiff with anxiety as well as his at-attention stance. "Until it got light enough to see. Just before I woke you."

"We could've gotten names. Descriptions. Plans of attack." Ben paces along the edge of the creek near their temporary camp. Some yards behind him are the graves they dug earlier that morning—one for Private Carroll, the other for the dead Reb bushwhacker. *Tom Whittier,* Billy thinks. *You know who he was. Don't lie to yourself.*

Corporal Schuyler, laying on a jury-rigged stretcher, moans softly in what passes for slumber. Billy dosed him a little while ago with as much laudanum as he dared, mixed with the last of the captain's whiskey ration. The sole remaining member of the squad is packing up Schuyler's bedroll. A hot, sick wave, as if from swamp fever, rolls over Billy. It could have been Dorrie's bullet that did for poor Carroll, or ended up in Schuyler's shoulder. Schuyler might yet lose the arm, or the use of it. What has Billy done?

He can tell Ben. Explain, absolve himself a little. Ben will be outraged that he let a Reb go free, but it will blow over. He hopes. He draws breath just as Ben turns toward him with icy fury in his eyes. "*What,* Private?"

"He was just a boy." The lie springs unexpectedly to his lips. He can't take it back now without making his situation more precarious than it already is. The memory of the little girl who tagged behind him and Tom whenever she could is too strong in him for truth. "Not even old enough to shave. He couldn't have told us much. And he didn't take his weapon." He nods toward camp, where two extra rifles lie amid the squad's. "Unarmed, he was no threat. Would you really have seen him hanged?"

"I'd see the lot of them hanged if I could." Ben speaks with a ruthlessness that leaves Billy cold as a dive into the creek. He's doubly glad now that he didn't confess the truth. "Whatever it takes to teach the lesson of God—that rebels and slavers cannot exist in this Union. We will scourge them from our midst, as we should have done long ago."

"And then who'd be left?" A challenge, quiet but steady, presuming on their shared past—not quite a friendship, but something akin. "How sharp a sword must we be in God's hand, and how deep the wound we inflict?"

"You of all people know what they deserve. I'd think you'd want justice."

"So I do. Tempered by mercy. Doesn't the Bible tell us so?"

Ben's glare holds for another moment. Then, incredibly, he smiles—a hard and mirthless thing, but Billy sees an easing in it, slight as the breeze off the water. "Spoken like Josiah's son. Or were you like this before?"

"Let's just say I've learned a bit in the past fourteen years."

"Well." Ben stares back at the camp, the graves, the pile of bedrolls and rifles next to the coffee pot, and the dead fire. "Too late to make any difference. If you don't recall dropping off, we've no way to tell how long your rebel boy's been gone." He gives Billy a sharp look. "You came from around here, didn't you? That Reb wasn't some fellow you knew back then?"

Billy laughs—a dry, forced sound. "I was ten when we left Tennessee. From the look of him, that Reb would've been half my age at most. And I didn't have much acquaintance with white boys from the next plantation over."

"No." Ben's tone is parched as dust. "No, I don't suppose you did."

Billy resumes his at-attention stance. "Will I be disciplined, sir?"

Ben's face registers the shift from almost-friend to subordinate, as well as the reason for it. "Not this time, Private. But it can't happen again."

"It won't." Not with Tom Whittier dead and Dorrie gone into the night. God have mercy, he'll never see her again.

SIX

April 24, 1872

Making a pot of tea gave Rivka something to do, a needed distraction from the turmoil inside. Her stomach felt tight, her fingers clumsy. It took concentration to measure the tea, pour the hot water, set the lid on the pot, and fetch cups from a cabinet. By the time she had everything ready, she felt able to face Aaron with at least surface calm. He would need that from her until he recovered from the worst of the shock.

She looked up and saw the mulatto woman—Ada—in the doorway. The boy hovered just behind her. "Let me help you," Ada said. Her soft voice had a Southern lilt. "I can get the pot. Nat, you bring some cups. One in each hand, and mind you take care."

The boy obeyed, eyes cast down as he slipped past his mother into the kitchen. He glanced at Rivka, partly curious and partly wary, as he took two cups from the counter. She found herself seeking signs of Aaron in his face, and closed her eyes against a wave of fatigue. Too much at once—Aaron alive and here, in the company of this strange Negro woman who spoke to and touched him with the closeness of a dear friend. Or a lover, or a wife. And this boy. Theirs? Too old, surely. Unless he was younger than he looked.

The two remaining cups felt cool in her hands. They anchored her as she followed Ada back into the parlor.

Aaron hadn't moved from the sofa. Pale and hollow-eyed, he barely noted their entrance. Sympathy for him warred with resentment, an unexpected emotion that brought shame with it. Rivka forced her feelings down, poured a cup of tea and handed it to him. "Drink," she said, as if to a small child. "It will help a little."

"Papa is dead," he said, as if repeating what she'd told him would make it comprehensible.

"Yes."

"And his killer is in prison."

"Yes."

He blinked, then looked at her as if seeing her properly for the first time since she'd spoken of the murder. "And you...?" He stopped and looked down at his tea. "I shouldn't ask. I have no right."

It hurt her to see him like this. He had always been so strong, so sure of things. Very like Papa, before the blistering fight between them that sent Aaron storming away to enlist. And now he could hardly look her in the face, or get a word out without floundering. She patted his hand. "Drink your tea."

Ada stood. "Nat and I'll just step outside a minute."

Aaron looked up. Rivka saw fear in his face. "Ada—"

She hugged Nat with one arm. "We'll be all right." Then, to Rivka, "Where should we..."

Rivka gestured toward the kitchen. "That way. There is a yard, and then the shul." They left the room before she could ask what Ada meant by *we'll be all right*, why Aaron looked afraid.

Aaron gulped tea, gripping the cup in both hands. A little color came back to his cheeks, but the fear didn't leave him. Rivka sat next to him. There was so much she wanted, needed, to ask, and she knew so little how to say any of it.

Aaron broke the silence as he set his cup down. "I got your letter."

She looked at him, surprised. "Which one?"

"About Mameh. I'm sorry. I should have been here. But I couldn't leave."

"I wrote every week," she said. "Papa wrote, too. Once. After Mameh died. You never wrote back. We thought you were dead."

"I never got Papa's letter. Only yours. Just the one. I wrote an answer, but didn't have the courage to send it." He closed his eyes and sagged against the sofa. "He must have despised me. The son who couldn't offer a word in his mother's memory. Couldn't even write to say I was still alive and whole. All those years. When we were coming here, I thought...I hoped—" His voice broke. "He seemed so strong when I left. I thought he would go on forever. I thought I'd have a chance...he'd take us in, keep us safe, I could make him understand...and now..."

Rivka took his hand. "Tell me. Let *me* understand."

He squeezed her fingers, then pulled away. She sensed him drawing inward, as if summoning the will to speak. "We had a farm in Virginia," he said finally. "I bought it with wages I saved working for the Freedmen's Bureau. The Bureau helped the freed people in the rebel states—made sure they had food, somewhere to live, medical care, schooling. Anyway, the farming didn't go well. I'm not cut out for getting a living from the soil. I'm not sure what I *am* cut out for. Except teaching." His bleak expression softened. "Nat was one of my students. The Bureau set up schools, all across the Southern states. They couldn't learn to read or write, the colored people. It was against the law. Imagine, a law that says people can't learn to read! So I taught them. And I met Nat, and then Ada." His affection as he spoke her name was so clear, Rivka felt as if she were witnessing an embrace. "And she stayed with me."

*As a wife, or...*Rivka couldn't finish the thought, let alone voice it. "And then what?"

He let out a slow breath. "The first years went well enough, until the Federal troops left. Then things turned ugly. Men rode out at night, white men, burning and looting and sometimes killing. They didn't like us teaching the Negroes, or aiding them in legal claims against whites. They wanted to drive us away. And we had no protection, except whatever we could manage ourselves." He gave a bitter laugh. "If President Lincoln had lived, maybe it would have been different. As it was, Ada and I became targets. A Yankee Jew and a mulatto woman and child, living openly as family—they could not stomach this, the night riders. They burned our home over our heads. We kept them from killing us, but we had nothing left, and we didn't dare stay."

"Where did you go?"

"Alton." The name came out shakily, and he swallowed before continuing. "Joseph suggested it. Joseph Levin—he was in my company during the war. And then we'd worked together for the Freedmen's Bureau in Virginia. Ada and Nat and I followed Joseph back to Illinois. There was a parcel of land next to his, cheap for the asking. He'd written me about it, and we took it."

"What happened?"

He took a long time to answer. Then, "They got Joseph. And tried to kill me."

Rivka felt bewildered. "Who did? Not the same people, surely. They wouldn't follow you all the way from Virginia. Would they?"

He shook his head. "No. It was others. But of the same kind. I should have expected it. We knew there were Reb sympathizers in southern Illinois during the war. But the war was five years over by then. And Joseph said nothing of any such troubles. He must have thought he could face them down by refusing to be afraid. But he was wrong."

"And now?"

He gulped more tea. "Now we're here. Where we'll be safe and I can think what to do."

"You don't sound like you believe that."

He shrugged and fixed his gaze on the street outside, hazily visible through the parlor curtains. She touched his arm. "Has one of those men come after you? Is that what you're afraid of?"

His utter stillness, and lack of reply, gave her the answer. "Why?" she asked.

He let out a shuddering breath. "Because I recognized him. I saw his face back in Alton, the night they attacked our farm. Ada saw him, too. And…" He wet his lips. "And then we saw him here. At the train station. If he saw me, or any of us…"

"You can describe him? You know his name?"

"I don't see what good that does." He sank back again, as if telling his story had exhausted him. "The best we can do is hope he missed us, and get lost in Chicago. Here among our people, where they might not think to look for a white man with a mulatto family."

"Aaron." She leaned toward him. "You must go to the police. They can find this man and arrest him."

"What will they do? *Can* they do anything, if he hasn't committed some crime here? And why would they take my word against his about what happened in Alton? They surely won't take Ada's. Not even in free Illinois."

She gave him a small smile. "I know someone who will."

SEVEN

The walk back to North May Street was long, but pleasant despite Hanley's errand. As he crossed into the West Division and traveled farther from the city's more crowded regions to those with wider streets and larger houses, untouched by the Fire the previous autumn, the shouts and hammering of workmen and the smell of horse gave way to birdsong and the fresh scents of spring. The blue sky and greening trees seemed out of joint on a day when a man had died so horribly in what should have been his sanctuary. Hanley felt for Will Rushton, who'd lost a part of his past...and for Ben Champion as well, he realized, though he'd never known him. He'd known and served with men like him during the war. That was enough.

Marcus Thomashaw, the neighbor Hanley sought, lived with his family just south of Ben Champion's place. Given how shaken Marcus Thomashaw was by the events of early morning, Hanley reckoned there was a good chance the man had stayed home from work. He'd meant to go straight there to talk with him again, but his steps slowed as he neared Champion's house. Another look at the crime scene wouldn't come amiss.

The house was undisturbed, just as he and Schmidt had left it. He went up to Champion's room and looked around, but nothing new called attention to itself. Back downstairs, he stopped off in the study for another search through the desk. The narrow top drawer held cards printed with the address of Champion's law office in the South Division. Hanley pocketed one. He looked through the rest of the drawers, more leisurely than last time. A corner of newsprint, peeking out from beneath sheets of stationery, proved

31

to be a clipping from the *Chicago Times,* with a headline that piqued Hanley's interest. THE CHICAGO CONSPIRACY, he read. *More Plotters Arrested, Discovery of Four Boxes of Muskets in Charles Walsh's Barn, Statements of Prisoners.* He skimmed the article.

Yesterday afternoon the excitement in some parts of the city approached nearly fever heat…another large capture of arms was made in a barn belonging to Charles Walsh, now a prisoner in Camp Douglas, and located in the rear of Adams Street, between State and Clark Streets…The assistance of Capt. John Nelson and some of the policemen of the South Division was called into requisition…another accession was made to the rebel raiders at present confined in the old Trinity Church, Madison Street…about two hundred in all who have been captured…"came to Chicago last Friday; a man brought me and four others, and paid our fare; told us we came to release the prisoners at Camp Douglas…the man told us we would be supplied with the best of arms, and we should be well paid for it, and he would have our expenses paid…"

The printed words recalled a story passed through the ranks of the Chicago Irish Brigade during the war that the Rebs had plotted to take over the city. Where was the Twenty-Third then…the Shenandoah Valley? It was hard to remember. So many battles across so many states, an endless hellish blur of rifle and cannon fire and choking smoke and screams of wounded men. So many marches, the constant dull agony of aching feet and an overwhelming desire for hot coffee by a campfire someplace out of the rain. Hanley eyed the date on the clipping. November '64. Another memento, though something of an odd one. Unless Champion had played a role in the Northwest Conspiracy trial? But that was a military affair, and held elsewhere. Cincinnati or someplace, he thought.

Nothing else stood out amid the circulars, concert programs, and bills with the word *Paid* scrawled across them in a clear, bold hand. Champion's, surely. The law office was worth a visit, to find out what cases Champion had been working on. He tucked the clipping inside his sketchbook and left for the house next door.

ભ

Number 15, the white clapboard where the Thomashaws lived, was large and needed a coat of paint. Scraggly rosebushes by the porch looked mostly brown, though Hanley saw green on a few branches. He reached the porch steps in time to see a young woman herding three children outside. She looked harried, with the faded prettiness of a flower past its best. From inside, he heard an infant's angry shrieks.

"Oliver, you keep the girls out of mischief," the woman said. Her accent struck Hanley—soft and rolling, with a Southern lilt. "First we'll weed the garden, and then y'all can play Indian wars or whatever you've a mind to. No making mud pies in the vegetable garden or the flowerbeds, and don't get any dirtier than you can help."

Hanley started up the steps. "Mrs. Thomashaw?"

She looked up, frowned and shook her head. Pale gold hair slipped loose from a twist at the nape of her neck. "Mrs. Thomashaw won't be wanting whatever you're selling today," she said, sounding weary. "Try across the street."

A hired woman, he guessed. This was the kind of neighborhood where folk could afford things like that. Up close, she looked older than he'd first thought, nearer to thirty than twenty. "I'm a police detective," he said as he pulled his badge from his pocket and held it where she could see it. "There's been an incident next door. I need a few moments of Mr. and Mrs. Thomashaw's time."

"Daddy's at his office. Mommy's with Grant," said the boy, a curly-haired moppet Hanley figured to be seven or so. "His tummy hurts and he won't hush up. I saw the wagon this morning. Did you put somebody dead in it?"

Revulsion crossed the woman's face. "Hush, Oliver. Y'all go on, now."

"But Mary—"

"You want me to call your mama out here? And her with that sick baby? Bad enough we never got you to school today." She shepherded the boy and the others across the porch. "Garden's waiting."

As the children scattered, she threw Hanley a troubled look. "You can go in, I guess," she said, and turned away.

Hanley thanked her and went inside. The baby's screams hurt his ears. He followed the sound to a spacious kitchen, where he found Mrs. Thomashaw walking her baby up and down amid scattered bread crusts and bacon rinds, unwashed dishes, and spills across table and floor.

"The chamomile isn't helping, Mary, you may need to go for the doctor—" She broke off as she saw Hanley. "Who on earth—"

He gave her his warmest smile as he showed his badge and said his name. "I'm sorry to intrude, but I need to talk with you about Captain Champion."

The baby shrieked in her ear. She flinched and patted his back. "Can you come back later? I can't think right now. I hardly had a wink of sleep all night, and heaven knows where Mrs. Flynn's got to...she's usually here by ten—" The infant let out an enormous belch and went limp on his mother's shoulder. "Thank goodness," she said softly. "None of my others had colic this bad. A little chamomile tea, that's all it usually takes. Not with Grant, though. Poor thing. Do you have children, Detective...what did you say your name was?"

"Hanley. And no. Not yet."

She gave him a sudden, brilliant smile. "Let me just put him down."

While she took her baby upstairs, Hanley looked out the back window at the older three children puttering in the garden. The hired woman—Mary—stood by a gnarled fruit tree, watching them. Hanley saw her lean against it, head lolling and shoulders sagging as if only the slender trunk held her up. One hand went over her eyes and stayed there.

"Well, then." Mrs. Thomashaw re-entered the room. "How can I help you, Detective Hanley?" Concern crossed her face. "I saw the wagon come earlier. Did something happen to Captain Champion?"

Hanley nodded. "He's dead, I'm sorry to say. If you were up for much of last night, you may have seen or heard something that can point toward his killer."

"You don't mean that dear man's been murdered?" She groped for the back of the nearest chair. "Why, just last week he played catch with Oliver. We were having a backyard picnic, and Rosemary got an ant bite and went into hysterics over it, and so of course Janet had to have hysterics too, and Captain Champion happened to be outside having a smoke, and he saw us and came over, and—"

"Mrs. Thomashaw." He held up a hand as if to block the flow of words. With the baby bedded down, she was almost too much at ease. "Let's sit, and I'll ask you some questions."

"Anything to help." She pulled out a chair and sank onto it. "Poor Mary. She'll be dreadfully upset."

"Why is that?"

Mrs. Thomashaw's cheeks pinked. "She…rather liked the captain…I think. Though I could be wrong."

"Did the captain return those feelings?"

Her blush deepened. "I can't say. It's not the sort of thing one asks about. And she's only the hired girl. Of course, if he'd said anything…I mean…I'd have spoken up for Mary, if I'd thought it was needed. But I didn't think it was."

Only the hired girl briefly annoyed him, but he let it pass. He decided to ask Mary herself before he left. Mrs. Thomashaw seemed most concerned with her children. If there had been some relationship between her hired help and Champion, she might not have noticed. "Did you see or hear anything unusual last night? Say, anytime from half past eight on."

Buried amid chatter about her children and her husband, Mrs. Thomashaw's story offered two tidbits that might be of use. She and Mary had been up all night with the baby and she hadn't paid heed to much else, but she did recall glimpsing light through the shutters of Champion's upstairs window around nine o'clock—a usual occurrence, she said. She'd also heard someone pass the house around ten. Light footsteps, moving quickly but not running. She remembered the hour because she'd just managed to settle Grant for the first time, and the grandfather clock struck ten just as she was going back to bed a few minutes later. Yes, the baby's room was at the front of the house. She'd rather Hanley didn't go in, but she'd be happy to show him from outside.

Out on the sidewalk, Hanley looked up at the double window. It offered a good view of the street. Anyone walking past the Thomashaw residence could have been heard from there. Ten o'clock…eleven hours before Hanley and Schmidt saw the body. Will Rushton had said Champion could have been dead that long. Were the footsteps the murderer's? He thought of a woman bought for the evening, working in tandem with a jilter, a sneak thief, the latter surprised in mid-robbery by a mark less distracted than he should have been. Then killing out of panic, with a weapon off the bedroom wall, because neither of the miscreants had anticipated the need. Possible. "What about earlier in the day? Do you recall anyone coming to Champion's house in the afternoon or early evening?"

"I'm afraid not. Grant woke up inconsolable from his afternoon nap...his stomach again...and then Oliver got a splinter in his finger while I was getting the supper things ready...he *will* keep trying to build towers with that rough wood Marcus—my husband—got to build a rabbit hutch...so Mary and I had a bit to contend with. A parade with a brass band could have gone into the captain's house anytime from two o'clock or so onward and I'd never have noticed. Though I suppose Alice must have come, as she usually does."

"Alice?"

"Alice Lockwood. His secretary. She comes on his half-days. Tuesdays and Saturdays, unless he's in court. Generally from three to six. She's helping him with his memoir." Mrs. Thomashaw looked stricken. "She won't know what's happened. It'll be a terrible shock."

"His memoir...he was writing a book?" Hanley thought back to the rigidly neat desk, nothing in it or on it that looked remotely like a book in progress. And a woman at Champion's house yesterday, the day he died.

She nodded. "About the war. He spoke of it to Marcus once or twice. My husband served in the Ninth Illinois, the cavalry. He was decorated for bravery."

"How far had Captain Champion got with it, do you know? Was he just starting?"

"Oh, no. It was nearly finished. I believe he had a publisher interested, though I can't recall exactly. Alice had been working with him for some time on it."

"How long?"

She thought a moment. "It must be nearly a year now. Yes. I remember I first saw her last summer, not long before Grant came. He turned eight months on Monday, and he's a perfect angel when his stomach isn't bothering him. Why, just yesterday, he—"

A shriek from the backyard cut her off. "Mary! Make him *quit!* I'm telling Mama!"

Mrs. Thomashaw sighed. "God grant me patience. I love them, but...I hope I've been of some help, Detective. Is there anything else you want to know?"

He could think of several things, all questions he could just as well ask later. "I'd like a quick word with Mary."

She blushed again. "I'll tell her."

EIGHT

The woman and boy came quickly when Rivka beckoned. She had the feeling Ada had been watching for her. Ada had beautiful eyes, gray with hints of green in their depths. Right now, they held a deeper concern than she was permitting to show on her face. For her son's sake, Rivka guessed. "I will show you where you can sleep," Rivka said.

"How is Aaron?" Ada said.

"Better."

"That's good." Ada hesitated, then drew breath and continued. "Did he tell you..."

Rivka felt a blush rising. "Yes." She'd hardly been able to look him in the face when she finally asked the question. They *were* married, he'd said. By the Freedmen's Bureau, with his friend Joseph Levin as witness. His defiant look and tone made it clear that was good enough for him—though it wouldn't be for the neighbors, Rivka knew with a sinking heart. For herself, she didn't want to think about it. Not when there were easier, more practical things to deal with.

To fill the awkward pause, she kept talking as she ushered Ada and the boy inside. "You'll want to rest. We don't have a washing-room, but I can get water for you. There is bread and butter if you are hungry, or I was just going to cook potatoes." She thought of Tanta Hannah and fought back panic. Putting Hannah off for midday dinner had been tricky enough, even telling her no more than that Aaron had returned. How she would react to his being in the company of two strangers, mulattoes, *goyim*—and one of them his wife!—she didn't know.

The small spare room upstairs was undisturbed except for the dusting Rivka gave it every so often. The boy—Nat—would need fresh sheets, and a fresh blanket as well. His clothes looked worn and travel-stained. He would need a new shirt and trousers. Rivka felt overwhelmed. The day had brought too much to take in.

She dredged up a smile for Nat, who hovered just behind Ada. "For you," Rivka said, gesturing around the little room. It held a bed, a washstand, and a small bookshelf Papa had made in the first weeks after the Fire. He had built it in silence, speaking only to ask Rivka for more nails, and filled it with mementos of Aaron's—a few books and some carvings, the only possessions of his they had saved from the flames. A memorial, she'd thought then…or a talisman, a sign of stubborn hope that Aaron still lived and might come home someday.

Now, Nat glanced at his mother, who nodded. Slowly, he walked to the door and looked in. A wisp of a smile crossed his face when he saw the bookshelf. On top of it was a palm-sized carving of a fish. He went to it and traced a scale with a finger. "This is real good. Looks alive, almost."

"Aaron made that. He was fifteen. He caught a salmon in the lake that summer. He wanted to remember it always."

Nat dug in his trouser pocket. "I made this. He showed me how." He held up a small wooden frog, then placed it next to the salmon. "There. Now they's friends."

"You can stay here and rest awhile," Ada told him.

The boy nodded. Rivka led Ada down the hall and stopped at the door of her father's room—her parents' room until her mother died. She felt heat rising in her cheeks again and hoped the other woman didn't notice. "You and Aaron will be here," she said. "It should be comfortable enough."

A glimmer of warmth showed in Ada's careworn face. "I'm sure it will."

ଓଃ

Will Rushton's steps slowed as he approached the red brick house on the corner of Erie and Noble Streets. For more than half of his thirty-five years it had been his home and his haven. Even the Great Fire hadn't taken it from him—the flames that devoured so much of the city had scarcely touched the West Division. Today, for the first time he could remember, he hoped to find the house empty.

As usual, no one was in the front parlor. Aunt Abigail rarely bothered with social calls on days she wasn't at her clinic. Uncle Josiah was at his office and wouldn't be home before seven thirty. The study was likewise empty, and he heard no sounds from the kitchen. Cook's afternoon off, he remembered. She'd be across town with her daughter now, celebrating the recent arrival of her first grandchild.

He called out softly when he reached the top of the stairs, but got no answer. He let out a breath he hadn't known he was holding and went to his bedroom. His shirt and trousers smelled of the city morgue. He changed to clean ones, went down the hall to the washroom, and splashed cold water on his face. He gazed at himself in the mirror, watching the wetness trickle down his cheeks and off his chin. He began to catalogue his features, a ritual he hadn't needed in years. Now he found it comforting, and that very comfort disquieting. *High forehead, slender nose, narrow cheekbones. Wide mouth, thin lips. Wavy hair, black. A hint of olive in the skin. Gray-green eyes.* He lingered over the eyes, then tore his gaze away.

He went back toward his bedroom, moving slowly as if in a dream. Partway down the silent hall, he stopped by a small, framed oval photograph of Frederick Douglass. "Ben Champion's dead," he whispered to it. A distant part of him recognized how strange it was that he half-expected an answer.

He reached his room, went in, sat on the edge of his bed. He ran a hand through his hair, then let it fall to his lap.

After a time, he opened the drawer of his nightstand. He took out a folded letter and sat awhile longer, the letter loosely held between his fingers. He'd read it countless times since receiving it eight days earlier.

Dear Will,

Meet me at Tremont House for lunch Friday? I know your mind on what we've discussed, but I still hope to persuade you. Recent events give us much to talk on.

Ben

He got up, went downstairs to the kitchen, found the safety matches and struck one. He held the letter over the sink and touched the match to one edge, then dropped the paper and watched it curl to ash. For a long time he stared at the blackened remnant, stark against the gleaming white porcelain.

NINE

Mary hadn't moved from her spot against the fruit tree. She acknowledged Hanley's approach with a glance, then turned her head to watch the children as they weeded the vegetable bed. The sag of her shoulders suggested bone-deep fatigue.

"Rough day?" Hanley asked, in the soothing tone of a priest at confession.

"You don't need to pussyfoot," she said without looking at him. "I know he's dead."

Her bluntness startled him, but he kept himself from showing it. "How?"

"Saw the wagon. Not much else y'all could have loaded on it." She fixed him with a penetrating gaze. "You want to know about me and the captain. But I don't have to tell you."

Blunt and hostile, over a question he hadn't asked. He leaned an arm against the tree. "That sounds like you knew Captain Champion pretty well." He watched for a reaction, but her face stayed still as stone. "Did you have an understanding with him?"

She let out a whuff of air that might have been a laugh. "You mean the kind that comes with a ring and a promise? No."

"Were you friends, then? Or lovers?"

"Don't you dare ask me that." She pushed away from the tree and stalked toward the garden where the children were. Oliver had turned to watch them, interest clear on his face.

"Miss…Mary," Hanley said as he caught up with her. "We *will* have this conversation. Inside the house might be better, or on the porch. Or you could come with me to the police station."

She stopped and stared at him. He kept his gaze level, letting her see that he meant what he said. "Tell me your full name. Where you're from. How long you've worked for the Thomashaws."

She took a few steps back toward the house. "Mary Olcott. Loudoun County, Virginia. Almost nine months. And I'm a loyal American, in case you meant to ask."

"When did you first come to Chicago? Were you looking for Champion? Did you have a prior acquaintance with him?"

"I didn't come here on account of Ben. I came for work. Seemed like anybody could find a way to live in Chicago."

A neat sidestep, he thought, while noting her use of Champion's Christian name. "So *did* you know him, before working here?"

"Ben Champion took a kindhearted interest in a Southern girl with no family or friends. I needed a way to support myself, and he found me the job at the Thomashaws'. Sometimes we met and talked, because he wanted to know how I was. What other people might think was going on doesn't make it true."

"He got you this job? How did that happen? How did you know him well enough to go to him for help finding work?"

"My brother knew him. In the war." Pain flashed across her face. "He's dead. He fought for the Union. Our neighbors didn't like that. They burned us out. I left with the clothes on my back and the egg money in my pocket."

"And you went where?"

"I don't like talking about those days." She looked past Hanley, toward the vegetable garden. "Oliver! No digging in there!" She strode across the grass, grabbed the boy by the arm and hauled him up from the dirt. "We're going in to change your clothes. And then you're going to sit awhile, all quiet by yourself." She marched him inside. The back door banged shut behind them.

The two little girls—neither older than five, by Hanley's guess—stared at him from the edge of the lawn. Hanley nodded to them and went in search of their mother, to find out what she knew of exactly how Mary Olcott had spent the night.

CB

Hanley left the Thomashaws' a short while later. Champion's neighbors on the other side were out of town, he'd learned, so for the moment there was no one else especially useful around to talk to. A few minutes' brisk walk would bring him to the horsecar stop at May and Madison Streets, or he could save the nickel fare and go on foot back to Lake Street Station. His feet were complaining after the day's tramping he'd already done, and he decided to indulge himself. The horsecar would get him back and started on his case notes all the sooner.

As he turned onto the boulevard, he saw a figure approaching. A woman, walking quickly. He noticed more detail as she drew nearer—fair hair and skin, plain gray dress, a simple straw hat. Not old, though some years past prime marrying age, he guessed. She passed him with a hastily averted glance, as if deliberately avoiding his notice. Resident or visitor, he wondered. He lingered to see which house she'd approach, and was startled to see her turn in at Champion's front walk.

It dawned on him suddenly who this might be. He turned and called out to her. "Alice Lockwood?"

She halted and glanced up, looking startled. "May I know who's asking?"

Another Southerner. He hid his surprise as he took out his badge. "Detective Frank Hanley. Chicago Police. If you've come to see Captain Champion, I'm afraid I have bad news."

She took the shock of it better than Hanley expected. No screams or fainting—she paled a little and turned away, then rallied enough to look him in the eye. "Is...is he still..."

He guessed what she meant to ask. "No. The body was taken away some hours ago."

She closed her eyes briefly. One hand went to the high collar of her dress and fidgeted with it. Abruptly, she moved her hand back down, gazing past Hanley over the sidewalk and lawn.

"I'm surprised to see you here, Miss Lockwood," he said. "I'm informed you usually come Tuesdays and Saturdays. Were you here yesterday afternoon?"

It took her a moment to answer. "Yes. Yes, I was."

"And you're here now because...?"

"We..." Her hand went to her collar again. Hanley noted the nervous gesture, filed it away for further thought. "The captain asked me. We made arrangements for an extra day's work. I'm...I've been helping him with his book."

"So I'm told. Since when?"

"Since last summer. I answered an advertisement."

Last summer fit with Mrs. Thomashaw's account. Alice Lockwood's excuse for coming here today was plausible enough, if convenient. With Champion dead, there was no one to confirm or disprove it.

He studied her a moment, relying on his long-honed skills of observation as a con man and then a cop. Plain garments, well made but not expensive. A general air of refinement told him she was educated, likely better off once but fallen on harder times. Plenty of such people in Chicago since the Fire. Which might explain her somewhat unusual position with regard to Champion—a woman secretary, alone with him in his house for six hours a week. He thought of Mary Olcott, in whom Ben Champion had taken a "kindhearted interest." Not so different from Miss Lockwood. The dead captain seemed to have a bent toward rescue, and toward Southern women. "Tell me about your work with him. Was all of it done here?"

She nodded. "Twice a week. Afternoons. He spent mornings at his office."

"And you did what?"

"Read and wrote, mostly." She stared across the grass again. "I'd read over what he wrote the day or evening before and make a clean copy. Sometimes he'd mark it up more. Or he'd read it out loud and ask me what I thought."

That was a surprise. "He trusted your judgment."

She shrugged. "I suppose."

"Where is the manuscript now? We didn't find it when we searched the house."

"I believe he sent it to his publisher last week."

Hanley looked out toward the boulevard. It sounded like Alice Lockwood was more than a copyist, if Champion had sought her comments on his book. To do that, especially with a personal memoir, implied a certain intimacy of thought, at least. Champion's unbuttoned shirt and stockinged feet came to mind, along with Schmidt's question—*Had a woman with him?* Maybe it wasn't Mary Olcott he should be looking at. "Where were you living before you came to Chicago?"

Her cheeks pinked. "Richmond. Though I don't see why it matters."

The Confederate capital until its fall. Hanley's regiment was at Appomattox then, but he recalled men weeping and shouting *Glory to God!* when word came. "You were Secesh?"

She glared at him. "I *was* secessionist. Now I'm just trying to live. May I go?"

Had Champion known? Surely not, or he wouldn't have hired her. "You were here yesterday as usual, you said. When did you leave?"

"At six. As I always do."

"Did Champion have any visitors that you recall?"

"No. Callers didn't drop by while I was here. That was working time."

"Did he mention if he was expecting anyone?"

"No."

"Someone stayed for supper, though. Was it you?"

She moved away from him. "No. I left at six."

"Did you see anyone coming toward the house? Or pass anybody, say, on your way to the horsecar stop?"

She hesitated, her hand rising to her collar again. "No one I'd recognize. Though..."

"Go on."

"He might have been coming to any house along here."

"Who?"

"A man I saw. Six houses down or so. We passed. I nodded, but he didn't take notice. He looked...upset."

"Describe him. Old, young, tall, short...?"

She frowned, as if in thought. "Older...past sixty, I'd guess. His hair was graying. Longish, almost down to his collar, but thin on top.

A bony sort of face. He dressed like a gentleman." She paused. "I truly would prefer to leave now."

"That's fine," Hanley said. "I'll walk you back to the horsecar stop."

She looked startled. "You needn't trouble—"

"It's no trouble, Miss Lockwood. I can't leave you here by yourself."

Her lips made a thin line. "Very well." She moved swiftly toward the boulevard, her low-heeled shoes tapping lightly on the boardwalk.

Silence reigned on the short journey to Madison Street, Miss Lockwood not inclined to speak and Hanley content to think over their encounter. Alice Lockwood was hard to read, and her obvious tension had many possible sources. He wondered again how much she'd told Champion about her secessionist past, and why she'd spent the past several months helping an abolitionist-minded Yankee write a memoir of the Union victory. Why she was in Chicago in the first place, come to that. Two Southern women in Champion's orbit, one with a story not easily checked, the other with no story she was willing to share. Whether any of it mattered was another question altogether. The man she'd passed on her way to the horsecar stop last evening—did he matter? Or was he simply a resident of the neighborhood, with no connection to Champion whatsoever?

"Where can I find you if I need to talk to you again?" Hanley said as they reached the horsecar stop. A westbound car was approaching, less than a block away.

"Mrs. McKinley's boardinghouse. Number 29 South Robey Street."

He pulled out his sketchbook and wrote the address as the horsecar drew up to them. "Thank you, Miss Lockwood. I'll be in touch."

TEN

Nearly three by the clock on the shelf within her view. Just over half an hour until English class ended. Rivka listened with partial attention as eight-year-old Chava Klein read from "The Song of the Bee" in *McGuffey's Second Reader*. The rest of her thoughts were with Aaron, and his refusal to tell her any more about the incident in Alton. He was terribly afraid, that much was clear. But he and his family were surely safe enough now, even if their attacker had seen them in the train station. Chicago was a big city—and Hannah and Jacob between them could make sure everyone around Market Street knew whom to watch for. Aaron would tell Onkl Jacob everything, of course...but not her, which rankled. As if knowing even the name of the man who drove them from Alton would be too much for her, when knowing of the incident itself was not.

She had not found Hanley, either, on her brief trip earlier to Lake Street Station. He was out on a case, no telling when he would be back. "If you want to leave your name, miss..." the officer at the lobby desk had said, with a look she belatedly recognized as admiring, "I'll tell him you came by." More disappointed than she should have been, and too flustered to leave word, she'd thanked the man and left. She would try again tomorrow. And the day after, and every day after that if need be, until she saw Hanley again.

Silence roused her from her thoughts. Chava had finished. How long had Rivka been woolgathering? "Thank you, Chava," she said. "Leah, please read the next two verses."

Leah Zalman stood and opened her book. Her clear voice echoed through the tiny room. Not even a proper schoolroom, an annex tacked onto Nathan and Zalman's tailor shop. Onkl Jacob had used it to store bolts of cloth. Her students didn't have desks—just a long table where they sat, a bookshelf where the readers and slates were kept, and a tiny coal stove in one corner. And its own entrance, so the girls would not disturb Jacob and Moishe at their work.

Rivka watched Leah, noted how neat her hair was, how smooth and clean her cotton dress. She read effortlessly, with poise unusual in a ten-year-old. She was as confident as her brother Moishe was timid. What a contrast she made to the boy Nat. A wary child, that one. Not surprising, given what he'd been through. She'd never met any colored people until today. None of them in Chicago lived near Market Street. And now she had two living under her roof, as family. A sister-in-law and a nephew, or as good as. She shook her head at the strangeness of it.

"Fraylin Kelmansky?"

"What?" She realized Leah had seen her gesture and misunderstood it. "I'm sorry. That was very good, Leah. Rachel, please continue, with Lesson Twenty-Four."

Red-haired Rachel Demsky stood, opened her book and promptly dropped it. She stammered an apology as she picked it up, then began to read the brief story on sheep shearing in a halting voice. Rivka felt for her. She knew Rachel hated reading aloud, was embarrassed by all the mistakes she made. But the girl needed the practice. *Not more than four sentences*, she decided, *and extra tutoring once a week. If I can get her parents to agree.*

She focused her attention on Rachel, ready to rescue the child if needed. Thoughts of Aaron, Hanley, and the Alton incident faded.

ങ

Her offer to tutor Rachel did not go well. The poor girl looked more embarrassed than ever and muttered something about asking Mameh before she fled out the door. Rivka gathered the readers and set them on the shelf, then went to collect the slates and chalk.

"Let me help, Fraylin," a voice said in Yiddish from the schoolroom doorway. She looked up, slate in hand, and saw Moishe. He gave her a shy smile, then walked to the table and picked up a piece of chalk. "Where does it go?"

Surprise made her hesitate. Moishe never came into the schoolroom. A sneaking thought suggested he was here to see her, but she pushed it aside. "Here." She retrieved a narrow wooden box and set it on the table. "I don't wish to keep you from your work, though."

"We are not so busy now." His eyes rested on her a bit too long. Flustered, she picked up three more slates. His soft footsteps as he moved around the table, collecting pieces of chalk and setting them in the box, seemed loud in the quiet.

She stepped past him and retrieved the last slate. He reached for a piece of chalk and rolled it toward three others he had gathered. "I have heard..." he said, then stopped as the chalk rolled off the table, struck the floor and broke. He bit his lip and crouched down to retrieve the pieces. "I'm sorry. I didn't mean to..."

"Never mind." She felt for him suddenly, shamed as he was by his own awkwardness. He reached up to drop the broken pieces in the box and tipped it over. Chalk showered down, one stick leaving a white mark where it struck his shoulder.

Color rose in his cheeks as he grabbed for the fallen sticks. "I am so sorry, Fraylin...I only meant to help..."

"It's all right." She knelt near him, keeping her eyes on the scattered chalk as she joined him in gathering it up. "This will only take a minute."

They reached for the same piece and their hands brushed. He snatched his hand away. The bell at the front door jangled, announcing the presence of a customer in the shop. Moishe stood abruptly. "I should go," he said, and left the schoolroom.

She stayed where she was a moment longer, eyes on the broken chalk in her palm. She closed her hand over the pieces and dropped them in the box, wishing she could as easily shed the burden of expectations that had settled on her like a heavy winter's snow.

A short while later, arriving home, she saw Ada in the kitchen, lifting the meat fry pan off its hook. A chopped onion and butter sat on the counter by the stove, where a large pot was steaming. The scent of boiling beans hung in the air.

"Not that one," Rivka said, more sharply than she'd intended, as she set down her books and hurried over. She felt herself blushing as she took the fry pan from Ada, who looked bewildered. She set it down, then fetched the dairy pan from its place. "This one."

Ada frowned as Rivka handed it to her. "They're just the same."

"They're not. We...I'm sorry, I thought Aaron would have said..." An odd, hollow feeling in her chest made it difficult to explain what should be simple—dairy pan for dairy, meat pan for meat. But Ada was Aaron's wife. If she didn't know which pan to use for what, it was because Aaron had not told her. Which meant he no longer kept *kashruth*. For how long, she wondered, and wanted very much to sit down and just breathe for a while.

"Why don't you show me, then," Ada said quietly.

Rivka set the dairy pan on the warm stovetop lid. "You wanted to add onions? I do that myself." It was easier to begin with something other than kashruth to focus on. "I learned it from Hannah Nathan. My mother tried to teach me to cook, but I didn't listen very well." She scraped off a dot of butter and dropped it in. "We use different pans for dairy—butter, milk—and meat. They can't go in the same one. Dishes, too. We keep them separate. Otherwise, the food isn't...right to eat."

Ada scooped up the onions. At Rivka's nod, she scattered them in the pan. They spat as they hit the melted butter. "Aaron never told me that." She watched Rivka with a guarded expression.

Explaining why it mattered suddenly felt overwhelming. What else had Aaron not told his wife? Ada likely had no idea of the trouble they would be in once everyone knew she was here, the *goyische* mulatto woman married to the rabbi's lost son. Rivka pulled out a chair and sat at the table. "This is how we do things. Only Aaron doesn't any more. I...I hadn't expected that."

Ada settled next to her. "Lot of things today you weren't expecting, I guess."

She couldn't answer. They sat in silence, listening to the onions sizzle. The scent of them, and of the beans, was a comfort.

"Aaron won't tell me about the man at the train station," Rivka said. "The one who led the attack on you in Alton. He said you saw him, too."

Ada looked at the bean pot. "He'll have his reasons."

"Will you tell me?"

Ada got up, went to the stove and stirred the onions. "These are about done." She wrapped her hand in a corner of her apron, lifted the pan, and scraped the onions in with the beans. "I need to find Nat. It's time for his reading lesson." Without looking at Rivka, she turned and left the kitchen.

Rivka stared after her. One hand found the end of the strap that held her books together, and she toyed with it. A simple question was all she'd asked, yet neither Ada nor Aaron would answer it.

It made no sense, she thought in sudden frustration, and went to put her books away upstairs.

ELEVEN

January 1865

The Liberty Inn is full of gray uniforms tonight. Dorrie counts three dozen in the common room, maybe more. The local farmers, in their homespun shirts and breeches, look faded and worn among them. As faded and worn as Dorrie feels.

How she wants to be one of the soldiers, laughing and drinking and trading stories. Still fighting Yankees and proud of it, instead of hiding her face and scraping a living in this tiny Virginia town just over the Tennessee border. But she can see the strain beneath the guffaws and boasts—the sneaking, cold fear that God is not on the side of the South after all. Gettysburg was the first proof. There've been others in the year and a half since. How many more are to come?

She won't think of that now. She buries her fears in her work, carrying trays of beer from table to table and to groups of men standing in corners, until she feels ready to drop where she stands. This job is one step up from selling herself—but it's better than starving out the winter, when nothing grows and all the wildlife has fled the advance and retreat of armies. She was lucky to get it when she stopped here five months ago, footsore from her long journey home—though it isn't home anymore, not after what happened there—and then through the mountains to this place. No Yankee soldiers here, certainly not any who'd recognize her, especially now that she's a woman again.

She takes hold of another tray and waits as Joel the barman fills a brace of beer mugs. The tray's edge—smooth, rounded wood—feels slick and cool. Like her rifle. The desire to heft the gun again comes on her like an illness. Cold sweat breaks out on her forehead, and she leans hard against the bar. The rifle is gone, gone on that dark hillside by a creek in East Tennessee. Gone like Tom, like Father, like home. Searing images crowd into her brain—her father gut-stabbed by a Union soldier's sword, leaking red blood while her useless screams echoed off the parlor walls. Her brother, blank-eyed and still, by the Union campfire, his pale fingers curving upward from the dark earth.

"You all right, honey?" Joel's soft voice sounds in her ear. His thinning hair and bent back make him look years older than the thirty he is. More than once since starting work here she's heard him curse the afflicted spine that keeps him from joining the army. Instead, he serves liquor to soldiers passing through and hangs on every word he can coax from them about battles they've fought, victories they've won. So far, the war has bypassed this little place. Sometimes Dorrie wonders how long they've got before the bluecoats come here, too. Her palms itch with the need for her rifle. Or a pistol, or even a knife.

"Dorrie?" Joel touches her hand. When she looks up, both his hands are wrapped around a beer mug. The strength of his grip tells her he wishes he had hold of her that way. He's sweet on her, though she can't imagine why. She never was a beauty, and now her face bears the mark of the hard living she's endured. Her hair is a barely respectable length, and she's gone skinny from too many months of foraging off the land or forgetting to eat what meals she can afford.

He nods toward the door to the storeroom. "You take a little rest in the back. Maggie can handle things on her own for a bit."

The storeroom smells of dust and spilled beer. She shuts the door behind her, grateful for the lessening of noise. The lamp she sets down on a nearby barrel casts weird shadows across the rough brick walls. The fitful light makes hulking ogres of the beer barrels and casks of port and wine. Bottles of whiskey and bourbon—got here somehow through the Northern port blockades—wink at her from a precious few stacked crates, their sides opened for ease of access. She could grab a bottle and drown her miseries in the burn of liquor. The owner, who rarely shows, will never know—and Joel, who knows the Liberty better than his own face, will never tell. She reaches toward the nearest crate, then lets her arm fall. Bourbon won't settle the sickness inside her.

She shuts her eyes against the dance of shadows. It reminds her of the Union camp, of the firelight flickering over Tom's slack face. He wasn't meant to die. He promised he wouldn't. *God's on our side, Dorrie.* He told her that after he joined up, standing by the parlor fireplace, tall and proud in his gray uniform. That grin on his face, the one that said he could do anything he dared to. *He'll keep me safe while we teach the Yankees a lesson they won't forget.*

Outside, in the common room, she hears glass shatter, followed by a swell of drunken laughter. Maggie needs help. She straightens slowly and leaves the storeroom. The lamp, turned out to save kerosene, goes on a shelf between storeroom and bar. She pastes a smile on her face, takes a full tray from Joel and walks it to the table he nods toward. Half a dozen soldiers sit there, the youngest still a boy, no older than sixteen. He's scrabbling on the floor in a puddle of spilled beer and broken glass. With a cry of triumph, he grabs the still-intact bottom portion of the glass and raises it to his mouth. A shard floats in what's left of the beer.

Before he can drink it, an older soldier blocks his arm with a chuckle. "Don't bother with that none. We got us some fresh right here." He looks at Dorrie when he says it, and she knows he doesn't mean fresh beer.

She quenches a shudder and hands the mugs around, then turns back toward the bar. Joel's steady gaze locks with hers, warm and welcome amid the chaos and din. He's watching out for her. If she had a heart inside her instead of a bruised stone, she'd find some way to let him know she's grateful.

As she reaches the counter, a blast of cold air announces another customer. Faded brown homespun shirt and trousers, scraggly dark hair and mustache. Another farmer, out to forget his troubles for an hour or two. As Dorrie waits for Joel to refill the tray, the farmer comes up to the bar. "Whiskey," he tells Joel as he pulls out a handful of scrip. "Best you got."

At the sound of his voice, Dorrie stiffens. A sideways glance lets her look him over. His hair is longer, and the beaten expression on his face is nothing like the boaster she once knew, but the eyes are right. The eyes, the long nose, the square stubbled jawline. When he reaches for the whiskey, she sees the puckered scar on the back of his hand, and she knows. Jefferson Holt. Tom's best friend from his army company, who left with him to fight the bluecoats on home ground, help him take back their house and land from Union troops. Who she fought side-by-side with for nearly a year across miles of Tennessee country.

Who ran off and left Tom dead. Left her as good as with the Yankees.

Rage rises like bile in her throat. He tosses back the whiskey, demands another, and she thinks of turning on him—striking the next glass out of his hand, screaming his name and his betrayal.

Through the red fury, a small cold voice whispers, *And then what?* She can see it happen, unfolding in her head like some mad waking dream. *Who's this crazy woman? I don't know her, never met her. Don't know what she's talking about. Must be drunk. Somebody send her home to her man, or her daddy, or whoever she belongs to.*

She'll be ridiculed, shamed. Joel won't throw her out, but word will get round and she'll be fired. Where will she go then? She's barely managed to get this far.

Holt's second whiskey comes, and he drinks it down. Dorrie watches his throat work, the bulge of his windpipe, his bobbing Adam's apple. How can this coward, this traitor, be alive and whole when Tom is dead? How can he have money for good whiskey when she has barely enough to feed herself?

Her tray is full again. Moving like a puppet, she heads away from the bar, toward another group of thirsty soldiers. There's nothing she can do. Nothing at all.

Cß

February 1865

The cold creek water makes Dorrie shiver in the thin light from the scattered stars. Kneeling at the water's edge, she splashes all the bare skin she can reach around her chemise—her arms and shoulders, her neck, the tops of her breasts where Jefferson Holt groped them. She can feel him washing away. Leaving her clean, truly clean for the first time in what feels like forever.

The wind bites her wet skin. Her dress and shawl will warm her, at least enough to do what's needful. She holds that thought to her like armor against the cold sick feeling that lurks in the back of her head.

She's seen dead men before. Even killed a few. But never so close as this, and never someone she knew.

She runs her wet hands over her arms and upper body, over every part of her Holt touched before she sank the hunting knife between his ribs. Goosebumps roughen her skin. She hauls herself to her feet and wraps her arms around her chest, then heads toward the spot where she left the wheelbarrow. Oddly, she thinks of Joel. He would've wanted to do what she's just done. She saw it in his face, that evening at the Liberty near three weeks gone when Holt shoved her against the wall for "a little kiss," his rough hands squeezing her breasts till she cried out in pain. Then Joel's footstep, his sharp voice—"Leave her alone!"—and Holt turning to sneer at him, calling him half-man, cripple. Terror threatened to drown her then. No one could help her, and she couldn't help herself. A weak woman, too weak to fight the bastard off without a weapon.

The hunting knife remedied that. It cost more than she'd thought, but the power it gave her was worth the price.

She plucks her dress and shawl from the barrow handles and puts them on. It was so easy to take him in the end. So easy to pretend she wanted him after all, so easy to go with him into the back room at the general store where he stocked boxes once a month to make ends meet. She'd worn the knife in a sheath around her thigh, easily accessible once her dress was off. With his hands fumbling at her chemise and his mouth smothering hers, he'd seen no threat until it was too late. Gorge rises as she remembers the taste of his tongue in her mouth—tobacco and old coffee and rotgut whiskey. The thick, ropy feel of it against hers, then its hard thrust almost to the back of her throat as she drove the knife home. His fall tore the knife from her grasp, the blade biting deeper as he hit the floor. She'd expected blood, but the knife kept it inside his body. She'd watched until the last light left his eyes and the stench of loosened bowels told her he was dead. Then she'd rolled him up in a blanket snatched off the shelves and lugged him out the back entrance, where the wheelbarrow was.

He's crumpled in there now, the lower part of one long leg flopping over the side. Hauling his dead weight into it took nearly every ounce of her strength. His heel kept up a steady drumbeat of small thuds as she pushed the barrow toward the creek, some hundred yards from the back of the store. Now, she looks over the bulging outline of his shrouded corpse one last time. Grim satisfaction comes to her, a sense of a dirty job well done.

She grips the barrow handles and maneuvers her load closer to the hard-frozen muddy bank. She flips back a corner of the blanket, grasps the knife hilt and yanks. The blade resists, then comes free. She wipes it on the grass, takes a moment to brace herself, and heaves the barrow sideways. Holt's body topples into the creek. The swift-running water will carry it away. Far enough, she hopes, for her to be well gone before anyone finds him.

She drops the knife in the barrow and heads away from the creek back toward the general store. The barrow is easy to push now. A laugh edged with nerves escapes her. She feels jittery, as if she's had too much coffee in too short a time. She felt this way the first time she shot a man, on patrol in the woods with Tom and Holt and the rest. A craving for drink hits her—good whiskey, smooth as silk and strong enough to sting the eyes. There's a bottle like that at the Liberty. In these dead hours of night, she could sneak in and get some. Just one swallow, enough to steady her. She reaches into her skirt pocket, feels the bulge of the small leather sack there. It holds all the wages she has left, plus the few small valuables she rescued from home. *Just one drink…*

She pockets the knife and leaves the barrow where she found it. The road nearby is a dusty track, pale in the starlight against the dark earth that surrounds it. Westward, it leads to the Liberty. Heading east, it winds through the foothills all the way to Richmond.

The papers say Richmond is under siege. But not fallen yet, despite Grant's best efforts to crush the heart of the Confederacy. There's a railroad there. Maybe a pawnbroker's, too, where she can turn the things she's carrying to good use.

She thinks of Tom, sees him grinning at her. Beckoning her down the road. She sets her feet on it, heading away from the Liberty, going toward the far horizon where the sun will rise.

TWELVE

April 25, 1872

Hazy morning sunshine cloaked Hanley in warmth as he walked eastward down Monroe on his way to Lake Street Station. The wet-mud scent of the Chicago River grew stronger as he neared its banks, while the rattle of wheels and clopping of hooves rose in volume. Carters' drays vied for space with horsecars and hackney cabs on the bridge up ahead, while on both sides of the river a steady stream of workingmen headed toward the building sites that were popping up like weeds with the advance of spring weather. Shopgirls and housewives were out as well, the latter with baskets over their arms on their way to greengrocers and butchers. Hanley reveled in the bustle of it all. He felt renewed along with the city, ready to embrace any challenge the day might bring.

Ahead of him, new structures lined the street as far as he could see—a few wooden shop fronts and small houses not yet weathered by wind and rain and last winter's snows, scattered amid hulking giants of brick and stone. The four-story bulk of the Bryan Block, at Monroe and LaSalle, gleamed in the sunlight. A monument to Chicago's resilience, the newspapers said. More likely to the spirit of moneymaking, Hanley thought, giving the building—mostly tenanted by real estate and insurance agents—a cynical eye. There'd been no shortage of new arrivals since the Fire, and the easing of winter's grip had brought more—bankers and builders, thieves and footpads, a spring freshet of human beings all looking to make their mark.

He slowed as he reached Canal Street, just west of the river. The tracks that ran next to it were empty, though a distant whistle warned him the next train would be passing soon. He could turn here, or cross the river and go further east before turning north to Lake Street. The tracks remained clear, the approaching train still a faraway dark splotch. Without giving himself time to think about it, he crossed the tracks and the bridge, and kept straight on toward Market Street.

The little Jewish neighborhood, with its frame houses and shops, looked just the same. He wondered what Rivka was doing now. Fine day like this, he'd be out digging the garden if he didn't have work. He could imagine Rivka doing that. Kneeling in the soil, trowel in hand, dark hair sliding loose from the kerchief she always wore. Turning the earth with the fierce strength of new beginnings, making a space where something could grow.

He shook himself. She was probably doing the day's shopping, or setting up for baking like Mam did on Thursdays. Not that Rivka Kelmansky's daily activities were any of his business. A lumber cart passed by. Hanley crossed the street in its wake. Ahead of him, he saw a slight woman in a black dress and kerchief. His steps quickened, and he called himself a fool even as he hurried to catch up with her. Then she turned into a greengrocer's shop, and he saw her face. Not Rivka after all.

The sharpness of his disappointment made him angry with himself. Rivka Kelmansky was no more to him than the daughter of a murder victim. A murder he'd solved. He'd no reason to think he'd ever see her again.

Some of the warmth had gone from the day. Putting his mind firmly on work, he hurried on toward Lake Street.

CB

Sergeant Thomas Moore, chief of the twelve-man detective squad, glanced up from the case notes he was reading when Hanley arrived in his office. "So what have you learned?"

"Ben Champion was stabbed to death with his own bayonet. By someone who knew what they were doing." Hanley recounted what Will Rushton had told him about the time of death, along with everything else he and Schmidt had learned about how Champion spent his final evening. "Given where he was killed, and with his boots off and his shirt undone, he may have had a woman with him. A high-class jilt, working with a sneak thief to rob the place while their mark was otherwise occupied, only it went badly wrong. Or someone snuck into the house and ambushed him. Though anyone lying in wait with murder on his mind would have brought his own knife, or even a pistol, unless he was afraid the neighbors would hear the shot. Plus, they'd have had to wait quite a while. Champion was home from three o'clock on, along with a private secretary, name of Alice Lockwood. He'd have heard a break-in attempt if—"

Moore interrupted him. "A woman secretary, at his home?"

Hanley nodded. "She was helping him with his war memoir. Which I didn't find, though it could be with his publisher. One of his neighbors mentioned it, said it was nearly finished." He gave Moore a wry smile. "I met Miss Lockwood as I was leaving North May Street. She didn't mention anyone calling on Champion in the late afternoon or early evening yesterday. He had a guest for supper, though. The dirty dishes were still there. Could've been Miss Lockwood, though she claims she left at six. If anyone saw her go, she'll be easy enough to rule out. Unfortunately, I've no one else to rule *in* yet."

"Neighbors not much help?"

"Not so far. Mrs. Thomashaw heard someone passing by around ten last night. She and the hired woman were up with a sick baby." He frowned. "The hired woman, Mary Olcott—there's something there, but I don't know what. She claims Champion got her the job with the Thomashaws, said her brother knew him in the war. Supposedly the Olcotts were loyalists in Virginia, run off by local Secesh after the brother was killed. I don't know yet if he was in the Union army or an irregular. There were plenty in some of those counties, on both sides." He paced across the room. "Mrs. Thomashaw thought Mary felt some attachment to Champion, though Mary herself didn't say much about it. Sidestepped my questions pretty neatly, in fact. She was around all night, though—taking turns walking the baby, making chamomile tea." He paused. "Funny thing, Alice Lockwood was Secesh. She admitted to it in our conversation."

"Did your victim know her background?"

"I doubt it. She'd not likely advertise it, especially when working for a Union soldier writing a book on the war. Must've needed the job, or else had quite the change of heart in the past few years."

Moore leaned back in his chair. "How's Schmidt working out?"

Hanley grinned back. "Like a hound on a scent. He's a quick thinker, and he's thorough. He found these, as a matter of fact." He dug in his pocket, pulled out the gold mourning ring and the broken chain, and handed them to Moore. "Hidden in the grass by the edge of the walk, like somebody lost them there."

Moore examined the jewelry. "Our killer, leaving in a hurry?"

"Could be. I'll ask Champion's cleaning woman if she's seen that ring before. I went to talk to her late yesterday, but her husband said she was at Mass. She was pretty shaken up by the whole thing."

Moore handed the ring and chain back. "She might know about a woman, too."

Hanley tucked the jewelry away. "You know Ben Champion was Will Rushton's commanding officer? They served together in the Eighty-Second Illinois."

Sympathy flitted across Moore's face. "Poor Rushton. Must have been a shock. Does he know anything useful?"

Hanley shook his head. "They'd lost touch. I'd not expect him to be much help, unless the reason for this murder goes all the way back to the war...but if that's so, I wonder why it took so long to play out. It's not impossible. I just don't think it's likely."

"Could be someone Champion knew then, that he didn't have a problem with until now."

"Or someone from one of his law cases. Or maybe even his abolitionist days, depending on how active he was. Though again, that's a long time ago."

Moore gave him a thin smile. "Fine Irishman you are. Don't you know the past is never dead?"

Hanley's answer came quick and sharp. "Unless we want it to be."

"I didn't mean your past. But what about the Secesh? Or people hereabouts who hated abolitionists for trying to bring some dignity to the black man that they thought should be reserved for whites? The kind who beat up and shot people for daring to say slavery was wrong. You think that past is dead to them?"

"Sounds like it's not dead to you." Hanley knew what Moore was talking about, though not what was driving him to raise it now. They didn't talk about it much—it was simply a part of their shared history. The occasional Negro who arrived for a meal or a few hours' sleep, Mam sending young Hanley with a message to a tavern a few blocks distant. Then Moore turning up, later in the night or just around dawn, to shepherd the fugitive away. Hanley'd known even then not to ask where. "You're not going to tell me you knew Champion? From before the war?"

Moore shook his head. "No. There were plenty of us working in Chicago, and it was safer not to know everyone else by sight or name. But I hate the thought that he might have died because of something he did back then, that someone couldn't let go."

Hanley frowned. "There would still have to be something more recent. Something that happened, something that changed. A person with a killing grudge doesn't wait this long for a convenient time to act on it."

"So go find out." Moore's smile took any sting from his words. "And take Schmidt with you when you can."

❦

Hanley was thinking of what Moore had said as he walked downstairs to the station lobby. About the past not being dead, about Secesh and grudges and old hatreds. He knew some folk could never let things go. He'd served with his share of Irishmen who hated the English, including fellow Americans with even a hint of English blood. Because of the Famine, for all it was a generation gone, or older grievances still as fresh to them as yesterday. Yet he couldn't understand it. He felt it in the songs and tales Mam had raised him with, along with her steady hand and sharp tongue. But when the music and stories ended, that feeling went away too. *As it should*, he thought as he pushed open the heavy front door. This was America, where people looked forward. Where you could make what you wanted of yourself, provided you worked at it and were plenty stubborn. Wasn't he living proof?

He went out into the sunshine and headed down the boardwalk, his mind more on the conversation with Moore than on where he was going. What sort of past did Champion have? Did any of it matter, and how much?

"Detective Hanley!" A familiar voice. Feminine, low-pitched and clear. He blinked, feeling stunned, as a workman hurried past and left a clear view of the boardwalk ahead. A slight young woman stood a few feet away, in a black dress and kerchief, a determined look on her strong-boned face. The look combined worry and warmth, as if despite whatever clearly troubled her, she felt glad to see him.

The sight of her made him so happy, he spoke before he thought. "Rivka," he said. And then could have kicked himself.

She didn't look offended, or even seem to notice his use of her given name. She came straight up to him. "I need your help. It's my brother, Aaron. Someone is trying to kill him."

THIRTEEN

It took Hanley a moment to collect his wits. "Where is your brother now?" he asked, taking refuge in police procedure from a surge of warring emotions. He wanted to soothe away the worry in Rivka's eyes, then go find whoever was threatening her brother and pound him to pieces. He jammed his hands into his coat pockets. He would need to spend time with her, of course, investigating the crime she'd just dropped in his lap. Possible crime—he didn't know what had happened yet. His eagerness at the prospect came with a touch of guilt, but not enough to quash the feeling.

"At home," Rivka said. "He is well for the moment. But afraid."

"I'd best see him now, then. Will he talk to me?"

She looked hesitant for the first time. "We can only try."

He wondered, as they hurried down the boardwalk, why he hadn't heard of Aaron before. Until a minute ago, he'd no notion the man existed. Why hadn't Rivka's brother turned up when Rabbi Kelmansky was murdered last winter? No one had so much as mentioned him then, Hanley recalled. He wondered what the story was, and why the man was here now.

The parlor of the little house on Market Street was much as he remembered, neatly kept and full of books. Two people sat on the small sofa—a dark-haired, bearded man in a plain shirt and trousers, and a mulatto woman in a blue calico work dress. The man—Aaron Kelmansky, Hanley guessed—perched on the sofa's edge, his body stiff and tense. He wore a skullcap and held a book with Hebrew lettering on the spine. The woman was mending a boy-sized shirt. She hid it well, but the set of her shoulders suggested unease to match Aaron's.

66

Her presence surprised Hanley. What was a mulatto woman doing in Rivka's house?

Rivka walked over to her brother, who stood with his book in hand. "This is Detective Hanley," she said. "Talk to him. He can help."

Aaron gave her a questioning glance, then studied Hanley as if taking his measure. Hanley sized Aaron up in turn. Tall as himself but slimmer, an openness to his face despite the guarded look he wore. A man used to trusting, Hanley thought, until necessity taught him otherwise. "I understand someone tried to kill you, Mr. Kelmansky. Tell me about it?"

Aaron looked down at his book, fidgeting with its pages. The mulatto woman set down her sewing, watched him for a long moment. Her face was the hue of light caramel, fine-boned as a white woman's and taut with anger. She had striking eyes, gray-green. "They ran us off," she said finally, in the soft rolling tones of a Southerner. *Another one*, Hanley thought. "Figured we'd be easy pickings. We weren't."

"And you are?"

"Ada Kelmansky. Ada Whittier that was, if it matters."

They were married. Hanley did his best to keep his amazement from showing. He turned to Aaron. "Who ran you off, from where? When? How many men were involved?"

Aaron swallowed. "Four of them," he said. "Only one I can put a name to, though I can guess some of the others. They attacked our farm in Alton. And the man—" He stopped, his eyes on Hanley's face, what little hope there was in them leaching away. "You can't do anything, can you? There's no point in my going on. You can't help."

Hanley let out a breath. He knew what he had to say next, had known it the moment Aaron mentioned Alton, and he hated the necessity. "The problem is jurisdiction. I work for the city of Chicago. What happens in Alton is for the Alton police to sort out."

"But…" Rivka's dismay made Hanley feel hollow. "The man is here. In Chicago." She turned to Aaron. "You saw him. You told me so."

"Yes, but he hasn't *done* anything."

"That you know of," Hanley heard himself say. Somewhere, a

67

skeptical part of his brain was telling him to leave it—what was he even dealing with here, some fellow visiting the city like a hundred others on any given day?—but Rivka was counting on him. She trusted him to do something to help her brother, and do something he would. "Did he see you? Does he know you're here?"

"I don't know. If he did, what then? Does something have to happen?"

"Depends on who he is and what he's here for." Hanley fished his sketchbook and a pencil out of his coat pocket. "Tell me what happened in Alton, and when, and who this man is."

"Lucas Errol." Aaron paced across the small parlor. "He owns a factory that makes farming equipment, plus some warehouses by the Mississippi. I think he's in river shipping as well. He does a good business, good enough to give away money and get his name in the paper. A leading citizen." His tone was bitter. "Joseph never trusted him. Joseph Levin, my friend. He's dead. Errol killed him."

Swiftly, Hanley took notes. "Go on."

Aaron continued to pace. "It was Monday night. Joseph came to supper. We'd scarcely sat down when we heard horses. Four riders, coming fast. We knew what that meant. There'd been rumors in town. Joseph and I had our service revolvers. Ada took the rifle, and we went out to face them down." He halted near Ada and laid a hand on her shoulder. She reached up and covered his fingers. The intimate gesture discomfited Hanley, but he suppressed his reaction and kept listening. "Three of them rode straight toward our house," Aaron went on. "Ada shot first. She knocked the lead man clean off his horse."

She scowled. "Didn't kill him, more's the pity. Just gave him a souvenir to carry 'round." She glanced up at Aaron. "Aaron and Joseph shot the second man. He didn't get up again. His friends dragged him off. We still don't know if he's dead or alive."

"Was Lucas Errol one of the friends?"

Aaron shook his head. "He was the fourth man. He just sat there on his horse, watching, while the others charged us. When they went down, he turned tail and galloped into the dark. Joseph went after him." He hunched his shoulders, as if the memory hurt him. "A minute later,

I heard a horse screaming. Then a shot. I ran toward the sounds. I saw Joseph not ten feet into the trees around our farmland. Down, still, shot through the neck. The horse was I don't know where. He'd thrown his rider. I saw the man on the ground, a pistol in his hand. There wasn't time to bring up my gun. I threw myself at him. We grappled. He dropped the pistol. I knocked it away into the leaves. His mask came off as we struggled, and I got a good look at him."

"Then what happened?"

"He hit me," Aaron said. "Hard to the jaw. I fell back and he ran off. I felt dizzy, and it took me a few minutes to get up. I went to Joseph…" His voice cracked. "He was dead."

His gaze went distant. Hanley could guess what he was seeing—his friend's corpse sprawled on the damp ground, killed by a coward no better than the Rebs he'd fought. Hanley's own memories of the war rose—dead bodies in blue and gray, scattered across the earth like wheat stalks cut down by a careless God. Worse, the men still living—bloody limbs and shattered bones and faces taut with agony, begging for the swift mercy of a gunshot to the head.

He banished the memories with an effort. "Where did you serve?" he asked.

"Eighty-Second Illinois Infantry. Company C, the Concordia Guards." Aaron's shoulders straightened, and for a moment Hanley glimpsed him as he must have looked on the parade ground. "Every man of us a Jewish patriot."

Ben Champion's regiment, and Will Rushton's. But not the same company. Neither Champion nor Will was Jewish. The Eighty-Second was mostly raised in Chicago, if he recalled, just like his own regiment. Some joined up later, farm boys from west and south of the city, Peoria and Springfield and Alton. He wondered if Champion had kept up with any of his squad-mates, the men who'd served directly under him. Those who survived the war would've known him well enough to give Hanley a sense of the man.

He brought himself back to the problem at hand. "What does Errol look like?"

Aaron described him with the precision of a soldier's report. "Six feet or so, large-built, running to paunch in the belly. Thinning blond hair, neat beard and mustache. They're darker, markedly so, more of a medium brown. He dresses like a rich man. He had on a brown suit when I saw him at the train station."

"That'd be the Chicago & Alton," Hanley murmured, mostly to himself. "I don't suppose you saw him with anyone? Someone meeting him, maybe?" If Errol had met a local, finding that person might give Hanley something to hang jurisdiction on. Slim a hope as it was, he refused to discard it.

Aaron shook his head. "In the crowds, I couldn't tell. He was right by the train. As soon as we saw him, we moved off as fast as we could."

"What time was this?"

A quick, uneasy glance at Rivka. Before Hanley could wonder at that, Ada answered. "Around noon Tuesday. Seemed like we were on that train forever."

Aaron was staring down at his book again. Rivka's gaze rested on him, a slight frown on her face. Then she shook it off and glanced at Hanley. The hope and trust he saw in her eyes made his heart skip. "I'll see what I can do," he said, looking last and longest at Rivka as he took his leave of them.

FOURTEEN

Enlarged heart," Will Rushton said. His voice sounded unnaturally loud in the big, open examining room at the city morgue. "Mr. Schultz died of a heart attack."

The coroner nodded. "I'll let the family know." He headed toward the doorway that led to the inquest room down the hall, where the Schultz family waited. At the threshold, he halted. "Why don't you take the day? You look like you could use some time off."

"I'm fine." Will managed a smile as he took a needle and suturing thread from his autopsy kit. The last thing he wanted was time on his hands.

"If you're sure..." The coroner lingered, as if awaiting an answer. Will kept threading the needle. After a moment, the other man left.

Will started closing up the dead man's chest. His hands moved automatically while his thoughts drifted where he didn't want them to go. Ben Champion's death was a weight on his mind, dragging everything toward it like gravity. *What am I going to do?*

He strode to the sink, rinsed his hands, poured a glass of water and gulped it like whiskey. The water did nothing to settle his churning stomach. The sound of footsteps made him twitch like a startled horse. He gulped more water and set the glass down, eyes on the examining room doorway.

He'd half-expected Hanley. Instead, Uncle Josiah stepped through it, one hand over his nose and mouth. Will couldn't say a word, even to greet him. In his fine suit, his gray hair immaculate, if too thin on top and too long for fashion, he looked thoroughly out of place. He lingered by the doorway, as if steeling himself against the odor of death that Will scarcely noticed anymore, then lowered his hand and moved further in. Upon reaching Will, he clapped him gently on the shoulder. "Don't look like that. It'll be all right."

Hope blazed up. "You found the note?"

Josiah's hand dropped and he glanced away. "Not yet. I'll have another look around the office when I get there."

"Nothing at the house?"

Josiah shook his head.

Will paced away from him. "I never should have gone to the Tremont. I should've known it would all go to hell, the stubborn son of a..." His own words, hanging in the chilly air of the morgue, made him flinch. He'd been grateful for that stubbornness once, for Champion's conviction that it was his job to right the wrongs of the world. Will had the life he had because of it. Until that same damned stubbornness threatened to take it all away. "The detective on the case—I know him. Frank Hanley. He's dogged, and sharp as a pin. I lied to him. He'll find out about Tremont House, someone will remember me, and then—"

"He won't find out." Josiah's voice was sharp with what he clearly meant as conviction, but to Will it sounded more like fear. "I'll see to that."

಄

Rivka hurried down Madison Street, empty shopping basket swinging over one arm. She would have to buy something, of course, in time to bring it home before her afternoon English class. She had told Aaron she was going to the butcher's, which wasn't exactly a lie. With three people turning up unexpectedly, she would need more food. Aaron didn't have to know where else she planned to go. As skittish as he was, it was a kindness not to tell him.

The Chicago & Alton Railway depot was less than a block ahead. She didn't know whom to approach once she got there, or even what to ask. But she wanted to learn what she could, give Hanley something to start with. And also, possibly, begin to find out what Aaron wasn't telling her.

She did her best to recall details about Lucas Errol as she hurried along.

Height, build, coloring, clothing. A well-off businessman, prominent in Alton. There had been talk, Aaron said, of his running for mayor when the current one's term ran out. She knew what train the man had come on as well, thanks to Ada. It surprised her to learn that Aaron and his family had been in Chicago since Tuesday afternoon, yet had not reached her doorstep until late Wednesday morning. "Why didn't you come here right away?" she had asked him, while he stood with his back to her, studying the bookshelves as if the answer to every trouble lay in the black-spined volumes there.

After a long silence, he'd answered, the words sounding pulled out of him. "I was afraid."

"You thought Papa would turn you away."

He'd shrugged in response, still unable to look her in the eye.

She reached the depot and went inside, where a surge of motion and noise engulfed her. Steam, smoke, the shriek of train brakes, and the clanging of bells blended with the dull roar of the crowds that swept through the cavernous space. Passengers disembarked or dashed for trains they wanted to board. Men and women milled around ticket windows or in clumps on the main floor. Children ran and shouted amid the throngs. A large man in a homespun jacket and flat cap jostled her as he passed, without a word of pardon. Someone else knocked against her empty basket, throwing her off balance. She stumbled, and a stranger's hand reached out to steady her.

"Whups there, miss," the stranger said. A man's voice, deep and smooth. His hand on her shoulder was the dark brown of a chestnut hull. "Don't be goin' over, now."

She looked up and saw a tall, thin Negro in a porter's blue uniform and gold-rimmed cap. His other hand gripped a pushcart loaded with luggage. He smiled at her, showing a gap in his bottom teeth. "Gotta be careful in the crowds. You have a nice day now, miss."

"Please," she said, as he started to leave with his load. "Can you tell me where the train comes in from Alton?"

"Platform Four, over there," he said, with a nod and a gesture. "You want tickets, or you meetin' somebody?"

"Meeting someone." Lucas Errol, arriving from Alton, wouldn't have bought a ticket here. But someone like this porter, working near

73

the train platform, might have noticed him. He surely had business in the city, and Hanley had asked if Errol met anyone at the train station. Maybe Errol came here regularly. "Do you work here every day?"

He nodded. "And I best get back to it." He touched his hat and moved away, dragging the cart behind him.

She followed. "What about Tuesday?"

He frowned, looking puzzled. She could guess what he was thinking—*Who is this strange girl, asking me questions?*—and her face warmed, but she didn't know any better way to start.

"I was here then, yeah," he said.

She thought quickly. "My cousin was supposed to be on the ten o'clock train from Alton Monday night. It would have gotten here Tuesday, around noon or so. But he has not come to our house, and we've had no word..." Her story sounded thin, but the porter looked sympathetic, so she plunged on. "If...if there is any chance someone saw him here that day...or did not see him, then we will know what to do next. Simply wait to hear from him again, or go to the police. In case something happened." She wished Hanley were here. He would know how to do this without sounding ridiculous.

The porter was shaking his head. "Lotta folks go through here in a day. You're lookin' for one fella, gonna be hard to notice. He look like you much?"

"Hardly at all." She described Lucas Errol as best she could, especially his light hair and darker brown beard.

The porter's face didn't hold much hope. "Sorry, miss. Can't say I remember him. I got a lot of ground to cover. Less'n I was right by the train when it come in, I wouldn'ta seen him."

Her face must have shown her feelings. He gave her a sympathetic smile. "Tell you what. You go on over to Platform Four—that's the Alton train, just got here—and ask the conductor. Name of Bert. He's on the Alton to Chicago run regular. He might remember somethin'. You tell him Isaiah sent you." With a friendly wave, he moved off.

Isaiah. A good name. She watched him go, then tightened her grip on her basket and headed toward Platform Four.

The conductor proved more helpful than Rivka had dared hope. He remembered Lucas Errol, who apparently came to Chicago at least once a month, and also a man who'd met him. That was unusual. "'Nother tall fellow," he said as they ambled down the train's length. He kept his gaze mostly on the engine, with occasional glances toward her as he spoke. "Taller than your cousin. Over six foot by my guess, and thin to boot. 'Specially in the face. Well dressed. Taller one had red hair, with an overgrown mustache and sideburns. Those caught my eye—you don't see 'em much now. Clean-shaven or a neat mustache and beard, that's the fashion nowadays."

"Do you know the other man's name?" She doubted it, but it was worth a try.

He shook his head with a smile. "Bless you, no. Not like he was President Grant, or Governor Palmer, or some such. Just a fellow meeting a friend."

"A friend?"

"Seemed like. They shook hands like it meant something, clapped each other on the back." He glanced down at her with a puzzled look. "The blond fellow's your cousin, you said?"

She nodded, thanked him and left the platform. She would have to hurry to Klein's and then home if she hoped to be on time for English class. The noise and chaos of the depot, so overwhelming before, buoyed her as she headed toward the doors to the street. She had succeeded, at least a little. Hanley would know how to make use of what she'd learned.

As she walked back toward Market Street, she wondered whether he would be proud of her.

FIFTEEN

C an't say as I know the man." Gentle Annie Stafford scowled as she shifted forward in her chair just enough to pick up her tea. She cradled the china cup delicately, a graceful action at odds with her huge hands. Never a slim woman, Chicago's fattest brothel-keeper had taken on even more weight in the years since Hanley had last seen her—in this same room, him in his patrolman's uniform, accompanying the detective who'd questioned her about a brutal robbery on the edge of the crime-ridden cesspool known as Little Cheyenne.

Annie had been happy to help, given that the bawdy house where the crime took place belonged to her younger and prettier rival, Carrie Watson. Hanley had already been to Carrie's place this morning—a landmark of sorts on South Clark Street, a lucky survivor of the Fire. He'd asked about Captain Champion, with no luck. On a whim he'd inquired after Lucas Errol also. Rich businessmen visiting Chicago tended to frequent the finer establishments of ill repute, but Carrie said she didn't know the name, and she valued her good relations with the police enough that Hanley believed her.

Now, sitting in Annie's parlor with its velvet-flocked wallpaper and overdone elegance, he felt as if he'd stepped back in time. He half-expected to run into his former self—not Officer Hanley, but the damn fool gambler, strolling in the front door with a night's winnings in his pocket and a good time with a girl on his mind. Before Pegeen, and the loss of her. Not that he'd ever been able to afford one of Annie's women. Ben Champion, though, surely could. "You never saw Champion here, or sent any of your girls to his home?"

Annie took a silver flask from her dress pocket and dumped a generous slug of something into her tea. The odor of gin stung Hanley's nose. "If I had, they'd not have gone there with thieving in mind, let alone murder. Bad for business if word got 'round."

"I was thinking of someone acting independently. Using you as cover for the robbery, murder being an unplanned consequence."

"Using my reputation, you mean." Her eyes flicked to the bullwhip that hung from an ornate lamp-bracket on the wall. The story of how she'd used that whip to "persuade" gambling prince Cap Hyman to marry her back in '66 was part of Chicago criminal lore. "Anybody trying that would soon regret their folly." She took a genteel sip of her gin-laced tea. "Sorry, Frank. If it's answers you're looking for, I haven't got them. Not about your murder victim, or this Errol fellow either."

"I had to ask." He drained his own cup. Such a simple solution, it would've been. A break-in gone wrong, the miscreants found and arrested, case closed. If Champion had a taste for prostitutes in the first place, though Annie didn't think so. He certainly seemed drawn to women, especially women in trouble. And Hanley'd figured he might as well ask her about Errol while he was there...a bird in the hand, and all. "Thanks for your help."

Annie fixed him with a sharp-eyed stare. "Just be sure the higher-ups remember it." Then her expression softened. "I never thought I'd say this, but the honest life suits you. More's the pity. Good-looking, open-faced fellow like you, a natural bunco man...waste of talent."

"Oh, it's not wasted." He set his cup down and stood. "I'll drop a word in the right ears about how cooperative you've been. Trust me for that."

Her belly laugh surprised him. "I do, Frank. I surely do."

He stepped out of the brothel and started down the street, marveling at the quiet on South Clark at this time of the morning. The higher-class vice dens did some daylight business, but far less than at night, and the gambling hells were pretty much closed until much nearer the supper hour. A solitary figure ambling up the boardwalk, in a gentleman's frock coat and the latest in fashionable hats, was the only other person out and about. *Which fine establishment is he going to, or did he come from?* Hanley wondered. He nodded to the fellow as they drew closer to each other, idly noting the overdone mustache and flowing red sideburns that only emphasized the horse-like leanness of the man's face. Not often you saw men wearing sideburns nowadays.

Sideburns looked startled, then abruptly glanced away. One gloved hand fumbled at his coat collar, turning it up as if to hide behind it. The futility of that made Hanley smile. He wished the fellow good morning, then stopped to watch as he turned in at Gentle Annie's. *Early customer. He'll have his pick of the girls...if any are awake.*

With a chuckle and a shake of his head, Hanley walked on.

03

A short while later, he rode a jolting horsecar south on State Street toward the end of the line. From there, just under a half-mile's walk would bring him to the Prairie Avenue neighborhood, a wealthy enclave for Chicago's better heeled, where Captain Champion's law office was. High-priced chambers in the midst of rich clients weren't exactly what Hanley'd expected of an idealist who went to war to free the slaves, though Champion might have needed the money to keep up his house. Life in the man's own neighborhood of North May Street didn't come cheap. And he'd heard of other lawyers taking up temporary offices in various parts of the city while they waited for the downtown buildings where they normally worked to be rebuilt.

A whisper of envy flashed through his mind. Suddenly he was fourteen again, trapped and desperate and bitterly jealous of the easy life some people had. What he wouldn't have given to live in a fine big house on a quiet tree-lined street. No worries about how much food was left in the larder, where they'd get more if Mam's customers didn't pay for the shirts and dresses she mended and sewed. No lying awake at night, wondering where he could find a job that paid more than a few coins a day. And then later, after he'd landed work on the docks, lying awake with a sick stomach, wondering how long before some copper caught him stealing. Or Mam did, and shriveled his soul with a look that said she'd raised him for nothing. All the strength and pride she'd taught him turned to thieving, her only son bringing her to shame.

His cheeks burned at the memory. But that time was long gone, by his own choice. It was only the visit to Little Cheyenne that brought the past to mind so forcefully. And, if sometimes he still wanted better than he could get on a policeman's wages, what of it? He'd learned to be satisfied with what he had. The war, and the second chance Sergeant Moore had bought him by taking him on the police force, had taught him that.

Braced against the occasional jolts and jerks of the ride, he took out his sketchbook and pencil, flipped to a blank page, and started to draw. He paused every so often to recall a detail here and there, but gradually the face of Lucas Errol took shape. Or at least a reasonable likeness, from Aaron Kelmansky's description. Aaron could judge it when Hanley next saw him.

At Twenty-Second Street he got off the horsecar and walked east, picking up a cold beef sandwich from a street vendor along the way. The bread wasn't a patch on Mam's, but the beef was tasty enough. He finished his lunch and dusted crumbs off his hands. Champion's law office was worth a look—for case notes, files, anything that might point to a lead in his murder. Better yet, a law partner, if Champion had one. With no notion where to find close friends of the dead man, a colleague might be his best bet for discovering what he could of Champion and his activities in the days and weeks before his death. That duty fulfilled, Hanley could take some time to keep his word to Rivka and search more for Lucas Errol.

He turned onto Michigan Avenue and headed southward, the breeze off the lakefront rich and damp in his nose. The sight of Lake Michigan, glimpsed between the buildings he passed, made him shiver, despite the sunny day. Would he ever see the lake without feeling the chill of it up to his shoulders, while a wall of flames roared like a monstrous live thing behind him? He glanced away, then stopped and made himself stare out at the patch of lake visible beyond him. Blue water, blue sky. Three puffs of white cloud, like sheep grazing in Heaven. Beautiful.

Peaceful. *The peace of the grave...* Impatient with his own fey brain, he shook his head and hurried onward.

Champion's law office was on Indiana Avenue just west of Prairie. With its tree-lined boulevards and midday tranquility, the area felt worlds away from the barely organized chaos of downtown Chicago, where the air rang with hammering and workmen's voices and tasted of brick dust and ambition. Hanley found the relative quiet, broken by an occasional passing dray or hack, unsettling. Funny to think he'd once dreamed of calling someplace like this home. In the years since, he'd come to prefer the bustle of human beings going about their daily business to the sleepy elegance through which he now walked. What had Captain Champion felt about the contrast, he wondered. Anything at all?

Soon enough he reached his destination, a gray stone row house with large bay windows and an arched door. Champion's office was on the first floor. The building manager, a barrel-shaped ex-soldier named Edison, gave Hanley's search warrant a cursory glance and then let him in. He hadn't known Champion especially well, he said when Hanley asked, but thought him a good tenant and a gentleman. Mr. Rushton upstairs, his partner, knew him better. They'd worked together for years, since before the war.

The surname caught Hanley's ear. "Mr. Rushton?"

"Josiah Rushton," Edison said as he unlocked the door to Champion's office. He moved with a slight limp, as if from a badly healed wound. Minié ball, Hanley guessed, and lucky it passed through. Had it hit bone, the man would be missing the limb. "He's a lawyer, too. Used to take fugitive slave cases, won 'em more often than not. Champion helped him on some, I think, back in the fifties."

Josiah Rushton was exactly who he'd hoped to see. Hanley wondered if he was related to Will. Mr. Rushton was at dinner, Edison said, but ought to be back soon. "I'll leave you to it. Just let me know when you're finished."

The office was spacious and flooded with light from the bay window, which faced the street. The room held a large oak desk, a padded leather chair, two straight-back chairs, a long bank of cubbyholes stuffed with papers, and several shelves full of law books. A photograph hung on the wall opposite the desk. Hanley recognized one of Matthew Brady's famous shots—a long line of Union cannons being guarded by a Negro soldier.

Unlike at Champion's home, the desk was littered with papers. Hanley sifted through them. He saw case notes in the same bold slant as on the paid bills in Champion's study, correspondence in similar and different writing. A calendar held notations over the past two weeks, all in Champion's distinctive script. *Deposition, S. Harlow. Hearing, 1 p.m. Lunch, Tremont, noon.* He pulled out his sketchbook and made a note of that last one, as it had taken place the Friday before Champion died.

Next, he jotted down the gist of a pair of recent cases Champion seemed to have been working on. One involved a couple's adoption of the wife's eight-year-old niece, the other, two brothers disputing who should inherit the family butcher-shop. He noted their addresses, though a butcher-shop hardly seemed worth killing over.

As he moved the butcher-shop papers aside, a telegram caught his eye. He picked it up. Dated April 16th, just over a week ago, it had been sent from the Alton, Illinois post office. He read the brief message. *Captain Ben—Rec'd your letter. Found more to testify in Farnham. New development here—urgent we discuss. Arriving Thursday morning train. George Schuyler.*

Hanley set the paper down. The salutation *Captain Ben* indicated Schuyler knew Champion fairly well, most likely from the war. If he'd served in the Eighty-Second, his name should turn up in the rolls. Schuyler's telegram seemed to refer to a current case. Hanley searched the assorted notes again, looking for the names Schuyler or Farnham, but found nothing. The adoption papers were six weeks old, those on the butcher-shop dispute five. He searched the first two desk drawers, but found only stationery, envelopes, two fountain pens and an unopened bottle of black ink. As he reached for the next drawer, movement from the doorway caught his attention. He looked up.

The new arrival had a craggy, clean-shaven face and thinning gray hair that nearly brushed the shoulders of his well-cut suit. He topped six feet, and could have passed as an older brother of Chicago's eccentric former mayor, Long John Wentworth. Hanley thought fleetingly of the man Alice Lockwood had described, who'd passed her on the street the evening Champion died. There were similarities, but nothing to make him certain. As Hanley drew breath, the stranger spoke—politely, but with an edge of authority. "May I ask who you are, sir, and what you're doing in my colleague's office?"

SIXTEEN

Hanley fished out his badge. "Detective Frank Hanley, Chicago Police. I'm investigating Captain Champion's murder. You'd be Josiah Rushton?"

The man nodded. His wary look gave way to raw grief. "I saw the paper this morning. Ben..." His throat worked, and he glanced down. "No one should die like that. Ben least of all."

"I'm sorry for your loss," Hanley said as Josiah came further into the room. "Are you any relation to Will Rushton? Police surgeon at the city morgue?"

Josiah took a moment to answer. "He's my son." He pulled at his shirt collar as if it itched. Hanley noticed a wedding band on one finger. "Nephew, really. On my wife's side. We adopted him after he lost his parents. You work with him?"

Hanley covered his surprise with an easy grin. "Best man the department's ever had at that job, my sergeant says." He let the smile fade. "Will didn't tell me you and Champion were partners. He seemed to think you hardly knew each other."

Josiah shrugged. "We don't discuss my work much. Ben's name rarely came up."

Hanley nodded acknowledgment. The omission seemed curious, but not worth pursuing just now, when he had potential leads to dig into. "I'd appreciate your helping me out. I've been looking through the captain's papers, hoping to find something useful, but..." He gestured toward the littered desktop. "They're a mess. I don't know what's important and what's not. Can you tell me about cases he was working on recently? Anything he was worried about?"

"You think that's why he was killed? A case?" Josiah wet his lips. "I suppose it's possible. Though I don't like to think of any of our clients..."

"Murdering someone?"

Josiah's mouth twitched in a brief, grim smile. "As you said, Detective." He walked toward the desk, hands in his pockets. "I'll do the best I can. What do you want to know?"

It took ten minutes to dispense with the adoption and the butcher-shop. "The Sperlings have their final adoption hearing next week. Ben didn't have a lick of trouble with that case. The Harlow brothers... Sam's a blowhard, but Ben told me he'd settled him down. Sam came by here last week, full of bluster about how he wanted things handled. Ben wasn't worried. And frankly, I can't imagine either of the Harlows having the gumption to kill anyone."

Hanley picked up George Schuyler's telegram. "This is pretty recent. Mr. Schuyler refers to testimony in Farnham, but I haven't found anything else with that name. Do you know about it—or about Schuyler? Telegram says he was coming here last Thursday. Did he?"

Josiah read the telegram, a slight frown on his face. "Farnham and Chandler. They're gunmakers in Alton, or they were during the war. They've gone back to making farm implements—threshers, reaping machines. Ben was bringing suit against them under the False Claims Act."

Hanley tensed. "Because of their guns?"

Josiah nodded. "A bad shipment sent to the Eighty-Second Illinois. Ben's regiment. Two companies got them. The guns jammed up, or broke in soldiers' hands. Some exploded when fired. Ben saw it happen."

Hanley felt a surge of anger. The Eighty-Second wasn't alone in that misfortune. Men in his own unit and others had been crippled or killed that way—their fingers or hands blown off, some bleeding out before their comrades could tie off a tourniquet. "How many men died?"

"At least ten he could prove, from what Ben said. He was looking for others—witnesses and survivors. I think Schuyler was one. I know he was helping Ben find more. He served in Ben's squad in Company A." Josiah folded the telegram and set it down. "Schuyler was here last

Thursday. Ben took him to dinner. I couldn't tell you for certain what they talked about, but he came here a few times over the past several months, bringing depositions for Ben to review. Poor fellow—one arm was absolutely useless. Bent, like from a break badly set. He couldn't move it at all."

Hanley pulled up a straight-backed chair and motioned Josiah toward the other. "Tell me everything you can about Farnham and Chandler."

Josiah sat. "As I said, they made guns during the war. Some good, some not. Ben traced the bad ones to them through requisition lists—they tell which shipment came from which manufacturer. The tricky part is proving malfeasance, or at least neglect. Plenty of gun factories weren't set up to be any such thing—they made farm machinery, or stoves, or parts for train cars. After Fort Sumter, when we needed guns and cannon faster than we could make them, they had to change things almost overnight. Not surprising it didn't always go well."

"And the False Claims Act?"

"Lets any citizen with knowledge of a possible scheme to defraud the government start legal action against those responsible." Josiah smiled. "I prosecuted a case like that in '63. Bad pork. The shippers knew—they'd got it cheap because it was spoiled and made a killing on a government contract. The shipping manager blew the whistle on them."

"So Champion had a viable case against Farnham and Chandler?"

"Definitely. He didn't confide the details, but he did tell me that much."

New development here, Schuyler's telegram said. Something more than the usual depositions? "I'd like a look at the Farnham case papers, if I may."

Josiah hesitated. "It hasn't gone to trial yet. You understand, much of this is confidential."

"You tell me what is and what isn't. Whatever is, doesn't leave this room."

After another moment, Josiah nodded and went to the bank of cubbyholes against the far wall. He took out one of several rolled-up sets of papers, untied the red ribbon that bound them, and eyeballed them, then put them back and took out another. Then another. With a look of increasing dismay, he searched through the contents of surrounding cubbyholes. Finally, he looked at Hanley. "They're gone."

℃ℬ

A second, painstaking search for the papers turned up nothing. Josiah looked steadily more agitated as they went through the cubbyholes and Champion's desk. Aside from Schuyler's telegram, they found nothing related to the Farnham case.

Hanley closed the last desk drawer and turned to Josiah. "Could Champion have taken them home?" Though he didn't recall seeing anything there that looked like legal papers, and the name *Farnham* had rung no bells. He hadn't found much of anything among Champion's personal papers, in fact, which bothered him now more than it had at the time.

"Maybe." Josiah frowned. "He didn't often do that, though."

"His desk was a mess when I came in. Was that usual? Or could someone have been here?" Champion's desk at home was strikingly neat. Maybe someone had been *there*, and taken something away with them.

Josiah pulled at his collar. In his eyes, Hanley caught a flash of panic. "I...it's possible, I suppose. But God knows who, or when."

"When were you last in the building?"

"Yesterday."

"Your regular working hours?"

"Yes."

"And you saw nothing amiss when you left—no one around who shouldn't have been? What time did you leave, by the way?"

"I don't remember anything out of the ordinary. I left at my usual time, half past six."

Hanley went into the hall and called for the building manager. Edison appeared shortly, an inquiring look on his face. "How late were you here yesterday?" Hanley asked.

"Till six thirty." Edison glanced at Josiah. "Locked up after Mr. Rushton when he left."

"Other than Mr. Rushton, did you see anyone around?"

"Nope." He frowned. "There's copper pipe in the basement I've been laying—it wasn't touched. Not much else here to interest thieves."

A few brief questions accounted for the keys. Edison kept his with him. Josiah displayed his on a watch-chain and said he'd never missed it since Edison gave it to him. Presumably Champion had one as well, somewhere among his effects.

They went outside, where Hanley examined the street door. He saw faint scratches by the keyway, almost imperceptible to anyone who didn't know what to look for. "Hook pick. Rake pick, too, maybe. Cracksman's tools." He turned toward Josiah. "You're sure you saw no one last evening?"

"No one."

"What about Tuesday?"

Josiah looked startled, then wary. "I don't recall anyone hanging around here that evening, either."

∞

The law office had been interesting, in unexpected ways. A lawsuit that could bankrupt its target, missing case papers stolen from the law office or Champion's home. Definitely a promising lead. The Harlow brothers, by contrast, offered nothing to sink his teeth into. Hanley had gone to the butcher-shop and found Sam Harlow exactly as Josiah Rushton described him. The "blowhard" was forthright, even belligerent at first, about his visit to Ben Champion's office. "'Course I talked to him. You've got to keep after people, you want things done right. Maybe I got a little hot, but…" He mopped sweat off his face with the back of a hand half again as large as Hanley's own. "Anyway, I'm sorry he's dead. He was a good lawyer. Now I've got to start over, and God alone knows what that paper shuffler of Charlie's will pull in the meantime. Charlie and me, we've fought since we were kids. Don't know why. Just rub each other the wrong way." He scowled at Hanley. "But I'll tell you this, Charlie didn't kill anyone. Hasn't got it in him. Faints at the sight of blood, the lily-livered idiot. I'll swear to that in court if I have to."

Charles Harlow, found at his lawyer's office a few blocks from Ben Champion's, was Sam's opposite—thin and weedy, with spectacles sliding down his nose. He and his lawyer had dined late on Tuesday at a local chop-house, with dozens of fellow customers and a waiter as witnesses. None of which meant he couldn't have hired a murderer, or gotten himself to North May Street in the small hours to do the job, but the lawyer claimed confidence that they'd have won in court, and his words had the ring of conviction. Hanley crossed the Harlows off his short mental list of suspects. Maybe Champion's murder *was* an attempted robbery, despite what the madams and Union Street cops had said, and somewhere in the city were a terrified prostitute and her jilter waiting for Chicago's finest to knock on their doors. Or it had something to do with the Farnham lawsuit and the exploding guns. He should find this fellow Schuyler, see what he was all about and what "new development" he'd found in Alton.

The word *Alton* lingered in Hanley's mind. Aaron Kelmansky, the assault on his farm…Monday, the night before Ben Champion died… No, he was reaching. Wanting an excuse to see more of Rivka, prove her faith in him by linking her brother's attackers there to a heinous crime here. The thought of her made his heart flutter, and he cursed himself for a fool. Nothing could come of it. He wasn't even sure he wanted anything to. He would help her with the problem she'd dropped in his lap, but no more.

Hanley passed the return trip idly sketching Josiah from memory, with the notion of showing the sketch to Miss Lockwood when he saw her again. Could Josiah have been Champion's supper guest? Unlikely. He hadn't mentioned it, and there was no reason for him not to. By horsecar, hack or omnibus, the crosstown journey from Indiana Avenue to North May took at least an hour. Not much time for supper if Champion was retiring—or dead—by nine.

Schuyler seemed a likelier guest, if he'd stuck around. All Hanley had to do was find him.

The city directory was no help, he discovered when he stopped off at Lake Street Station to look Schuyler up. The squad room was mercifully quiet, only four detectives present, catching up on paperwork amid the reek of old coffee and dust. A couple of them gave him a nod as he entered and crossed to the bookshelves against the far wall. Plenty of Schuylers in the directory, but no George. He shoved the thick volume back into place with a sigh. City residents weren't obligated to list themselves—those who did so, did because they wanted to. Or maybe Schuyler lived in Alton, and went back there before Champion's murder. Will might know, or he could try the temporary city hall at Adams and LaSalle. Word among war vets on the force was that some Illinois regiments' muster rolls had been salvaged and ended up there after the Fire. The roll for the Eighty-Second would at least show where Schuyler hailed from.

He was turning toward the squad room doorway when the grinning desk sergeant poked his head around the jamb. "Lady here to see you, Detective Hanley," he called.

Who...? Not his sister, Kate, or his mother. The desk sergeant knew them by sight. He hurried through the doorway and stopped short. Rivka was waiting for him.

"Miss Kelmansky." Thank God, he'd remembered the right mode of address. Her hesitant smile faltered, and he felt a moment's nervousness. "Has something else happened? I'm sorry, I haven't had time yet to look much for Lucas Errol..."

The smile came back, and now he swore he saw a glimmer of mischief in it. "That's all right. I have."

SEVENTEEN

Y ou went to the Chicago & Alton depot?" Hanley was looking at Rivka as if she'd done something extraordinary—sprouted chicken feathers, or turned to stone.

His surprise nettled her, an unexpected feeling. Did he not think her capable of walking one block across the bridge to the train depot and asking a few questions? "Yes. I wanted to *do* something."

"You would," he said, a smile playing around his mouth. She felt a blush rising, and her irritation melted away. "Here." He gestured toward the doorway behind the lobby counter, through which she glimpsed the corners of a few desks and a tall window in need of washing. "Come into the squad room and tell me about this fellow Errol met."

She followed him, curious to see where he worked. The squad room was a drafty barn of a place, with dusty floors and battered furniture and a round-bellied coal stove in the corner. A dented tin pot sat on top of it. The smell of coffee hung in the air, dense as fog.

Hanley led her to his desk, one of four grouped on the left-hand side of the room. Two were occupied by men in rumpled shirts and trousers. Fellow detectives, she guessed. One was reading a sheaf of notes. The other glanced up and nodded at Hanley before going back to the form he was filling out. Hanley pulled his chair to one side, dusted it off and gestured for Rivka to sit. On his desk she saw stacks of papers, a leather-bound logbook, an inkwell and penholder, a clean coffee mug, and a framed drawing of two women. She recognized Hanley's mother from their brief meeting last winter. The younger woman was less familiar. His sister, perhaps? She recalled he had one. Pretty, certainly. It *could* be her. Rivka felt a pang of something she wasn't quite willing to call

90

jealousy. Over what? A picture belonging to Hanley that was none of her business.

"I don't know the man's name," she said as she settled into her chair. Hanley lounged against the side of his desk, an arm's length away. "But the train conductor told me what he looked like."

Hanley straightened, snagged a chair from an empty desk, and set it down next to her, then pulled out his sketchbook as he sat. "Describe the man, as best you remember."

She did so, watching in fascination as his pencil flew over the blank page. His hands, large and long fingered, moved with unexpected grace. When she mentioned the red hair and flowing sideburns, Hanley paused, frowning as if he'd thought of something, but he said nothing as he continued his task. "Who taught you to draw?" she asked, then bit her lip. What an idiotic question, and far too personal.

"My mother. She grew up...well, not rich, but a lot better off than my da. Her family wasn't too happy when she ran away with him." He broke off, a look on his face as if he'd said too much. "There." He pushed the sketchbook toward her. "Did I get everything? Thin face, mustache, sideburns?"

"I think so." She rested her fingers on the drawing's bottom edge. "I did not see him myself, so it's hard to say..."

"Your brother might have, though. Or his...his wife." He stumbled slightly over the last word. "They might have passed him in the crowd, just another stranger in a sea of people." He eased the sketchbook from her and flipped it shut. "Are they at home now? Maybe this'll jog their memories."

ॐ

"I'm sorry." Aaron, standing in the little front parlor with the drawing in hand, shook his head. "I don't recall this man."

"Maybe Ada, or Nat—" Rivka began, but his sharp headshake cut her off.

"They won't recall him either. All we wanted was to leave the train station, fast." He handed the sketchbook back to Hanley. "I apologize, Detective. We never should have troubled you about it."

Hanley turned to another page. "What about this one? I drew it from your description of Lucas Errol. Is it a good likeness?"

Aaron spared the second picture a moment's glance. "Yes. But it doesn't matter."

Rivka felt uneasy. He sounded so brusque, could hardly look Hanley in the face. He'd been far more open this morning, despite his fears. What had changed? "Aaron—"

"Rivka, please. Leave it. We've wasted the detective's time long enough."

She glanced over at Hanley. He was watching Aaron with an alertness she remembered from the investigation into her father's death—tamped down like a banked fire, but ready to blaze into life. "You don't want me to look for Lucas Errol, then...or for this fellow, whoever he is?"

"Yes. I mean, no. I don't want you looking for them. There was never much chance of your being able to help us anyway, as you yourself said." Aaron began pacing the room. He passed by a small table, where a folded newspaper lay next to one of their father's books, open and face down.

She saw Hanley's gaze shift to the newspaper. "Evening edition?"

Aaron stopped pacing. "This morning's. Jacob brought it." He shrugged. "Nothing much of interest in it. I've been gone from the city too long, and we don't plan to stay."

 C8

Rivka saw Hanley out, then went back to the parlor. Aaron stood staring out the window, one hand on the sill, positioned so his silhouette couldn't be seen through the lacy curtains. Mameh had made those—an irrelevant passing thought, her mind's attempt to distract her from her growing anxiety. "Why did you send Detective Hanley away?"

The hand on the sill curled into a fist. "We never should have come here. We'll go in the morning. I'll find out when the first train leaves."

He was making no sense. She wanted to shake him, but clenched her own fists to keep back the impulse. "You've hardly been here more than a day. Now you want to go away again? I don't understand."

"Good." He turned to leave the room, but she blocked his path.

"You can't go. How will you get money for tickets? Where will you—"

"I have money. I sold our plow horse."

"Where will you go? What about Ada? You don't even know what she thinks. And Nat, what about him? He's a child. How is it good for him if you run from here, like you did from Alton?" She broke off as her own words registered. "Did something else happen there? I know there's something you're not—"

"Nothing else happened." He stepped around her, toward the parlor doorway.

"Here, then," she said as he walked into the hall. "Something happened here. What?"

He stalked off toward the staircase. "Nothing. *Leave* it."

She hurried after him. The story he had told before, of armed men shooting and killing to drive them off their farm, was bad enough. What could be so much worse that he thought Chicago wasn't safe, either? "Don't go in the morning," she said, catching his wrist. He halted at her touch. "Give it a few days. A little time to see what happens. After ten years' absence, is that so much to ask?"

He stood motionless, saying nothing. Rivka counted heartbeats in the silence. Four of them passed before he answered her. "I don't know."

EIGHTEEN

April 8, 1865

Richmond is full of Union blue, her streets teeming with Yankee soldiers who walk around as if they own the place. *So they do,* Dorrie thinks bitterly as she watches out the window of her cramped hired room above a tavern. The owner and his family tried to flee, but Confederate soldiers burned the bridge over the James, and Jeff Davis commandeered the last train to Danville in the middle of the night. That left nothing for Richmonders to do but curse Davis for a coward and await the victorious Yankees' arrival.

The rumor mill has run wild for days with conflicting reports. Davis is re-establishing the capital in Danville and is determined to continue the fight; or the bluecoats nabbed him and threw him in prison, intending to parade him down the streets of Washington like a captured slave. General Lee surrendered and is under tight Union guard; or Lee will never surrender, and is gathering Richmond's defenders to stand against the Yankee conquerors. Lincoln is offering amnesty to Confederate soldiers who lay down their arms; or Lincoln is arming the darkies, and they'll come any moment to round up "Johnny Rebs" at gunpoint.

Dorrie recalls the blue-clad Negro soldiers, the first Northern troops to enter Richmond as the city burned. Rank upon rank of darkies with guns, marching in tight formation under the Union flag. The sight of them took the solid earth under her feet and turned it upside down. Negro soldiers, dressed like whites. Armed like whites. Acting like whites. Showing the people of Richmond what the new rules are, the new order for a conquered South. The bluecoats have set them free. They and the Yankees can do whatever they want, with no one to stop them.

She sees Negro Richmonders on the sidewalk below, with their dusky skins and patched clothes. Not that her own clothes look any better. Thin cotton petticoat and brown dress of cheap calico stolen off a washing-line outside the last little town before she reached Richmond nearly two months ago. Some of the darkies mingle freely with white folk, trusting the bluecoats to protect them should anyone object. All that blue, everywhere she looks.

Dorrie briefly closes her eyes. Her stomach is empty, has been since yesterday morning. Her sewing work, which barely keeps her in brown bread and coffee, has dried up while captive Richmond adapts to its Union masters. Most of Richmond's commercial district lies in smoking ruins, engulfed by the fire set when retreating Confederates burned the armory and the riverside tobacco warehouses. Union army sutlers, with their wagons full of provisions, have replaced the lost butcher-shops and bakeries and general stores...at least for those who have Union greenbacks to pay with.

Dorrie's own money might as well serve as curling-papers for her hair. She eases her little leather bag from her pocket and takes out a scroll-shaped silver brooch. A gift from Tom. She clenches a fist over it, so tightly the edges dig into her palms. Maybe one of the sutlers has a wife or sweetheart back home and will give her a few days' food for it. Her cheeks burn at the thought—she, Dorcas Whittier, daughter of Edward Whittier who owned one of the finest plantations in East Tennessee, reduced to begging Yankees for bread!—but pride fills no bellies.

She sets her jaw, and her hand rises to the thin gold chain around her neck. She wears it low down, well beneath the scar there. It holds the mourning ring Tom wore, that she took from his dead body. A thick gold band with leaf-patterned edges and a groove down the middle that cradles a narrow braid of their mother's dark hair. Dead in childbirth, Mama. Bearing her. She wasn't meant to know that, but the house slaves loved to gossip, and none of them noticed little Dorrie peeping round the kitchen door.

She holds the ring up. The red-gold strands she took from Tom's head and added to the braid gleam in the weak morning light. Is he dead because of her, too? Did he see the Yankee soldier club her down that terrible night, forget his own peril long enough for another bluecoat to shoot him? She doesn't even know which bluecoat it was. It might have been the scar-faced captain. Guilt swamps her in a wave that leaves her shaking. "You shouldn't have left me," she whispers, as if Tom were there to hear her. It can't be her fault, or his own, that he's dead. One more wrong to lay at the Yankees' feet.

Her growling stomach recalls her to her purpose. She lets the ring drop, musters her courage and heads downstairs to the street.

Soldiers swarm around the sutlers' wagons, a sea of blue stippled with brown and tan and mourning black—Richmonders in shabby shirts and trousers, or dresses five seasons out of fashion. The crush of people, and the stink of smoke that still hangs in the air this close to the burned district, rob Dorrie of breath. She catches a glimpse of the Stars and Stripes flying over the Capitol dome nearby and turns her eyes away. Food is all that matters. She pushes through the crowd toward the nearest sutler's wagon and wedges her way into line.

An endless time later, her turn comes. The sutler is built like a liquor barrel, with a woolly brown beard and a greedy look. Good. She can use that. "Give me a loaf of bread and four slices of cold beef. And a sack of tea, and half a dozen eggs." She can make the bread last three days, and some of the eggs will serve as payment for her room until she finds a way to get Union money. She shrinks from the most obvious one. She hasn't yet sunk that low. The thought of Jefferson Holt, crumpled on the storeroom floor with her knife in his belly, gives her a flash of strength. What he couldn't take, she's damned if she'll give for greenbacks. Surely not to the bluecoats. The idea makes her gut-sick.

"Ten dollars." The sutler speaks with a harsh Northern accent. He eyes her up and down, as if calculating the worth of her thin body underneath her dress. "You got cash?"

"I have this." Dorrie holds up the brooch. "Real silver. Worth double what you're asking, so I want change along with the food." She holds his gaze, daring him to disagree.

His answering gust of laughter smells of onions. "You got a damned nerve, I'll give you that." He braces his meaty arms on the sides of his cart and leans toward her. "But I don't need no gewgaws. What else you got?"

Her hand closes over the brooch. "I've got this. Now give me what I asked for."

He leers at her. "You come back after dark and ask for Scully. I'll give you something then. If I like what you give me first."

Fury wells up, overriding common sense. She spits in the sutler's face.

The chatter of the crowd ceases, and she feels a breath of air as those closest to her move away. The sutler stares at her as he wipes his cheek. "Get out of here. Or I'll see you in prison for assaulting a soldier."

She wants to punch his sneering face, grab his throat and squeeze it until something breaks inside. She wants her hunting knife to sink into his fat neck, or her rifle to shoot him dead with. All she can do is turn away. The crowd closes around the space she leaves behind. She takes a few steps, not knowing where she's going. Just away from the sutler, and anyone who saw her degradation.

A hand brushes her shoulder. She stiffens and looks up, ready for a fight. A Yankee soldier is staring down at her. She expects scorn, but sees none. He's young, though not a boy, with reddish hair a shade darker than Tom's. "Are you all right, miss?" He talks like a Northerner, but with a flavor of something foreign in it, as if he grew up speaking something other than plain English.

She doesn't trust herself to speak, merely nods. Kindness from a Yankee isn't something she's ready to deal with. Another soldier comes up, this one with a thin beard. "Trouble, Emil?" the new man says.

"Not for me." Emil addresses his next words to her. "If it's food you need, you'll do better over there." He gestures toward another sutler's wagon twenty feet away.

"I've no money." The admission, which she hasn't meant to make, comes out in a harsh whisper.

The bluecoats exchange glances. "I can spare a little," Emil says. "What about you?"

The other man shrugs. "Dollar or two. I was lucky at cards last night." He digs in his trouser pockets and comes up with a couple of bills, holds them out to her.

Dorrie stares at them. White paper, scallop edged in green, with a swirl of green links framing the numeral one. The swirl makes her think of chains. She should take the money, thank these two soldiers. She wants what the greenbacks can buy her so badly that her need shames her all the more. She hasn't even her dignity left, standing here in this dusty street with these young men in blue. Coming to her rescue, when she wouldn't need rescue if it weren't for the likes of them.

The street fades away. She's back home, in the hall by the parlor, a blue uniform filling her vision, sour breath in her nostrils and a harsh voice in her ears. *Give me what I want, bitch. Think you're so high and mighty, well, you ain't. You're nothing but a Reb.* Her scream raw in her throat as rough hands grope under her dress. Running footsteps. Papa shouting. The hurting hands off of her. A drawn blade in one of them, her father on the floor, his blood bright red on her skirt and her sleeves and her palms—

Someone touches her elbow. She flinches, sees Emil staring at her. "Come on," he says. Numb, she follows him toward the wagon.

The bluecoats buy her bread, eggs, and tea. She tries to hand Emil the brooch, but he won't take it. "Please," she says, and her voice breaks.

"Mueller!" Cheerful and hearty, a man calls out from behind them. They turn, and another bluecoat hurries up. Brown-haired like the soldier with Emil, he has a fuller beard and a rounder face. There's something wrong with his left arm. It's bent, and doesn't swing even a little bit. A war wound, she guesses, and wonders which Southern bullet he owes it to.

Emil's face splits in a broad grin. "Schuyler! We thought you'd gone home to Alton."

"I came back." He claps Emil on the shoulder with his good arm. "Signed up with the Freedmen's Bureau. They need everybody they can get. Clerks, teachers, doctors, legal aid...I told the captain already, he said he'd spread the word through all the companies in the Eighty-Second Illinois..."

The three men move off. On the far side of the street, they meet up with two more bluecoats. As the taller one turns to welcome the newcomers, she gets a good look at him. Blunt-cut hair, butternut brown; an old knife scar across one sharp cheekbone; full beard, long nose, deep-set eyes. Beside him is Nigger Billy like a slighter, younger shadow.

She can't move, can only stare. The scarred man's face in the campfire light. Those eyes full of contempt as he laid open her neck and his harsh voice threatened her with death. Billy, after, dropping hardtack and a canteen at her feet and telling her to get gone by sunrise.

They haven't noticed her yet. Dorrie ducks her head to hide her face, rearranges her purchases in the burlap sack the sutler gave her. Her hands are shaking. Best not touch the eggs, she'll break one. From the corner of her eye, she sees the scar-faced man and the others walking off down Broad Street. There's an inn over that way, where the owner hawks sandwiches and beer while proclaiming his loyalty to the Union and his hatred of slavery. Never mind that he owned two slaves, who ran off to the Union lines the day the colored troops entered the city.

She hurries toward the sanctuary of her room, thanking God for her narrow escape.

NINETEEN

April 26, 1872

Hanley began his Friday morning with a trip to city hall, where persistent inquiry eventually netted him a box full of muster rolls salvaged from the October flames that had ravaged the Merchants' Building, General Sheridan's former military headquarters. The roll for the Eighty-Second Illinois Infantry was the fifth one he pulled from the jumble of papers, with Company A near the top of the list, below commissioned officers and non-commissioned staff.

Enlisted men were grouped by rank. He spotted George Schuyler under *Corporals*, his residence given as Alton. Ten to one he lived there now. Hanley wondered what the chances were of getting his boss to authorize an Alton trip. Will Rushton was listed as a private, Champion as a first lieutenant with a field promotion to captain in 1863. Hanley noted that fact in his sketchbook, then gave the muster rolls back to the harried-looking records clerk with thanks and left the building.

A quick visit to Gentle Annie's on South Clark netted him nothing about the red-haired man with sideburns who he'd seen there the previous morning. "He gave his name as Mr. Smith," Annie told him. "Wanted a girl and paid for one, like they all do."

"Is he a regular customer?"

She shrugged. "He turns up every so often. Which means he can afford my prices, at least sometimes. That's all I know of him."

Which was pretty much what Hanley had expected. He tamped

down his brief disappointment. Rivka's description aside, the fellow might not be the same man who'd met Lucas Errol at the train depot. Even if he was, nothing said he had anything to do with the assault on Aaron Kelmansky's Alton farmstead.

He embarked next on a hunt for the law office thief. After an hour or so asking questions around the riverside docks and saloons, his patience was rewarded with a hint passed up from "a fella who knows a fella who heard maybe" that Crowfoot Abe—a talented cracksman Hanley knew from the old days—might recently have pulled "an easy job on Indiana Avenue, by where them rich folks live." He knew where he'd find Abe this time of day, and cursed the power of memory. He didn't want to go there, but it was the only lead he had on the break-in. So he helped himself to cash from the box in the Lake Street squad room and headed across town to the Skibbereen Club.

The mingled odors of bad drains, moldy sawdust, and mouse droppings hit him like a fist as he walked in the door. He halted just inside to let his eyes adjust to the gloom. He couldn't help glancing toward the corner table where Paddy Moroney used to sit and play endless games of cards. Paddy was dead, his throat slit because he'd spoken too freely to Hanley during the Kelmansky murder investigation. That the man who killed him was in prison now, his vice empire swallowed up by the city's other gambling princes, was cold comfort. Paddy had been like a brother to Hanley when they were boys, taught him how to fight and how to laugh at the absurdity of the world. No matter that he was poorer than dirt, too often drunk, and still thieving off the riverside docks to support himself and his children, the loss of him cut deep.

Crowfoot Abe sat at a table not far from Paddy's usual, nursing a whiskey and chewing a piece of toast. Rope thin and barely past five feet, he was tough as old leather and bad-tempered as an army mule. His thick hair, prematurely white, stood out in the dim room. Hanley ordered a beer—"and no water in it this time," he said as he slipped an extra two bits across the bar. Drink in hand, he ambled over to where Abe sat, hooked a chair out with one foot and dropped into it. Abe's plate held smears of egg yolk. Hanley jerked his head back toward the barman. "He still serving breakfast?"

Abe gulped whiskey to wash down his toast. "You don't mind, I like eating alone."

"I won't stay longer than I need to." Hanley sipped his beer. It wasn't watered, but neither was it good. He swallowed, wiped his mouth with his sleeve and leaned his elbows on the table. "How long that is, depends on you."

Abe glared at him. "I don't feel like talkin' to a damn cop."

Hanley turned his beer mug. Light from the table lamp glinted off the glass. He'd given some thought to his approach on the way here. "You pull a job on Indiana a ways south of Twenty-Second a couple days ago? Break-in at a lawyers' office?"

Abe snorted as he swabbed up egg yolk with his last chunk of toast. "Sure. And I also robbed the Merchants' National Bank. Take me away, officer."

"It's not you I'm after. If it was, we'd be taking a walk right now. You wouldn't have pulled that job on your own. You steal what you can sell, and you can't sell a bunch of law papers. Somebody paid you to take them. I want to know who."

"And I don't want to tell you." Abe bit into his toast, chewed and swallowed. "Last fella talked to you too much ended up with a cut throat."

"Sean Doyle's no threat to you from prison. And even if he was, you can handle yourself. Or isn't that true anymore?"

"I don't squeal. You forget that?"

"Tell you what." Hanley pulled a battered pack of playing cards out of his coat pocket. "How about we have us a little five-card stud while you think it over?"

Cʒ

A while later, Hanley was three dollars down and Crowfoot Abe looked almost cheerful. "I'm not asking you to squeal on one of our own," Hanley said as he dealt out another hand. "The stolen papers are about a lawsuit, rich gents cutting corners. Good men died because of it. You got this job from some rich bastard, didn't you?"

Abe gathered his cards with a smirk. "You already know so damned much, why're you talking to me?"

"Making sure of things. I don't like to make a move until I know I'm right."

"Always were a careful sonofabitch. Sitting in the background, watching us all, not saying a damned word. Unless somebody got you drunk." Abe grinned and nodded toward Hanley's partly finished beer. "You ain't drunk enough to win yet, though."

"I'll take my chances."

"Ah, hell." Abe set his cards down and tossed back the last of his whiskey. "I'll tell you this much. Out of kindness, and 'cause I won plenty off you already." He gave Hanley a sharp look. "Not sayin' this happened, mind...but if it did..." At Hanley's nod, he continued. "Say some fella come up to me at O'Banion's Saloon, down on Custom House Place. And say he says he's looking for a cracksman. Heard I was one of the best, and would I bust into some office and swipe a bunch of papers. Says I'd know 'em by the name Farnham. And say he pays me a hundred to get 'em and bring 'em to him. He wouldn't say why, and I wouldn't ask."

The amount made Hanley raise an eyebrow. A hundred dollars was a month's wages for a patrolman. "Some spender," he said.

Abe snorted. "Ain't my business to care what he does with his money. Fella like that, he'd be a gent, like you said. Soft hands, clean, nails trimmed, not a mark of a hard day's work on 'em. And he'd talk like he had more schoolin' than the usual ten-cent players who come to O'Banion's. We get them high-and-mighty types there sometimes. Bored with the fancy places where they usually go to lose their money. They want to rough it some. This fella, though—sayin' he spoke to me, which I ain't—he'd a' been lookin' for me special. Somebody musta gave him my name."

"He give you his?" Likely not, but sometimes people were stupid. It never hurt to ask.

Abe laughed. "You kiddin'?"

Hanley set down his own cards and pulled out his sketchbook. "Tell me what he looks like. And where those papers ended up."

෬

Another bad beer and a dollar in losses later, Hanley left the Skibbereen Club. The sky was clouding over, and he could smell rain along with wet earth, damp wooden boardwalks, old garbage, and horse manure. At the nearest intersection, he stopped for traffic and studied his sketch of Abe's "employer." Bare seconds after Abe started talking, he knew who it had to be. The red-haired gent with the florid mustache and sideburns, who'd scuttled past him into Annie Stafford's bawdyhouse the previous morning. The same man Rivka had told him about, who'd met Lucas Errol three days earlier off the noon train from Alton.

Abe had delivered the stolen case file to Sideburns—"Not sayin' I did, mind"—late Wednesday night at 354 Custom House Place, a cheap panel-house bordello four doors down from O'Banion's Saloon. Panel houses catered mostly to farmers and grangers—commission merchants who dealt in bulk grains, meats, and produce—who got off the trains at the nearby depot on Van Buren. Country folk with a little money and less sense, who bought themselves a touch of city wickedness so they could feel like men of the world. Not the kind of place where a soft-handed, smooth talker like Sideburns should normally take his pleasures. If he was a sometime regular at Annie's, he'd likely chosen the panel house for its anonymity, one dive among many where he could count on seeing no one who knew him—at least, no one who mattered. Or maybe the seediness of it attracted him. Some men liked that kind of thing.

The location might be another reason. Custom House Place was in the First Precinct, lorded over by Captain Michael Hickey of the Armory Station on Harrison Street. Mike Hickey was known for corruption, though so far he'd been slippery enough to leave little proof that would stand up in a courtroom. Especially one whose judge he'd bought. If Sideburns—whoever he was—knew enough to go to O'Banion's for a cracksman, he surely had other connections as well, that could buy Hanley trouble. Why had he wanted the papers related to the Farnham lawsuit badly enough to pay a thief a hundred dollars for them?

He frowned at the sketch. Sideburns had to be involved in the exploding-guns case. Nothing else made sense. Was he a defendant? And what about Lucas Errol, a wealthy Alton businessman with a reputation to protect? The Farnham and Chandler factory was in Alton. Was Aaron Kelmansky's night rider involved with the lawsuit? Either way, Errol and Sideburns had just become prime suspects in Hanley's murder investigation. And he had some pointed questions for Aaron as well.

A gap appeared between drays. Hanley crossed the street, thinking now about Ben Champion. Half-dressed when he died, on his way to bed. Surely not circumstances where he'd be face-to-face with a man he was prosecuting for fraud. Sideburns had met Crowfoot Abe on Tuesday night, the night Champion died. Could Abe...but no, Abe wasn't a killer. And even if someone paid him enough to make murder as well as theft worth his while, he'd never have left Champion's gold cufflinks behind. He'd have gone through the house like a one-man locust swarm, picking up whatever he could carry away.

Hanley walked on. Whatever the truth, he'd come closer to it once he identified Sideburns and found the stolen legal papers. Custom House Place was nowhere to go without backup, though. A spatter of rain struck him, and he picked up his pace. Rolf Schmidt would come with him. Schmidt was a good cop, solid in a fight—and not always married to the rules. For the scheme taking shape in Hanley's mind, that could only be an advantage.

TWENTY

T he little schoolroom felt hot and close. The afternoon was warm for late April, and the girls were wilting in their high-necked, long-sleeved calico dresses. Sweat made Rivka's scalp itch under her kerchief, and she wished she could snatch it off. The back door, propped open, let in some air, but not enough on this windless day. It was hard to concentrate. Even Leah Zalman had stumbled over a few unfamiliar words, and the less fluent readers made mistake after mistake that left them flustered and red faced.

From her place at the head of the table where they worked, Rivka eyed the clock. Two thirty. Maybe she should end class early. The girls' mothers would welcome an extra hour of help before Shabbos started at sundown, and no one seemed to be learning much. Rachel Demsky was reading aloud, faltering even more than usual. "Clouds...that won... der...no, *wander*...th...thr...?"

Muffled shouting from outside halted her in mid-sentence. The shouting grew louder, though Rivka couldn't make out words. Only the tone, rough and angry. With surprise, she recognized one of the voices as Onkl Jacob's. Some dispute in the tailor shop? Surely not. Onkl Jacob would never shout at a customer.

Rachel had turned toward the shop door. She looked frightened. An uneasy murmur swept through the room. Rivka pushed her chair back and stood. "Everyone read silently on page twenty-six. Leah, please keep an eye on the class. I'll be back in a moment."

Three customers were in the tailor shop, huddled together and staring out the large front window. Neither Jacob nor Moishe was in sight. Rivka recognized Lazar Klein the butcher, wearing a coat with one sleeve off, the other pinned on at the shoulder. She followed his gaze and saw Onkl Jacob in the middle of the boardwalk, facing down a dozen men. Strangers, and not Jews, to judge from their appearance. The men stood in the street shouting at Jacob, their faces distorted with anger.

Rivka hurried to the front door. Moishe hovered just outside it, twisting his window-cleaning rag in his hands. "Tsuris," he said, with a worried look toward the confrontation. *Trouble.*

She stepped outside. She could hear the shouts clearly now. *Jew filth! Nigger lovers!* Onkl Jacob was yelling back. "Get away from my shop! Go home! Get out of here!" The mob's raw hatred made her skin crawl. These strangers must know about Ada and Nat. Had they been seen? Perhaps on Wednesday morning, when they first arrived, or—

A chunk of stone whizzed past Jacob's head and thudded onto the boardwalk just short of the shop window. Jacob moved toward the men, fists clenched. "I said, go away!"

Another stone flew, then more. Ugly laughter came from the mob, along with jeers and taunts. "Give us the niggers!" one shouted. Another called out with a leer, "Give us the girl!" With a flash of horror, Rivka realized they meant her.

Two of the men advanced across the empty street. One held a broken brick. The other knelt briefly and picked something up—a cast horseshoe, a thick curve of iron with a bent nail sticking out. Rivka hurried forward and caught Jacob's arm. "Onkl Jacob, come away—"

The horseshoe sailed through the air and struck Jacob in the face. He staggered backward. The broken brick thudded against his shoulder, sending him down on one knee.

More laughter from the men. The two in the lead moved closer. Bricks and stones rained on the boardwalk inches from where Rivka and Jacob stood. Behind her, Moishe cried out as a stone hit him. Rivka's taut nerves shrieked at her to run. She bent to help Jacob up and saw the horseshoe a foot away.

She grabbed the shoe and flung it toward their attackers. A fist-sized rock next, then another. She saw it strike the lead thug on the hip, heard him swear, and felt a surge of triumph. Someone was shrieking like a crazy woman—*Go, get away, leave us alone!* Was that her voice? She had gone mad, and she didn't care. It felt good to scream at them, throw things, fight back.

Loud shouts in Yiddish filled her ears as Moishe ran up beside her. Grabbing whatever came to hand—rocks, bricks, street debris—he hurled it at their assailants. A brick struck one man hard enough to spin him partway around. A jagged-edged rock struck another in the head. He dropped to the dusty street and lay still. The attackers fell back, then fled.

"*Hashem.*" Moishe pressed a hand to his mouth. His white shirt bore a dusty splotch where a stone had hit. "Did I kill him? *Hashem...*" He staggered toward the fallen man and sank down beside him.

Trembling and sick, Rivka turned back toward Onkl Jacob. He was still kneeling on the boardwalk, blood running down his face where the horseshoe nail had torn a jagged gash across his cheek. She ran to him and helped him up, then moved them both slowly and painfully toward the shop door, Jacob's arm anchored around her shoulders. "I'll get Hannah," she said, breathing hard with effort and aftershock.

Lazar Klein opened the door, and Rivka maneuvered them inside. Moishe came in just behind and moved to take Jacob from her. "Someone go for the doctor," Rivka said. "And take the girls home. Can you stay with him, Herr Zalman, while I get water?"

Moishe nodded and led Jacob to a chair where waiting customers usually sat. Rivka made it as far as the door to her classroom, where she stopped a minute to breathe. She couldn't let the girls see her like this. Her kerchief had slipped, and sweat plastered strands of hair to her cheek. Her hands trembled as she tugged the kerchief back into place and tucked the loose hair underneath.

When her breathing slowed, she stepped into the classroom. Eight frightened faces looked up at her. "Go straight home, all of you," she said, as calmly as she could manage. "Herr Nathan has had an accident. Herr Klein will walk with you. You can go through the shop. He'll meet you there."

She waited long enough to see Leah Zalman take charge. She followed the girls into the main room, grabbed a scrap of waste cloth from the cutting table, and headed toward the rain barrel just outside the back door, where she soaked the cloth, wrung it out, and hurried back in.

Onkl Jacob looked pale, his jaw set. Anger, or pain, or both. Moishe stood next to him, one hand on his shoulder. Gently, she washed the cut on Jacob's cheek. It wasn't as deep as she'd feared. The blow from the horseshoe must have been glancing. The doctor might not be needed after all. "I'll get Hannah," she said again as she tucked the damp cloth into Onkl Jacob's hand.

He gripped her fingers, pressing the cloth between them. "And then go to Aaron," he said. "Tell him I must talk with him before Shabbos begins."

CB

She smelled the charred wood before she saw it. The odor reached her a few yards from home, carried on the wind like a warning. She hurried onward, then stopped abruptly in front of her house. The parlor window was an empty hole, framed by the scorched remnant of her mother's fine lace curtains. A sobbing breath escaped her, and she ran to the door.

A crack split the air as she barreled through the doorway. Something buzzed past her ear like an angry bee. She threw herself sideways, caught a heel in her skirt, and went down hard on her knees. Terrified and furious, she scrambled up, determined to meet this new attack on her feet.

"*Hashem in himmel…*" Aaron's voice. Shocked, trembling, he stood with a pistol in hand not two yards away. Behind him, Ada and Nat huddled on the sofa. He lowered the gun, barely able to keep hold of it. "Rivka…I'm sorry…I thought…"

"Never mind that." Her hands were shaking. She clasped them hard to steady herself. "You're all right? All of you?" At his nod, she continued. "They came to the tailor shop as well. A mob with bricks and stones. Onkl Jacob was hurt. He sent me to bring you there."

TWENTY-ONE

Y ou don't recognize him, either?" Hanley said. He'd come back to Lake Street Station to make the night's arrangements with Schmidt, and taken the chance to ask around about Sideburns as well.

Moore frowned at the sketch. "Not to put a name to." He handed the drawing back to Hanley with a shake of his head. "I've a sense of something, but I can't place it. He dressed well, you said?"

"And can afford what Annie Stafford charges for her various amusements."

"Gentleman gambler's my guess. I might have run across him at one of the pricier gambling hells. Though I don't recall booking him. Maybe he's one of those smooth-tongued types that always talks his way out of trouble."

"Bunco-steerer?" Hanley tucked his sketchbook away. "Though if he is, he's new in town. None of the squad knows him, either." He gave Moore a crooked smile. "I'll try Eddie Norris at the First Precinct. He owes me a favor, after letting me damned near get shanked in the Armory jail. What Eddie hasn't learned about vice in the South Division isn't worth knowing."

He left the station and hurried down the boardwalk toward Market and Madison Streets. With Sideburns connected to the Farnham lawsuit, and Lucas Errol connected to Sideburns, it was time for another word with Aaron Kelmansky about the attack on his Alton farm. After that, Eddie Norris, who should be at home and awake for the next few hours before his evening shift started.

He reached Rivka's block in time to see her coming out of the house next door to her own, Hannah Nathan a step behind her. Then the smell of charred wood hit him, leaving a bitter taste on his tongue. Alarmed, he hurried forward. Three more strides brought him near enough to see both women's white faces, and a gap edged with scorching where the Kelmanskys' front window had been.

He fought down instinctive panic. "Miss Kelmansky, Mrs. Nathan. What's happened?"

Hannah Nathan answered first. "Someone threw fire at Rivka's house. A mob came to Jacob's shop, screaming insults and threats. Jacob was hurt. We are going there now."

He turned to Rivka. "Is Aaron all right? And his family?"

"For the moment." She swallowed. "I came to tell him about Onkl Jacob, and…"

He made a split-second decision. "I'd like a word with him." *And this time he'd best talk to me.*

"Rivka…" Hannah gripped her arm.

Rivka eased out of her grasp, then clasped her hands. "Go to Onkl Jacob," she said gently. "Aaron and Detective Hanley will come soon. Tell him we are on our way."

Hannah hovered another moment, clearly torn, then murmured something in Yiddish and hurried off down the street. Hanley turned his attention to Rivka. "Tell me what happened."

"Some men threw bricks and stones at us outside Onkl Jacob's shop. A dozen at least. They called us—" Even in the warm afternoon air, he saw her shiver. "They threatened us. They wanted Ada and Nat. Onkl Jacob was hurt…not badly, but…"

She'd said *us*. Three times. He felt a chill as the implication sank in. "You were there?"

"Yes." She crossed her arms over her chest. "I was teaching, and I heard the shouting. I went to see what was happening, and then I saw Onkl Jacob and went out—"

"Why, in the name of God?" he snapped, suddenly furious. "Facing down a gang of thugs…Lord knows what they'd have done to you. What possessed you to risk yourself like that?"

She looked startled, then angry. "I should have left Jacob to face them alone? I went out to *help*. Anyone would have——"

"All right. I'm sorry." He shoved clenched fists into his trouser pockets. Beneath his anger, and the fear that drove it, he felt a sneaking admiration. In her place, he'd have done the same thing.

He took a deep breath, then another. "And here? Do you know what happened?"

She shook her head. "I came to tell Aaron, and I saw...that. No sign of who did it."

"Let's hope your brother knows," he said, and followed her inside.

They met Aaron by the base of the stairs. He looked exhausted, and dismayed at the sight of Hanley. "Detective. What are you doing here? I told you, we don't need your——"

Hanley stepped forward. "You do now. Someone threw an incendiary device here. Who was it? Did you see them?"

"No." He closed his eyes briefly. "Just the brick through the glass, with lit rags soaked in kerosene. I was too busy putting the curtains out to notice anything else."

"But I'm guessing you have some idea who's responsible."

"I don't know anything. I only want us to be left alone."

Past Aaron, Hanley saw Ada move into the kitchen doorway, a dishtowel in her hands. Rivka drew breath, but stayed silent. He wished she were elsewhere, wished he could have spared her what he had to say next. "It's a bit late for that, Mr. Kelmansky. Your night rider Lucas Errol just turned up in my murder case. And now someone's attacked you and your neighbors. Would you have any notion why?"

Aaron's expression reminded Hanley of a rabbit with a hawk circling overhead. "No. I wouldn't. I'm sorry."

For Rivka's sake, and Ada's, Hanley kept his tone gentler than he might have. "I don't believe you. Not the way you look right now, not after you shut down on me yesterday afternoon. That morning, you were nervous but willing to talk about Lucas Errol and the assault on your farm. Six, seven hours later, all you wanted was for me to drop it and go away. What changed? Is it to do with what happened in Alton?"

Aaron's jaw tightened as Ada moved beside him, the dishtowel taut around her fingers. "I told you what happened in Alton. We were attacked, for the obvious, ugly reasons that I am a Jew and my wife and stepson are Negroes. That's all I have to say." He started up the stairs, so quickly that he'd reached the top before Hanley could collect himself and follow.

He caught up with Aaron in a bedroom just off the staircase. Aaron had opened a bureau drawer and was pulling clothes out of it, a cotton shirt and a pair of homespun trousers. Light, hurried footsteps sounded behind Hanley, and he turned as Ada drew level with him, Rivka in her wake. They pushed past him into the bedroom, where Ada took the shirt and trousers from Aaron's hands. "Put those away. There's nowhere else to run to."

Aaron sank onto the bed. After a moment's silence, Rivka spoke. Her voice sounded small in the stillness. "Aaron? What's the matter?"

He said nothing, merely shook his head.

Hanley took a step into the room.

"Go away, Detective," Aaron said without looking up. "There's nothing you can do for us. There's nothing anyone can do."

"That was before. If Lucas Errol is implicated in a crime here—"

A floorboard creaked. Aaron's gaze shifted past Hanley at the sound, and his bleak expression gentled. Hanley turned his head and saw a boy hovering in the hallway. Aaron's stepson, surely. Mulatto, about twelve by Hanley's guess. His face was wary, his body poised as if to fight or run.

Hanley looked back to the bedroom. Aaron seemed calmer now, resolute. He picked up the shirt, folded it and laid it on the bed.

"The assault in Alton, where your friend Mr. Levin died," Hanley said. "That wasn't just hatred, was it? Did you know about the exploding guns that went to the Eighty-Second? Your regiment, if I remember. Did your company get them? Was Lucas Errol involved in the lawsuit about them and trying to shut you up, through intimidation or murder?"

Aaron grabbed the trousers. "I can't answer that."

"Can't, or won't?"

Aaron sat still, the trousers crumpled in his hands. Then he looked around—at Ada, at Rivka, then at the boy. Finally, he met Hanley's eyes. "Not here. Not now."

"Tonight at the station, then."

"I can't tonight. Our Sabbath begins at sundown."

"All right. Sunday." That was an ordinary day for Jews, if he recalled. He could skip Mass. Mam would be scandalized, but work came first.

Aaron hesitated. "In the day…I would rather not…"

Hanley restrained his impatience. "Come Sunday night. Eight o'clock. It should be dark by then."

Aaron hesitated. He raised a hand, narrow fingers toying with the edge of the small skullcap he wore. Then he nodded.

CB

Rivka walked with Hanley back downstairs. He was silent, as if lost in thought. She glanced at him, wondering what to say about Aaron, or if to say anything at all. He looked troubled, eyes shadowed and mouth set in a grim line.

"What did you mean about exploding guns?" she asked when they reached the bottom of the staircase.

He hesitated, then seemed to come to a decision. She saw sorrow and anger in him, tightly reined in, as he told her. His words conjured ugly pictures in her mind—the flash of fire and smoke, the sudden rush of blood from a soldier's mangled hands. She closed her eyes, but the images wouldn't go away. Aaron knew of this and would not speak? Didn't intend to, despite his wordless promise to Hanley upstairs? She knew that gesture, those fumbling fingers at his kippah. Confusion gripped her. This wasn't like him. It was…inexplicable. What could he know that was so terrible, to drive him to such behavior?

"There's more to what happened in Alton than your brother told me," Hanley said, as if he'd read her thoughts. "I don't know if he'll tell me the whole truth on Sunday, but he might tell you. Can you talk to him? It'll help him and his family. He just doesn't see that yet."

She glanced at the floor. It needed sweeping. "Until Wednesday,

I hadn't seen him in ten years. He still remembers me as a girl of fourteen."

"I know it won't be easy. But…" He trailed off with a harsh sigh. The floorboards creaked as he shifted his weight.

She felt a flash of annoyance, along with a dry mouth. First Aaron, now Hanley, who didn't want to tell her something. "But what?"

"Let's just say the more I know, the more he'll tell me. And the easier things will go for him."

Her eyes widened as the implications sank in. She fiddled with her kerchief, suddenly nervous. "I cannot promise anything."

"I'm only asking you to try. I'm sure you'll manage."

"You trust me so much?"

"Yes." He said it as if he meant a great deal more. She looked up, but he'd glanced away, a faint flush on his cheeks. "I'd appreciate anything you can do," he said as he met her eyes again.

03

They went to the tailor shop next, where Onkl Jacob was. He kept calm as Hanley questioned everyone there about the rock-throwing mob—how many men, what did they look like, did Jacob or Moishe or Rivka recognize any non-Jewish neighbors among them. Focused and persistent, he drew out details from each of them that they hadn't known they remembered. Moishe kept close to Rivka throughout, as if his presence could safeguard her from the frightening memory of the assault. He had picked up the horseshoe after the attackers fled, and Hanley took it from him with somber thanks.

"Do you want to press charges?" Hanley asked.

Jacob shook his head. "There was no damage done, and no one was hurt except me." He brushed the gash on his cheek. "It will bring us too much trouble for not enough gain. But if you and some others you trust can keep an eye out, we would be most grateful."

"We'll keep you safe," Hanley said. "That's a promise."

TWENTY-TWO

May 1865

Monroe, Virginia. That's what the paper in Billy's hand says. He reads it over, still not quite able to believe what it tells him.

Ada is alive. His sister is alive and well and in Virginia. How far from Richmond? He doesn't know Monroe, couldn't find it on a map if you paid him a gold eagle. Is it close? Could he go there, could he find her, could he—

His thoughts halt as if they've dropped off a cliff. For a moment he can only stare at the paper as if it's all of existence. The white, white paper covered with black letters and lines. He can't go to Monroe. Can't find Ada. Can't see her, let her see him, let her know—

It's enough just to know she's alive, isn't it? Enough to know that the sister sold away before he turned ten didn't die of overwork, or disease, or ill use, or in unattended childbed in a slave cabin somewhere in the Deep South. Arkansas, Louisiana, Alabama. He used to have nightmares about that. Stories told to frighten children into behaving—"You'll be sold downriver, picking cotton, or cutting cane, until your fingers bleed and your body screams for mercy. And they won't let you stop until you're dead." That didn't happen to Ada, for all his fears. How long has it been since she went away? Eighteen years, by God. Would he even know her if he saw her again?

Foolish question. Of course he would. Big sister, best friend, except for Tom—

He won't think about Tom, shuts out the sudden vision of a sprawled dead body by a campfire in East Tennessee. Ada is alive and well and in Virginia...

A fellow soldier passes through the doorway with a murmured "Excuse me." Brought back to awareness of his surroundings, Billy steps to one side, out of the way. The Spotswood Hotel, one of the few structures left standing in what was Richmond's business district, before the retreating Rebs set fire to it, has been commandeered as a temporary office by the Freedmen's Bureau, which is taking shape and doing its work for the newly freed Negroes of the South despite Andrew Johnson's best attempts to stop it. The thought of that man brings a slow burn in Billy's gut, as if he's eaten a peck of raw onions and washed them down with corn liquor. He can't call Johnson "President," even in thought. *Papa Lincoln, you should have lived. You should have lived to guide us safely through what's left of the night.*

The Negroes call him that—Papa Lincoln, or Father Abraham. Billy could laugh at the irony of it. Black people, calling a white man "father" and meaning it with all their hearts. *The Negroes.* Hot shame surges through him that he can think of them that way, as something utterly separate from him.

"Billy?" A hand claps his shoulder. He looks up and sees Ben smiling down at him. Even now, though he's long since grown to manhood from adolescence, Ben Champion towers over him. Ben must see something in his face, because the broad smile fades. "Everything all right? Did you find her?"

He nods and holds out the paper, not trusting himself to speak. Ben Champion is the only person in Richmond just now to whom he dares reveal anything of what he's been doing. Ben is the only one who knows the truth.

"Monroe." Ben's voice is soft. "That's near Lynchburg. A hundred miles or so from here."

Billy stares at him, then starts to laugh. "A hundred miles. My God..." How close was she to so many places where the Eighty-Second fought over the past three years? In Virginia, in East Tennessee...the latter too close for comfort to where he and Ada were born, the plantation both of them called home, until Ada was sold and the rest of the family escaped to the North.

"I have to see her." He's surprised to hear those words come out of his mouth. "I have to see her, know for certain she's all right, not...not homeless or hungry or..."

Ben gives him a long look. "We won't be heading back to Chicago and muster out for another week at least. You want leave, you have it."

One week. Seven days. And there's a train to Lynchburg, if the tracks are repaired. The army has had men working on it since Richmond fell and the Rebs surrendered, more than a month ago.

Seven days. It'll be enough.

ΩΩ

Monroe, reached on foot after the six-hour ride to Lynchburg, is a sleepy hamlet surrounded by farmland. Former plantations, given over to what were called "contraband camps" during the war and have since been renamed "freedmen's villages"—small settlements of thirty to fifty cabins, built by the slaves and refugees who fled there for sanctuary, on the land that once belonged to white masters. There's something fitting in that.

The cabins are neatly kept, built of planed lumber that must have been requisitioned by the Union army. In the bright May weather, the garden plots near each cabin are thriving—half-grown tomato plants, summer squash, and snap pea vines nodding in the warm spring breeze. Billy halts partway down the long drive that draws a graceful curve between the cabins on one side and a man-made pond on the other. There are no birds on the water, no ducks or geese or swans. Any that once belonged to this plantation were hunted and eaten by hungry locals long ago. For a moment he envisions a carriage rattling up this drive, pulled by a matched team of high-stepping bay horses, conveying well-dressed visitors to this place. What would its former owners think, seeing it become home to those whose sweat and blood once watered this land—theirs through toil even then, though no law let them call it so?

He has no idea which of the cabins is Ada's. He sees a woman weeding her garden near one, another hanging out washing, still another planting late seeds along with three children digging beside her. The closest woman, the one weeding, is too dark to be his sister. The others, too far away to tell. He strolls further down the drive, keeping an eye out. This is a foolish thing he's doing—but the cabins are some yards from the roadway, enough distance to let him pretend he's just a Yankee soldier passing through. Even if he sees her, Ada won't know it's him. She won't expect him in a soldier's uniform. He has no plans to reveal himself. All he wants is to see with his own eyes that she's well.

He reaches a footpath that cuts through the grass toward the cabins. They're only a few yards away at this point. Too close? As he hesitates, the back door of the nearest cabin opens and a young boy comes out. High yellow, wavy dark hair, a fishing pole over his shoulder. He can't be more than six or seven. "Bye, Mama," he calls out, then heads for the footpath. He notices Billy and stops. He takes in the uniform, Union blue, and gives Billy an open, friendly smile. "Help you, mister? You lookin' for somebody?"

"I, um…" Before Billy can get anything else out, the cabin door opens again. Framed in the gap is a woman—mulatto like the boy, tall and graceful in a dark blue work dress.

"Nat, come back and wash—" Her voice dies as she catches sight of Billy. She eyes him with a puzzled frown.

He should nod and keep going down the drive. *Just a soldier, ma'am, nothing to do with you. Good day.* He can't move, can hardly breathe. The woman's face, her voice—both familiar despite the passage of time—imprison him as amber does an insect.

Her frown gives way to a questioning look. "I'm sorry, do I know…" She takes a step forward, then another. He still can't move, can only stare at her, blinking unexpected moisture from his eyes.

Amazement crosses her face—then a stunned joy, as if she's lit from within. "Billy?" She takes another step, one hand out. "Mother of God…"

He moves toward her without meaning to, drawn by that hand and the look in her eyes, and catches her up in a fierce embrace. "Dear Lord," she says when they break apart. Her fingers brush his cheek. "God in Heaven, Billy, I can't hardly believe it's you."

TWENTY-THREE

April 26, 1872

Eddie Norris lived on Taylor Street, several blocks from the rebuilt Armory Station near Pacific and Harrison. Interrupted at an early supper of barley soup and biscuits, he was less help than Hanley had hoped. "Not a gambling prince, your fellow," he said, eying the drawing of Sideburns. "Leastways, not in Little Cheyenne or Custom House Place. I've gotten to know 'em all pretty well by sight, even the new ones who've come since the Fire. Those sideburns and that mustache, I'd remember." He handed the sketchbook back to Hanley. "Could be a regular customer just about anyplace, but I've never busted him. I can ask around the Armory, see if anyone else has."

"Just don't let on who you're asking for." Bad blood between Hanley and Captain Michael Hickey, the First Precinct's commander, had only deepened in the two years since Hanley's transfer from the Armory to Lake Street. It didn't help that Hanley had beaten out Captain Hickey's handpicked favorite for promotion to the detective squad less than a year ago. He thanked Eddie and left, then lingered outside the Norrises' small frame house in the late-afternoon sunlight. Mrs. Flynn, who cleaned for Ben Champion and some of his neighbors, lived on Jackson near Sherman Street, not too far away. She'd be home now, doing her own household chores or making supper for her family. He should go there, ask her what she knew about her dead employer. All the questions he'd set aside in the excitement of the stolen lawsuit papers and the hunt for Sideburns—visitors, women, general habits and temperament, even the gold mourning ring and broken chain Rolf Schmidt had found in the grass by Champion's front walk.

Yet he felt reluctant to move. That stretch of Jackson Street had been part of Conley's Patch, until the fire that started in Catherine O'Leary's barn reduced the whole area to scorched dirt and smoldering pine ash. Even now, almost six months on, he'd no desire to pass through old haunts, or see what had become of the neighborhood that was his world for the first nineteen years of his life. Even going off to war hadn't taken the Patch out of him, though it made a good beginning. The Fire did the rest, offered through disaster a chance for a real fresh start. Here, now, standing outside Eddie Norris's place, Hanley felt a superstitious dread. As if walking through the Patch, picking up its dust on his shoes, would make him fit for nowhere else once again.

"Stupid damned fool," he muttered, and made himself turn north and east. It'd save him another trip to this part of the city the next day. And Mrs. Flynn might help him rule out a thing or two, more definitely than Eddie Norris had done.

She looked surprised to see Hanley when he arrived, and smoothed her water-stained apron, as if embarrassed to be caught in her workaday state. "I'm just making boxty," she said, patting a wisp of flyaway hair into place with one roughened hand. "If you don't mind talking while I check the potatoes..."

"Not a bit." He followed her into her small kitchen. The Flynns lived in the front section of a one-story frame house, a double-cottage arrangement as common in Conley's Patch before the Fire as after. A strong boiled-potato scent nearly masked the fainter smell of cow from the detached barn behind. "I came to ask about Captain Champion. I won't take much of your time."

"That poor man." She picked up a chopping knife and stabbed it into the steaming pot on the stove. "Hanging's too good for whoever killed him. I know that's an awful thing to wish for, but I don't mind saying it this once."

He took out his sketchbook and turned to the picture of Sideburns while she fished peeled potatoes out of the boiling water and dropped them in a waiting bowl. Crowfoot Abe might not be a killer, but it didn't mean the man who hired him wasn't one, and Champion could have been killed as late as one o'clock Wednesday morning. "Would you recall seeing this gentleman at Captain Champion's recently? Say anytime in the week or so before the captain's passing."

She eyed the sketch, then shook her head. "No. I don't recall him."

He turned the page to Lucas Errol's picture. "How about this man?"

"No," she said after a long moment, as if she wished she could say *yes.*

"That's all right, Mrs. Flynn." He gave her a smile meant to reassure as he put his sketchbook away again. "How many days a week did you work for Captain Champion?"

"One full, one part. Early Wednesdays"—she bit her lip, clearly recalling the horror of this past Wednesday morning—"and Saturdays. The Thomashaws next door are my other Wednesday family, from ten or so till three...sometimes later, if the missus and Mary have their hands full. I'm there Tuesdays as well. Fridays I'm at Mr. Markham's for the washing."

Markham was the neighbor on the other side, out of town since Saturday. Between his house and the Thomashaws', Mrs. Flynn spent four days at or near Champion's every week. "You spend a lot of time on North May Street. You see quite a bit, I imagine."

Her eyebrows rose as she pulled a potato masher from a drawer. "I'm no gossip, Mr. Hanley. I'll tell you that right now."

"But you might have seen who came to Captain Champion's house on Tuesday, the day he died. What time that day were you next door at the Thomashaws'?"

"In the morning. I start at eight, and I'm generally done by one o'clock."

One o'clock. Too early to have seen Champion's supper guest arrive, or Alice Lockwood leaving. Thoughts of Alice brought Mary Olcott to mind as well. Mrs. Flynn worked with her for two days every week. "The Thomashaws' hired woman said she knew Captain Champion from the war. Did she ever talk about it? About him?"

"Hardly ever." She thumped the masher into the steaming bowl of potatoes. "I asked her once about her people, where she was from. Making conversation, you know. She told me she didn't like to talk of it.

Said she'd lost too much. In the war, I took it as. The poor thing looked that upset…I didn't ask again."

"What about Miss Lockwood?"

The masher thumped down with extra force. "What about her?"

Mindful of her earlier remark about gossip, he framed his next question with care. "You worked for the captain on Saturdays. Miss Lockwood was there Saturday afternoons. Did she and Captain Champion work well together?"

"I know what you're asking." Pink bloomed in her cheeks, and she focused all her attention on the potatoes. Hanley, recalling his own days helping his mother cook, until his sister grew big enough to do it, felt a sympathetic ache in his arms as he watched Mrs. Flynn grind away at the bowl. At this rate, there'd not be a lump left in the mash the size of a coat-button. "Is it because of where he died? In his bedroom…like he was?"

"I have to think of every possibility, Mrs. Flynn." He waited a moment while that sank in. "Was there anything between Miss Lockwood and Captain Champion? Or him and Miss Olcott, that you know of?"

She set the masher down and brushed hair off her forehead. "He spoke to Mary sometimes, but just friendly-like. Was the job all right, how was she getting on. Now, that Miss Lockwood…" She added a handful of flour to the mashed potatoes, then pulled a wooden spoon from a drawer and stirred them. "There was nothing improper, mind. Not while I was around. She'd set her cap for him, though. Careful about it, she was, but a woman knows these things."

"How did the captain take it?"

"Oh, he liked her right enough." Mrs. Flynn dusted flour off her hands. "He was always a gentleman…but he'd watch her sometimes, with a look like he'd been walking in a desert and she was a long glass of water. I suppose he couldn't help it, what with them working so close on that book of his. And she's pretty enough, for all she must be thirty if she's a day. No beauty, but all right." She grabbed a box of salt, shook a pinch into her palm, and tossed it into the bowl. "I wonder sometimes why she's got no man or family. Mary neither, come to that, and she must be near the same age. I had four babes by then, three living and one in the churchyard. She might've lost 'em in the war. But it's not the kind of thing you ask, and they never said."

He thought of the mourning ring, back at Lake Street. "Could you come down to Lake Street Station tomorrow? I've something for you to look at. Officer Schmidt found it at Captain Champion's."

"I suppose." She made a wry face. "With the captain gone, I've no work to be at except for my own house. When should I come?"

They settled on two in the afternoon, late enough for her to finish the bulk of the day's chores, yet early enough to get home and make supper if she rode the horsecar back. "We'll cover your fare, since you'll be there on police business."

"Police business." She sounded breathless, as if unexpectedly invited to a Sunday social. "Isn't that a wonder."

"One more thing, Mrs. Flynn." Caught up in the question of Champion and his secretary, he'd almost forgotten about George Schuyler, who'd come into town on urgent business the Thursday before the murder. "Do you recall a visitor to the captain's home while you were around last Friday or Saturday? A man with a crippled arm."

"I do," she said. "He was with the captain Friday afternoon. I saw the pair of them going for the train." The eager look left her face, and she bit her lip. "He gave me my Saturday pay before he left, even though he said I needn't come while he'd be out of town. Came over to where I was hanging out Mr. Markham's washing and handed me the money—for my trouble, he told me. As if he ever made me any. Then he went back inside. Wasn't half an hour later he and his friend left."

Champion had left town mere days before his death? "Did he say where they were going?"

"No. Just that he'd be back Monday latest. He sent a note he was back in the Monday afternoon post." She faltered, hands bunched in her apron. "I wish I'd known that day was the last time I'd see him alive. I'd have...I don't know...said something. A prayer for his soul, maybe."

Something about Friday nagged at his memory, but he couldn't place it. He left her soon afterward, new questions on his mind. Had Schuyler and Champion gone to Alton the weekend before Champion died? And, if so, why?

TWENTY-FOUR

With the daylight waning and his feet sore, Hanley headed home for supper. He needed fortification before heading out later with Schmidt to Custom House Place.

He spent an enjoyable couple of hours eating fried lake whitefish and talking over the day's news with Mam, then teasing his sister, Kate, over the primping she was doing for a first night out with her new beau. Gerry O'Donnell, recruited to the police force after the Fire last October, was one of the few young men Hanley felt comfortable letting near Kate after her last disastrous experience with a swain. "You don't want to look too gorgeous, you'll blind him," he said, as he lingered by the kitchen table. Kate had propped a small mirror against the wall nearby, and was curling her bangs with a slender length of iron heated on the stovetop.

She stuck out her tongue at him. "Go away, Frankie. I've got to finish my hair."

He gave an exaggerated flinch at her use of the nickname he disliked and moved away. At the doorway, he turned back. "You do look pretty. Gerry'd best appreciate what he's getting."

Her cheeks went pink above her bright smile. "We're only going to the dance by Saint Pat's."

A fleeting thought of Rivka there, dancing with *him*, brought a flutter in his chest. *Fool's notion*, he told himself, and banished it. "Enjoy yourself. And don't be home too late." It was good to see her so eager, so unafraid. Hanley went upstairs to change clothes for the night's work, grateful that for the moment all was right with *some* things in the world.

ca

Custom House Place by night was a fraction less dismal than by day, with darkness cloaking its ramshackle saloons and panel houses. The smells of urine, stale liquor, and spring mud laced with rotting vegetable scraps rose from the boardwalk, which sported an array of stains—old dishwater, spilled beer, and the occasional darker splotch of blood from a street brawl. A departing train clanged and whuffed from the depot on Van Buren. Hanley imagined the bunco-steerers descending on the fresh crop of suckers like flies on a dead dog. The cardsharps, cons, and whores at the surrounding establishments of vice would soon have plenty of work.

The fading train sounds gave way to tinny piano music, spilling out from O'Banion's Saloon. As Hanley and Schmidt passed it, a burst of raucous laughter echoed over the street. "Having a good time in there," Schmidt said. "Too good?"

Hanley shook his head. "We're after different fish tonight."

Schmidt made a face as if he'd tasted something bad. "This fella we're after...he a customer where we're going? Must be damn fool, buying a girl in that lousy place."

"He may not be there." Though Hanley hoped he would be, and that he'd put up a fight. A little time at home with his family had tamped down the edgy need to hit something, but not enough. The mob attack at the tailor shop and the incendiary device through Rivka's window, Aaron Kelmansky playing stubborn, and too many questions without answers had started gnawing at him again the minute he left home. Schmidt's brief, skeptical report on the known toughs he'd chased down at Hanley's request—"Wouldn't say if anybody paid 'em to make trouble, they don't know nothing"—had only made it worse. He needed an outlet, the rougher the better.

More piano, out of tune, came from inside Number 354. A shift in the wind brought outhouse stink to Hanley's nose. He coughed, spat to one side, and entered the bordello. Schmidt followed.

Tobacco smoke and murmured conversation rose above what

passed for music in the dimly lit parlor. Unlike Annie Stafford's, there was little elegance here—just enough pretense at it to show up how shabby this dive of a bawdy house was. Hanley saw the usual collection of ten-centers waiting for an inexpensive girl—stout grain merchants in their Sunday best, farmers in homespun with mud-splotched boots, shop clerks out for what they could buy of a night on the town. Dahlia Ford, the brothel owner, presided over it all like a debauched Queen of Sheba. Bony as a starved plow horse and decked out in red silk, she sat at the piano massacring "Sweet Adeline." Two farmers and a middle-aged granger seated nearby listened with rapt attention.

Another familiar figure lounged against the wall, eyeballing the room—Knock-down Jimmy, Dahlia's hired muscle. Six-foot plus and broad as a barn, he fixed hard brown eyes on Hanley and Schmidt as he straightened and moved to block their path. Schmidt drew level with Hanley, one hand on the butt of his truncheon.

"Miz Ford?" Jimmy said.

She broke off in mid-note, then turned at Jimmy's nod. Her eyes, puffy from too much drink and too little sleep, narrowed as she caught sight of Hanley. It took her a moment to place who he was. Then a tight-jawed, artificial smile crossed her painted face. "And what can I do for you this fine evening, sir? You and your friend here?"

"Business," Hanley said. "Somewhere private."

She turned to her small audience. "Excuse me, gentlemen. Do think up some more songs for me, won't you? It passes the time so pleasantly." Her attempt at a girlish laugh, as she rose from the piano stool, made Hanley think of glass breaking.

Jimmy moved to accompany them, but Dahlia shook her head. "Keep an eye on things out here. This won't take long." She led the way through the parlor toward a door in the far wall. They passed a whip-thin youth running a shell game, with another farmer as his patsy. The man's liquor glass held dregs, and he was red faced and shiny eyed as he laid down his money. The youth's glass was full, and he moved the shells with a sober man's precision. Hanley had run similar cons once, with dice and cards instead of walnut shells and a dried pea. Shameful, how easy the rubes were to fleece. He paused long enough to lean a heavy hand on the shell man's shoulder and drop a brief word in his ear—"Let him win"—then followed Dahlia through the doorway.

In the hall beyond, he saw three closed doors and a staircase that led to more bedrooms where girls waited. The creak of bedsprings and occasional soft grunts filtered into the hallway. The sounds put Hanley even more on edge, though at least the girls here were willing. *Sort of.*

Dahlia shut the parlor door, then rounded on Hanley and Schmidt. "Hickey send you, did he? He's got a nerve. I already paid up for this month. I don't know what you think you're getting out of me, but—"

"Answers," Hanley said. "About a customer of yours. He was here Wednesday night, after ten. Took delivery of some papers from a known cracksman and thief."

She shook her head. "I don't give names, Mister—"

"Detective. And you do when I ask you. You forget who I work for?" He didn't work for Captain Hickey anymore, hadn't for two years and better, but Dahlia wasn't privy to the inner workings of the Chicago Police Department.

Her eyes narrowed. "What's this fellow done? Cheated him of his cut?"

"Never you mind." He took out his sketchbook, flipped to the drawing of Sideburns and passed it to her. "This is him. Is he a regular?"

She frowned at the sketch and drew breath as if to speak. The nearest bedroom door opened and Sideburns walked out. Unsteady on his feet, he halted abruptly when he saw them.

A girl's voice, too hard for its youth, followed him out. "Not *my* fault your flag's at half-mast, you cheap bastard!"

Sideburns blinked and flushed red. His gaze flicked from Hanley and Schmidt to the far end of the hallway, where a back entrance was just visible.

Hanley stepped toward him. "Don't. You'll only buy yourself trouble."

Schmidt moved to flank Hanley. Both of them were close enough now to tackle Sideburns. Hanley watched that knowledge play across the man's face, watched him make the fool's choice and fling himself, wobbling, toward the back door. Hanley was on him in three steps. They landed hard, Sideburns face down beneath him. Hanley grabbed his arms and yanked upward.

Sideburns yelped. "All right! Leave off!"

Hanley kept his grip tight. "So you can run again? No chance. Tell me your name."

"None of your goddamn—"

"Clement." The girl appeared, draping herself in the bedroom doorway. Her plain cotton chemise was misbuttoned, and she wore no corset underneath. She aimed a look of disgust toward Sideburns. "Clement Berwick. Comes here every couple weeks." At Dahlia's fierce glare, she folded her arms across her ample chest. "He cheated me. And you. He's done it before."

Dahlia's glare shifted to Berwick. She started toward him. "You lousy rotten—"

As Schmidt blocked her path, Hanley got up and hauled Berwick off the floor. "Come on. We're taking a little walk."

α

"Armory's the other way," Berwick said, as they turned northward up Clark Street. He spoke like a drunk trying to sound sober.

Hanley steered him along, Schmidt assisting from the other side. "You could use a good long stroll in the fine night air. Clear your head."

Except for a pair of night shift detectives, Lake Street Station was deserted when they arrived. They marched Berwick past the lobby desk and down the hall toward the holding cells. Both of them were empty, an unexpected mercy on a Friday night. "I take care of the arrest," Schmidt said as Hanley muscled Berwick into the nearest cell.

Berwick's gust of a laugh stank of whiskey. "Arrest? For what? Cheating a whore? Being with one? No one gets arrested for that. I've got *friends*. You're—"

"We're not arresting you," Hanley said. "Yet."

Schmidt caught Hanley's eye. Hanley gave him a small nod. Given the location of Custom House Place and the consequent odds that Captain Hickey was among Berwick's *friends*, he didn't want the man's name coming up on any arrest reports until he had something more serious to charge him with than buying a girl.

Schmidt ambled a few paces away, slouched against the wall, and busied himself with his fingernails. Hanley leaned against the cell bars. "So. You were at O'Banion's Saloon this past Tuesday night. With an acquaintance of mine. You paid him to steal some papers from a law office on Indiana Avenue. Why?"

Berwick folded his arms. He'd started to sober up, but wasn't there yet. "I don't have to tell you anything."

"The papers related to a lawsuit. Farnham and Chandler. Exploding guns, dead Union soldiers. The kind of thing a man'd pay to keep buried. You did. A hundred dollars. Are you a defendant in that lawsuit, Mr. Berwick? Or connected with someone who is?"

"I don't know what you're talking about."

"If I had a nickel for all the times I've heard that, I'd be richer than Marshall Field. What's your connection to Farnham and Chandler, and why did you want those papers so much?"

Berwick pursed his lips. "I go to O'Banion's to gamble. Are Chicago's finest going after mere players now? I understood you prefer to catch the sharpers...when you bother arresting anyone at all."

"You've been misinformed."

"So tell me the fine and I'll pay it." A heartbeat's pause and Berwick continued, with a meaningful look at Hanley. "I just need to know to whom."

Hanley straightened. "That sounds like a bribe. Now, why would you offer me that, if all you did at O'Banion's was gamble...and all you did at Dahlia Ford's place was cheat a whore? You never hired a cracksman, never took delivery of legal papers you didn't steal...about the lawsuit you're not involved in." He paused, feigning thought. "Maybe it's your friend Lucas Errol who's involved. In the lawsuit, in theft, in worse."

"I don't know anyone named—"

"You don't lie well when you're drunk, Clement. You met Lucas Errol off the train from Alton Tuesday afternoon. There's a witness. A whole depot full of them, in fact. Are you both defendants in this lawsuit? Conspirators to defraud the federal government—"

"I'm his lawyer," Berwick snapped, then flushed red.

"Some truth at last. So tell me about Farnham and Chandler. Lucas Errol is the defendant, I take it, responsible for those bad guns and dead men?"

Berwick drew himself up. "You can't ask me about that. Attorney-client privilege."

"This is my station. I can do whatever I want."

"I can make trouble for you. And I will."

"Clement." Hanley shook his head. "Mike Hickey can't help you. You're not officially here."

Berwick gave him a cold look, then tugged at his shirt cuffs as he moved away from the bars. "My client is an innocent victim of a suit brought by a vindictive Union officer, because Mr. Errol supported state's rights during the late unpleasantness between North and South. Lucas was a junior partner at Farnham and Chandler. He didn't make those guns, wasn't in charge when they *were* made. Things happened. Men died. But not because of Lucas Errol. A man can't be crucified in court for backing the losing side."

Hanley snorted. "Lucas Errol's no innocent. Which Ben Champion, your 'vindictive Union officer,' stood a good chance of proving with what was in those papers. Or he would have if he hadn't been murdered Tuesday night."

Berwick stiffened. "I don't know anything about that."

"No, because you were at O'Banion's hiring a thief. Though you could've hired a murderer as well. Who else did you talk to at O'Banion's that night? They know me there, they'll tell me, if I make it worth their while." He paced across the cell, watching Berwick from the corner of his eye. "Or was it Lucas Errol who went to Ben Champion's house that night and killed him, and you had to clean up his mess? Which makes you an accessory. He was here in Chicago when the murder happened. He could've—"

131

Berwick lurched forward with a wild swing of one arm. Hanley caught it and spun him around, using his weight to press Berwick against the cell bars. "You damned fool. Drunk, disorderly, *and* assaulting an officer. You'll be staying here awhile."

"Go to hell," Berwick spat.

Hanley yanked his arm upward. The man yelped. "Tell me everything you did at O'Banion's," Hanley said. "Everyone you spoke a word to. And exactly where both you and Lucas Errol were last Tuesday night. I want every damned minute accounted for."

TWENTY-FIVE

March 1867

The prison washhouse smells of steam and soap and wet cloth. Dorrie hauls a dripping sheet out of the long stone washtub and wedges one edge into a wringer. Her hair, damp from the humid air, flops into her eyes. She lets it lie. The other women doing laundry all look as she must—like scarecrows in a hard rain, scrawny and bedraggled. There's nothing left of her, not even enough for a desperate man to pay for.

She turns the wringer crank, ignoring the ache in her arms. After nearly two years of doing this every day, she's likely strong enough to strangle someone with her bare hands. That scar-faced Yankee captain, for one. She couldn't get away from him. First that night in East Tennessee, then Richmond, where she fled for sanctuary. But God brought her enemy there, revealed her to him, let him do her harm once again. A cruel joke, like Abraham with Isaac. She's never realized before coming to this place how terrible God is, to treat his own that way.

No choice, she tells herself. That thought gives her a strange comfort. Poor Emil. The Yankee soldier who was kind to her, who helped her buy food. She hated him for it at first, but a meal or two changed her mind. Then the food ran out, and it was sell herself or starve. And the only men with real money were the bluecoats. The thought of lying with any of them made her ill, but she wasn't ready to die yet. So she went looking for Emil, the one bluecoat whose hands on her she might just be able to

133

tolerate. She haunted the sutlers' wagons and the taverns, until she finally saw him at the White Horse—alone, half-drunk, a letter in his hand.

She gathers up the wrung-out sheet, wetting her plain prison dress further, and carries it to the drying rack, where she drapes it as best she can. The sight of her own hands—red as raw beef and wrinkled as dried fruit—makes her laugh, a harsh bark. She's beyond crying. Has been since Tom died. She chokes the feeling down and heads back toward the washtub.

Ivy is there, hand on one hip, staring at her like she's a bad smell. The woman's name doesn't suit her. Forty if she's a day, Ivy's red faced and blowsy even on prison food, with sagging breasts and three teeth missing. Hard to believe Ivy and she are both here for the same offense. Who'd have paid cash money for *that*?

"Y'all think something's funny?" Ivy says. "Miss High-and-Mighty, doin' darky work like the rest of us. That funny to you?"

Dorrie stares at her. From the day they met in this damned place, Ivy hasn't let up about her being a fine lady. Dorrie has calluses aplenty on her hands, from living rough in the woods and from sewing in Richmond, but other things give her away. The way she talks, how she carries herself. Ivy loves the notion of a fine lady brought low. Dorrie can't think why. She's done nothing to Ivy, or any of them. She's kept to herself, waiting out the time. Only another month to go. Then she'll be rid of Ivy, rid of laundry and cheap prison fare and fleas and bedbugs. Not that anything better awaits her outside.

"I said, that funny to you?" Ivy is louder now, angrier. She thinks Dorrie's ignoring her. Suddenly, it is funny. Dorrie feels a grin stretch her face, hears a laugh burst from her throat. Her laughing gets louder, faster, echoing off the walls. Her vision blurs, and she can barely breathe. She waits for Ivy to shake her or slap her. But there are no grabbing hands, no sharp blow. She blinks hard and sees Ivy still by the washtub, staring at her like she's crazy. Ivy crosses herself, and she laughs harder. Dorrie the crazy woman. Don't get too close, it might be catching.

Behind her, the washhouse door creaks open. The warden, a hatchet-faced woman with a temper to match, calls her name. "Whittier! Come with me. Now."

Her laughter cuts off. The sudden silence presses against her eardrums. She wipes her eyes with her soap-spattered sleeve and follows the warden out.

Anxiety makes her feel cold as they walk down the corridor. Her hand creeps toward the neck of her prison dress. Tom's mourning ring on its chain is still there, the only possession she's managed to hold onto. She touches the chain for comfort. "Where are we going?" She can't help thinking of Captain Scar. Not satisfied with bursting in on her and Emil in the cheap room at the White Horse, her half-naked and Emil with his pants undone. He must have seen them leaving the common room, and feared she would rob or harm the boy once their business was finished. The captain had pulled her away from Emil and thrown her to the floor, his voice harsh in her ears: "You won't take a penny or anything else from one of my men, you thieving Reb whore." Next thing she knew, he was hauling her to the local jail with her chemise still around her waist. The only mercy was, he didn't recognize her as the boy Confederate he'd captured almost a year before. Not even by the neck scar he left her with. He's figured it out, she thinks now with a shiver. Figured it out and come to take her someplace where she'll die a traitor's death—

"You're getting out," the warden says without looking back at her.

Frightened, she fumbles. "I have another month...I thought..."

Now the warden looks around. "You want to stay here? Well, that's just fine. I'm sure we can find you a fresh cot somewhere, though you'll have to go down to one meal a day. Food's tight, and you'd be an extra mouth. But suit yourself."

They're still walking, so Dorrie knows the warden doesn't mean a word. "Why am I getting out early?"

"Somebody asked. Special." The warden's tone warns her off from inquiring what she means. Money's changed hands somewhere. Who would pay to set her free? Would Captain Scar pay to take her away and murder her?

The answer awaits her in a sparsely furnished room where visitors usually come. Joel stands near the dusty window, one hand resting on his walking stick for support, the way he used to rest against the bar when he got tired. She never would have expected him. He looks the same as he did at the Liberty Inn—skinny shoulders and bent spine, gray eyes in a fine-boned face. Those eyes are shining at her now, as if she's some treasure he'd thought lost until this moment.

"Dorrie," he says. She watches him take her in—her skinny frame in the dirty prison dress, her lank hair and roughened hands. He must know why she's here, what she's done with herself since she left—though not the murder she committed, or surely he wouldn't have come. Yet he looks at her as he might at a precious object, broken by mischance and left in the dirt. Hoping he can dust her off and make her good as new.

He holds out a hand. "Let me take you home."

TWENTY-SIX

April 27, 1872

Early Saturday morning, Hanley found Sergeant Moore in his usual spot at Lily Stemple's eatery, enjoying a cup of strong coffee and homemade biscuits before the work day began. Hanley poured his own mugful from the pot on the cast-iron stove, dropped a coin in the jar nearby, and joined his boss, telling him everything that had happened with Clement Berwick the previous night. "I booked him for assaulting a police officer. I figure I've got a couple of days before Mike Hickey gets wind of it. Berwick says he left his client at the Tremont House around eight the night Champion died, has no idea of the fellow's whereabouts after they ate supper together. Nor did he pay anyone to steal anything. He did make sure to say he's certain Lucas Errol had nothing to do with the murder. His client is an innocent man, a fine upstanding churchgoer and pillar of the community in Alton, and it's a tragedy that now he won't be vindicated in court."

"I thought Champion had a partner," Moore said. "The lawsuit might not be dead along with him."

Hanley sipped coffee. "I'd like to get my hands on those papers, see what's in them that Berwick paid a hundred dollars for. Errol probably has them now. Any chance of my getting a warrant to search for them?"

"If Errol, or his lawyer, didn't toss them in a rubbish pile."

"Why pay so much just to chuck them away? No, they wanted to see what Champion had." He tapped a finger against his mug. "Champion was looking for witnesses, collecting depositions. Maybe Berwick wanted to find those people. Bribe them or threaten them to change their testimony in court. Bury the depositions, different stories or no story on the stand...I'm betting they'll keep those papers, at least for a while." If not, he'd be on the next train to Alton, to find George Schuyler. That suggestion could wait until later, though. The trip took fourteen hours and would cost the department money. With only twelve detectives to cover the whole city, chasing a lead out of jurisdiction required a damned good excuse.

Moore ate the last bite of his biscuit. "Judge Carruthers might oblige, but he won't be in chambers for another hour at least. If Lucas Errol has money to pay a lawyer, that makes them both people to reckon with, even without Mike Hickey in Berwick's corner. Not the best choice for arrest under questionable circumstances. You'd best hope you can make something stick."

CB

A quick trip to O'Banion's, nearly empty in the bright light of morning, confirmed Berwick's alibi for the night of the murder. Hanley found the owner wiping beer glasses with a rag that looked capable of touching off a cholera epidemic. "Fella was here, all right," O'Banion said, after Hanley slipped him a silver half-dollar from petty cash at Lake Street. "Lost himself a packet, but he switched over from faro to dice and goddamn if he didn't win most of his stake back. Some luck." He spat into a glass, then swiped at the wet spot. "He asked after Abe when he first got here, maybe nine o'clock. They talked awhile. Then your fella come over to the faro table. Didn't move for a solid hour. Abe was drinking. Bought himself a whiskey, the good stuff, so somebody paid him something."

That matched Abe's account—thirty dollars up front, seventy more on delivery. So much for Berwick's claim they'd merely "passed pleasantries." Dahlia Ford, roused from sleep at Number 354 just down the street, grudgingly confirmed that a large roll of tied-up papers and several greenbacks had changed hands at her place late Wednesday night. "I hope that bastard Berwick rots in jail. The nerve, him cheating me." She lowered her voice. "He was in with Mike Hickey, you know. Back in the war. Running a racket, getting bond-jumpers to join the army for the enlistment bonus. Then they'd run back to Hickey, pay him a cut and go do it again somewhere else. Him and that Berwick used to laugh about it. I never turned them in, 'cause I had my interests to look after, but the stories I could tell you…" She tapped a finger against her nose.

"What stories?" Past history, nothing he should be wasting time with now, but the prospect of dirt—even old dirt—on Mike Hickey was too tempting to resist.

She looked dismayed. "Never mind. I didn't say a word. If you squeal to him, I'll—"

He fished the last dollar from his pocket. "If I like what I hear, I won't tell him a damned thing."

σ

For the next little while, Hanley listened while Dahlia talked. "The Order of American Knights," she said, her voice scarcely above a whisper. "Hickey and Berwick used to bring those damned Copperheads here. They came, oh, three or four times in '64. I remember the last time particular." She tapped her nose again. "I'd just took over running this place, and there was the Democrats coming to town for their convention."

He recalled the stories from that time, eagerly devoured in the midst of combat by the Chicago Irish Brigade, to whom politics from home was as intoxicating as whiskey. Rumors that this presidential candidate or that one was a sure winner or loser against Abe Lincoln. Rumors of Copperheads converging on the city, some of them said to be working in secret to scotch a Union victory. And rumors of trouble, centered on Camp Douglas, the sprawling encampment outside the city limits where Confederate prisoners of war were kept. "I remember it clear as sunrise. Late July, two years to the day Mr. Ford passed on, God rest him. Mike

Hickey wanted one of my back rooms. No girls, just the space. He said there'd be men coming, and I should send them to where he was. Must've been a dozen at least, all in one cramped room hotter than hell, so hot they had to prop the door just to breathe. Well, I had to check on my girls who were in the other rooms, so I couldn't help but overhear..."

"What?"

She gave him an expectant look, her gaze flicking to the dollar in his palm. He waited a moment, then handed it over.

She tucked it away in her wrapper and leaned toward him. "Something about guns, and how they had almost all the money. To buy them, I guess. Berwick said that. I didn't hear who they meant to pay, or what they meant those guns for. And then nothing came of it, so I forgot about it. Copperheads always were big talkers. But the police *did* find guns later, in that fellow's barn in November, and the papers were full of stories about the American Knights meaning to take over Chicago and make us all Confederates, and I got to thinking..."

Hanley drew in a breath. "Are you saying Mike Hickey was involved in the Northwest Conspiracy?" Those newspaper stories, he remembered too—Southern ne'er-do-wells and sympathizers converging on the city, determined to release and arm the Reb prisoners at Camp Douglas and turn Chicago into the capital of their so-called Northwest Confederacy. The loss of the city, with its vital rail links for troop and supply transport, would have devastated the Union war effort, maybe enough to let the Confederates eke out a victory.

"I don't know." She looked worried now. "They didn't meet here after July, and it was months later those stories came out. But he could've been."

He certainly could, Hanley thought as he headed west toward Union Street Station where the police court was. Judge Carruthers should be there by now, and with luck he'd get his warrant. Not that Mike Hickey's—or even Clement Berwick's—actions back in '64 had any bearing on his current case. He couldn't even use Dahlia's story against Hickey without proof of wrongdoing, more than the word of a madam who regularly paid Mike Hickey off. Still, it might prove a useful thing to know.

TWENTY-SEVEN

Judge Carruthers wasn't in chambers, Hanley found to his chagrin. The man was home with a spring chill, his housekeeper having sent a note. Balked on two fronts, he lingered outside the police court and pondered his next move. Go to Tremont House after the stolen papers anyway, without a warrant to back him up? Sweat Lucas Errol about where he was after eight Tuesday night? He shook his head, frustrated. Errol wasn't a petty thief or informant, or other lowlife easily pressured by police. Better to tackle him with a little leverage in hand.

A westbound horsecar got Hanley to North May Street around eleven. He had a good stretch of time before he needed to be back at the station to show Mrs. Flynn the mourning ring.

The ring bothered him, now he thought about it. It had the look of a man's ring, and had fit Champion's hand at the morgue, but if it was his, why hadn't it been on his finger, or on his dresser with his cufflinks? Had whoever killed him taken it and then dropped it during their hasty retreat? The chain nagged at him, too. A man's ring worn like a locket seemed more like a woman's adornment. Which brought him back to his jilter theory—or to Alice Lockwood, if Mrs. Flynn's notion of things between Champion and his secretary was correct. Or even to Mary Olcott. Then again, the ring might have nothing to do with the murder. Some visitor of Champion's might have lost it unawares anytime beforehand, or simply had no chance to ask after it.

He put the ring from his mind and mounted the steps of the Thomashaws' front porch.

ଓଃ

Marcus Thomashaw, playing ball with his son Oliver in the back yard, looked as if he'd spent a wakeful night with a pillow over his head. His hair stuck out at odd angles, and it clearly took him some effort to think through the questions Hanley asked. "I didn't get home until seven last Tuesday," he said, tossing a brown leather ball toward Oliver, who leaped for it, missed, and went chasing it through the grass. "I generally don't. I don't recall seeing anyone at Champion's that evening either, arriving or leaving. Doesn't mean they mightn't have, though." The ball whizzed through the air, a wild looping throw that landed just short of Marcus's feet. He scooped up the ball and lobbed it back.

"Your wife mentioned hearing someone pass by your house on foot around ten Tuesday night. Were you awake at the time? Do you recall the same thing?"

"I was awake, all right." He smoothed his rumpled hair, to little use. "Hard not to be, with poor Grant and his stomach upsets. I know Susanna—my wife—and our hired girl, Mary, were up and about." He frowned as if in thought. "I don't remember footsteps, but someone went out the back door about that time. Maybe an hour after I went to bed, which was around nine. Grant had gone quiet for a bit. I thought at first it was Mary, going for the doctor in case the poor mite started up again. But whoever it was came back within, oh, ten minutes at a guess. Could have been Oliver, sneaking out for a look at the stars. He's interested in things like that." He glanced fondly at his son, who'd gone after the ball but gotten distracted by something in the grass. "Stars, plants, animals, anything to do with nature. Too bad he doesn't tend as much to his schooling."

A few questions asked of Oliver made clear he hadn't left the house, nor seen or heard anything of use. Nor had Marcus, apart from the back door. The Thomashaws' bedroom was at the rear of the house, so he wouldn't have heard the footsteps passing in front in any case. Oliver trotted over to his ball and started tossing it by himself, apparently not discouraged by his repeated failures to catch it. Hanley turned his attention back to Marcus. "How well did you know Ben Champion? I'm told you and he had a talk and a smoke on occasion. Were you friends?"

"Friendly acquaintances, more like. My family only moved into the neighborhood a couple of years ago. Captain Champion welcomed us with a bottle of fine whiskey for me, and some tulip bulbs for Susanna. Said his mother had prized them, grew them around their house. Apparently the family's lived here for ages."

Marcus had served in the cavalry, if Hanley recalled right. "Two soldiers trading war stories?"

"That and politics." Marcus gave him a wry smile. "Sometimes one desperately wants a conversation that doesn't turn on the antics of one's offspring, or what makes the sky blue. Champion was an intelligent man with plenty of opinions. He didn't like the way things were going, I can tell you that. The Democrats wanting to act like there was no rebellion, President Grant and the Republicans hardly much better. There's even talk of shutting down the Freedmen's Bureau and leaving all the Negroes in the South high and dry. Ben was furious about that. What did we fight the damned war for, he said, if we're not going to keep a just peace—if we let evil have its way in the South again, and the freedmen can go to blazes? He hoped his book might change things, like Mrs. Beecher Stowe's did. Change some attitudes, at least."

"His war memoir, you mean? Did he tell you much about it?"

"Just that it was about the men he led in the Eighty-Second Illinois Infantry. He said people needed to know. People in Washington, he meant. Politicians." The last word came out with an edge of disgust. "He said they were good soldiers and it might surprise some folk to learn that." Marcus frowned. "You know, it didn't strike me at the time, but that seems an odd thing to say."

Hanley shrugged. "A lot of the men who signed up weren't trained. Plenty hadn't ever held a gun. I was one of them."

"Bull Run." Marcus gave a mirthless laugh. "Imagine, people bringing their families to watch that battle. Picnic dinners and blankets on the grass. As if men dying for their country were entertainment." He shook off the bleakness his words had conjured up. "At any rate, Champion had high hopes for his book. Too high, I thought, though

143

I didn't tell him so. How much can a book do at this point? But he'd lined up a publisher, had it nearly ready to send them, so—"

"Then it wasn't at his publisher's yet?"

"Not that I know of. He expected to finish it up this past week." He gave Hanley a questioning look. "I don't suppose I could send it for him? He told me who his publisher was, said they'd signed a contract and all. Seems a shame not to see his work through."

"We didn't find it," Hanley said. "Would he have kept it somewhere other than his home or office, do you know?"

"I suppose he could've given it to Miss Lockwood, to read over one more time. I can't think where else it might be."

ଔ

Champion's desk was as empty as his house, nothing that looked like a manuscript anywhere in it. Hanley went back through every room, searching for a safe or a strongbox the right size to hold a stack of paper, but found none. Champion's upstairs closet yielded a carpetbag and a portmanteau with a lock. Not typical places to keep important documents, but who knew? Hanley hefted each in turn. The carpetbag was empty, but there was something in the portmanteau. Not too heavy. Maybe the right weight for a sheaf of paper a few inches thick.

He pulled the portmanteau out and set it on Champion's bed. No key in the miniature lock, nor one attached or anywhere on the closet floor. Where had he seen a key the right size? He had, he was certain of it. Too small for a door-key, oddly shaped...He strode to the nightstand and yanked open the narrow drawer. There it was, the key he remembered from his first search of the bedroom.

He snatched it up and went back to the portmanteau. The key turned smoothly in the tiny lock. Inside was a pair of shoes. Hanley swore under his breath. Where was the damned manuscript? Or a copy—there must have been one, hadn't Alice Lockwood said she copied whatever Champion wrote since her last working day? He took a slow breath, thinking it through. The manuscript might be with Miss Lockwood.

Yet she hadn't had it with her when she came to Champion's house the morning after his murder. They'd made special arrangements for her to work that day, she'd said. He closed his eyes, conjuring up how she'd looked. Nothing in her arms, no parcel or satchel…only a string purse dangling from her wrist, too small to contain anything beyond whatever young women normally carried about. A handkerchief, a hair comb, money for the horsecars. If Champion gave her the manuscript to read over, why hadn't she brought it back?

He left the bedroom and headed down the stairs. A thought occurred to him as he reached the bottom, and he made a final search of the two places he hadn't yet looked.

He found what he was after in the kindling-basket—a collection of scrawled-on papers in a short flat stack beneath a scattering of twigs. Nowhere near enough to be an almost finished book, but a few lines on one page told him these were discards from it.

Spent the day camped near a small river, awaiting the return of our scouting party. We knew Rebel bushwhackers were in the area. The only question was how many, and how close by…

He went back upstairs, fetched the carpetbag, and stuffed the papers into it. God knew what a war memoir had to do with Champion's murder—probably nothing—but that it appeared to be missing, when it shouldn't be, was enough to rouse Hanley's instincts. Something was out of place here. Time to find out what.

TWENTY-EIGHT

Luck was with Hanley when he reached the boardinghouse at 29 South Robey Street. He met Alice Lockwood coming out the front door, dressed as if on her way somewhere. "Miss Lockwood, I'm glad I caught you," he said. "I need a little of your time."

"I..." She looked flustered at the sight of him. "I was just on my way out. Perhaps anoth—"

"This won't take long. Where were you headed?"

"Oh..." She shrugged. "Just out. Such a fine day, not one to waste."

He nodded toward the north end of the block. "There's a park over there. We can talk on the way."

She replied with a terse, "Very well," and preceded him down the boardwalk.

Robey Street was a pleasant neighborhood, a step up even from his landlady's area on West Monroe. Champion must have paid Miss Lockwood a fair wage for her to afford a room here. He fell into step beside her as they proceeded.

"I'm still wondering about the war memoir," he said. "Champion's neighbor tells me it wasn't quite finished. But you led me to believe he'd sent it to his publisher."

She licked her lips—a quick, nervous gesture. "I understood he was preparing to send it."

"So you don't have it? But if the memoir *was* finished, why did Captain Champion ask you to come and work on Tuesday? And why were you going to his house on Wednesday?"

"He...he wanted me to help him tidy up his notes."

"Who's the publisher?"

"I don't recall."

"But you were his secretary. You never corresponded with the publisher on your employer's behalf?"

"Ben preferred to handle that himself. He liked to be in control."

He let a brief silence fall and eyed her as they continued down the boardwalk. Her jaw was set, her shoulders tense. He decided to throw her off balance and tie up a loose end at the same time. "You mentioned an older gentleman who passed by you on North May Street Tuesday evening," he said, taking out his sketchbook and turning to the page with Josiah Rushton's likeness. "Would this be him, by any chance?"

"I don't know," she said. Too quickly, and with barely a glance at the sketch.

He'd expected a "No." Why on earth was she lying about this? As far as he knew, she didn't know Josiah Rushton from Adam. "I'm sorry, Miss Lockwood, but I don't believe you."

She glared at him. "A lady doesn't lie, Detective...and a gentleman does not so accuse her."

"I'm not a gentleman. I'm a cop."

She stopped in the middle of the sidewalk. "Are you threatening me?"

"A man is dead. I'll do what I have to, to get at the truth."

Silence again. Then she let out a slow breath, the fight draining from her along with it. "I have my reasons for speaking as I did. Must I confess them?"

He said nothing to that. After several seconds, she continued. "I saw that man. Just not on the street, and not when I said. And I don't know who he is." She glanced toward the little park that lay half a block ahead of them now. "Can we go there and sit? I'd prefer to be comfortable while I tell you."

"All right."

They reached the park, and he brought them to a halt at the first empty wrought iron bench. "Here's as good a place as any. You may as well start."

She sat, shifting to accommodate her bustle. He settled next to her. She smoothed her skirt. He stayed still, not saying a word.

"That older gentleman…" A flush rose in her cheeks. "I saw him later that night."

"How much later?"

The flush deepened. "I'm not sure. I wasn't paying attention to the time. Must we go further with this? It isn't fair to Ben. He's not here to defend his reputation."

Or yours, Hanley thought. "You stayed for supper?"

"Yes." A slight smile, as if at the memory. "Scrambled eggs and fried potatoes. Ben learned plain cooking during the war. He was good at it. He had whiskey—one glass. I had water. We weren't…careless. Overconsumption of liquor wasn't involved."

He eyed her silently for a moment. She sat flagpole straight, though the heightened color in her cheeks gave the lie to her coolly defiant expression. Every inch the lady, despite the brazenness of what she wasn't quite confessing to. She must have grown up rich—she had the iron reserve he'd seen in other well-off people, those who'd never known a time when their money didn't give them the unquestioned right to do what they pleased. He was inclined to believe at least some of her story, as he doubted any woman would lie about her own willing seduction. "So when did the older gentleman turn up?"

"A while after supper. Ben and I were…upstairs. Please don't ask for the details. Surely some things can be kept private."

That was all right with Hanley. What concerned him just now was the timing of Josiah's visit—if it happened the way she was telling him. Josiah hadn't said a word about being at Champion's house Tuesday night. "Was it dark out yet?"

"I don't recall."

Otherwise occupied. "And when he arrived?"

She shifted her weight. "We heard knocking at the front door, and someone calling for Ben. He knew who it was. I could tell by his face. He…he said he'd go settle it, and asked me to wait." One hand smoothed a wisp of hair at her neck. "I heard him go down and open the door. They had words, Ben and this man. Hard words. When I heard the man shout, 'You can't do this, I won't let you,' I couldn't help myself.

I looked out and saw him." She shivered. "He was so angry. I thought he'd strike Ben, hurt him. And I didn't know what to do. I couldn't help. That man couldn't even know I was there. I knew then I couldn't stay. If anyone saw me leaving…if anyone thought…they might use it against Ben somehow. So I…I gathered my things, and… The man must have left, because I heard Ben come back upstairs. We met on the landing. I said I should go. He let me."

She fell silent, eyes focused on a nearby tree that was starting to bud. He let the silence stretch a time. She'd looked and sounded sincere, yet she'd lied to him before with a little truth mixed in. Nothing to say she wasn't doing it again. Because she killed Champion? But if she'd willingly gone to his bed—or started to—then why stab him to death? With a bayonet. A soldier's weapon, a soldier's thrust. Not something a woman like Alice Lockwood should be capable of. And what about Josiah? Was any of this story true?

"I take it no one saw you leave, again," he said, not bothering to hide his doubt.

"You think I'm lying? About *this*?"

"Maybe you weren't willing. Maybe Champion forced—"

"God!" She stood and took two swift steps away from the bench, arms pressed to her stomach. "I've no more to say to you. I've told you the truth. Now leave me alone. For the love of Heaven, *leave me alone*."

TWENTY-NINE

Hanley made it back to Lake Street barely in time to meet Mrs. Flynn, who was waiting for him. His mind still on the encounter with Alice Lockwood, he thanked Mrs. Flynn for coming and beckoned her into the squad room. He'd fetched the ring and chain from the evidence box earlier, and now held them out to her. "Do you recall seeing these among Captain Champion's things when you cleaned house for him?"

She gave the jewelry a puzzled glance. "I don't think so. I'm sure he never had a ring like that. He never wore one for his parents after they died. He said it was better to honor their memory by carrying on their work." She lowered her voice. "They were abolitionists, you know. Before the war and all."

He set the ring and chain on his desk. "You've known the family a long time?"

"For near twenty years before Mr. Charles and Mrs. Minna passed on. Nineteen I was, new married, and Pat and me wanting to earn all we could so as to put by for a family. They were fine folk, the Champions. Paid well, always had a kind word and a smile. They didn't mean for me to know about the Negroes they took in...but there was a little boy came down sick and his mam wouldn't leave him, and I never got Mrs. Minna's note telling me not to come that day. It broke my heart to see them, poor things. Half-starved, feet bleeding from walking miles across rough country, jumping at every sound. Especially after that slave law. They weren't safe anywhere then. They'd stop for a meal or a few hours' sleep and keep running, all the way to Canada."

He knew what she meant by "that slave law"—the Fugitive Slave Act, passed in 1850 in a futile attempt to settle the furor over the slavery question. It required Northerners to aid slaveholders in recapturing their escaped "property," even paying magistrates twice as much to declare a black man a slave as to let him go free. The effect had been to turn every Negro north of the Mason-Dixon Line into a potential kidnap victim.

He thought of Sergeant Moore's suggestion that Champion might have died because of something in his past that someone couldn't let go. The law office building manager had mentioned Champion helping fugitive slaves. Maybe the notion wasn't so far-fetched after all. "I heard Captain Champion worked on fugitive slave cases."

"Him and Mr. Rushton, until the captain enlisted in '61," she said. "Josiah Rushton and his missus were great friends with the captain's parents. Right after that slave law went in, Mr. Josiah took the captain on as a clerk. Quite a young man, the captain was, but even then wanting to help the Negroes any way he could. Mr. Josiah knew a hundred ways to talk a Negro free, or hold things up so other folk could get them away. By the time the judges sorted out who belonged to whom, the Negroes would be long gone from the courthouse or the jail."

Intrigued, Hanley pulled out his chair and gestured for her to sit. Josiah and Champion apparently had a closer relationship than he'd thought. Certainly more than Will Rushton had implied. *I think my uncle worked with him once or twice...* He found himself wondering when the Rushtons had adopted Will. As a child or a youth, surely. Long enough ago for Will to have a notion how close the two families were. And Josiah, raising Cain at Champion's house the night he died...if Hanley could believe Miss Lockwood this time around.

"Did Champion ever talk about any case of his and Mr. Rushton's that led to trouble? Anything that came up again recently?"

She bit her lip. "I'm sorry, I don't know. I heard bits and pieces, but I don't recall any names, or anyone I could put a face to. It was all so long ago. Something was heavy on him these past few weeks, though. I could see it in his face. But he never said what." Her breath caught. "It's still hard to believe he's..." Hastily she crossed herself. Hanley fished a handkerchief from his pocket, checked that it was clean, and handed it to her. With a murmured thank-you, she dabbed at her eyes. "If there's any more I can do to help," she said as she handed the handkerchief back, "you just say the word."

 C3

Hanley stayed in the squad room awhile after she left, slouched in his chair, fiddling with the mourning ring and thinking. A piece of jewelry Champion didn't own, fallen in the grass by his front walk. Josiah Rushton supposedly at Champion's home the night of the murder, shouting and threatening him. Will Rushton, speaking as if his uncle and Champion hardly knew each other, even though that clearly wasn't the case. An out-of-town trip, most likely to Alton, site of the gun factory whose owner Champion was suing for causing the deaths of Union soldiers. A possible link through the defendant's lawyer to the Northwest Conspiracy. The attack last Monday night on Aaron Kelmansky's Alton farm, and whatever he wouldn't talk about in front of his sister, wife, and stepson. A missing war memoir. Someone leaving the Thomashaw house by the back door, someone else hurrying past it in front, during the hours Champion might have died. How did it all fit? Hanley felt pulled in a dozen directions, unable to make sense of the pile of fragments he'd collected.

Back to basics. Who had reason to want Ben Champion dead? Alice Lockwood's story explained the man's half-dressed state, but could she have killed him with a single bayonet stab—let alone had reason to, if she'd wanted to share his bed? A thug hired by Berwick or Errol might know how to kill with one blow, but someone like that would have brought his own weapon—and surely would have alerted Champion when breaking into the house, unless he climbed in through the second-floor bedroom window. No bully boy would go to that trouble, and Hanley couldn't see Errol—a rich businessman, accustomed to paying others for what he wanted—doing so, either. Mary Olcott, who lived next door? He'd found hints of intimacy between her and Champion, but all secondhand. Enough to make her a woman spurned, lashing out in rage? But a bayonet, wielded like a soldier? Not something a woman would know how to do. Unless…

He swept the ring and chain into his desk drawer—time enough to return them to evidence later—and left the squad room.

∛

Mary Olcott answered at the Thomashaws' house, her expression guarded. Behind her, little-girl voices squabbled over whose turn it was to dry the dishes. "If you want the Thomashaws, they aren't here. They went to the lakefront with Oliver to watch the boats."

"I came to talk to you."

"I've children to mind and washing-up to do. Good day, Mr. Hanley."

She started to close the door. Hanley blocked it with his foot. "It won't take long. Just a few questions about the night Captain Champion died."

He saw fear in her eyes, swiftly masked. Then she stepped outside and closed the door. "Go ahead, then. Before they break something in there."

He began with the expected. "Did you see or hear anyone around Champion's house Tuesday evening? Anyone coming or going, say between six and ten o'clock?"

"I don't recall."

He leaned against a newel post, arms folded. "You're sure? It was a nice evening. Warm enough to have windows open."

"I was getting the children to bed." She glanced toward the closed door. "They make plenty of noise."

"Keep you busy."

"Yes." She took a few aimless steps across the porch. "Mrs. Thomashaw can tell you. I settled the other children and then helped her take care of Grant. He was screaming fit to..." She faltered. "...to wake the dead."

"Yes, Mrs. Thomashaw said how busy you were. Stirring up the stove, brewing chamomile, getting the little girls back to sleep. You were all over the house that night. Did you leave it?"

"Why would I leave, with all I had to do?"

"Someone did. Around ten, or a bit after."

Her chin went up as she locked gazes with him. "Not me."

"Not even for a few minutes to catch your breath?"

"No."

She was trying too hard at sincerity. She *had* left the house, he was certain. Gone next door to Champion's? "Tell me again how you met Captain Champion. And how you found him when you came to Chicago."

She looked bewildered. "What's that got to do with anything?"

"You met him in Virginia, I think you said? Loudoun County?"

"I don't see—"

"In the war. Through your brother. You said they fought together. But a Virginia man wouldn't have served in the Eighty-Second Illinois."

Her smile was bitter. "You heard of Mosby's Rangers?"

Surprise made him straighten. "The Gray Ghost. Attacked Union soldiers and supply lines all through the war. Nobody ever caught him."

"My brother tried. He died for it. Mosby's men ambushed him. Ben Champion was the Union commander he reported to about Confederates in the county. He ought to've been safe, Ben promised us that, but..." She ended with a shrug.

He let the silence hang. In the first years after the war, stories had come out of just such people as Mary was describing. Union loyalists in Confederate territory, fighting their Secesh friends and neighbors, sometimes inducted into the Union army, but often simply irregulars. Not all those in the news accounts were men, either. "Did you fight, too? Some women did. I've read about it in the newspapers."

"What I did then has nothing to do with now."

"Did you blame Champion when your brother died?"

She stood so still, it looked as if she'd stopped breathing. Other sounds filled the silence—the breeze through the leaves, the faraway clopping of hooves from the horsecar stop a block away, the crack of breaking china.

"God in heaven!" She strode to the door, flung it open and hurried inside. He heard two little girls' voices raised—one scolding, the other weeping. He started after her, then halted just inside the door. Between crying children and broken crockery, she'd have every excuse to evade him some more. He loitered on the porch, listening to the murmur of voices from the house. When the voices stopped, he waited for the sound of her footsteps returning. Hearing nothing, he went inside.

He found Mary by the trash bin, dumping jagged pieces of a saucer into it from a dustpan. The little girls were nowhere in sight. "I need an answer," Hanley said, as if the interruption hadn't occurred. "Did you blame Ben Champion for your brother's death?"

Her hand tightened around the dustpan handle. "You won't believe me, whatever I say. If that's enough to make you arrest me, then go right ahead."

THIRTY

Full dark had just fallen when a knock came at Rivka's door. She opened it and saw Moishe, still in his Shabbos suit, hands deep in his trouser pockets. "Herr Zalman," she said in surprise. "You're early."

"Jacob and Hannah are just coming," he said. He made no move to enter, and she realized he was waiting for her to invite him in.

She stepped back and gestured him inside. "Aaron is upstairs. I'll tell him to come down—"

"Fraylin." The hesitant word stopped her halfway to the stairs. She turned back. Moishe had taken a handkerchief from his pocket and was toying with it. "I...I wanted to say...you were very brave yesterday. At the shop. You saved Jacob's life."

Remembering the chaos and terror of those moments, she shook her head. "I didn't think, I just...you must have felt it, too." It still surprised her that Moishe had joined her in hurling rocks and curses at their attackers. She wouldn't have thought he had it in him.

Unexpectedly, he looked her straight in the eyes. The intensity in his face startled her. "You should not have had to do that. I should have helped Jacob first." He took a step toward her. "Someone should protect you. It isn't right that you should—"

"Please," she said. Whatever declaration he was working up to, she didn't want to hear it. "Don't distress yourself. Onkl Jacob is all right. I'm sure there will be no more incidents."

"Fraylin Rivka—"

"I should get Aaron," she said, and fled upstairs.

ოჳ

156

By the time she came down again, the parlor was crowded with nearly a dozen people. Jacob and Hannah Nathan; Lazar Klein, the butcher who served as cantor; Yitzhak Demsky, the baker and head instructor at the boys' school; and the other foremost members of the Market Street community. With no rabbi yet sent to replace Rivka's father, authority fell to Jacob to make important decisions—but the one being made tonight affected them all, and so he had called this meeting. Tonight, he and those here would decide about Aaron and his family.

From just inside the parlor doorway, Rivka looked around at them. She knew every one, had since she was a child back in the old country. Yet now she saw them through a stranger's eyes. What would they do about Aaron? How would they choose? Her own uncertainty frightened her. She remembered the men with bricks and stones, their ugly faces and harsh voices. Then coming home to the shattered front window and the harsh burnt odor where the incendiary device had left its mark. Aaron, panicked enough to shoot at whoever came through the door. Despite what she'd told Moishe, other such incidents were likely to happen as long as Aaron and his family stayed. Yet, surely Jacob and the rest would not turn him away, or Ada and Nat either. Not when they were in danger, not when—

"I knew this was a bad idea." Mrs. Zalman shot a glance at Rivka from her seat at one end of the sofa. "Letting a young girl live in this house on her own. Of course she made an error in judgment, allowing those people to stay here." Her gaze flicked to where the parlor window had been, the gap boarded over with wooden slats. "And we are all saddled with the consequences."

Moishe drew breath, but hesitated a second too long. Tanta Hannah spoke first, more gently than Mrs. Zalman deserved. "Sarah, this is Aaron we're speaking of. The son of our *rebbe, alav ha-shalom.*" *May he rest in peace.*

"And a fine thing he has done in his father's memory," Mrs. Zalman snapped. "Were it up to me—"

"It isn't." Rivka knew she shouldn't make trouble, but the words came out before she could stop them. Defiant, she plunged on. "Everyone here will decide. After Aaron speaks, for himself and his family."

Moishe was blinking at her like an owl. She left the room before he could say anything, or Mrs. Zalman could reply.

Aaron had stayed upstairs with Ada and Nat. They were sitting on the edge of the bed, Aaron and Ada holding hands, Nat huddled next to his mother. "They're ready for you," Rivka said. She gave Ada and the boy a mute look of apology. The attacks here and at the tailor shop were not their fault, yet Mrs. Zalman talked as if they were. How many would agree with her?

To her surprise, all three of them followed her out. "It's their fate being decided along with mine," Aaron said in response to her questioning look. "They have a right to be there. Nat, too. If he were Jewish, he'd be a bar mitzvah in a year. A man."

Looking at the boy's set face, his expression too old for his years, Rivka had to agree. They went downstairs together, Rivka in the lead, Aaron holding tight to Ada's hand.

A murmur went around the parlor at Ada and Nat's appearance. Jacob rose from his chair. The gash from the horseshoe nail showed dark red on his bruised cheek. "Aaron, this is not how we do things—"

"They have a right to hear what will become of them." Aaron ushered his family toward a corner of the room where there was a little space left to stand. He turned to face Jacob and the rest, one arm around Ada, a hand on Nat's shoulder. Rivka took her place beside them.

After a moment, Jacob nodded. "Then let us begin."

Aaron glanced down as if gathering his thoughts. He took a deep breath and straightened his shoulders. "My family and I came here because we have nowhere else to go. We were burned out of our farm in Alton. Attacked because my wife and son are mulatto and I am a Jew. We need safety and a roof over our heads, for at least long enough to decide what to do next." He closed his eyes, and when he opened them and continued, his voice was ragged. "I know we have brought trouble to you. I didn't intend that. I also know this is not what you would have expected of me...a Christian wife and stepson..." He trailed off, then again seemed to gather himself. "But I ask you to shelter us. Because who else will?"

If not me, then who, Rivka thought. She felt a fierce pride in her brother. He would face down the world, if he had to, for what he believed was right.

"So you *have* brought us trouble." Mrs. Zalman again. "Why should we suffer for one who walked away? You were born among us. Raised among us. But you married a *goy*. How do you live now, Aaron? What are you? How much have you thrown away for this woman and her son?"

"Mameh," Moishe said, too softly for her to heed.

"Does that matter, when we are in need?" Aaron replied. "What would my father say if he were here?"

"He would take you in," Rivka said. "He would want you all safe and alive. Trouble or not, danger or not. Nothing else matters next to that." She looked around the room, at the six men and four women who would decide Aaron's fate. "They ran when we threw their own stones back at them. Moishe and I against six times as many, and they ran. Do what my father would have done. Let Aaron and his family stay."

"But at what cost to us?" Yitzhak Demsky spoke gruffly, as if not entirely easy with what he had to say. "Aaron is one thing. Whatever his personal decisions, he belongs here. But this woman and her child—"

"My name is Ada," Ada said, quiet but firm. "My son is Nathaniel."

Demsky's cheeks reddened, but he kept going. His gaze stayed on Jacob as he spoke. Rivka had the sense he felt afraid to look anywhere else. "They should not be here. They do not belong. Can they not go and be with their own kind? There are Negroes in the city. They should go there. If they stay here, they will bring more trouble." He spread his hands. "You all know what happened Friday. Who knows how much worse it could get? I read the papers. Something happens somewhere almost every week because of the Negroes. Riots, murders, attacks... Aaron just told us it happened to him. If we harbor them, it will happen again to us."

Hannah gave Jacob a troubled glance. "Jacob says he was not much hurt..."

"This time," Demsky replied. "What about next time?"

Aaron drew his family closer. "We won't be separated. And if I go live among the Negroes, I will become a target." He swallowed. "Not from them, but from those who burned our home in Alton. One of those men is here. I can't let him find me."

The room erupted then, everyone talking at once. Except for Jacob, who sat still with his head bowed and his hand over his eyes. Rivka watched him, every nerve alert. He knew about Lucas Errol. Aaron had told him everything. Her heart pounded in her chest. Jacob was the *gabbai*, who took care of the shul, and had the greatest authority next to the rabbi. His word carried weight. Whatever their misgivings about Christians and mulattoes in their midst, if he spoke for sheltering Aaron and his family, the others would surely be persuaded. She watched him reach up and rub the gash on his cheek with one finger, back and forth and back again.

"You should have told us," Demsky said. "If this man is hunting for you, then you have put us in even more danger."

"So we should put Aaron and his wife and child in even greater danger? To save ourselves?" Hannah spoke again, leaning forward on the sofa's edge. She stumbled slightly over the words *wife and child*, but that she said them at all gave Rivka a glimmer of relief. If Hannah could say that, when Onkl Jacob had been hurt, then Jacob could not be far behind. She hoped. He hadn't moved in the past minute, still sat motionless with his head bowed.

"How can that be right?" Hannah went on. "To help ourselves at the expense of others. Even if they are not our own."

Demsky scowled. "We don't know anything will happen to them."

"Yet you are sure something more will happen to us if they stay," Rivka said. "Both cannot be true. Which is it, Herr Demsky?"

He turned a fierce glare on her. "You should keep silent. A girl like you—"

"He is my brother," she answered with equal heat. "They are my family, too." She hadn't expected to say that, but she felt the truth of it as soon as the words left her lips. The swift, warm glance Ada sent her way gave her new strength, made her stand a little taller.

Jacob raised his head. "Enough. Yitzhak and Hannah have raised two points. How much danger are we in, and do we have the right to safeguard ourselves at any cost?"

"We may be in less danger than we think," Rivka said. "Aaron has talked to the police. To Detective Hanley." She felt a slight flush in her cheeks as she said Hanley's name. "He knows who this man is and what he looks like, and has asked others to watch out for him. They will help protect us against any who would do us harm."

"Police," Mrs. Zalman muttered. Next to her, Moishe stared at his hands. Rivka couldn't guess what was in his mind, didn't want to try. Many of the others looked thoughtful. They remembered what Hanley had done for them last winter, finding and jailing the man who murdered their rabbi. Rivka began to breathe a little easier.

Jacob looked Aaron in the eye. "You spoke with Detective Hanley?"

"Yes. He agreed to do what he can."

Jacob nodded. He said nothing for several seconds. Then he took a deep breath and spoke. "We are commanded to love the stranger, for we were strangers in the land of Egypt. We are also taught that whoever rescues a single life, has rescued the entire world." He looked up and gestured toward Ada and Nat. "They are strangers here, and their lives are at risk. We cannot turn them away simply because we are afraid. And, as Rivka says, there may be less to fear than we believe." He glanced at Aaron, then back at the others. "We should let them stay until the danger has passed."

The air in the room felt charged, as if a thunderstorm were building. Then Hannah spoke. "I agree with Jacob. Let them stay."

Moishe spoke in favor next, with a nervous glance toward his mother. Of the rest, only Mrs. Zalman and Yitzhak Demsky objected. Rivka reached for Aaron's hand and gripped it hard. He and Ada and Nat were safe for the moment. She thought of Hanley then, and hoped he could keep them that way.

THIRTY-ONE

May 1871

The green hillside smells of spring, of flowers and grass and recent rain. Dorrie stares at the fresh earth near her feet. An unbroken swath, dark as night, is mounded over Joel's body. She wishes she could mourn, but the cold stone in her chest won't let any feeling touch her.

Nearby, the pastor murmurs a final prayer. His words wash over her like the breeze, soft and meaningless. A little silence follows, and then a light touch on her shoulder. "There's coffee and food at the house," the pastor says. "My wife's seen to things. If you'll come…"

"No. Thank you." The words don't feel like hers. Nothing feels like hers—not the grave, not the pastor and his useless Bible words, not the few mourners who've long since departed. Not even the grass and the sun, shining too bright in the blue sky. "I'd rather be alone awhile." She can't face people yet. She doesn't want to stay here, either, or go back to her own little house a quarter mile from the white frame church where Joel's been laid to rest. If she had it in her to move, she'd run away, far enough to escape the memory that hasn't left her alone for the past three days.

The pastor clears his throat. "I'll tell her you'll be along. God bless and keep you in your time of sorrow." The rustle of his black frock coat tells her he's leaving. The silence in his wake is so deep, she could fall into it and never climb out.

Next thing she knows, she's kneeling in the grass, one hand on the sun-warmed slab of wood that marks the grave. Joel's name, a pair of dates, the words *Abide With Me*—these are all that's left of him above ground. She runs her hand across the wood. A splinter pricks her finger, a tiny nagging pain that scratches at her stone heart. She pulls the splinter out. A drop of blood wells up. The breeze carries the distant sound of children laughing. She knows where it comes from, and her stomach gives a sick lurch as memory takes hold.

The hired boy from the tavern down the street came to get her, his thin chest heaving as he burst through the door of Willard's Dry Goods where she helps sell fabric. "Trouble at the Star," he gasped out. "Mr. Joel and some men, and that Yankee. You better come." She followed him to the Sun and Star, to two bodies crumpled in the dusty street. The Yankee from the darky school outside town lay moaning and barely conscious, a discarded thing, a little way off from the townsfolk gathered around the second body. All she could see of that one was a blond head and an outflung arm in gray calico.

The tavern owner, a burly man with a perspiring face like a side of beef, stepped forward to block her path. "It just happened, missus, nobody meant it—we was after teaching that Yankee a lesson, but your man, he just got in the way—"

"Let me through." She pushed past him, choking on her own frantic breath. Gray calico work shirt, the familiar curve of a bent spine. A dark stain against the gray, a larger one in the pale dust beneath the sprawled form. A hunting knife coated in red a foot or so away.

"I never meant to do it." This new voice was thin and reedy like a half-grown boy's. She looked up from Joel's unmoving body and slack face, saw a skinny youngster in his teens, white-faced and sweating. "I went for the Yankee. But Joel was there, just *there* all of a sudden, and I couldn't stop—"

From beyond the small crowd came a breathy moan, halting words in a clipped Northern accent: "Help me…God help me…"

The tavern owner moved away from Joel. Another man followed. Then came the dull thud of a kick striking home. More men moved over and shouts filled the air, rising like heat haze amid a drumbeat of kicks and blows.

Dorrie stayed put, one hand in Joel's hair, the other pressed to the red wet patch on his shirt. She willed that hand to rise and fall with the rhythm of breathing, but there was no motion beneath it. No motion at all.

∞

A week drags by. Dorrie must have eaten and slept, but she can't remember. Everything is hazy, except for the bank man. She remembers him too well.

The paper he brought when he came the other day sits on the dirty kitchen table. She hasn't kept the table scrubbed, doesn't see the point. That paper proves her right. The table, the kitchen, the little house Joel paid to have built, their small garden—none of it is hers. Joel's earnings from the Star were paying for the land, but with those gone, she can't hold onto it.

"We'll give you till the end of the month," the bank man said, slick as bacon grease. "It's the least we can do." He's a Northerner as well, one of the countless number that have come south since the war ended to make fortunes off others' misery. Now he's going to take her home away. It wasn't much, nothing compared to the plantation house where she grew up, but it was hers. Hers and Joel's. And so what if she didn't love Joel? She was grateful to him, cared for him as best she could. All he ever asked of her was kindness, a few comforts, and a willingness to share his bed. She owed him that, and she gave it. Now everything she has is gone again. There's nothing left for her here. Not Joel, not home, not even any kinfolk who might take her in.

She wanders outside to the garden, green with young pea and squash vines and the shoots of carrots and potatoes. She won't be digging those come autumn. What would the slaves from the Whittier plantation think of her now? Or her father, or Tom, or even her mother, gone in childbed so long ago. A harsh breath escapes her, born of a bitter thought. She does have kin left, of a sort. Nigger Billy, who ran away with his slave family when she was scarcely old enough to remember him. Then he turned up as a soldier, serving with white men and taken for one—or so she guesses, from what little she observed on that bleak night in Tennessee when she and Billy crossed paths. Her half-brother, though no one ever acknowledged it. A house slave given the easy jobs, even allowed to learn his letters with Tom in the hopes of spurring Tom to greater effort. When she'd asked her father if the slave gossip was true, he'd ordered her mouth washed with soap. That, as much as anything, told her the answer was yes.

Where is Billy now? He was kind to her, even on the night of the bushwhacker raid. He helped her then, for the sake of who they both once were. She sinks to the dirt at the garden's edge, gripped by a need sudden and powerful as a summer downpour, to see Billy again. He needn't see her. She doesn't even know if she wants him to, can't think that far. But she can't stay here. Why not go where Billy is? Go where there's one person connected to her by blood, even if half of it is darky blood. Where one person knows who she is—who she *was*—and might just give a damn.

Fingers digging into the warm earth, she conjures up the memory of Richmond. She last saw Billy there, with—

A shudder wracks her. Captain Scar. If he's where Billy is, maybe she'd best stay away. Her fear shames her, the shame blazing into anger. Captain Scar won't stop her, whatever she decides to do. He's taken enough from her already, he and every other Yankee who ever did her harm. She imagines laying open his neck with a blade, the way he did to her. Humiliating him, making *him* helpless and afraid—

With effort, she schools her breath. Richmond. Billy in uniform. The other soldiers with him, laughing and talking. One clapping Billy on the shoulder, saying, "Home to Chicago." Is that where he's gone to? The first city of the West, some folks call it. A place people go to start over. And there are Southerners there. She's read the papers, she knows plenty of people in Chicago sympathized with the South and wanted to sue for peace. She can go there, find work, find a place to be. Maybe find a man to protect and care for her.

Is Billy living as a white man now? The thought gives her a queer turn. There's a wrongness to it, a sense of something warped in the fabric of what should be. Still, it's none of her business. She has enough to do, just surviving.

She stands, brushes her skirt clean, walks back into the house. The pay she's owed from the dry goods store should cover train fare and let her live while she looks for work, provided it doesn't take her too long. Another thought of Captain Scar chills her, but she puts it from her mind. In a city so big, she won't run across him. God can't be so cruel, or so capricious, as to place her in that man's path again.

THIRTY-TWO

April 27–28, 1872

Hanley set the murder case aside long enough to enjoy his Saturday evening at home with Mam and Kate. Their landlady, Ida Kirschner, celebrated the end of her Jewish Sabbath with singing around the piano, inviting as many of her boarders as cared to join in. Hanley had recently taken up his fiddle again, after the months following the Fire, when he'd been unable to face playing it. He found his musical talents in demand, and thoroughly enjoyed running through his repertoire of dance tunes, drinking songs, and the ballads his mother loved that left not a dry eye in Ida's parlor.

Father Gerald's homily the next morning drew on the Old Testament verse about loving the stranger, "for you were strangers in the land of Egypt." The text, long familiar to Hanley, struck him now in a new light. He'd never considered its source in the Hebrew Scriptures, and he found himself thinking of Rivka hearing the same words in her little pine-board temple. Did they hold special meaning for her now, with her brother's mulatto wife and stepchild under her roof? Strangers, indeed. He still had trouble accepting the notion of a white man married to a Negress. The sneaking thought came that his discomfort was unworthy, not so far removed from the hatred of the night riders who had driven the Kelmanskys from their Alton farmstead. He shook it off, turning his focus on the assault itself. Something more than hatred was behind that. He felt suddenly impatient for the evening, when Aaron Kelmansky would come by the station and finally tell him the whole truth.

ଔ

Tremont House, open for business on Michigan Avenue in a building that miraculously survived the Fire, was one of the few hotels aspiring to any sort of elegance as the city continued its revival. Hanley's steps echoed as he crossed the floor, a little dazzled in spite of himself by the gilded trim and crystal in the lobby. How many weeks' wages would it cost to stay in a place like this for even one night? And the Tremont was nothing on the short-lived Palmer House that opened last September and burned two weeks later, or so he'd heard. The sheer waste of it made him shake his head as he approached the lobby desk. The clerk presiding behind it showed Hanley his best officious manner but, after seeing Hanley's badge, reluctantly confirmed that Mr. Lucas Errol was a current guest of the establishment, had been since Tuesday afternoon. A little more prodding earned Hanley the room number—"Mr. Errol's usual when he has important business in the city"—along with the observation that Errol might be in the hotel dining room finishing his midday meal.

"Much obliged," Hanley said, and followed the scents of grilling steak, lamb, and roast chicken in search of his quarry.

He halted in the dining room doorway and collected his thoughts as he looked for Errol amid a sea of well-fed men in dark suits, seated at tables swathed in gleaming white. The low-pitched hum of their conversations blended with the muted clink of cutlery against china. Sunlight poured in through the front window, giving a warm glow to the dark-paneled walls and striking glints off silver and glasses as the customers ate and drank. Hanley wished he had a warrant, but he couldn't wait for one. Berwick could be sprung by Monday and, after that, the stolen papers might well end up in a rubbish heap. He would just have to bluff and hope it netted him something.

He spotted his man at a small table against the far wall. With a nod toward an approaching waiter—"I've found my party, thanks,"—Hanley ambled over.

Errol looked up as Hanley pulled out a chair. Beneath a veneer of politeness, he was clearly annoyed at the interruption. "Excuse me, but I don't think I've had the pleasure...?"

"Detective Frank Hanley. Chicago Police." A quick check of Hanley's pocket confirmed he had enough change for a cup of coffee, even overpriced as it surely was here. He seated himself, turned upright the empty cup at his place, and poured from the ornate silver coffeepot in the center of the table. "Not much left," he said affably as he set the pot back down. "You might want to order a refill. Lucas Errol, isn't it? I've been wanting to talk to you."

The man's cool gaze shifted from Hanley to the coffeepot, betraying nothing. His pale blue eyes and light hair gave him a washed-out look, despite the darker beard. His light brown suit coat, of fine-woven and expensive wool, sported fashionably narrow lapels, and his mustache gleamed with oil. "About?"

"Let's start with why you came to Chicago."

Errol sliced into a lamb chop. The bone from another, eaten down to gristle, lay on one side of his plate. "Why is that any business of yours?"

"I'm investigating a murder." Hanley leaned forward, elbows on the pristine tablecloth. "Of the man who was suing you under the False Claims Act. You sold exploding guns to the Union army. Ben Champion was going to jail you for it. Until he ended up dead last Tuesday night."

Errol ate a piece of lamb, then speared a chunk of potato. His movements were delicate, fussy, as if he never labored at anything more difficult than handling a knife and fork. "Champion *was* suing me. I won't deny that. A tragedy, how he died. But I had nothing to do with it." He gave a chilly smile. "I had no reason to want him dead. He'd have lost the case."

"That's not what I hear."

Errol ate the piece of potato and washed it down with ice water. "Then you hear wrong. Good afternoon, Detective."

Hanley sipped his coffee. It was mellow and rich, much better than the harsh brew at the police station. "You were in the city Tuesday night. Did you go to North May Street?"

Errol's eyes narrowed. "I was here. Dining with my lawyer."

169

"Mr. Clement Berwick, yes. We've met." Hanley sipped again, savoring the taste. "He says he left you here at eight o'clock. What about afterward?"

Errol gave a short laugh. "It's a long journey from Alton. All I wanted after Berwick left was a decent night's sleep."

"Can anyone confirm you were here all night?"

"Ask the night clerk if he saw me leave. He didn't. He'll tell you so."

"I'll do that." Hanley watched him cut the last sliver of meat from his chop, working at it as if the task required all his concentration. "So... what's in the Farnham and Chandler case papers you and Clement stole?"

Errol sawed at his chop. "I don't know what you're talking about."

"Clement confessed. As did the thief you paid. Quite the sum, I'm told."

The meat tore free. Errol stabbed it with his fork. "Whatever Berwick did, under the impression he was helping me, is no fault of mine. I can't be held to account for him."

"Then how about for your own actions? Assault and attempted murder, for example."

Errol laughed. "Of Champion? That's not *attempted* murder. Whoever did that, succeeded. And it wasn't me, or anyone to do with me."

"I'm talking about Alton. Where Ben Champion went this past weekend in connection with his lawsuit against you. Where you led a band of night riders in an assault on a farmstead last Monday night. By midday Tuesday you were here...and Tuesday night, Ben Champion was dead. You're telling me that's all happenstance? I don't think so."

"I'm not responsible for what you think." Errol glanced around and raised a hand. "Waiter! My bill."

"You were seen," Hanley said. "Monday in Alton, Tuesday on North May Street." Pure bluff, that last, but he had to shake something loose from the man. "The night clerk here won't save you. I'm sure there's more than one way out of the building."

Errol's face reddened. "I went to bed. I slept until Wednesday morning. As for Alton, if you're so certain I committed a crime there, telegraph the Alton police and get them to arrest me. But you'd best have solid proof."

"What's in those stolen papers, Lucas? What did Ben Champion find in Alton, that you killed him for?"

"Waiter!" Errol's sharp call brought a young man in a white coat scurrying over. A few terse words, and the bill changed hands. Errol eyed it as if looking for an error, then dug a wallet out of his suit coat. "You think I don't know how things work in this town? I may not be from here, but I know people who are. And they know people who know how to deal with people like you. I had nothing to do with any murder, or theft, and if you harass me about it, I will take steps." He tossed a greenback on the table and stood, sucking in his belly paunch as if to look taller. "Do I make myself clear?"

Hanley stood as well. "Clement and his friends can't help you, Lucas. I'll get a warrant for those stolen papers, and I *will* find out where you were Tuesday night. Save us all some trouble if you tell me right now."

Anger crossed the man's face, along with a hint of fear. "I don't have to tell you anything. And if you come around again, you'd best have your goddamned warrant in hand."

ೞ

The waiter came to collect Errol's payment, frowned as if dissatisfied, and moved off. Hanley lingered, finishing his coffee. Lucas Errol had been somewhere Tuesday night that he didn't want to admit to. Champion's house? Who might have seen him, and how had he gotten there? Hanley toyed with the cup handle. From Tremont House to North May was a long trip on foot. Hackney cab, maybe, or horsecar. There'd be a minor risk of a driver remembering Errol, but with the number of passengers throughout the day and evening, the man might easily have been lost in the shuffle. As to the stolen papers, Judge Carruthers had best get over his spring chill soon. Once Captain Hickey learned of Berwick's arrest, he wouldn't hesitate to—how had Errol put it?—"take steps." The man had done it before, damned near permanently.

He frowned and drained his cup. Nothing left in the pot when he shook it. Could Champion's missing war memoir figure into the Farnham case? The Eighty-Second had gotten the exploding guns. Maybe Champion had written about them. If so, Errol might have stolen the missing manuscript, as well as the legal papers. By now, Hanley was nearly certain someone had.

"'New development,'" he muttered. Nothing in Champion's memoir would be new to Champion himself—though it was Schuyler who'd used that phrase in his telegram. Hanley still didn't know what that was about. He pushed back his chair just as a voice nearby said, "Sir?"

He turned and saw the waiter, hovering with a slip of paper in hand. "Your bill," the young man said. "For the coffee."

Of course Errol had contrived not to pay for the portion of his order that Hanley'd drunk. The charge made Hanley's eyes widen, but he had enough to cover it. He handed over the necessary coins, plus a couple extra to make up for what he guessed was Errol's stingy tip. "Were you here last Tuesday evening?"

The waiter nodded, with an appreciative look at the money. "Normally I work the luncheon shift, but we were shorthanded, so they asked me to stay through supper. Why?"

"The fellow I was with just now—was he here then, do you recall?"

"Do I." The waiter pocketed Hanley's bill and payment. "He had a disagreement with his dining companion. Mr. Clement Berwick comes here with clients fairly often. A lot of them do, lawyers and bankers and such. Their dispute seemed to be about a legal matter." Briefly, he looked embarrassed. "Sometimes one can't help overhearing..."

"I imagine. Do you remember anything specific?" When he looked hesitant, Hanley said, "It could have a bearing on a murder case."

Eagerness lit the waiter's eyes, then vanished in regret. "I don't recall much. Just 'We have to do something,' and needing to find something. Or someone. I'm not sure which, now I think about it."

Some*thing*, Hanley thought, would be whatever Errol and Berwick expected to find in the Farnham case papers. Some*one* might be Aaron Kelmansky. Apprehension made his shoulders knot. Maybe the rock-throwing mob and the incendiary device through Rivka's window on Friday afternoon hadn't happened by chance. Lucas Errol might not know who to hire for mayhem, but Berwick would.

He thanked the waiter and walked away, then turned back. A minor thing, probably, that he'd just now recalled from Champion's office calendar, but Hanley liked to be thorough. "Did you serve luncheon on Friday, a week ago? April nineteenth, I think it would've been."

"I did, yes."

"Captain Ben Champion ate here that day, I'm told. Do you recall him?"

The waiter looked somber. "Yes. I was sorry to read of his death. He comes…came here fairly often. Always tipped well. He did that day. And paid for the other fellow's meal, even though the man barely touched it before storming out."

Not Lucas Errol, probably. As far as Hanley knew, the man wasn't in Chicago then. Not Berwick either, or the waiter would've said. "Did you know this other fellow?"

The waiter shook his head.

"What did he look like?"

"My height, about, with dark wavy hair. I wondered, when he first came in, if he was a foreigner—he had a bit of a Spanish look. That hint of olive in the skin, you know. Of course, when he talked I could tell he was as American as anybody."

"I don't suppose you heard his name?"

"Not his full name, no. But I did hear the captain call him 'Will.'"

 C3

As he walked out of the hotel, still chewing over what the waiter had told him, it took Hanley a minute to recognize something was out of place. A large, enclosed vehicle loomed near the front entrance, drawn by a patient horse that stood with its head down. No windows Hanley could see, and the words *Police Patrol* were painted along the side. What was a paddy wagon doing in front of the Tremont?

He had his answer when a burly man in blue climbed off the seat next to the driver and strode over to him. "Francis James Hanley," Captain Hickey said, with a hard-eyed wolf's grin as he grabbed Hanley by the arm. His fingers dug into Hanley's elbow. "You're under arrest, for assault and battery against one Clement Berwick."

THIRTY-THREE

S unday dinner was Will's favorite—roast beef with new potatoes and baby onions—but he couldn't eat more than a few bites. "Are you not well?" Aunt Abigail asked him, her face full of concern. Uncle Josiah, at the other end of the dinner table, carefully sliced a potato into bite-sized pieces.

Will shook his head and managed a smile. "Overtired, that's all. Had a lot of work lately."

Her concern deepened. "Cholera? We've seen some cases at the clinic." Outbreaks often started in late spring, Will knew, with everything thawed out from the winter and the temperatures sometimes reaching near-summer heights.

"No. Very little illness, in fact. Violence and misadventure." He sipped his wine and tried not to gag on it. "I'll be fine with a little rest."

She nodded, speared an onion and ate it. Will glanced at Josiah. "Any word yet on who broke into Captain Champion's office?"

"No." Josiah paused. "It's been harder than I thought to find all of Ben's important papers. The theft certainly didn't help."

A chill bloomed in the pit of Will's stomach. He attacked the slice of beef on his plate, then stopped. The sight of the knife blade cutting through the pink center reminded him of the stab wound in Ben Champion's torso.

The knife clattered against the china. To his adoptive parents' startled faces, he said, "I'm sorry. I'm not feeling well after all," and fled the dining room.

Upstairs, in his room, he halted by the bed. His head pounded with tension. *I sent the damned reply to Ben's office. Where is it?*

Two dozen words, plus his name, that would damn him if Hanley found it. Especially after Will lied to him about having no contact with Ben Champion since muster out in '65. He could recite the note from memory. *Ben—You know my mind about the book. I ask you again not to risk this. I will come Friday in hopes of finally persuading you. Will.*

He found himself staring at the pattern on his quilt. Crossroads—four dark green squares joined at the corners, bracketing a cream-colored diamond. He didn't care to dwell on where and when he'd learned the meaning of that particular pattern. That time was gone. That Will was gone. *Forever now, please God.*

He paced the room, taking in its details to avoid thinking of less comfortable things. Bedstead, dresser, desk and chair, shirt rack, all dark mahogany. Bookshelves stuffed with medical texts, volumes of poetry, and a few favorite novels. Papers on the desk, notes for a book he'd thought of writing on the uses of science in criminal detection. Would he ever dare publish it? Ever dare risk what small measure of fame such a book might bring his way?

People will know, he'd told Ben. *Despite all your promises, sooner or later they'll figure it out. And then what happens? To me, to Abigail and Josiah—*

A soft knock at his door broke his train of thought. "Will?"

Josiah. "Come in," Will said.

Josiah entered and shut the door behind him. "Your mother's worried."

"My mother is in Canada." He saw Josiah flinch at the words, but an instinctive apology died unuttered. What use was there in apologizing for the truth?

Josiah drifted toward the desk, where he toyed with a few papers. "Calm yourself and go talk to Abigail," he said after a lengthy pause. "Ask her about the clinic. Bring up the news, or the weather. Just let her know you're all right."

"I'm not."

The silence between them was longer this time. Josiah leafed through Will's notes, while Will stood in the middle of the floor with his arms crossed over his chest. *Like a shield,* he thought. *A barrier against harm.*

"I told you I'd make this right," Josiah said finally. He turned toward Will. "And I will keep my word. Just as I kept it to your mother twenty-two years ago."

The mention of his mother made Will's throat ache. He hadn't heard from her since she'd fled the States in 1850. They'd talked it over, agreed it wasn't safe to write. Was she well, happy? He managed to get out one word, the word that mattered most. "How?"

"I don't know yet." Josiah reached out toward him. "You trusted me with your life once. Can't you trust me again?"

Will stared at Josiah's hand. Soft, smooth skin, pale as milk except for the faint blue of an old man's veins beneath. Age had deepened the lines on it, but the hand was still rock steady. Still vital, still strong.

He closed his own over it as if it were a lifeline.

;

"What do you think he'll do if you don't show?" Rivka stood by the desk in their father's study where Aaron had parked himself. "Shrug and forget about it? You lied to him. Or you will have, if you don't go to the police station tonight. You think nothing will come of that?"

He turned away from her, jaw set, and stalked toward the door. "Whatever does, it's better than dying."

Dying? "Aaron..." She grabbed his arm as he passed her, but he shook her off and kept going. She hurried after him, only to have the back door slammed in her face. Breathing hard, she wrenched it open—then stood in the gap, watching her brother stride across the yard and vanish through the door of the shul. Was there any point in pursuing him there? He would only keep refusing to talk, even scold her for bringing contention into the house of Hashem. She clenched her fists and pressed them to her forehead. A pulse beat at her temple, partly anger, mostly fear. Between danger from Lucas Errol, danger from whoever sent the mob and threw the incendiary device, and now danger from Detective Hanley—who had promised to protect Aaron, but might be obliged to jail him instead—she didn't know anymore where to turn.

Fighting an impulse to cry, she stepped back inside and shut the door. She'd set a soup pot of chicken bones to boil an hour earlier for that evening's supper. An onion, three carrots, and a knife lay on the chopping board by the stove. She made no move toward them. Except for the soft hiss of the simmering stock, the house was silent. After a moment, she heard the murmur of voices. Nat and Ada, upstairs, taking turns reading aloud. Of course—it was Sunday, the Christian holy day. Unable to venture out to a church, Ada and her son were reading their scriptures together.

Rivka brushed suddenly clammy hands against her skirt, then headed upstairs herself. At the top of the staircase, she listened a moment, then crept across the landing into her parents' room.

No one was there. She searched it quickly and thoroughly, keeping an ear out for footsteps or the cessation of voices from down the hall. She found what she was seeking in the pocket of Aaron's oldest-looking trousers—a small cloth pouch, which held greenbacks and some coins. Enough for a train ticket, maybe for three, to someplace within a hundred miles or so of Chicago. Likely not back to Alton—nothing was left for Aaron and his family there except worse danger. She refolded the trousers and went to her own room, where she tucked the money pouch into the toe of a winter boot at the back of her wardrobe.

She was partway downstairs again when a shadow passed the curtained front window. She froze in sudden panic. A gentle tap came at the front door, followed by a muffled voice speaking Yiddish. "Fraylin? Are you there? Is anyone home?"

Moishe. A different kind of anxiety gripped her, and for a moment she thought of staying where she was. But Moishe deserved better from her, especially after standing up to his mother on Saturday night. She should thank him, at least. Better yet, Aaron should. She thought of fetching Aaron from the shul, then decided against it. In his present mood, he was nothing to inflict on anyone.

Moishe's hesitant smile when she answered the door made her think of a puppy unsure of its welcome. He held a cotton shirt, sturdy and well made. "For the boy," he said. "Herr Nathan gave me the cloth. No charge."

She took the shirt and thanked him, touched by his kindness. He must have worked all morning on it, starting as soon as he reached the tailor shop. "It was no trouble," he said, then cleared his throat. "How… how are you, Fraylin? I mean…how are all of you?"

"We are well, thank you." A small, awkward silence fell. Moishe glanced away, but didn't move from the doorstep. He seemed to be waiting for something.

She heard herself talking to fill the quiet. "I should thank you also for Aaron and his family. It can't have been easy, going against your mother."

The look he gave her held a touch of defiance. "I do not always agree with Mameh. Nor do I need her consent for what I choose to do." His expression softened, in a way that made her nervous. "It is good you should know that."

She couldn't let him say any more. "Thank you again for the shirt," she managed to stammer, and bade him farewell as she closed the door.

THIRTY-FOUR

Shoved into the paddy wagon by Hickey and the driver, Hanley stumbled through a puddle of sick where some poor bastard had lost his breakfast. The dim enclosure reeked of stale sweat and worse. He caught himself against a wooden bench, scraping his palms on its rough surface. From outside, he heard the driver climb onto the box and chirrup to the horse. The paddy wagon lurched. The motion threw Hanley sideways and he sat down hard on the bench. He steadied himself, then banged on the wall by the box. "Berwick assaulted *me*! I can prove it!"

No response. Hanley banged some more. "You've no right to do this! Let me out, you son of a bitch!"

He heard a guffaw, then indistinct words. The wagon was moving in stops and starts. There must be heavy traffic. Hanley slumped on the bench, nursing his bruised knuckles. No use beating on the wall and shouting, except to keep Mike Hickey entertained. He took shallow breaths, in and out, trying not to gag on the foul air. The coffee he'd drunk in the hotel dining room threatened to jump back up his throat. Damn Hickey. He must have a spy at Lake Street Station, to have gotten wind this fast of Berwick's Friday night in the lockup.

He eyed his shoes and felt another queasy jolt, only partly from the half-digested egg spattered across the dark leather. He fished out a handkerchief—thank God they'd saved emptying his trouser pockets for when the wagon reached the Armory jail—and wiped off the muck, then tossed the handkerchief down. He knew what was waiting for him at the Armory. Booking as a criminal, confiscation of his badge, plenty of harassment, and a beating while he waited in a cell for a hearing on the trumped-up assault charges. Get him in front of one of Hickey's pet judges and he wouldn't stand a chance.

The wagon picked up speed. He heard horsecar bells, creaking wheels, and clopping hooves from delivery wagons, carts, and drays. The sounds washed over him as he racked his brain for what to do. No good trying to get out—the wagon walls were solid, the one small window barred, the rear doors locked from the outside. He'd have to depend on Moore, and Schmidt, if it came to court proceedings. Which wouldn't happen until Monday at the earliest, depending on how long it suited *Captain* Hickey to keep him in jail.

Despite the stifling air in the wagon, a chill seeped through him. How much did the bastard know? That he'd been waiting outside Tremont House to arrest Hanley said he knew something. The story Dahlia Ford had told, about the Order of American Knights back in '64, came too clearly to mind. If Mike Hickey had any inkling she'd blabbed about that...

Knifed in lockup. Captain Hickey had turned a blind eye to that once before, during the Kelmansky murder investigation last winter. Why not see to it himself, if enough was at stake? Hanley thought of Rivka then, and his heart sank further. He'd promised to help her brother, but so far he'd failed. What would happen to Aaron—to her—if he was gone?

A loud shout came from outside. The paddy wagon's sudden halt threw him to the floor. Horses neighed, a high thin sound like a woman's scream. The wagon lurched forward, and Hanley heard the driver curse. He hauled himself up and pressed his face to the barred window. A lumber cart stood hard by, the big gray that drew it stomping between the shafts while the cart-driver swore and shook his fist at something ahead that Hanley couldn't see.

The paddy wagon lurched again. He heard the wet smack of a whip against horseflesh, then another screaming whinny and something heavy falling and breaking. Something wooden, a large crate or barrel. The wagon tilted upward as the horse that drew it reared in terror. Hanley fell hard against the doors. The impact knocked the wind from him. An iron band squeezed his midriff and he fought for breath while the wagon swayed and plunged. Finally, the locked muscles under his ribcage loosened, and he gulped air as a drunkard gulps whiskey.

From close by came a thud, like a rock hitting the side of the wagon. He turned his head toward the sound and gaped. Not a rock. A rectangle of daylight where one rear door had swung open.

He dove through the gap, hit the street hard, staggered to his feet and ran.

ᘓ

The stitch knotting his side made every breath an ordeal by the time he reached Moore's house in the West Division. Mike Hickey wouldn't hesitate to go after him at home, but he figured sending bully boys to trouble the chief of detectives was more risk than the man was prepared to take. He knocked and was admitted by Moore's housekeeper, Mrs. McGrath, who blanched at his ripe odor but otherwise took his disheveled appearance in stride. "He's in his study, Frank," she said. "Go wash up first. I'll bring coffee. You look like you could use it."

He thanked her and limped down the hall to the water closet, where he splashed his face and neck and wetted down his shirt. He raised the window a couple of inches and draped his coat over the sill to air it, then headed toward the study. Nasty bruising at shoulder, hip, and knee from his rough landing in the street was making itself felt, more so now than it had during his frantic run for sanctuary. At least the stitch was easing up. It felt more like a two-inch push knife now than a Bowie sunk between his ribs.

"Good God, Frank!" Moore looked up from his Sunday paper as Hanley entered the room. "What happened to you?"

"Mike Hickey. And a lucky traffic accident." He told Moore all about it—Dahlia Ford's tale, what happened at the Tremont and after—as he sank into the nearest sofa corner and tried to get comfortable. A losing battle. "I don't know if he's just helping Berwick out by getting me away from the man's client, or if there's more to it. After last winter's little stay in the Armory, I didn't want to risk my life along with my badge."

Moore wore the look of a man solving a puzzle. "Dahlia Ford named both of them—Mike Hickey and Berwick—as American Knights? And they talked of buying guns in '64?"

Hanley nodded. A soft knock at the study door announced Mrs. McGrath with the coffee. Hanley noted with gratitude that she'd included a plate of scones—he was unexpectedly ravenous, and helped himself to one with thanks as she withdrew. "You were on the force then. You know anything about it?"

"Better than that. I was there."

ଓ

The early morning breeze carried the smell of horses to Moore's nose as he led his fellow patrolmen across the trampled grass. "Quiet as you can, boys," their captain had said, his voice hushed in the chill November air. "We don't want a single Copperhead slipping away. Especially Walsh. He's the snake's head. Chop that off, and the traitors are done for."

Ahead of them, Charles Walsh's weathered barn was still and silent. No sign of life anywhere near it, nor the usual foot traffic on this stretch of State Street. Moore felt the familiar burn in his throat, part excitement and part unease. Was the tip good, that Walsh and his fellow conspirators were gathering here, so near the heart of the city? What if they were gone—no men, no rifles, just patient horses and cows chewing their hay? The Copperheads had tried this before, back in July, or so rumor had it. The conspiracy to take over Chicago had melted away then—called off for God knew what reason before any arrests could be made, though the rabidly pro-South Chicago Times claimed the plot wasn't real to begin with. A wild-eyed Republican fantasy, the paper termed it, an excuse to smear good men who only wanted an honorable end to "Mr. Lincoln's misguided war."

Not this time, *Moore told himself*. This time, we'll have them.

Five feet from the barn doors, the murmur of voices reached his ears. He halted and motioned to his men to surround the building. The nearest patrolman gave him a fierce grin, hefting a massive fireman's axe as he moved into position. Moore eyed the squad, listening to what words he could make out from within. Rifles...every prisoner...Camp Douglas. *One hand raised, he counted silently to three. Then he chopped his hand downward.*

The men with the fire axes charged forward and struck at the doors with bruising force. The wood splintered and gave way. Confusion reigned for the next minute—cries of alarm, startled faces, running men in homespun shirts and trousers, blue uniforms shouting in pursuit. A heavyset patrol officer tackled one man, while another pointed his pistol at a white-faced conspirator and ordered him to stand still. A blur of motion caught Moore's eye a scant second before someone cannoned into him. He hit the floor with a whuff, then struggled partway up in time to see a lanky figure ducking into the barnyard. Pale cotton shirt, dark trousers, no cap on his red hair. Not a cop. Moore lurched to his feet and dashed after him.

The fellow had a head start, but not enough of one. Moore threw himself forward, landing hard against the fleeing man's back and knocking both of them to the ground. The Copperhead swore and scrabbled for purchase in the grassy packed dirt. As Moore grabbed for his shoulder, he rolled over and rammed a knee into Moore's gut. Moore gasped and loosened his grip. The Copperhead threw him off with a vicious kick toward his face, then staggered upright. Moore swiped at his ankles, but missed. By the time he got to his feet, the fellow was across State Street and vanishing around the nearest building.

He cursed then, the words tasting bitter as the blood on his tongue. He spat in the dirt, wiped his lips, and turned back toward the barn. They weren't finished yet—there were rifles to find and criminals to book. He'd track down that red-haired bastard later, if the man was fool enough to show himself anywhere Moore might run across him. Face long and bony as a horse's, flowing red sideburns framing a hawk's nose and muddy brown eyes. No, he'd not forget him any time soon.

೫

"That's where I've seen Berwick before. On that raid." Moore added a spoonful of white sugar to his coffee. "He and another fellow got away. I didn't know his name then…but I remember him." He raised his cup, with a wry smile. "You don't forget a bust like that one, especially when people years later are still calling it 'the raid that saved Chicago.'"

Hanley sipped his own coffee, invigorated by more than the hot brew. "Where did the rifles come from? Dahlia said the conspirators talked about money. Did Berwick, or someone else from the American Knights, buy them—and from where?"

Moore shrugged. "We never found out. God knows there were enough gun factories to choose from. There was talk at the time that they'd come from downstate, southern Illinois being full of Reb sympathizers, but no one had any proof."

Hanley set his cup down. "What about Alton? Farnham and Chandler. Ben Champion's lawsuit. What if he found out about more than exploding guns? His friend Schuyler, who was helping him—he found something in Alton, urgent enough to telegraph Champion about, not a week before the murder. Urgent enough for Champion to leave town with him that weekend. Champion got back to Chicago on Monday, and a day later he's dead."

"You talk to Schuyler yet?"

"Haven't found him. He's an Alton man, so it's likely he still lives there."

Moore poured himself more coffee. "Sounds like this is a perfect time for an out-of-town trip."

CȈ

There was one more thing Hanley had to do before leaving the city. A quick detour home to change clothes and throw a few things into a carpetbag, then a journey by horsecar, and a few minutes' brisk walk brought him to Market Street, tranquil and empty in the waning light of early evening. The front parlor window at Rivka's house was boarded up, and he saw no evidence of fresh attacks. Relieved at that, he knocked on the door and waited.

No one came. He knocked again. "Mr. Kelmansky? Detective Hanley. There's been a change of plan. We need to talk."

After several seconds, he heard footsteps. Light and quick, a woman's tread. The door opened and he saw Rivka, white faced. Beyond her he caught a glimpse of Ada huddled in a corner of the sofa.

Unease made his nerves tingle. "What's happened? Where's Aaron?"

Rivka stepped back from the doorway. "He's gone," she said. "Please... you have to help us find him."

THIRTY-FIVE

ow long has he been gone?" The urgency in Hanley's tone did nothing to ease Rivka's fear.

"I don't know." Seated next to Ada on the sofa, she held Ada's slim, cold hand in both of hers. Nat, mercifully, had gone upstairs to study and would hear none of this. "He went to the shul not long after dinner. When he didn't come home, I went to see if he'd stayed for the minyan—" She halted, caught in the memory of the men's shocked faces when she walked in on them at prayer. And then, when she explained, a different kind of shock as they all realized no one had seen Aaron since mid-afternoon. "Jacob and Hannah started going door to door, looking for him. But then—"

"What did he have with him? Money, clothes, food?"

"Clothes off the line." Ada spoke in a rough whisper. "A shirt and trousers. I washed them this morning." She pressed her lips together, and her grip on Rivka's fingers tightened. "But no food. And no money." She raised her other hand to show Hanley what was in it—the small bag Rivka had retrieved from her winter boot. "All we have is in here. Not a penny missing."

Hanley frowned at the bag. "Why didn't he take it?"

Rivka swallowed to moisten her dry mouth. "I took it first. I hid it."

He stared at her. "You knew he meant to run," he said after a long moment. "Or you figured. And you didn't think you should tell me?"

Sudden anger flared. "I should tell you *what?* That my brother lied when he said he would come to you? What happens when people lie to the police, Detective Hanley—and the police know it?"

"After last winter, I'd think you could trust me," he shot back. "All he had to do was quit stonewalling—"

"Stop." Ada's sharp voice cut through the air. "Aaron is gone and we have to find him. That man Lucas Errol will kill him else."

In the small silence that followed, Hanley looked around for a chair, pulled one near Ada and sat. "Tell me why."

She fumbled in her skirt pocket and came out with a piece of paper. Without a word, she held it out to Hanley.

He took it. Plain notepaper, folded in half and wrinkled. He unfolded it and read the few lines written there in a slanting scrawl: *You have what I want. Come to Twelfth and Clark by the rail line or your family will pay. Sunday, four o'clock.*

"He didn't run off," Ada said.

It was well past four by now. Hanley looked up. "When did you get this? From whom?"

"I don't know. Not who, not when." Ada swallowed. "Sometime after we first got here. Could've been Friday, when they broke the front window. I found it just before you came. I was putting clean sheets on the bed. Aaron hid it in his pillowcase."

Twelfth and Clark. He knew the place, vaguely. A scrap of waste ground between the river and various railroad lines, right before they swung off South Clark on their final approach to the depot. A switching tower was there, maybe a storage shed or two, all suitable as spots for someone to lay in wait. "You're sure he went there?"

"I'm not sure of anything. Except that we need help."

Rivka slipped an arm around Ada's shoulders. Ada relaxed against her, like a tired child. Hanley ran a hand through his hair and she noticed a scrape at the base of his palm, saw for the first time that he held himself as if something hurt somewhere.

"What does the note mean?" he said. "'You have what I want'?"

"Those rifles," Ada said. "It has to be about those damned rifles."

Hanley nodded. "The bad guns from Farnham and Chandler. I already—"

"Not those." She straightened and looked him in the eye. "The ones that were stolen and brought to Chicago in November of '64."

ℭ

Jacob, Moishe, and some of the other men formed search parties to check with other observant Jewish communities—one on South Clark Street, the other west of the river. "Just in case he went there, rather than where he was meant to," Hanley told them. "I'll go to Lake Street Station, organize a squad. We'll let you know what we find at Twelfth and Clark."

Rivka stepped up beside him. "I'm coming with you." She caught a glimpse of Moishe frowning at them, but ignored it.

Hanley scowled at her. "Absolutely not. It's a godforsaken part of town, no place for a woman. We don't even know if Aaron went there. He could be holed up somewhere else, out wandering the streets, or... it's too dangerous."

"He's my brother." She moved past him, toward Lake Street. "Shall we go?"

"Riv—Miss Kelmansky, you can't just—"

She paid him no heed, simply started walking. He hurried to catch up with her. "You should go home, stay with Ada," he said.

"And do what?" She tightened her kerchief against the rising wind. "Pace around the parlor like a caged lion in a menagerie? Make tea neither of us will drink? Pretend everything is all right, now that we've handed it off to the men?" She picked up her pace, driven by fear and a nagging pang of guilt. "I shouldn't have confronted him. I just..." No words were adequate to say how helpless she'd felt, unable to break through Aaron's stubborn insistence on keeping the whole truth concealed. So she kept walking in silence, matching Hanley's long-legged stride.

He was silent for the rest of the block. As they reached the intersection, he spoke. "You confronted him..."

She eyed the near-empty street. A lone horse-drawn omnibus pulled away from the corner three blocks down. "About coming to see you tonight," she said softly. "He wasn't going to. I wanted him to keep his word."

"He said nothing to you about any of this? What Ada told us...no hints at all?"

She shook her head. "He talked to Onkl Jacob, the day they came. I know he spoke of Errol then, because Jacob knew about him. But how much he said of what they found out in Alton..."

The wind gusted off the river as they neared Lake Street. Rivka shivered, less from the stiff breeze than from rising fear. She tried not to think of the worst possibility, to focus only on the small comfort that at least she and Hanley, and the search parties, were taking action. They weren't helpless, sitting and waiting for terrible news. She thought of Ada, and Nat, and her throat caught. If anything happened to Aaron, what would become of them?

They reached the station, and Hanley gestured for her to precede him up the stairs. Each step felt harder to take than the last. He came up beside her and reached for the doors. The glow of the gaslights on either side threw his face into sharp relief—set jaw, grim mouth, eyes worried but determined. Whatever they found out in the next few minutes, Hanley would see it through.

"Do you think—" she said.

"Let's not worry about that yet."

Rivka nodded and followed him inside.

ᘓ

They found nothing at the place by the railroad tracks, nor any clear sign Aaron had been there. Six patrolmen with lanterns, plus Hanley and Rivka, combed the street corner, the ramshackle building Hanley said was a switching tower, and the nearby ground that sloped gently toward the river. The tower was empty, as if abandoned. The ground held blurred footprints that might have been anyone's—no trace of a scuffle, nothing that might be blood. She'd flinched when Hanley mentioned that to the men. The darkness, the emptiness, the whisper of the river, and the distant murmurs of the searchers, pressed down on Rivka until she could scarcely breathe. At one point she found herself staring at the dark rushing water, eyes straining to glimpse amid its churning a shape she half-expected and yet would give her life not to see.

"He's not here. I don't think he ever was." Hanley spoke gently as he stepped up beside her. She shivered, her gaze still on the river. He slipped an arm around her shoulders. She relaxed into his warmth. "We'll find him," Hanley said. "Alive and in one piece."

She drew away, putting an inch of space between them. "You don't know that."

"Until and unless we find otherwise, there's hope." Lightly, he touched her shoulder. "We're finished here. Come on."

The patrolmen drew ahead of them, starting the long trek back to Lake Street Station. "Where now?" Rivka managed to say as she and Hanley reached the boardwalk again.

He gave her a wry look. "If I said home, I'm guessing you'd ignore me."

She couldn't answer. That Aaron wasn't here, injured or worse, should have been some solace—but that might only mean no one had found him elsewhere yet.

"He may be fine," Hanley said. "Holed up somewhere, having a meal or a drink or a cup of coffee while he works things out."

"He doesn't drink," she said, as Hanley steered them northward. "And he'd no money. And—" She broke off. She'd meant to say, *And he wouldn't eat anywhere not kosher,* but that might not be true anymore.

"Could have earned some odd jobbing, if he took off in the afternoon and never went by the rail tracks. There's plenty who'd hire an able-bodied man to clear brick and scrap from a building lot for a couple of hours. He could get enough to buy himself supper, at least." His expression turned grimmer as he stared down the street.

She touched his arm. "What is it?"

He glanced at her. "When Jacob and Hannah went looking for Aaron...did they ask the neighbors if anything was missing?"

Shock robbed her of speech. Then anger swept through her. "My brother is no thief!"

"Your brother is terrified for himself and his family. If he never went to Twelfth and Clark—if he never intended to—then he's also angered Errol or whoever wrote that note, and he knows it. Who's to say what he might do?"

"I won't hear this." She strode blindly away from him, her footsteps making hollow thuds on the boardwalk.

Hanley followed her. "The quickest way to disappear is a train ticket. But you can't earn enough for that in an afternoon. He'd have to steal if he meant to vanish that way."

"Then let us go to the train stations. And we'll prove you are wrong."

"Fair enough. There's a depot up ahead at Van Buren. We'll start there."

Their lantern and the gas lamps every few yards shed just enough light to see by. Rivka peered at houses and storefronts as they passed, afraid of spotting a huddled shape in the shadows. She wouldn't look at Hanley, didn't want to see pity in his eyes. Didn't want to acknowledge that he could be right. Staying angry helped stave off the fear that made her want to break down and cry.

No one recognized Aaron's description at the Chicago, Rock Island & Pacific depot. Her sense of triumph as the last ticket agent shook his head was short lived. Chicago had an abundance of rail lines...or Aaron could be hiding somewhere...or hurt...or...

"Now what?"

Hanley shrugged. "Other depots. Restaurants and taverns. Cheap boardinghouses. Any place he might eat or snatch a few hours' sleep. Or home, to see if anyone's found him."

She didn't trust herself to speak until they were outside again. "Not home," she said. He would find a reason to leave her there, or there would be no word...or there *would* be word she didn't want to hear.

"Rivka—"

"No. Don't reason with me. I can't *be* reasonable. Not—" She forced herself to put her fear into words, to give it shape she could grapple with. "He could be dead."

He took his time responding. In his face she saw regret, and respect. "Yes."

The weight of it settled on her like a stone. Her feet hurt, and she felt exhausted beyond measure. "A few more blocks," she said.

He gave a small sigh. "There's a tavern just past Adams. As likely a place as any."

The dark pressed in as they headed onward. Every noise seemed magnified. When Hanley offered her his arm, she took it. The feel of him reminded her of the moment by the river, his touch the only warmth amid her cold terror for Aaron. They reached the empty yard next to the tavern, where outhouse reek made her catch her breath. A lantern on a hook over the back door threw jagged shadows across the patchy grass.

Staring into the yard, Rivka abruptly halted. She felt Hanley stiffen as he saw it too. Pale homespun, caught by the lantern light, covering a human-shaped lump next to the outhouse wall.

They hurried over. Hanley knelt by the body and gently turned it. A shocked cry escaped Rivka at the sight of Aaron's battered face.

Hanley's hand went to Aaron's neck. "He's alive. Let's see how badly he's hurt."

She knelt by Aaron's shoulders and gently straightened his arms while Hanley worked on his legs. His shirt was torn, his knuckles bruised and swollen, his breathing labored as if his lungs couldn't work right. Rivka choked down terror and cradled his head in her lap. He was alive—but for how long?

In Your hands, Baruch Hashem, she thought—but he seemed very far away.

THIRTY-SIX

June–August 1871

Chicago is all noise and chaos, whuffing trains and rattling horse-drawn cars and more buildings and people than Dorrie has ever seen. The hot summer air feels thick in her lungs, smelling of horse manure and river mud and lake water. She spends her first day wandering the streets, goggle eyed at the sheer number of shops, houses, eateries, and saloons. Richmond was nothing like this. Tall buildings of brick and stone loom everywhere—banks, hotels, Field & Leiter's department store, McVicker's Theatre. She halts and stares awhile at the gleaming façade of a nearly finished building, men swarming over it like ants at terrifying heights. How do they do that without succumbing to the terror of falling?

"That there's the Palmer House," says a voice close by. She turns and sees a grizzled newspaper vendor in a red cap, who grins as she catches his eye. "Potter Palmer's buildin' it for his wife. A wedding present, they say. Must be nice havin' that much money."

It is, she could have told him. She knew what that felt like once upon a time. Long gone, those days. Sometimes, with all that's happened since, she's not sure if her memory of them is even real.

બ્ઝ

Her first attempt to find work doesn't go well. The fellow in charge of hiring at Field & Leiter's seems receptive at first, but his face changes when she opens her mouth and her Southern drawl comes out. Secesh, he's thinking, and in no hurry to help one of *her* kind. She's had enough of taverns—maybe a smaller shop will take her on. But she has no luck there, either. Her living arrangements don't permit taking in laundry, and sewing doesn't pay enough for rent. Without references, no rich family would hire her as a tutor or household help, even if she had any aptitude for the latter sort of work.

Desperate, she bargains with the flint-eyed German woman who runs the boardinghouse where she stays—a break in the rent in exchange for help at meals. Living with Joel, she learned simple cookery—fried potatoes and eggs, flapjacks, pea soup, boiled beans. She cooks and serves up, and does her best to deflect the notice of the men daily at the table. Sober-faced Germans, mostly, talking with thick accents and shedding city mud from their boots when they come home for supper. A few Southerners live here as well, transplants like herself, though none Dorrie cares to appeal to. None are gentlemen, and they all remind her of Jefferson Holt—onetime braggarts beaten down by harsh experience and simmering with resentment. She takes care not to be their target, and sleeps with a kitchen knife under her pillow. If any of them makes a move, she'll do for him like she did for Holt back in Virginia years ago.

Two months drag by, her living hand to mouth and wondering if she'll ever have better. Where she might turn for *better,* she hasn't an earthly notion. She won't go to Billy, she knows that now. The half-formed thought of doing so that brought her to this Northern city by its vast, cold lake was a phantom of her grief- and shock-addled brain. Does he even know she's kin to him? He might, if he paid heed to slave women's stories. How the world has changed, that Dorcas Whittier could ever have thought to claim kindred with a Negro. But he's not Nigger Billy anymore. He's a white man now. He must be, from what she saw during the war—the white Yankee soldiers, in Tennessee and in Richmond, treating him like one of their own. Some days, she resents this beyond sense or sanity. God has brought her low and him high, for no reason she can discern. Tom was wrong, she thinks on her worst days. Saying God would teach the North a lesson. There is no God—or if there is, he hates her.

Neatening the parlor on an early August afternoon, she picks up a discarded copy of the *Chicago Tribune*. The headline across the folded-back page reads, *Situations Wanted*. One of the tenants must be looking for work. Dorrie casts an eye over the columns, not expecting much. Halfway down the third one, an advertisement catches her eye. A flicker of interest rises as she reads it through. *Reasonable pay offered...North May Street...Apply in person by August 10th.*

Two days from now. Why not present herself and see what happens? She won't have lost more than the nickel fare for the horsecar, not even that if she walks. She doesn't want to stay here, eking out a living with the constant fear of catching the wrong eye. Perhaps God will throw a little miracle her way—though she hasn't been on speaking terms with him since Joel died, all because a Yankee didn't have the sense not to come where he wasn't wanted.

She quells the familiar burn of anger, tucks the paper under her arm, and heads upstairs to make sure her Sunday dress is presentable.

⅓

When the door opens at the house on North May Street, the sight of the person on the other side steals the breath from her. No miracle, this. A cruel joke, like everything else the Almighty has let happen to her since the start of the war ten years ago. The man before her is one she still sees in nightmares of a Union scout camp, a long and wicked blade at her throat, Tom lying dead in the flickering firelight. Captain Scar.

Somehow, she gets through the conversation that follows. Somehow, she answers his questions—truthfully where she can, inventing where she must—in a steady voice that sounds as if it belongs to someone else. He speaks to her gently, not at all like the monster she knows him to be. He'll send to her by city post within a few days, he says, after the decision is made. He doesn't connect her with the boy soldier he captured and tormented on a Tennessee hillside in May of 1864. Or with the ragged, desperate woman in Richmond a year later, whom he made sure was sent to prison for whoring. How blind he is, how trusting. If she had her kitchen knife, she could cut his throat before he knew what happened. Perhaps this isn't a cruel joke after all. Perhaps there's purpose in it. Hasn't she always been told God moves in mysterious ways? Is that why she's been thrown into *his* way again—as the instrument of God's vengeance for the wrongs he's done?

For now, she dissembles. He mustn't suspect a thing of her until she knows why this has happened, what she's supposed to do. Through the whirl in her head comes a moment of clarity. If she gets this position, she'll kill him. Work for him a few days, just long enough to accustom him to her presence, and then...or no. Listening to him speak, seeing in his face a glimmer of the want she's seen in other men, she thinks of something better. She'll use that want, fan it from a spark to a flame. Take the time to make him hers, and helpless, then strike him down. Yes. That's fitting.

That night she dreams of Tom. Not dead on the dark hillside, but alive and a boy again, laughing as he runs with her across the grass. Behind them, the rambling brick plantation house glows in the afternoon sun. In this dream, nothing's gone from her. There are no bluecoats, no violence, no deaths. In this dream, all is as it should be.

She wakes to a crushing sense of loss, bitter as ashes in her mouth. And to words from the Bible that ring in her head: *Vengeance is mine, saith the Lord.*

THIRTY-SEVEN

April 28–29, 1872

anley caught the last night train to Alton, arriving at the depot with five minutes to spare. "I've informed the superintendent," Moore said as he and Hanley reached the platform where the train stood, belching steam and coal ash. "He wasn't best pleased to be interrupted on a Sunday, but he agreed to suspend any disciplinary proceedings Mike Hickey might start against you until the situation's looked into."

Hanley gripped the handle of his carpetbag tighter. "He knows damned well what Hickey is. Why——"

"Because that's not the way it works." Moore's patient tone nettled Hanley, though he supposed he'd asked for that reminder. Knowing what Mike Hickey was and proving it were two different kettles of fish. *And both of them stink to Heaven.*

"I'll handle things here," Moore went on. "Schmidt'll speak for you, under oath if need be, and his reputation is solid as rock. That's *if* things get that far. Captain Hickey counted on controlling the situation. He may back off, now he's lost that."

Hanley wasn't reassured. "You'll see to Mam and Kate? Make certain they're all right while I'm gone?"

"We'll take care of it. Telegraph me if you need to. I'll pay the charge." Moore clapped him on the shoulder. "Good hunting, Frank."

Cʒ

Too keyed up to sleep, Hanley spent the first thirty minutes of the journey southward staring out the window, even though there was nothing to see but the blank dark of the countryside. George Schuyler should be easy enough to find once he got to Alton. He was a law clerk, Ada had said, who drew up the purchase deed for the Kelmanskys' farm. "He and Aaron found out they were both in the Eighty-Second during the war. They swapped stories, got to be friends. Year or so after, George came to Aaron, said his old captain was looking into bad guns that killed some soldiers in Aaron's company and another. Asked would Aaron help him find survivors, witnesses. Well, they found more than they bargained for."

She hadn't known much beyond that—only that it had to do with stolen rifles ending up in Chicago, intended for the Northwest Conspiracy. "Aaron didn't tell me more, and even that much, I had to drag out of him. He said the less I knew, the safer I'd be."

Hanley could piece together the rest. Champion had gone to Alton three days before he died and brought something back with him. Something Lucas Errol and his crooked lawyer expected to find among the Farnham case papers, that was worth a hundred-dollar payment to a thief. Something they now thought Aaron Kelmansky might have. A deposition, a written confession, from someone. Could Errol have gone to Champion's home the night of the murder, thinking what he sought might be there? Not knowing his lawyer was making other arrangements, panicked at the thought of discovery…Hanley let out a breath. The bedroom was the problem. If Champion had died downstairs, investigating sounds of a prowler after Alice Lockwood left…

If she *had* left. He had only her word for that.

Irritated, uncomfortable in the second-class seat several inches too short for his lanky frame, he opened his carpetbag and dug out a fistful of paper. He'd tossed the discarded pages from Champion's war memoir into the bag on impulse before he left home. Since sleep eluded him for the moment, he might as well read to pass the time.

Despite the occasional word or phrase crossed out and rewritten, the pages weren't hard to decipher. Champion wrote with clarity and precision, his skills no doubt honed by his practice as a lawyer. *"The Eighty-Second Illinois, first mustered at Springfield, was a heart-stirring sight,"* Hanley read. *"Here we stood, sons of all nations and all walks of life, come together to defend the truest ideals of our Union."*

As Champion described the regiment's journey to its first station in Virginia, Hanley found himself remembering his own early days in uniform. The bright sunshine that June in Chicago, when the city's proud Irishmen first stood together in ranks and received their rifles as members of the Irish Brigade. Hanley had gotten one, the first gun he'd ever held. The smooth feel of it in his hands, the slim, long deadliness of it, had fascinated him. He'd used a cosh before, sometimes a knife—tools of the trade for a gambler and con man, handy for protection or doing harm short of fatal. A gun was purely for killing. He'd wondered then if he could fire his rifle at another man, a man he didn't know. A man who'd surely kill him first if he didn't.

The thought of the green boy he'd been then made a grim smile tug at his lips. He'd learned to kill soon enough. The fierce desire to keep breathing did that to you. Though he never got used to the sheer carnage of the war. Few soldiers did, and those few, you learned to stay away from.

He skimmed the next couple of pages. It was all so familiar—raw recruits, endless drill, long marches through rain and mud, or heat and dust, with indifferent food and a tent at the end if you were lucky. If not, nothing to eat and a bedroll on the hard ground. Here and there, he saw names of places where the regiment had fought or made winter camp—Fredericksburg, Hartford Church, Stafford Court House. Partway down the fourth page, the words *Loudoun County* caught his eye. He read the paragraph more closely. *"...in Loudoun County, Northern Virginia. The local people were sharply divided; just as many were loyal as not, and those who stayed true to the Union often faced persecution from their rebel neighbors."*

Here was at least some confirmation of the story Mary Olcott had told. The Thomashaws' hired woman claimed her brother died in

Loudoun County fighting Confederates, and acted as a spy of sorts for Ben Champion while the Eighty-Second was stationed there. Hanley kept reading, looking for the name *Olcott*. He found general references to local militias on both sides, though the only militiaman singled out was given no surname. Champion described him as the subject of a prank often played on new recruits—persuading them that "picket duty" meant balancing atop an actual picket for several hours, so as to better view the surrounding countryside. *"Poor Samuel, a local boy, took some razzing from his fellows before they would trust a Virginian—but he bore it in good part, and stood his 'picket duty' manfully for nearly four minutes. The feat so impressed the rest that they deemed him worthy to share their dinner of fried hardtack and boiled peas."*

He smiled slightly and kept going, until the final paragraph on the eighth page caught his attention. *"There were many who acquitted themselves well on the field of battle, especially during these trying early days. One of the best was a young soldier I cannot name. I knew him, served with him, even called him friend; yet he must remain anonymous, for reasons both complicated and ignoble."*

Maybe this, and not poor Samuel What's-His-Name, was Mary Olcott's brother. He might have joined the Union army in the field, as many loyalists in rebel states did. Hanley continued reading. *"I tell his story in this volume for one reason—to aid the cause for which we fought this terrible war, so that all those who died for freedom's sake shall not have died in vain."*

The next page described the soldier briefly, though not in terms that made him easy to identify. Born in Tennessee, he'd moved to Illinois as a child and considered himself a Northerner. That let Mary Olcott's brother out, Hanley thought. He was quiet, more often found reading than drinking or playing cards—though when he did play, he usually won, and then stood his fellow players to extra food from the sutlers' wagons that followed the regiment from camp to camp—better meat, additional coffee rations, fresh-made pie. Hanley skimmed the rest of the page, which diverged into an account of the so-called Mud Campaign, followed by a long, dull winter in camp.

There was a break between this page and the next, which picked up with another anecdote about the nameless young soldier. He was a medical student, reading *Gray's Anatomy* as often as his Bible. Champion wrote approvingly of his nerve as he held an injured man steady on a makeshift operating table—a length of canvas spread over the bare ground inside the tent that served as a field hospital—while an army doctor amputated the man's forearm, shattered by a minié ball. *"Those of his persuasion are commonly supposed to be cowardly, but he did not flinch from his dreadful task. The life of his fellow soldier depended on it, and he would not let his comrade down."*

His persuasion, Hanley thought. Could Champion mean Aaron? But Aaron Kelmansky served with the Jewish company, the Concordia Guards. This soldier was someone Champion served side by side with. Was he colored? But a colored soldier wouldn't serve in the same company as a white man, unless...

He gave a soft whistle and set the page down. No wonder Champion had seen his memoir as another *Uncle Tom's Cabin*. It would make quite the story if Hanley's guess was correct.

He wondered, as he sat with the pages in his lap and stared out again at the passing darkness, who the anonymous soldier was. And whether he might be the one who'd spirited Champion's war memoir away.

ଔ

The air outside the Alton rail station smelled of the nearby waterfront. Noon sunshine made Hanley squint as he headed up Alby Street, ignoring the twinge of muscles stiffened from the long night spent folded into the second-class seat. His dreams, when he finally slept, had been full of cannon fire and blood, the kind of dreams he hadn't had since a year or so after muster out. It was a relief to move under his own power, to have something to do besides stave off memories he'd spent seven years doing his best to bury.

He looked around as he walked along. Though tiny compared to Chicago, Alton was larger than he'd expected, stretching for a good couple of miles from the river docks and warehouses that were the town's lifeblood. He could hear the deep-throated horns of riverboats, the voices of workmen floating from dockside and the ferry landing. Before he'd gone two blocks, the odor of damp gave way to the smells of coffee and frying ham. They led him toward Third Street, which ran northwest from the river's edge. A ways off, a towering hill loomed over the riverscape. A scattering of headstones at its top marked it as the city cemetery. He stared at the headstones—how many Union and Rebel graves were among them?—then turned away.

The Steamboat Tavern, recommended by the stationmaster as serving "the best grub in town," was on Third just off Alby. Hanley went in. A quick glance around showed seven or so scrubbed tables scattered across a well-swept floor. The aroma of coffee hung thick in the air. He ordered at the bar and sat down to wait. A short time later, fortified by coffee, ham, and eggs, he went to pay his bill. "I'm looking for a fellow," he said to the barrel-shaped man minding the till. "George Schuyler. He clerks for a lawyer here. Where might I find him?"

The man raised a bushy eyebrow as he took the greenback Hanley offered him. "George Schuyler? Top of the hill. Six feet under."

THIRTY-EIGHT

Breakfast was a bleak meal, neither Rivka nor Nat able to eat much. Rivka managed some tea and a boiled egg, and watched as Nat chewed down half a slice of toast before pushing his plate aside. His eyes looked haunted, and she wondered if he was remembering Alton. How much he'd seen there.

She laid a hand on his shoulder as she left the table—what could she say for comfort, that he wouldn't know was a lie?—and went to put tea and toast on a small wooden tray. Then she took the tray upstairs.

Ada didn't look up when Rivka entered the bedroom. All night, she'd spent in the chair drawn up by Aaron's bedside—even sleeping there, when she slept at all. Which wasn't much, Rivka had judged, listening to Ada's anxious breathing between fitful dozes of her own.

She set the tray down on the bureau. "I've brought you breakfast. We're out of sugar for the tea, I'm afraid." What had made her say that? Babbling about food when Aaron lay abed, pale and still as death. A lump rose in her throat. So many hours since they'd found him, and he still hadn't woken.

The first words of the prayer for healing—*mi shebeirach*—came to mind, but she couldn't go on. Even to Hashem, she could think of nothing useful to say. She brought the tea to Ada. "I put honey in. It will help if you have a little something."

Ada blinked, then focused on Rivka. "Help," she said dully. "Nothing will *help*. Nothing but God, and he isn't here."

"I don't know about that." Rivka's own voice was less than steady. "But I know you won't be much help to Aaron, or Nat, if you don't eat and drink." She lifted Ada's free hand—the other was wrapped around

Aaron's limp fingers—and pressed the tea mug into it. "Just a sip. Then a bite of toast."

Not until Ada took the full weight of the mug did Rivka let go. "Stubborn," Ada said, her face softening. "Just like him, the damn fool." She glanced away, lips pressed tight. Then, with a deep breath, she met Rivka's eyes again. "How's Nat? Did he eat?"

"Some toast and tea with milk. He's whittling now, in the kitchen."

Ada nodded. "Good. Keeps him from taking on." She sipped tea, then lowered the mug. Her gaze was back on Aaron, steady but without hope.

Rivka buttered the toast, giving immense attention to the task. She felt helpless and frightened, and furious at Aaron for putting himself in harm's way. If he had only talked to Hanley...and now he might not get the chance.

"When I first saw him..." Ada spoke in a dreamy voice. Rivka set down the toast and butter knife and turned to watch her. "He was surrounded by children," Ada went on. "Must've been a dozen, every shade of colored, from light like Nat to dark as plowed earth. He had a baseball and bat, looked almost new. They were jumping around, trying to knock the ball out of his hand. 'Everyone gets a turn,' he kept saying. 'Let everyone have a turn.' They were all laughing, him and the children. Tossing that ball around. And Nat..." She smiled, her eyes overbright. "Nat couldn't stop talking about his teacher, Mister Aaron. So one day, I decided I had to meet this man." She gave a breathy laugh. "First time in my life a white person spoke to me like it didn't matter what color I was. Some of the others, the Yankee whites who came—they acted like we didn't know how to put on our own clothes without them telling us. Aaron..." Her voice caught. "Aaron was different."

Was. Rivka shut her eyes against the sting of tears. Aaron would wake up. He had to. Hashem couldn't take her father and her brother in the space of four months. Not when Aaron had come back to her after so many years of absence. She felt lost and alone even with Ada a few feet away. Suddenly, fiercely, she wished Hanley were here.

She opened her eyes and made herself walk over to the bedside. Last night, after she and Hanley brought Aaron home, Doctor Gershon had examined him, bandaged his ribs, and left them a packet of willow-bark tea for headache. "He'll have a big one when he comes to. He may not remember much, either. Keep him calm and quiet, or he could hurt himself worse than he already is." As if anything could be worse. She could see and hear Aaron breathing, yet the strange thought crossed her mind that he might not be with them anymore. Perhaps his soul had already gone, and his body simply didn't know it.

She fought down panic as she leaned over him. The bruises on his face were purple and livid, made by fists and who knew what else. The thought made her shiver, though she suppressed it for Ada's sake.

"I remember a fellow when I was a girl, name of Jackson," Ada said. "Kicked in the head by a mule. He never was right, after. If Aaron's like that...I don't know what'll happen to us."

Rivka straightened. "You'll stay here."

Ada gave her a long look, part warmth and part regret. "We're not your kind, Nat and me. You know it. Your people know it." She glanced back at Aaron with a wistful smile. "He's just about the only one I know who never paid it any mind."

Three steps brought Rivka around the bed. She knelt by Ada's chair and looked her in the face. "If my people meant to turn you away, they'd have done it. And besides..." She took the woman's hand, tea mug and all. "This is *my* house. You and Nat can stay until *you* wish to go."

Into the brief silence that followed came Aaron's voice, weak and thready. "Ada?"

THIRTY-NINE

Schuyler's dead?!" Shock washed through Hanley, sharp as cold water. "How? When?"

The tavern-keeper handed him two bits' change, apparently enjoying the chance to impress an out-of-towner with a piece of juicy gossip. "Last Monday night. Throat slit like a prize pig. Somebody jumped him. Poor fellow didn't stand a chance with one crippled arm."

Hanley pocketed the change, his heart racing. "Anyone arrested?"

"Nope. Don't expect there will be, neither." He closed the till and gave Hanley a curious look. "What'd you want Schuyler for, anyways?"

"Business. Why do you think no one will be arrested?"

The man came out from behind the bar and headed toward the table, where he picked up Hanley's dirty dishes. "He was stirring things up that're best let lie."

The guns, Hanley thought. "Like what?"

He turned toward Hanley, plate and cutlery in hand. "Where you from, mister?"

"Chicago."

"Never been there. Thought about goin', to see what it's like." He walked past Hanley and set the dishes on the bar. "This ain't Chicago, though. Might be good you remember that while you're here."

ଔ

The local police were no help, as Hanley had expected after the tavern-keeper's veiled warning. The police chief, tall and lanky as Hanley and with a beard in need of a trim, told him bluntly the case was closed, and

205

no business of his. "Next train north goes out at half past one," he said, lounging in his chair and digging under his fingernails with a toothpick. "You can catch it if you hurry."

"I'm in no hurry. Your murder case *is* my business, unless I learn otherwise. I'm not leaving until I get the truth."

"Then you'll be staying a mighty long time."

"I'm a patient man."

Several seconds passed. Hanley didn't budge, nor did his gaze leave the police chief's. Finally, the man set down the toothpick. "Robbery," he said, his voice and face smooth and hard as granite. "Schuyler was assaulted on the street late at night, likely by a transient off the boats. His pockets were emptied of whatever money or valuables he had in them. No witnesses. I don't waste my men's time on fool's errands. Unlike the Chicago police, it appears. Alton may not be Chicago, Detective Hanley, but we're not bumpkins. We know our business." *And you stay out of it* was left unspoken, but Hanley got the message all the same.

號

Schuyler's employer, a local attorney named Matheson, offered little more. From him, Hanley learned that Schuyler was prompt, meticulous in his work, and a frequent customer of Donahue's, a local saloon where he often ate and had a beer or three in the evenings. "Some nights he'd stay there longer than was wise. Donahue's caters to plenty of local people, but we get all kinds off the riverboats, too, unloading cargo. One of them must've followed George out. The fellow's long gone by now, I expect." Matheson shook his graying head. "Killing a man over a few greenbacks and some change. He can't have had more than that. I don't know what this world's coming to."

"Were you here when Captain Champion came, the Chicago lawyer in the Farnham and Chandler lawsuit?" Swiftly, Hanley calculated days. "It would've been Saturday, a bit over a week ago. The twentieth, I think. Mr. Schuyler brought him here to meet someone connected with the case." Not knowing where the land lay, he chose not to mention the stolen rifles.

The lawyer shook his head. "They didn't come here. I wanted no part of it. George was with the captain that day at the Fair Oaks Hotel, by the train station."

"Do you know who they met with?"

"No. I'm sorry."

"Why did you want no part of it? Schuyler and Champion, and whoever they spoke to, wanted justice for dead soldiers and the families they left behind. What's wrong with that?"

Matheson grabbed a stack of papers on his desk. "I really can't tell you any more. If you'll excuse me—"

Hanley took a stab in the dark. "You know he wasn't robbed. Or you figure. Who killed George Schuyler, Mr. Matheson?"

"I don't know." Matheson's response was clipped, almost angry. Then his shoulders sagged. "Why rake things up, that's what I told him. Nothing good comes of it, even when we mean it to." He rubbed the bridge of his nose. "George was killed between here and Donahue's, not a hundred yards from this office. The night he died, someone went through our files. I don't know who, and I don't know why. I wouldn't have noticed, only they mixed things up with some papers I've been working on when they tried to put everything back."

☙

Nothing in Matheson's files had to do with guns, and the lawyer said no papers were missing. Schuyler must have written down whatever statement about the theft Ben Champion came to hear. That was standard procedure in legal matters, as Hanley understood it. No question Champion brought a copy back to Chicago. Had Schuyler made another? If he'd squirreled it away here without telling his boss, Hanley couldn't know whether the night-time office thief had found it.

A quick trip to Donahue's, roughly a block away, confirmed Schuyler's presence there the night he was killed. He'd left, said his frequent drinking companion, an elderly regular named Matty, around eight thirty. "Used to buy for me when I was skint," Matty said, staring morosely into a glass of beer. "I'm gonna miss George. Whoever done 'im musta got the drop on him. Havin' just one good arm didn't mean he couldn't shoot."

"He was armed that night?"

Matty nodded. "Never went nowhere without his army pistol. 'Specially lately. Like he was worried somethin'd happen to 'im." Another headshake. "Never tol' me why, though."

The police chief hadn't mentioned finding a weapon, or that one had turned up since. Stolen by whoever killed poor Schuyler, Hanley guessed— and not for the money in his pocket. If the local police gave a damn, they could look for the pistol and maybe find the killer. Unlike Hanley, who had no resources here and no idea where to start.

Having gotten all he could out of Matty, Hanley went back to the law office and stood outside it, eying the staircase that wound up the side of the sturdy wooden building. The door at the top, to the second-floor room where Matheson said Schuyler lived, was closed. Hanley went up and tried the door. Locked, of course. He could break it down, though that wouldn't sit well with whoever had let the room to Schuyler in the first place. A complaint to the local police, and Hanley would be facing more than a barely civil suggestion that he park himself on the next train out of town.

He leaned against the outside wall and let out a slow breath. Schuyler was killed last Monday night. The same night as the attack on the Kelmansky farm. According to Ada, Aaron had first stumbled across the story of the stolen guns. Ten to one Errol knew that. In a small place like this, with people "stirring things up" about a leading citizen and his major business enterprise, word would get around. With Champion and Schuyler dead, Aaron was the only one left alive who knew the story's source. Who'd told it to him—and was that person alive or dead? No one to ask except Aaron, a long journey off and unconscious to boot.

What had the note said, that drew him away from the uncertain haven of Market Street? *You have what I want.* Damning knowledge, maybe on paper, as well as in Aaron's head. A chill spread through Hanley. Fourteen hours away by train, and who knew what could happen in the meantime.

Moore. He turned and left Schuyler's place, heading to the post office to send a telegram.

FORTY

Two more bodies had come in Sunday night and Monday morning—a portly middle-aged man without a mark on him, and a scrawny boy struck by a train. Prospecting for coal fragments, most likely, and got too close to the tracks. Will could scarcely bring himself to look at the child's mangled body. He spent his days determining causes of death, but the young ones depressed him. Would anyone come to identify this boy, or was he just another street orphan, destined for a short note in a morgue record book and a pauper's grave?

He shook himself and went to wash his hands. Normally, the sound and feel of the running water soothed him. Today, he watched it cascade over his skin and couldn't keep back the thought—*No darker than a farmer's tan. Not enough for anyone to notice.* His breath came fast as he dried his hands with a thin towel off the rack by the stone sink.

Work on the middle-aged man kept him too busy to think for a time. *Hydropericardium*, he wrote in his logbook, tracing each letter with care. Aunt Abigail had taught him penmanship, guiding his fourteen-year-old self through exercises. Her long, graceful hand around his, shaping, pressing. Milk-pale skin against olive-cast. A contrast she'd carefully never mentioned.

He gripped his pen until his fingertips ached. The dead man was pale as a gutted fish except for the red muscle visible where Will had opened his chest to look at his heart. The sight made his stomach roil. He knew what was wrong, and it wasn't the corpses he had to tend to. How long before Hanley found that reply note, found out about the scene with Ben at the Tremont House? He couldn't take solace in the passing of days, couldn't convince himself each one wasn't bringing discovery closer instead of farther away.

Footsteps in the hall made him start, and he turned toward the morgue doorway with a sense of dread. Not Hanley, thank God. It was his newest morgue assistant, with the afternoon post.

"This came for you, Dr. Rushton." The younger man held out a squarish brown-wrapped package. "I think it's your microscope lens." He sounded eager as a puppy hoping for a game of fetch. "When can you show me how it works? I don't mind waiting. You just say when you have the time, and I'll..."

God, yes. He'd promised that, hadn't he? A lifetime ago. "We'll figure something out." He forced a smile and took the package. "Later this week, say."

"Thanks!" The assistant left with a spring in his step, the silence in his wake more profound than before.

Will set the package down and sutured up the dead man's chest. Dealing with the mangled child was beyond him just now. Instead, he took the package to his small office, where he spent the next few minutes unwrapping the new lens and inserting it into the microscope. The task made him think again of Hanley—this time standing by Ben's corpse in the morgue as Will slid the bayonet into the fatal wound. A gold ring on a broken chain in Hanley's hand.

He straightened at the thought of the ring. Found in the grass outside Ben's house, Hanley had said. He'd thought for a moment he recognized it. But he'd last seen *that* ring on the finger of Tom Whittier, lying dead in the firelight after the failed bushwhacker ambush in 1864.

He found his mind turning toward that long-ago night by Blackbird Creek in the hills of East Tennessee. Dorrie, in shabby men's clothes and with her hair hacked short, bound to a tree while Ben Champion cut her with his bayonet blade and threatened her with the hangman's rope. Ben had frightened even him that night. God knew what Dorrie must have felt. Himself a while later, dropping hardtack and a canteen at her feet and telling her to get gone by sunrise. He hadn't untied her, but he hadn't stopped her from freeing herself. He left that decision to God. Seeing her on that hillside, bleeding and broken, he couldn't help thinking of the little girl she'd been. All red-gold curls and lace, following him and Tom everywhere.

He swallowed to moisten his dry mouth. Another memory surfaced, barely heeded at the time, but now taking on a horrible significance. Dorrie, free of her bonds, flitting in shadow toward the glow of the banked campfire and bending over Tom's sprawled corpse. Had she taken the ring from his hand? Will couldn't remember.

How could that ring have turned up at Ben Champion's place? He had to be mistaken. Dorrie Whittier would never come to Chicago. If she survived the war, she'd have gone home, found some sort of haven among friends or neighbors, like as not someone to marry and take care of her. That was what girls like her did. What they were raised for.

She couldn't be here. That ring couldn't be here. It wasn't possible.

൚

"Hanley's not here, Doc," the desk sergeant said in response to Will's query when he arrived at Lake Street Station. The man looked harassed. Beyond him, in the squad room, Will heard the buzz of voices. Agitated, some angry.

He nodded toward the sounds. "What's got them riled up?"

The desk sergeant shook his head as Rolf Schmidt's voice rose above the rest. "Horse shit. Hanley's still detective. He didn't do nothing wrong. We—"

"So where is he, then?" A booming voice, a sneering tone. "If he wasn't arrested for assault, why isn't he here?"

"Sergeant sent him on a case. Out of town."

"How the hell do *you* know? You're foot patrol. You don't know anything, you damned cabbage-eater."

"More than you. You want I should prove it?" A chair scraped across the floor amid a flurry of footsteps. The desk sergeant muttered, "Oh, hell," and ducked into the squad room.

Will caught snatches of what followed—*fight in the stationhouse and it'll cost you both your badges...dumb cabbage-eater thinks he can take me...not taking that from nobody!*—and made a snap decision. "Officer Schmidt," he called as he walked around the desk toward the squad room doorway, "I need your help with something, if you've got a minute."

ℭ

"Evidence room," Schmidt said. "Got what you need in a box someplace. Come on back." The high color was fading from his cheeks, but Will could tell he was still struggling to get himself under control.

The desk sergeant looked anxious. "Sergeant Moore don't like evidence going missing." He gave Will an apologetic look. "Be better if you ask him, maybe..."

"My case while Hanley's away," Schmidt said, a touch louder than necessary. "My problem. You come."

Will followed him to a small room halfway down the hall, full of stacked boxes and crates labeled with dates and names. A narrow wooden table near the door held a logbook and a pen stuck in an inkwell. Schmidt went to the nearest stack of boxes, eased one off the top, and brought it over. He nodded toward the logbook. "Write in there what you take and when, and sign your name. Bring it back when you're finished." His expression turned curious. "What you think you gonna see with that little machine you got?"

"I won't know till I look." Will made himself breathe slowly as he lifted the lid.

Schmidt nodded toward a small, cotton-wrapped bundle in a corner. "That's it there. The machine tell whose ring it is?"

"Maybe." Will unwrapped the bundle. The ring gleamed against the pale cloth, the chain curled inside it like a miniature snake. He re-wrapped it and picked it up, then filled out the logbook as Schmidt had directed. Hanley's signature was a bold scrawl just above his own. "So where is Hanley? And what's this about him being arrested?"

Schmidt scowled. "Sonofabitch Chamberlain don't know nothing. Sergeant Moore sent Hanley to Alton. A big lead in the case."

"The Champion murder?"

"*Ja*. Could even be who killed him. Some guy he was suing, didn't like it." Abruptly, Schmidt went quiet. "You don't hear that from me," he said after a moment.

"Not a thing." Will managed a conspiratorial grin and closed the box.

Schmidt hoisted it back into place. "You sign a paper at the desk, too," he said. "Ask the sergeant." He nodded for Will to precede him out of the evidence room.

Will felt light-headed, as if he'd skipped a day's meals. He wrote out the requisition form, made all the right noises, and after a while found himself outside with the jewelry in his hand.

The morgue, when he finally reached it, was blessedly quiet. He went to his office, laid the bundle next to the microscope, unwrapped it, and spent the next few minutes staring at it. The ring shone up at him—a thick gold band edged with a twined-leaf pattern that framed a deep groove. A standard design for a mourning ring. This one held a narrow braid of dark brown hair, enameled to preserve it. Around it wove a lighter coil, three or four strands of reddish-gold. Breathing faster, he slid the ring from its chain and laid it on the microscope stage just beneath the viewing lens.

He knew what he'd find as he angled the ring properly with one hand and adjusted the lens with the other. Delicate lines etched on the underside came sharply into focus: *I Will Remember Her.* Next to that, two sets of initials, *A. W.* and *E. W.*—Anne Whittier and Edward Whittier, mistress and master of the plantation where Will was born. The dark hair was Anne's, dead long ago of childbed fever after the birth of her daughter Dorcas. *Dorrie.*

Will swallowed and closed his eyes. Dorrie and Tom. The white half-brother and -sister he'd grown up with, played with whenever his duties permitted. He'd been a dab hand at polishing the silver in those days. Turning the spit whenever roast meat was wanted at the Whittier family table. And any other household chore a quick-witted, nimble-fingered slave boy who looked almost white could be told to tend to.

No one admitted they were kin, of course. Not to Tom, not to Dorrie. Such things weren't talked about, except in whispered gossip by the Negro women, who knew everything. Such blood ties might be acknowledged obliquely, through better treatment, better food, sometimes even a little learning…but the child of a slave remained a slave. To be worked, used, sold at the master's whim. Or given in payment of a gambling debt, as his full sister Ada was. Like a horse, or a gold watch, or the silver Will had polished until his arms ached.

He covered the ring, unable to bear the sight of it any longer. He'd return it to Lake Street Station before the day ended, but right now he couldn't stand looking at it, even in its wrappings, let alone picking it up. That ring had been on Tom Whittier's finger eight years ago. Dorrie took it before she fled. It shouldn't be here now, but it was. Which meant Dorrie was, too. Dorrie Whittier, whom he'd last seen passing for a boy and spitting fury at Ben Champion for taking her captive, for killing her brother. For being on that hillside, a survivor of the bushwhackers' ambush. For being the victor in Union blue.

He gripped the edge of the table. It couldn't be true, what he feared. And if it was, who did he dare tell?

FORTY-ONE

Rivka had cancelled the day's English class. She would do the girls no good with her mind stuck on Aaron and his condition. For the past few hours he had drifted in and out of coherence, complaining of a headache and not clear on where he was. Sometimes he was back in Alton, at the farmstead she'd never seen. Other times, he seemed lost in their childhood. "You've put your hair up, Rivkaleh," he said once, addressing her as if she were a little girl. "When did you do that? Does Mameh know?"

Dr. Gershon had told them this wasn't unusual. "A blow to the head does strange things. The vagueness comes and goes. With luck, his mind will clear in a few hours, or maybe days."

"And without luck?" Rivka had asked.

He didn't answer, merely shook his head. "Give him willowbark tea as he needs it. Keep him quiet. And pray."

Now, Rivka bent her head against the rain as she neared Lake Street Station. Hanley would want to know Aaron had woken, though only Hashem knew if her brother could tell him anything useful. Hanley would be there, she told herself. He had to be. One sight of him, tall and strong and reassuring, would steady her to face whatever lay ahead.

The desk sergeant, familiar by now, shook his head when she asked for Hanley. "He's out of town, miss. Should be back in a day or two. Did you want to leave a message for him?"

Suddenly shaky, she braced herself against the desk edge. "Only to come…" It was hard to think of the right words through the anxiety that gripped her, though there was no reason for it. Hanley would be back. A day or two made no difference, might even be a help as far as Aaron's condition went. "To come to the Kelmansky house on Market Street as soon as he can.

My brother is aiding him in his case, and may have something to tell him."

The sergeant rummaged in a drawer, unearthed paper and a pencil, and pushed them over to her. "You write that down, miss, I'll see he gets it soon's he comes in."

She wrote swiftly, steadying her hand by force of will. As she finished, the lobby doors creaked open behind her. For an irrational moment, she expected to see Hanley when she turned around. The new arrival was someone else. A slender man, middle-aged, with a neat mustache in a narrow face, capped by unruly hair. He held a slip of paper. It came to her that she knew him, though she couldn't recall his name.

At the sight of her, his grave expression deepened. "Miss Kelmansky," he said, striding toward her. "I'm Sergeant Moore, Chief of Detectives. I've just had a telegram from Detective Hanley. You'll want to alert the men among your people—your brother is in great danger."

CB

Rivka entered the tailor shop and looked around for Onkl Jacob. Moishe glanced up from the cutting table, where he was working on a man's coat, and gave her a shy nod. Before he could speak to her, Jacob came out from the storage room, a bolt of black wool balanced on his shoulder. He brightened when he saw her, swung the bolt down and leaned it against a nearby wall. "Rivkaleh! How is Aaron...any better?"

"He's awake." Tears pricked her eyes. "Doctor Gershon hopes he will recover."

Jacob came closer, concern in his face. "And how are you?"

"Well enough. But there is more danger than we knew." Quickly, she related what Sergeant Moore had told her. "Hanley went to Alton, but the man he went to speak to is dead. He fears Aaron may be next. The police can only arrange for a few men to protect us from Lucas Errol, or anyone he might send to do us harm. The sergeant wanted to know how many of our own we can organize. I said I would ask you."

Jacob pursed his lips and nodded. "We will take care of things." He patted her shoulder. "Don't worry. And tell Aaron not to worry, either."

As if that were possible. Still, she couldn't help feeling a touch relieved, if only because she was no longer alone. Jacob and the other men would do their best to safeguard Aaron long enough for Hanley to solve the case and end the threat once and for all.

She thanked him and left the shop. Moishe followed her out. "Fraylin! Wait a moment."

Part of her wanted to keep going, but that would be inexcusably rude. She stopped a few feet from the shop door. A loaded wagon rattled past. "What is it, Herr Zalman?"

"You are all right now? And Aaron? Truly?" He had walked outside with the coat lapel he'd been cutting and was twisting it in his hands, eyes wide and anxious behind his spectacles.

She managed a smile to reassure him. "Yes. I should get back to Aaron now."

"But there is still danger, you said."

"Onkl Jacob will take care of things. All will be well."

As she stepped away, he reached toward her, his fingers brushing the edge of her sleeve. Surprised, she halted. Faint embarrassment at his bold gesture gave way in his face to another look—hopeful, even ardent. Her breath came short and her heart began to pound. *Not this, not now...*

"There are other ways to be protected," he said. "If you...if you and I were—"

Words tumbled out of her mouth, anything to make him stop talking. "Please. It's too soon. There's...there's too much..."

His cheeks pinked, and he looked down. The lapel was crumpled in his hands. "I understand. I will wait until you are ready. Forgive me, Rivka."

He had used her given name. "There is nothing to forgive," she said faintly, and turned away.

છ

She got as far as the kosher baker's, three doors down from the tailor shop, before reaction set in. She leaned against the low-slung wooden building and made herself breathe slowly until the shaky feeling subsided. She had known this was coming, known it even before Papa died last winter, yet still she was not prepared.

He would wait until she was ready. And then what? She knew. If Aaron recovered fully, Moishe would ask him for permission to court her. If not, he would wait a little longer and then ask Onkl Jacob. And why wouldn't they say yes? Moishe was a good man, with steady work and the prospect of inheriting a thriving business. And he cared for her. Or at least for the woman he thought she was.

A gust of wind snatched wisps of hair from under her kerchief. Without thought, she tucked them back. She felt hollowed out. Things had always been this way. They always would be. What was wrong with her that it upset her so much? She felt like a prize sheep or goat, or some other valued possession to be dispensed by the men. *We only want what is best for you, Rivkaleh,* Onkl Jacob would say if she protested. *He is a good man,* Tanta Hannah would tell her. *And he has been so patient.* As if she was a reward for Moishe's admirable behavior.

Was there any chance Aaron might think differently? He had married as he wished. But he was a man.

The hard surface of the building hurt her back. She pushed away from it and wandered down the block, past all the neighbors' houses, toward her own. With Aaron inside it. And Ada. His mulatto, *goyische* wife. Jealousy flared up, hot and stinging. Aaron had chosen for himself, while she...

She passed the house and kept heading north. Not until the wet scent of the river breeze reached her and the red brick bulk of Lake Street Station loomed up did she realize where she was going. What had brought her back here, of all places? Hanley wasn't inside. He was in Alton, tracking a murderer. Cold fear gripped her like a hand at her throat. If he should be hurt, even killed, she wouldn't know. Not for days, maybe not ever. She was nothing to him, after all—just a girl he knew from a case he'd solved. Why would anyone tell *her* if anything happened to him?

She stood there awhile longer, fool that she was, gazing at the station's front door—even though she knew full well she wouldn't see Hanley coming out.

FORTY-TWO

Dusk had fallen by the time Hanley gave up on his efforts to learn more about Schuyler's murder. He had no intention of leaving Alton until he found out what he wanted to know, but that was proving harder than expected. He kept his inquiries discreet—out of his jurisdiction and damned near ordered to leave town, the last thing he wanted was more attention from the local cops.

He went into Donahue's and ordered a beer and a roast beef sandwich. That taken care of, he glanced around for Matty, but didn't see him. When the taverner pushed his supper across the bar, Hanley asked after the old man. "Gone home to sleep it off," the taverner said, and held out a hand. "That'll be four bits, mister."

Hanley dropped some coins into his palm, picked up the food, and took a seat at an empty table. The beer was decent, the sandwich too dry, but he ate it anyway. No sense wasting his money along with his time. Frustration at the day's failures gnawed at him, and half his beer was gone before he knew it. He slowed his pace—too much drink wouldn't help—and ran over in his mind what little he'd accomplished in the past several hours.

The Fair Oaks Hotel was a bust, the proprietor unwilling to acknowledge anything beyond Ben Champion's having stayed there on Saturday the twentieth. "Paid for one night," the fellow had said, his wary gaze fixed on Hanley's face. "Checked out on Sunday in time for the early morning train. I don't know what he was here for, or who he met. I run a hotel—I don't have time to stand by the registration desk all day, watching who comes in and out."

"What about staff?" Hanley asked. "Someone has to be here, don't they?"

The proprietor's tone sharpened. "I don't want you bothering them.

I've told you, we don't know anything about your man's business here." He wouldn't be budged—and with no authority outside Chicago, Hanley had no choice but to leave it at that.

He took another bite of sandwich and washed it down. Back home in the city, he'd know exactly where to go for information about a street crime—especially one that likely wasn't. In Alton he knew no one, had no connections, no pull. The one with pull hereabouts was Lucas Errol, and he'd apparently used it quite effectively to cover his tracks.

"Busy fellow last Monday night," Hanley muttered, eying the remnant of sandwich on his plate. First the assault on Aaron's farmstead, then a trip into town to…what? Break into the law office and search for the document he thought Schuyler put there? Knife poor Schuyler in the street? Hanley frowned. He couldn't see Errol, in his dandy's suit and oiled mustache, having the brute guts for that. And it was too much for one man to do, especially one who'd caught the late train out of Alton that same night. At least he'd verified that much. The stationmaster knew Errol by sight and recalled selling him a ticket. He hadn't remembered the Kelmansky family, which surprised Hanley until he thought about it. After the attack on their farm, they wouldn't have felt safe at the Alton rail station. If he were Aaron, he'd have gone on foot or by wagon to the next town up the line and caught the train for Chicago there.

He finished his beer, went to the bar and ordered another. The place was filling up now, the customers rowdier as well as more numerous. From the swirl of shouted drink orders and conversations around him, Hanley gathered at least some of the new arrivals had come off the cargo boats. There seemed to be a rivalry of sorts between the riverboat men and a few of the regulars, mainly boasts and cheerful insults tossed back and forth.

Back at his table, Hanley kept an ear cocked for any change in tone as he fished out his sketchbook and pencil and started making notes. Errol had been at the farmstead, with three accomplices, around supper time last Monday. After dark, from Aaron's account, but not long after. Had he hoped to drive Aaron and his family from their home so he could search it for the deposition or confession he thought Aaron might have? A grim smile tugged the corner of Hanley's mouth. Obviously, things hadn't gone according to plan—two of Errol's night riders had ended up shot, at least one seriously injured. While Errol sat on his horse and watched.

He traced an aimless spiral on the page. That left one able-bodied night rider to help Errol search the law office and dispatch poor Schuyler. Hanley frowned and tapped the pencil against the paper. Given what he was looking for, Errol would have searched those files himself. Whether his accomplices were paid ruffians, or men known and bound to him in some way, it wouldn't be worth the risk to rely on any of them. Could Errol have been part of the Order of American Knights? Alton and other river towns were hotbeds of pro-Reb sentiment during the war. Some of those ties might still be active, especially with the rise of violence against the freedmen across the formerly rebellious South.

"You're a cheat! A goddamn, lyin' cheat!" The hoarse shout brought Hanley to full alertness. Some ten feet to his left, a bull-necked fellow in a farmer's homespun shirt and trousers faced off against a string bean of a man with a rough beard and a riverman's cap. A deck of cards lay jumbled on the table between them.

"Say that again," the riverman said, in a dead quiet tone that set Hanley's teeth on edge. One of the fellow's hands was on the table next to an ace of spades. The other was out of sight. Hanley eased to the edge of his chair, ready to move if necessary.

"I'll say it again! I'll say it ten times! You're a goddamn lyin' cheat, a cheat, cheat, cheat—"

A knife blade flashed in the riverman's other hand. "You got three seconds to take that back. Or I'll open another mouth in your throat."

Hanley rose and was moving forward when someone near the riverman pulled out a cosh and thwacked the fellow over the head. He staggered, and someone else threw a punch. A third man grabbed the cosh wielder and slammed him into the wall. Hanley heard wood scrape behind him just in time to duck as a chair hurtled over his head. It struck the brawny farmer in the back and sent him sprawling over the card table.

"God *damn* it, not in my place!" The taverner's voice was drowned in the free-for-all, boatmen against locals against anyone unlucky enough to be nearby. Hanley pocketed his sketchbook and worked his way toward the door. It went against his grain to leave a fight, but there were too many combatants for him to help the taverner break things up.

The night air felt cool on his face as he slipped outside. Fresh and bracing with the damp tang of the Mississippi, it made a marked contrast to the odors of spilled beer, sawdust, and sweat he'd left behind. He lingered by the door, savoring the taste of the breeze and the relative quiet, broken only by muted noises of the fight and the gentle lapping of waves against the nearby riverfront.

Some instinct warned him of a sound that didn't fit. A rustle of cloth, a stealthy footfall. He half-turned in time to register a shadowy figure moving in close, a rough hand grabbing his shirt, hot sharp pain beneath his ribs.

His first confused thought was a stitch in his side, though this hurt a thousand times worse. He sagged against the wall, fought to stay upright, felt splinters tear his skin as he sank to his knees. Where had the shadowy figure gone? Vanished back inside Donahue's, into the night.

FORTY-THREE

Voices swam through the liquor fog in Hanley's head. "He don't look too good." Someone had poured whiskey down him, he couldn't remember who. Didn't do damn all for the pain he was in.

"Lost some blood. Not too much, lucky for him. Hand me that, will you?" Probing fingers near the stitch in his side, which had taken over his whole body and burned like live coals.

"'M in Hell," he muttered. "Mus' be." Just the place for a onetime thief and con man who'd let his first love get killed. Who'd let down someone else that mattered to him, let her down terribly. Rivka. He'd failed her, and now he was dead and in Hell, and he'd never be able to say he was sorry.

"Hold still." He felt a new pain amid the burning, a pricking sensation as if from a miniature red-hot poker.

Definitely Hell. Dull resentment flickered in his brain. "Not fair. 'M a cop now. Changed m' life, tryin' do some *good*. Doesn't 'at matter any?" If he could just see straight, look the blurry figure closest to him in the eyes, he'd give the Devil—or God—what for. It wasn't *fair*, damn it.

The red-hot poker went away. Something cool and wet pressed where it had been, and the burning lessened. "You'll be all right by and by," someone said. A man's voice. He knew it. Not well—it wasn't Sergeant Moore, or Rolf Schmidt, or Will Rushton. Whose? He'd heard it not so long ago...

The puzzle was too much for him. He gave it up and let the burning darkness claim him.

CB

He woke to a dry mouth, a pounding headache nearly as bad as the throb of pain between his rib cage and right hip, and the musty odor of a root cellar. "Easy," someone said, pressing him down when he struggled to sit up. That voice again. "You're among friends. You've suffered an injury. Don't strain yourself."

A second voice spoke. "You want some water, mister?"

"Please." Hanley hardly recognized his own voice, which rasped like a rusty hinge. He opened his eyes, blinked, made out a scrawny hand pressing a flask into his palm.

Someone else slid an arm under his shoulders and gently lifted. "Have a sip. Try not to gulp it. Take it slow."

The water was the best thing he'd ever tasted, washing away the bite of stale whiskey at the back of his throat. Making himself stop at three sips took effort. With his head finally clearing, he looked at the man who was propping him up. Startled, he recognized the proprietor of the Fair Oaks Hotel.

"What..." he murmured as the flask moved away. When the hotel owner tried to ease him back down, Hanley stuck out an arm and braced himself upright. The hard-packed earthen wall felt cool under his palm. He shook his head, winced, glanced around. Light from a lantern on a wall-hook showed him shelves embedded in the dirt, bushel baskets on the shelves. He smelled onions, spotted garlic ropes hanging from the ceiling. In the middle of the room, at a rough-built table, sat a thin fellow whose chest looked sunken under his brown calico shirt. Untidy dark hair fell across his forehead. "What am I doing here?" Hanley said to the hotel owner. "What are *you* doing here?" He nodded toward the thin fellow. "And who's this?"

The thin fellow cleared his throat. "Name's Prewett," he said. "Ern Prewett. You been looking for me."

CB

"I couldn't risk trusting you," said the hotel owner, who gave his name as Addison. "I'm sorry for that. I was coming to Donahue's to fetch Ern's supper, and I saw what happened. Only thing I could think of was to bring you here fast and patch you up. Lucky for you, it looks like your knife man missed anything that matters. I told Ern you came asking about that Saturday, when he met here with that Chicago lawyer, Captain Champion, and...well, I'll let him tell it." He gave Prewett a look, friendship blended with concern. "You do as much as you can, Ern. If you need to stop, stop. Mr. Hanley won't be going anywhere for the next little while."

Prewett coughed, pressed a handkerchief to his lips, coughed again and cleared his throat. "I met with George Schuyler last Saturday, him and that city lawyer and that Kelmansky fellow I first told my story to. Schuyler"—he coughed again, more wetly this time—"Schuyler wrote down what I said. Official-like, for court, he told me. Kelmansky was a witness. Seems you got to have a coupla those." He gave Addison a small smile. "Pete here, he was a witness, too."

"Witness to what? What did you tell Ben Champion?"

"That I stole rifles from Farnham and Chandler back in '64. Mr. Lucas Errol paid me to do it." Prewett shifted in his chair and gave another wet cough. *Pneumonia?* Hanley wondered with a thrill of fear, then told himself not to be ridiculous. If Prewett had an infectious disease, Mr. Addison would hardly linger here, or be bringing him supper. "I was a damn fool back then. Figured the Secesh had a point. Why go to war to make a bunch of Negroes free? Next thing you know, they'd be coming here for land, thinking they should have it just like white men. Let the South mind its business and we mind ours, that's what I thought." He shrugged. "The money didn't come amiss, neither. Enough with what I'd saved from factory work to buy my own spread. My daddy worked in town, but I never cottoned to storekeeping. A man feels free on a farm."

"You worked at Farnham and Chandler during the Rebellion?"

Prewett nodded. "Packing rifles for shipment. Easy enough to fix the records, make sure four crates went missing. Me and Errol loaded 'em on a wagon late at night, hid 'em under straw bales. He said his friends'd use 'em to take over Chicago, give the whole city and its rail lines to the South, and end the war right quick." A coughing jag shook him, longer than the others. Addison got to his feet, but Prewett held out a hand as if to forestall him. When the handkerchief came away this time, Hanley saw a dark smudge on it.

"It didn't happen that way," he said quietly. "The guns were found and the plotters arrested. Most of them."

Prewett grabbed his flask and gulped water. "Not Errol, though," he said when he could speak again. "Bastard didn't pay me the rest of what he promised, neither. Took me five more years to save up for my land. Five years I didn't have to waste, turns out."

"I'm sorry," Hanley said, and meant it.

Prewett took a shallow breath. "I'm a sick man. Doc doesn't know what with, but he knows he can't cure me. When word got 'round a while back that Schuyler and Kelmansky were looking into bad guns from Farnham and Chandler, seemed like the Almighty was giving me a chance to tell the truth, make things right with Him before we meet. So I found Kelmansky, and I told, and then I told Schuyler and that Champion fellow." He gave Hanley a sad little smile. "And now I told you. You do something about it?"

Cautiously, Hanley nodded. "I will."

☓

It took some doing, but eventually he argued Addison into letting him go to Schuyler's rented room. The lock was cheap, easily jiggered by lantern light and the narrow blade of a well-placed table knife. Heedless of pain from the stab wound that made him grit his teeth every step of the way, he followed Addison inside, then leaned against the wall by the door and looked around. No quilt or blanket on the bed, only a single worn sheet. A cedar chest in the corner might once have held clothes. A shirt lay across it, crumpled as if thrown there.

Hanley nodded toward the chest. "Let's open it up."

Addison did as requested, then shone the lantern inside it. Nothing but a pair of old shoes with cracked uppers and a missing heel. The shirt, when Hanley examined it, had worn cuffs, and its collar had been turned at least twice. He glanced up, and in the ring of light spied a bare hook on the wall that should have held a winter coat—even Alton got cold sometimes. "Someone went through Schuyler's things," Hanley said. "Took his coat, any decent clothes he had—to keep, or maybe to sell."

Addison raised the lantern and shone it around the room. Its glow revealed a table a few feet away, bare except for a kerosene lamp and an inkwell, and a shelf on the east wall that held half a dozen books. "So what exactly are we looking for?"

Hanley moved to the bookshelf. "Prewett's statement. Hopefully, Schuyler didn't hide it in a coat or trouser pocket somewhere. Shine that light over here." The other man obliged, and Hanley read the few titles in Schuyler's library. A Holy Bible, a few novels, a book about river birds, a volume of Walt Whitman's poetry. He picked up the Bible and shook it gently, but no papers fell out. He did the same with the rest, but had no better luck.

Where was Prewett's statement? Schuyler had written another copy of it—Hanley would stake his life on it, damned near already had. Unless Errol *had* found it and disposed of it...no, he wouldn't let himself think that. He eyed the books again. Bible, bird book, three adventure novels, Whitman poems. Something about the Whitman... He gave it a closer look. It was cleaner than the other volumes, all of which bore a visibly thicker layer of dust.

He opened the Whitman and turned the pages slowly, running his fingers across each one and eyeing their top edges in the lantern light. Two pages near the middle were uncut. They felt thick, as if something lay between them. Hanley touched the bottom edge, felt the slit there, pried the gap wider and pulled out what was inside. He unfolded the thin sheaf of papers and held it close to the lantern. Clear, slightly cramped writing—Schuyler's?—leapt out at him from the top page.

April 20, 1872

I, Ernest Prewett, do solemnly swear before all men here present that the story I tell is a true and correct account of what I and Mr. Lucas Errol did on the night of October 28th, 1864.

Hanley looked at Addison. "When's the next train to Chicago?"

Addison frowned. "You shouldn't be traveling yet. That wound needs time to—"

"There isn't any time." Hanley closed the book and set it back in place. "I've got to get there as soon as I can. A man's life may be at stake."

FORTY-FOUR

April 30, 1872

Will hadn't slept well, and left his bed early Tuesday morning in no condition to report to work. He hoped they wouldn't miss him for one day. The Whittier mourning ring, and Dorrie's presence at Ben Champion's house, continued to plague him. When had she been there? How recently? Recently enough to have—

"Will?" Aunt Abigail's voice came with her gentle knock at his bedroom door. "Do you want eggs for breakfast?"

"I...I'm not feeling well." He thought of opening the door, but suddenly didn't want to see her, or anyone. "Don't worry, though. A little rest will set me right."

"I'll send Cook up with tea and toast," she said. He breathed easier at the sound of her moving away, her footsteps receding down the stairs.

Alone with his reflections again, he stared out his window at the flowering dogwood by the side of the house. He was mad to think what he was thinking. Eight years gone since that night in Tennessee, when Dorrie Whittier was the sole survivor of a Reb bushwhacker raid against Ben Champion's scouting party. Eight years since Ben in his rigid, righteous fury threatened and tormented the boy militia fighter he thought he'd captured. Awful as it was, surely Dorrie couldn't carry a killing grudge for all that time. Yet he couldn't get away from the plain fact that she shouldn't be here, in Chicago, at Ben's home. In what capacity—a neighbor's or friend's wife, or some sort of employee?

He couldn't imagine her as a hired girl, but the war might well account for such a reversal of fortune. Whatever the case, she would have known Ben the moment she laid eyes on him. Remembering the aftermath of the ambush in Tennessee, Will felt certain of that.

And the bayonet. One thrust, quick and hard and deep. A soldier's strike. Dorrie had been with Tom, who surely knew how to fight. Tom would have taught her everything, made certain she could fight like a man. She could have struck that blow. She likely had the knowledge and, once, she'd had the rage. Did she still?

His breath came faster, and his hands were less than steady when he accepted the tray of tea and toast their cook brought him. He should tell Hanley, leave word to get in touch as soon as he got back from Alton. But if Hanley looked into Dorrie Whittier, Will knew what else he would find.

He gulped tea, winced as the hot liquid burned his mouth. He couldn't risk it. He'd barely escaped the threat of that damned memoir, though in the last way he'd have wanted. To risk exposure again as what he truly was, was suicide, professional and personal. How many who now called him colleague or friend still would, if they knew?

From downstairs, he heard the front door open and Aunt Abigail exchanging pleasantries with the postman. The door closed, and he settled wearily against his pillows. He didn't want more tea, was in no mood to eat. All he wanted was blessed unconsciousness and for all this to be over when he woke up.

He heard Aunt Abigail climbing the stairs, and this time made himself answer her tap at his door. "This came for you," she said, holding out a small white envelope. "The postman found it in our box. Someone must have left it early this morning."

After she withdrew, with a soft admonition to eat his toast, he sat on the edge of his bed and eyed the envelope. It bore his name in an unfamiliar hand. No stamp or return address. He opened it and took out the sheet of paper inside. And then he briefly stopped breathing.

I know who you really are, the note said. *I will keep your secret for a price. Come to Union Park tomorrow at noon, where I will prove what I say and tell you what to do. If you don't come, everyone will know what I know.*

He clenched a fist around the note. His fingernails dug into his palm, but the pain barely registered against the terror that swamped him. Who wrote this? Who left it? Why now, after all these years?

Ben's memoir. He wasn't safe after all.

He had to tell Hanley. He couldn't tell Hanley. He sat with the crumpled paper in his hand, staring out the window, unable even to get up and throw the blackmail note away.

FORTY-FIVE

The midnight train from Alton reached Chicago early Tuesday afternoon, nowhere near soon enough to suit Hanley. If he could have, he'd have pushed the damned thing to go twice as fast the whole way. The train had barely stopped when he got to his feet, disembarked, and strode down the platform, ignoring the stab wound that throbbed above his hip, determined to reach Lake Street Station and Moore as fast as he could.

His second telegram, at least, should have gotten to his sergeant before he did. *Found proof Errol involved re rifles, 1864. Am bringing back, today 2 pm train. Pick up Errol if feasible.* The hotel owner, Addison, had promised to send it first thing Tuesday morning, and Hanley trusted his word. If Moore had acted on it, they should have a few hours to sweat Errol before his lawyer noticed his absence and did something about it.

"Detective," the desk sergeant called as Hanley charged through the station doors, but Hanley had no time for more than a wave of acknowledgment on his way down the hall to the holding cells. One of them was occupied, watched over by the familiar figure of Rolf Schmidt in his patrolman's blue.

Even before the man in the cell turned at the sound of Hanley's approach, Hanley took in the smoothly trimmed sandy hair and well-cut suit, and allowed himself the luxury of momentary relief. "Mr. Errol," he said. "Good of you to drop by."

☙

"I warned you." Errol stood with his hands in his pockets, glaring at Hanley across the few feet of space between them. "I told you at the Tremont to stop harassing me. You have no right to keep me in a damned jail cell." He turned toward Sergeant Moore, who had joined them not long after Hanley's own arrival. "I agreed to come here with you against my better judgment, sir. I don't know anything about that man you say was beaten the night before last, and I've no notion why you think I do. I certainly wasn't expecting this kind of treatment." He puffed himself up like an angry rooster. "I wish to contact my lawyer. *Now.*"

"When we're finished here," Moore said, smoothly but with a hint of steel. "My detective has a few questions first."

"Am I under arrest?"

For answer, Moore nodded toward Hanley. "Detective?"

"Show me your hands," Hanley said.

Errol's scowl deepened. "What? Why?"

"Show me your hands."

Errol yanked his hands free of his trouser pockets and thrust them toward Hanley. "Go ahead and look, much good may it do you. I've told you, I had nothing to do with your beating victim. I don't even know the fellow's name."

Errol's hands were smooth and pale, no bruising or other marks on them. Which meant only that he hadn't beaten Aaron bare-knuckled. Remembering the finicky way he'd handled his cutlery in the Tremont dining room, Hanley found that easy to believe. "He owns a walking stick," Moore said quietly. "Officer Schmidt collected it for examination."

"Oh, for God's sake," Errol muttered.

"Where were you on Sunday, Mr. Errol?" Hanley asked. "Say, from noon onward."

Errol gave an irritated sigh. "At Tremont House. I dined there at half past twelve. I left two hours later, for a walk. After that, I ate a light supper at Kinzie's Chop House and then spent time at some of your finer establishments where liquor and card games are purveyed, though I can't pinpoint every single one. Overindulgence in drink will do that, you understand. I'm not proud of it, but it's no crime. I returned to the hotel late. If you want to know precisely when, ask the night clerk. We exchanged greetings. Is that sufficient for you?"

"When did you reach Kinzie's?"

"Sometime after five, or maybe six. I don't recall the exact hour."

"So you can't say where you were between half past two and maybe six on Sunday?"

"I was walking. By the river and then down Pine Street, if I recall."

"All that way? For three hours? And with or without your walking stick?"

"Walking clears my head," Errol snapped. "I've had considerable difficulties to deal with lately, as you well know."

"Oh, we'll get to those. Did anyone see you on this ramble of yours? Anyone who might remember you from Adam?"

"I don't know."

"Well. That's a problem."

Errol folded his arms, reminding Hanley of a petulant schoolboy. "Yours. Not mine."

"I know what you wanted from Aaron Kelmansky," Hanley said. "We have the note you wrote, demanding Aaron meet you late Sunday afternoon. 'You have what I want,' it said. Is that why your crook of a lawyer paid to steal Ben Champion's papers on the Farnham lawsuit? Did the pair of you think you'd find the confession Champion went to Alton to get? Only it wasn't there, so you resorted to desperate measures against the only man within your reach who knew about it. Tell me, did you intend Mr. Kelmansky to die, or merely to be terrorized into silence?"

Errol blanched. "I don't know anyone named Kelmansky. Or anything about a confession. To what? What terrible crime am I supposed to have committed?"

"Murder, for one," Hanley said.

The man had the gall to smirk. "Of Ben Champion. You tried that one before, Detective. I'll say it again—I wasn't anywhere near Champion's house the night he died. Anyone who says I was is lying."

"Not Champion," Hanley said. "Or, not only him. I meant George Schuyler. He was killed in Alton a week ago Monday. The same night you led a party of night riders against Aaron Kelmansky's farm there. This past Sunday afternoon, you lured Kelmansky into an ambush through your note threatening his family. All three of these men—Champion, Schuyler, Kelmansky—have one thing in common. They know what you did back in '64. They know you arranged the theft of the rifles meant for the armed takeover of Chicago by the Rebel prisoners at Camp Douglas that year. You and your cronies meant to build a Northwest Confederacy around *my* city. Fortunately, you failed. But people's memories are still fresh, Lucas. A respectable businessman like yourself—you can't afford to be tied to that kind of scandal, especially with your court case pending about the exploding guns you sold to the Union army. If Ben Champion tied you to the Northwest Conspiracy, he'd have won that lawsuit in a walk. You'd be bankrupt, likely imprisoned, certainly ruined."

"You should write dime novels." Errol's smirk had a ragged edge. "That's quite a tale, if any of it were true."

"I went to Alton," Hanley said. "I met the man you paid to steal those rifles. I have his story, in writing and in here." He tapped his temple. "You can't bury it, Lucas, no matter how many people you harm. It's too late for that."

"I don't believe you." The smirk was gone now, Errol's hands flexing and clenching as if of their own volition.

"His name is Ern Prewett," Hanley said. "You promised to pay him for stealing those rifles, but you reneged on the deal. He's a bit bothered by that. Shall I describe him, or have you heard enough?"

Errol closed his eyes. He looked ill. "I wasn't at North May Street the night Champion died."

"Then where were you?"

He sagged against the bars. "Annie Stafford's bordello. I paid for a girl. Louisa, I think her name was. Annie will know."

FORTY-SIX

Y ou lied," Hanley said, glaring at Gentle Annie Stafford from the middle of her parlor.

She narrowed her eyes. "I did no such thing. If a customer doesn't want to give his name, I don't ask for it. You never told me what your man Errol looked like."

"My mistake."

The sarcasm in his voice bypassed Annie, or else she chose to ignore it. She turned toward the girl, eighteen at a guess and dainty as a butterfly, who'd come down to join them at her summons. "That's all. Go on back upstairs and get ready for the evening."

The girl gave Hanley a swift, worried glance. "I'm not in trouble, Mrs. Stafford?"

"Not a bit. I'm sure the police are grateful for your help." She shot Hanley a sidelong look as she patted the girl's shoulder. "Go on, now."

Hanley left soon afterward. The wound in his side ached like fury, and he knew he should rest, but he couldn't. Despite a powerful motive, Lucas Errol hadn't killed Ben Champion, and wouldn't have known who to hire to do it. Berwick knew, but hadn't done that, from what Hanley's informants told him. So where did that leave the case?

On impulse, he caught the nearest westbound horsecar and rode it to North May Street. Another look at the crime scene, another talk with Champion's neighbors—something had to shake loose. He'd missed something, or paid insufficient attention to something he'd already uncovered. Like who left the Thomashaws' house around ten last Tuesday night, or whose footsteps Mrs. Thomashaw had heard going by in the front. They'd happened close together, now he thought about it—the light, quick footsteps and the backdoor sound. The same person, or two people? Had one of them seen the other? He let out a frustrated sigh. The elder Thomashaws weren't likely to know any more than they'd already told him, and their hired woman Mary Olcott was on his suspect list. Getting the truth out of her would be no easy task, and he had nothing to work with. Not even Champion's memoir. The pages he'd found told him nothing about Mary's, or her brother's, past connection to the dead man that might give her motive for murder.

The sun was low when he reached North May Street. Eased somewhat by the horsecar ride, the throb in his side had lessened, and he found the walk to Champion's less of an ordeal than he'd expected. The curtains were still drawn across the front window, and weeds had sprouted near the bushes that flanked the porch. He could feel the emptiness of the place from partway down the walk, seeping outward like water from a slow leak.

He unlocked the front door and went in. Inside, silence lay thick as the dust. It wasn't hard to imagine Ben Champion's shade here, lingering until justice was done.

He shook off his morbid fancies and headed toward the staircase. As he reached it, a floorboard creaked. He held still, scarcely breathing, and listened. Nothing. Yet that creak hadn't come from beneath his own feet. It had come from behind him, from Champion's study.

He strode to the study door, opened it, and froze. Josiah Rushton stood by Champion's desk, one hand resting on an open drawer.

"Detective," Josiah said. Beneath his surface calm, Hanley saw fear.

"What are you doing here?" The question came out harshly. "How did you get in?"

"Through the back door." Josiah's hesitant smile held no warmth. "I had to break a windowpane, I'm afraid. Not sure who I'd pay damages to. Ben had no living family that I know of."

"You broke in here...for what?"

Josiah licked his lips. "I'd rather not say."

"You don't have that choice." Hanley gestured toward the door, keeping his hard gaze on Josiah so the man would know he meant business. "Come on. We're going to Lake Street Station."

"I wasn't there." Josiah stared at the squad room's far wall. The place was empty save for him and Hanley, though there was no telling how long that would last. "Whoever claims otherwise is mistaken."

Hanley leaned forward to look him in the eye. It was past seven now, and with no more supper than a biscuit sponged from a fellow detective, washed down with rotgut station coffee, he was out of what little patience he'd had.

"You were seen at Champion's house the night he was murdered. You made a bit of a ruckus. Called attention to yourself." Though as he said it, Hanley knew it might not be true. Alice Lockwood he believed now, at least about Josiah showing up in a state. But she'd said he left. Had he come back? Mrs. Thomashaw had heard footsteps, quick and light, going away from Champion's house around ten. But light footsteps didn't square with Josiah's solid, six-foot-plus frame. And Champion was stabbed to death half-dressed, just after he came through his bedroom door. What in the name of God would Josiah have been doing up there? Hanley grabbed his lukewarm coffee and took a swig, hoping the bitter taste might clear his brain.

Josiah let his head loll against the chair back. "I wasn't at Ben's. I went home at my usual time and stayed there."

"Was anyone home with you that evening? Your wife, or Will?"

"I didn't kill Ben," Josiah said, without opening his eyes. "As God is my witness."

His pallor worried Hanley, in spite of his anger with the man. "I'll have to book you for the breaking and entering."

"I know." Hanley was struck by his tone. He sounded too weary to care. "If I might write a note to my wife? I don't want Abigail to worry."

"Why were you there today, searching Champion's desk? What were you looking for?"

"I can't tell you."

"Why not?"

Josiah shook his head. "That note to my wife, please? It's getting late. She'll be home from the clinic soon."

"Clinic?"

"For the indigent. It's near Cook County Hospital. Will sometimes—" Josiah clamped his jaw shut, as if to swallow back whatever he'd meant to say.

Hanley frowned. "What about Will? What does he have to…" He trailed off. The Tremont House. The waiter. Ben Champion lunching there the Friday before his death. With Will Rushton. The waiter had heard Will's name, described him in detail. Captain Hickey's attempt to arrest Hanley, his escape from the paddy wagon, and then the trip to Alton and everything that happened there, had driven it from his mind. "Will met Ben Champion a few days before Champion died," he said. "At the Tremont. They argued. Will stalked out. But he told me he'd lost touch with Champion. Hadn't seen or heard from him in years, not since muster out in '65. He lied. And you…Will talked like you barely knew Champion, but that's not true." Mrs. Flynn's story came crowding into his brain—*Josiah Rushton and his missus were great friends with the captain's parents…took the captain on as a clerk right after that slave law went in.* "That's not true, and he must've known it. He's involved in this, isn't he? And you know how. What aren't you telling me? What were you after at Champion's house?"

Josiah stared past him out the window. Hanley counted heartbeats in the quiet. "My wife," Josiah said finally. "May I please send her word?"

Hanley let out a sharp sigh, yanked open his desk drawer and took out paper and pencil. "I'll ask Will myself," he said, eying Josiah narrowly as the man pulled the items toward him.

Josiah glanced up, paler than before. He looked about to speak, but then pressed his lips together and bent his head over the paper. He scrawled the note, folded it, and held it out to Hanley. "Let's get on with it."

☙

"If you can't put Josiah at Champion's house during the right hours, we've no reason to hold him for anything but today's break-in," Moore said when Hanley reached his office after formally booking Josiah Rushton and escorting him to a holding cell. They'd moved Lucas Errol out of it just a few hours before, transferring him to Union Street Station, whose captain could be trusted to keep an eye on him, with Captain Hickey none the wiser. "That he *could* have been there that night isn't enough. Can you *prove* he was there late Tuesday night or in the small hours of Wednesday morning?"

"No." Hanley scowled. He knew what Moore hadn't spelled out—a prominent citizen like Josiah, with a sterling reputation, couldn't be treated like a common criminal. They'd only managed it with Errol because he was from out of town. For Josiah there had to be proof, and it had to be solid. "My sole witness says he left before she did. I've only her word for any of it. And Champion died half-dressed in his bedroom."

Moore frowned. "That sounds like a woman. You're sure the killer was in the bedroom, and Champion was returning there?"

"Body position says so. And the body wasn't moved. Champion died where he fell." An image of the bayonet wound, oozing blood across the bedroom floor, made Hanley queasy. The thrust had gone straight to the heart. A vivid picture crossed his mind of a sergeant he'd known in the Twenty-Third Illinois, choking on his own blood in the aftermath of a bayonet charge. It troubled him that he couldn't recall the man's name.

"So what about the women?" Moore said. "You mentioned two. The neighbors' hired woman and Champion's secretary?"

"Alice Lockwood, yes. And Mary Olcott. Both Southerners come north looking for work. Miss Lockwood was Secesh, Miss Olcott a loyalist from northern Virginia. Or so she says, and it may be true. Miss Lockwood admitted to being there under questionable circumstances. Claims she left Champion alive."

"But a woman wouldn't handle a bayonet like a soldier."

"Nor would Josiah Rushton, come to that. He was too old to serve in the war. As far as I know, he was never a military man."

Moore frowned. "Why would Josiah—or either of the women—want Champion dead?"

Hanley shrugged. "Some reason I haven't dug up yet. Or maybe no reason at all because none of them killed him." He felt worn through, wanting nothing more than a hot meal and a long sleep. "So what do we do about Josiah? He sent a note to his wife. I expect she'll be here shortly."

Moore sighed. "Let her take him home. He'll keep for a few days—long enough to find proof he killed Champion, or figure out who did."

σβ

The desk sergeant stopped Hanley halfway to the stationhouse doors. "Got a message for you, Detective," he said as he rummaged through a drawer. "Been trying to give it to you since you got back. That girl left it—the little Jewish one from Market Street. She came looking for you yesterday afternoon." He unearthed a slip of paper and handed it over. Hanley took it, unsure whether the flutter in his gut was anxiety or anticipation.

"Thanks." He unfolded the paper, but didn't have time to read it before the front doors swung open. Will Rushton walked in, followed by a spare, sixtyish woman who was surely Josiah's wife, and a short bewhiskered fellow in a trim gray suit whose age and bearing shouted *lawyer.*

"We're here for my Uncle Josiah," Will said. "We've come to take him home."

FORTY-SEVEN

Arrangements were quickly made, surety given for Josiah's appearance at police court in two days for a hearing on the breaking and entering charge, and then the elder Rushtons left along with their legal counsel. Will made to follow, but Hanley held him back with a hand on his arm. "You and I have something to discuss."

"Not here." Will darted a glance toward the squad room, where the night shift was settling in. He looked as if he hadn't slept in a week. "Please."

"All right," Hanley said slowly. Lily Stemple's was closed by now. Where else could they go? "The evidence room should be private enough, if that's what you want."

Will looked as if he might protest, but then gave in. "That'll do."

They walked down the hall, Hanley letting Will take the lead so he could observe him unnoticed. Will moved like a man going to his own hanging. The tension in his shoulders could've cut cloth. How was he involved in this mess with Ben Champion? They'd served together, he'd said. Something from the war? Hanley thought of Champion's memoir, with its account of the unnamed soldier. *His persuasion*, Champion had written. *I tell his story to aid the cause for which we fought this terrible war.* Hanley had only guessed it on the way to Alton Sunday night, but now he felt certain. Champion's nameless soldier was a Negro passing for white. Maybe Will knew who the man was and had lied to shield him from exposure.

They reached the evidence room, with its stacks of boxes and pigeonhole cabinets running up every wall. Hanley saw Will glance around, saw his gaze alight briefly on a box tower to the left of the door. Then Will turned to face him, and there was no time to ponder anything except the first question in his mind. "You told me you lost touch with Ben Champion after muster out, seven years ago. But you lunched with him at Tremont House the Friday before he died. Or you started to. I'm informed there was a shouting match and you stormed out. You want to tell me what that was about?"

Several seconds passed before Will answered. "I was at Tremont House," he said finally. "But I prefer to keep my business there private."

"Don't be stupid," Hanley snapped. With effort, he reined in his temper, eying Will's face without further word. Will would know this tactic, of course. Keep quiet until the sheer weight of the silence forced him to speak. Recognizing it wouldn't help him, though. A trickle of sweat ran down Hanley's back, making his knife wound sting. The aftermath of last night in Alton and fatigue from the long train journey fueled simmering anger at Will for making Hanley treat a valued colleague like a suspect.

Will was looking everywhere but at him—at the towers of boxes, at the gaslights on the wall, at what little could be seen of the floorboards. The room smelled of dust and mice. The stationhouse needed a cat to keep after the vermin. Hanley kept watching Will, not shifting his gaze even a fraction, until Will finally spoke. "You know, for an Irishman you're damned good at not talking."

Hanley ignored the jibe. "What did Ben Champion say that made you storm out of the Tremont House dining room?"

"Nothing to do with his murder."

"I'll be the judge of that."

Will jammed his hands into his trouser pockets. "I don't care to discuss it."

"For God's sake, man! Do you *want* me to haul you to a jail cell? Because I will if that's what it takes. I don't give a damn if anyone else raises a fuss about it. You lied to me about a murder victim. Why?"

"Not so loud." Will's voice was tight, his breathing fast and shallow.

"Then *talk*. Tell me why you lied about when you last saw Ben

Champion." An awful idea crawled into his brain then, and he did his best to shut it out. He knew Will, trusted him, had worked with him since joining the police force after the war. Even a passing thought that he could commit murder was preposterous. And for what?

"I…" Will swallowed, not looking at Hanley. The gaslight cast patterns of light and shadow across his face. He drew in a breath, then another, mouth open like a beached fish. His expression rattled Hanley. The man was terrified. Because he *had* killed Champion…or he knew who had?

"Was it to do with Josiah?" Hanley said. Will's adoptive father, guilty after all. "Is that why you acted like they hardly knew each other? Or was it that Negro soldier Champion wrote about?" He paused, but Will's face showed no change. "I know Josiah handled fugitive slave cases before the war. I know Champion helped him—the man was his clerk at the time. I also know Josiah was part of the Underground Railroad. Does he know who that Negro soldier is? Did he tell you? Is the man here in Chicago? Is that what the argument was about?"

Will closed his eyes. "God help me, I can't," he murmured, as if he'd forgotten Hanley was in the room.

Hanley wanted to shake him. He moved close enough to see the sheen of sweat on Will's face. His pallor was noticeable even in the gaslight, despite the olive in his skin. Hanley found himself staring. Funny, the color hadn't really struck him before. And Will's hair, pure black and wavy. *His persuasion*, Hanley thought. *A medical student, quiet but with steady nerve. Brought to Illinois as a child…the Rushtons' nephew, adopted as their son…*

"My God." The words came out of their own accord. "It's you. You're the Negro soldier."

Will's headshake was barely perceptible. Denying Hanley's accusation? Or the fact that Hanley had made it, and the inescapable implications?

Will Rushton, a black man. Hanley felt dazed, like he'd gone five rounds with a bully boy in a saloon brawl. It couldn't be true. He *knew* Will. Trusted his judgment, liked him. They'd even had drinks together a time or two…He couldn't stop staring, looking for final proof in the planes of Will's face, the shape of his mouth, his nose…

He shook himself, took a deep breath and asked the last question he wanted to. "Where were you the night Ben Champion died?"

☙

The horsecar ride to the South Division took longer than Hanley remembered. Each minute felt like eternity crawling by. Will slumped next to him, staring out the dust-streaked window. Hanley wondered what he was seeing, or if he saw anything at all. How had *he* failed to see what Will was? He couldn't wrap his mind around it. Will's jokes about his Spanish mother, that dead-black wavy hair…of course he was mulatto. Hanley felt like a fool not to have recognized it before.

"I was at the clinic," Will had said before they embarked on this journey. "Aunt Abigail's, on Meagher Street. We dined at home with Uncle Josiah and then went to the clinic together. I was there until past eleven. She'll tell you."

"She would," Hanley said, and marched Will out of the station. Damned if he'd trust the man's word after what he'd learned tonight. All of it. "She thinks of herself as your mother."

Will bit back an angry retort, then slumped a little and walked on toward the horsecar stop. Hanley kept hold of his arm the whole way, and until the car came, only releasing him when they sat side by side on the hard wooden bench.

The end of the line stop at Meagher and Stewart, near a railroad crossing, lay just ahead now. Hanley pulled the bell cord and hauled Will upright. Will said nothing until they reached the boardwalk. Then, finally, he looked Hanley in the face. "I'm not going to run. There are no fugitive slave laws anymore."

"You lied to me. And you have one hell of a motive for murder."

"I'm not lying now. And I didn't kill Ben. Josiah didn't, either. There's someone else—"

"Who?" Hanley snapped. "You have a name, a description? Some actual proof?"

Will held his gaze a moment, then looked away. Silent, they crossed the empty tracks and headed up Meagher Street.

Even at this hour, the clinic was a busy place. Hanley questioned a doctor and some nurses about Will's presence on the night of Champion's murder. One nurse vouched for his being there when she left at half past eight. The doctor hadn't arrived until the following morning, but clearly recalled the case notes Will left him on several patients, including three new admissions from the Tuesday night in question. Neither he nor the nurse had any apparent suspicion that Will wasn't as white as they. With obvious reluctance, the doctor agreed to let Hanley speak to a few patients Will had tended. "But briefly, Detective. These are sick people, and I won't have them bothered more than necessary."

A young man with a broken leg—"Accident at a construction site," he told Hanley—recalled Will giving him pain medicine at half past ten. That let Will out as the person who'd passed by the Thomashaws' house on the night Champion died. A middle-aged woman with healing burns all down one arm recalled Will changing her bandages a little before eleven.

"Aunt Abigail and I left at eleven thirty and took the horsecar home," Will said. "We arrived home a bit after midnight." His tone turned bitter. "I'm sure you'll find a driver who can vouch for us both."

"And what difference would that make? I only have your word for the time of death. Who's to say you didn't lie about that to protect yourself? Or to protect Josiah. Or you might be mistaken."

Will's cheeks flushed. "You're questioning my *work*?"

"Why shouldn't I?" Hanley said. "Why shouldn't I question everything about you? You've gone to some lengths to hide what you really are, for years. The Rushtons did the same. What wouldn't Josiah do for you, if your secret was threatened? And Champion threatened it with his war memoir. That's what you quarreled about at Tremont House, wasn't it? That's why Josiah went to Champion's place last Tuesday night—to stop him by any means necessary."

"No," Will said. "Uncle Josiah wouldn't—even if he *did* go there, he would never—"

"Then who else did? Who else had a reason, aside from you? He *was* there. Alice Lockwood told the truth when she—"

"Alice Lockwood? Who's that?"

"Champion's secretary. It doesn't matter. What matters is that Josiah Rushton has no alibi, and the pair of you have every motive to—"

"What does she look like? Alice?"

Hanley stared at him. "Why in the name of heaven are you asking me that? If you think distraction will work with me, then you're a damned fool."

"Does she have blonde hair? With a little red in it? She's close to thirty years old?"

Visceral unease crept up Hanley's spine. "What do you care? Why—"

"Because I know her." Will swallowed hard. "I know her. At least, I'm pretty sure. If she's who I think…"

Hanley let out a breath of a laugh. "Nice try. I don't believe you. You're so used to lying, it must be second nature by now. Pretending to be white, fooling everyone—were you laughing at us behind our backs?"

"For God's sake, Hanley!" Will turned away from him, head and shoulders bowed as he struggled with his emotions. Abruptly, Hanley felt ashamed of himself.

"We may as well leave," he said, a touch more gently. "I'm finished here."

Will raised his head. "You want proof of who else could have killed Ben? A name, a description? I have them now. You gave them to me. Come with me and I'll show you."

FORTY-EIGHT

April 30–May 1, 1872

T his is damned irregular," Hanley said as he followed Will up the steps of the Rushtons' house. "I don't even know what I'm doing here."

"Finding Ben's killer." Light shone on them from an upstairs window, the elder Rushtons clearly not yet retired for the night. Will unlocked the door and they stepped inside. He led Hanley to a front room and turned on the gaslight. A study—Hanley saw bookshelves, a newspaper rack, three comfortable armchairs, and a heavy desk of carved dark wood.

Will strode to the desk and took something from a drawer. An envelope, Hanley saw when he held it out. "This came with the morning post," he said. "Not sent by it—there's no postmark or return address. Someone left it in our mailbox yesterday, after the second post came."

"And this mysterious 'someone' killed Champion? Is that what you're asking me to believe?"

"Read it. Believe your own eyes, if nothing else."

Hanley took the envelope. A white rectangle, the kind sold with common notepaper. *William Rushton* was written on it. The same graceful writing flowed across the single sheet inside. He frowned at it, nagged by a sense he'd seen the hand before. He read what was written there, then read it again. He felt Will's gaze on him and looked up to meet his eyes.

"I couldn't think who wrote it at first," Will said. "But then you mentioned Ben's secretary, Alice Lockwood, and—"

That was where he knew the handwriting from—Champion's discarded manuscript pages. He could see them in his mind's eye, almost as clearly as the blackmail note in his hand. Expansive script like Champion's own, but more delicate where his was bold. Part of Miss Lockwood's job was to copy what Champion wrote, make it neat enough to read over. "So she dropped this here, when, in the dead of night? But how did she know your name, and where you live? Ben Champion never identified that Negro soldier he wrote about. How would she connect him with you? And even if she did, how does that prove she killed Champion?" Though even as he said it, other thoughts filled his brain. Alice was there that night. He had only her word she'd left Champion alive. Again, he recalled Officer Schmidt's question—*Had a woman with him, maybe?* The killer was in Champion's bedroom, had gut stabbed him when he returned to it…

"She had reason. And she isn't Alice Lockwood. I can prove that, too." Will swallowed. "Tomorrow morning, in my office at the morgue. Early as you can. Bring that gold ring you found by Ben's front walk."

Ↄໄ

He was at the City Hospital, the ring and chain in his pocket, by seven o'clock the next morning. Will met him in the examining room. The man looked even more ill than he had the night before.

"Give me the ring," Will said, when Hanley had followed him into his office and shut the door behind them.

"No. I'll do it." Hanley moved over to where the microscope sat on a table against the wall. Brief embarrassment gripped him as he realized he wasn't sure where to put the ring in order to examine it. The flat surface beneath the viewing lens? He slid the ring off its chain and set it on what he hoped was the right spot, then put his eye to the viewing tube.

The ring was a bright gold blur. He found a knob on one side of the apparatus and fiddled with it. His second look showed an even fuzzier gold splotch. Impatient, he turned the knob in the opposite direction. This time, he saw nothing but blackness.

"You have to adjust it carefully." Will spoke with cold control. "If I may, Detective?"

Flushing slightly, Hanley stepped aside. He watched Will make several minute adjustments to the knob, which must focus the lens. His movements were precise and competent, everything Hanley was used to seeing from him. Up until yesterday, Hanley had taken that competence for granted.

Up until yesterday, Will Rushton was a white man, came the sneaking thought. Hanley twitched, casting it off like a horse ridding itself of a fly. He had every right to judge Will Rushton differently now. The man had lied to him, misrepresented himself to everyone. He turned away from Will, seeking distraction until the damned microscope was ready, and remembered Rivka's message. He'd shoved it in his coat pocket the other night and forgotten about it. Now he took it out and read it. *Dear Hanley, Aaron is awake and may be able to speak with you. Please come when you can.* She'd signed it with her given name. He lingered briefly over that, and over the salutation, taking an odd joy in both, even as he told himself she didn't mean anything by them. At least, anything more than trust in his ability to help her brother. He would go there as soon as he was done here, he promised himself, talk to Aaron if he could, and then—

"There." Will shifted position away from the microscope, but kept the ring at a slant with one hand. "You can read the inscription now."

Hanley bent over the eyepiece. The tiny curving lines on the inside of the ring that he hadn't been able to make out now appeared in sharp relief: *I Will Remember Her, A. W., E. W.*

"Alice Whittier," Will said quietly. "And Edward Whittier. They owned the plantation where I was born."

Hanley looked up, for the first time absorbing an inkling of what it meant that Will was a Negro. "You were a slave," he said after a pause.

"Yes. We escaped when I was ten, followed the Underground Railroad to Chicago. The Rushtons helped us settle in, kept tabs on us after my father died." Will moistened his lips. "My stepfather, I should say. He married my mother as soon as he was able, when we got here. Slave marriages weren't recognized in the South. Nor was my relationship to my actual father, though the slaves knew. And I knew. I'm certain Edward Whittier did as well." Color stained his cheeks, but he went on. "Whittier turned to my mother whenever his wife was…unable. That ring is his. He had it made up after his wife died in childbirth. Her last child was a daughter. Dorcas…Dorrie…Alice."

"Alice," Hanley murmured, then frowned. "But this still doesn't tell me why she'd murder Ben Champion."

"I don't know for certain myself," Will admitted, fresh anxiety on his face. "But they crossed paths during the war. She was a bushwhacker, dressed as a man and taken for one. They ambushed our scouting party one night. She was captured. Her brother, Tom, was killed. They shot one of our men dead, sorely wounded another, and Ben…" Revulsion flickered over his face. "Ben hurt her. Threatened her with hanging and cut her while she was helpless and bound. I didn't recognize her until later that night, and I…" He swallowed. "I let her go. Dropped water and hardtack by her feet, told myself if she got free before sunrise, I'd take it as a sign God didn't want her hanged as a Reb just yet. I never knew what happened to her, after. Until now."

Hanley thought of Alice's story—the seduction interrupted by Josiah's unexpected arrival, her fear for Champion's safety. Her insistence immediately afterward that she had to leave, not for her own sake, but for his. If this ring was hers—if she was who Will said she was—then why in the name of God would she allow the man to touch her who'd taken her captive and done her harm eight years before? Could she have been unaware of who he was? But no—she'd spent months working on his war memoir, which surely contained an account of the ambush Will spoke of. That, if not her own memory, would have told her.

What had he himself suggested, when he went to her lodgings on Robey Street and then questioned her in the park nearby? *Maybe you weren't willing*, he'd said. She'd reacted so strongly, he'd shut his questioning down. She'd already told him what he went there to ask, that she didn't have Champion's manuscript...

"The memoir," he breathed. "That's what Josiah was looking for."

"Yes. He didn't find it. He told me at breakfast."

"Miss Lockwood has it. Or wants you to think so—'I will prove what I say'?"

"That's what I'm afraid of."

FORTY-NINE

Through her bedroom window, Rivka eyed the morning sky. The patch of it she could see was free of clouds. Another sunny day ahead. She had slept like the dead until an hour ago, when dreams of breaking glass and fire woke her.

Efforts to fall back asleep were useless. Her mind would not be silent—random thoughts flew through it, swift as leaves on the breeze. Moishe, reaching for her outside Onkl Jacob's tailor shop. *There are other ways of being protected.* Aaron, pale and exhausted, drifting between sleep and wakefulness as Ada held his hand. Nat whittling at the kitchen table, his face set and his food untouched. The scrawled note that had lured Aaron into danger: *You have what I want...your family will pay.*

She shifted position, easing a cramp in her side. Hanley had not come yesterday in response to her message at Lake Street Station. Would he come today? Or was he still in Alton? She closed her eyes and murmured a prayer to Hashem, to keep him safe and bring him home soon.

Her eyes felt gritty. She closed them and breathed slowly, in and out, but couldn't escape the whirl of thoughts in her head. With a sharp sigh, she sat up. She might as well go and make breakfast.

She dressed, ran a brush through her hair and pinned it, then tied her kerchief on and left the bedroom. A brief look in Nat's room showed the boy curled in a ball under his quilt, eyes shut, breathing deeply. Across the hall, Aaron and Ada slept also, her dark head on his shoulder, one arm thrown across his chest. Ada's hair was down. Long black waves framed her face and spilled across her pillow. Aaron's hand was just visible against her back. Rivka's heart gave an extra beat. She felt awkward, and envious, and fiercely protective of them both.

She went downstairs, where she stirred up the fire in the stove, set water to boil for coffee, and then walked outside to their small chicken coop. Both hens had laid eggs. She slipped them out from under the birds, cradling them in her palm, and took a moment to gaze across the small yard toward the street beyond. She saw a milk wagon rattle past, heard the iceman calling out his wares. Another day, with who knew what would happen in it. She looked up at the pale blue overhead and whispered the *Shehecheyanu* prayer: "*Baruch atah Adonai, Eloheinu melech ha'olam, shehecheyanu, vekiyemanu, vehigianu lazman hazeh.*" *Blessed are You, the Lord our G-d, Ruler of the Universe, who has given us life, sustained us, and allowed us to reach this day.*

Back inside, she heard footsteps on the stairs. Nat appeared seconds later, his hair tousled and his eyes brimming with sleep. "I'm hungry," he said, as if that surprised him.

Rivka summoned up a smile. "Eggs for breakfast. And coffee should be ready soon."

"Okay." He gave her a shy smile in return and went out the back toward the outhouse.

She placed the eggs on the counter, took the dairy fry pan down, and set it on the stove. Both eggs plus some toast should fill the boy up. She cracked them into a bowl and beat them to a froth, fetched and sliced some bread, and was reaching for butter in the icebox when a knock came at the front door.

Hope fluttered in her chest. Was it Hanley? She hurried down the short hallway, wiping her hands on her skirt, and answered. A patrolman stood on the step, not one she knew by sight. He nodded to her. "Morning, miss. Detective Hanley sent me to bring you to Lake Street. Right away, he said."

"I..." She glanced back toward the kitchen, where she could just see Nat approaching through the partly open back door, then abandoned thoughts of breakfast. If Hanley needed her, she would go. "Of course." She took a moment to adjust her kerchief, then stepped out and closed the door behind her. "Did he say why?"

"No, miss. Just that it was urgent."

She nodded and followed him down the boardwalk. Hanley must have found something in Alton, maybe something about Lucas Errol that would put the man in prison. Aaron and his family would be safe then. He would want to tell her that right away. Though it seemed strange he hadn't come himself with such news. Didn't he want to know about Aaron, whether he'd said anything of who attacked him in the tavern yard Sunday night? Perhaps he preferred to ask her instead of troubling an injured man. Though it seemed unlike him not to question Aaron himself.

Doubt crept into her mind as she kept up with the patrolman. They were nearing the intersection, where a large vehicle loomed. Rectangular, enclosed on all sides. The horse between the shafts stamped, and she saw painted letters across the side—*Police Patrol.*

As they drew even with it, the patrolman grabbed her arm. She drew breath to cry out, but the wagon doors flew open and a pair of brawny arms pulled her up into it as the patrolman shoved her hard from behind. Her cry was lost in the depths of the wagon—gloomy and close, the only light and air coming from a small barred window high up on one side.

The wagon lurched, and she fell against the wall. She braced herself and looked up. A stranger sat on the wooden bench that ran along the rear of the wagon. Broader in the shoulder than Onkl Jacob, he had the look of a man who fought with his fists and enjoyed it. His hard-eyed smile made her afraid.

"Morning," he said, with a sardonic edge. "May as well have a seat. It'll be a long ride."

She clenched her fists in a vain attempt to keep fear at bay. "Who are you? Why am I here...what do you want with me?"

"Never mind the first. As to the second and third, let's just say you'll be enjoying my hospitality for the next little while."

FIFTY

oon, the blackmail letter had said. *At Union Park.* Before
accompanying Will and Josiah on what might yet prove a wild
goose chase, Hanley had one last vital question to ask.

He arrived at the Thomashaws' residence just before nine. The
sharp cries of a baby in distress carried all the way to the front porch.
As he reached the door, Oliver Thomashaw yanked it open and darted
out, his schoolbooks slung over his shoulder.

"I wouldn't go in if I was you," he said, in the world-weary tone
of a grown man. "Grant has an upset tummy again, and Janet spilled
her milk, and Rosemary broke the glass trying to clean it up, and I am
going to school right now." The boy clattered down the steps and was at the
end of the walk before Hanley could ask him where Mary Olcott was.

He went in and headed toward the kitchen, drawn by the sounds
of wailing and the harried voice of Mrs. Thomashaw failing to impose
order. "Janet, hush now...Rosemary, no, stay away from the glass, honey,
you'll cut yourself...Poor little mannie, now you just spit out that big
burp and you'll feel so much better...Janet, stop crying and get Mama
a cloth, for pity's sake!" As he strode into the room, Mrs. Thomashaw
looked up. Her hair was falling down and the buttons on her shirtwaist
were askew. "Detective! I'm sorry, this isn't a good time..."

He could see that. "Where's Mary?"

The baby screamed in his mother's ear. She flinched as she patted
his back. "Gone for the doctor. She should be back any minute—"

Footsteps sounded from the porch. He went into the hall and saw
Mary coming through the front door, followed by a round-faced elderly
man with a genial smile. She halted at the sight of Hanley. The doctor

stepped around her, nodded to him, and went toward the kitchen. Mary stood still as if frozen to the floor.

"Miss Olcott," Hanley said. "Did you go to Ben Champion's house the night he died?"

She didn't move, barely seemed to breathe. He thought of a deer going still at the scent of danger.

"I don't think you killed him," he said gently. "But I think you saw who did. Did you go there?"

She shifted her gaze to stare past him. Then, "Yes."

"What did you see? Starting when you went out your own back door late Tuesday night."

She glanced down, silent. When she looked back up, he saw anguish in her eyes. "I needed a breath of air. The baby'd been screaming so, and the house was in such an uproar…after we got things settled, I wanted a minute of quiet. Just a minute. I was looking toward Ben's place, to see if there was still light in his window—and I saw her."

"Who?"

"Miss Lockwood. I didn't see her face. But there's no one else it would've been. Crossing the porch, running down the steps…I went around by the side yard and saw her passing by this house and into the dark."

"And then?"

Her breath came faster. "It was late. She'd no call to be there. There was no light in Ben's window. The front door was ajar. I went inside, I called out—" She swallowed hard. "No one answered. I went through the house. And I found him. Upstairs. With that godawful thing sticking out of him." She closed her eyes. A tear slid down her cheek. "I came home after that. Didn't sleep all night. Then you came in the morning and took him away."

Blessed quiet descended on the hall as the baby's screams subsided to whimpers. "Why didn't you tell me before?"

"I was afraid you'd think I killed him." Her voice was steadier now. He sensed relief in her, as if she'd shed a burden. "When the first thing you asked me was if we'd had an *understanding*…" The last word came out with a harsh emphasis. "Woman scorned, you thought. And why shouldn't you?"

"And your brother, spying for the Union in Virginia?"

"I never blamed Ben for that. Daniel hated the war, said it was poor boys fighting and dying for rich men's good. He wasn't the only one who felt that way, even though plenty called him a traitor for it. He got up a company to keep us safe from the rebels. Our neighbors, people we'd called friends." She hitched in a breath and kept going. "Whenever Union troops came through, Daniel helped them hunt the raiders down. The Eighty-Second Illinois was in Loudoun County for weeks in '63, late winter and spring. That's when Daniel met Ben. Ben was hell bent on stopping the raiders from preying on us loyal folk. He hated them and wanted to save us. If he could do that, the whole county might go over to the Union side. Maybe even secede from the rest of Virginia. There was talk even then about the western counties breaking away. Plenty of folks in Loudoun County had no love of slavery. Daniel and Ben hoped they could bring us all over, to the side of right."

Her face crumpled, and she put a hand to her eyes. "They got Daniel one night. Then they came and burned us out. They shot my father down like a rabid dog. The rest of us ran. I made it to the Union camp, alone. My mother and my little sister didn't. Lord knows where they are now. I surely don't. Ben didn't, either. I came to Chicago because I hoped he could help me find them. He did what he could for me. Not his fault it wasn't what I wanted."

He felt sympathy for her, so much it almost hurt, and left for Robey Street feeling bruised of soul.

CB

Union Park, an oasis of green in this West Division neighborhood, was sparsely populated when Hanley, Will, and Josiah arrived half an hour before noon. A young mother or nanny strolled down the path that led into the park from Ashland Avenue, pushing a baby carriage, while a little boy of four or so gamboled just ahead of her. An elderly man sat in the middle of the park, facing a majestic oak tree, an artist's easel before him and a paintbrush in his hand. Across the park, two women walked with their heads bent together in conversation.

"Take that bench," Hanley said, nodding toward the one nearest where Alice—Dorrie—would likely enter the park. "I'll take the next one." He carried a folded newspaper under his arm and wore a suit and bowler hat borrowed from Josiah, who was a close enough fit to him for their purpose. "We'll see what happens at noon."

"Dorrie will come," Will said.

"You'd best hope." Hanley gave the Rushtons a terse nod and watched them take their seats, then moved off and made himself comfortable on his own chosen park bench. He turned to face partly away from Will and Josiah, but made sure he had a decent view.

Time passed slowly. Hanley read his newspaper, keeping it high enough to shield most of his face while permitting him a view of the street. At last he saw a slender figure in a dove-gray dress approaching, fair hair visible beneath her hat and something large in the crook of her arm.

She drew close to the bench where Will and Josiah were, near enough for him to see it *was* Alice Lockwood, and also to see the thick, blocky sheaf of papers she carried. Both the Rushtons stood. Neither offered her a hand, or made any other greeting. The three of them looked at each other, silent, the air charged as if this was some deadly serious contest, with the one who spoke first the loser.

Finally, Alice stirred. "Billy," she said, with a bare nod at Will.

He took his time answering her. "I don't use that name anymore."

"No. You're white now." A twisted smile crossed her face. "You've done well for yourself since you left us. You can keep it that way if you give me what I want."

"Which is?" Josiah asked.

"Cash money. One thousand dollars." At Will's gasp, she gave a bitter laugh. "Blood money. Five hundred for me and five hundred for Tom. The man who should pay for him, can't. He's already paid another way."

"Ben Champion," Will said. "You killed him. Why?"

She tilted her head, studied him as if making up her mind. "I don't have to answer to you," she said finally. "To either of you. But you did me a good turn years ago, Billy, and you were a brother to me once. I loved you back then, when I was a little girl. So I'll tell you."

She paused. Moving slowly, so as not to betray himself by a rustle of newspaper or cloth, Hanley inched closer on his bench.

"He did me wrong," she said softly. "He killed Tom. Hurt me. Humiliated me. That night in Tennessee, when Tom died…then again in Richmond, where I was barely surviving. He made sure I was thrown in prison for selling myself to Yankee soldiers. Robbing them too, or so he thought." Her voice hardened as it rose. "You Yankee bluecoats took everything from me. My home, my brother, the life I should have had. You didn't even leave me my pride. *He* didn't leave me my pride. Someone had to pay for that. And when God brought me to Captain Ebenezer Champion, all this time after, I knew he was that someone."

Her smile then chilled Hanley. "'Vengeance is mine, saith the Lord.' I know you read your Bible, Billy. You understand."

Hanley still didn't feel that *he* understood.

"Why didn't you kill him straight off?" Will asked. "Why work for him for months, first?"

"I wanted him helpless, like I was to him back then. I thought I'd play with him for a bit, see if he might remember me and what he'd done to me. But he never did, not till the very last moment. When he unbuttoned my dress he saw the scar from where he'd cut me. I knew then the time had come to end it all."

Hanley set down his paper and stood. "Alice Lockwood," he said as he crossed the few feet between them and gripped her by the arm. "You're under arrest for the murder of Ben Champion. I'll take you to the station now."

Shock crossed her face and she fought to pull away, but Hanley tightened his hold. "It's over," he said. "Let's go."

ോ

260

He gave Alice over to the custody of Captain Miller at Union Street Station, with instructions to convey her to the Armory jail as soon as was practical. Until he knew for certain where he stood with Captain Hickey, he had no intention of running his head into that particular noose. The woman seemed lost, unable to comprehend that her victory over Ben Champion—symbol of every Yankee who'd wronged her—had led to this. "I won't go to prison," she'd said to Hanley, the only time she spoke on their mostly silent trip to Union Street. "Someone will come for me. Joel will come. Tom will. Or Billy." She'd turned and grabbed his wrist then, her voice as imperious as a queen's. "Tell Billy he's to come. He's to bring me home."

Quiet pity for her made him promise, though he'd little intention of keeping his word. He left her with Captain Miller's men and turned his steps toward Lake Street to report the case's conclusion to Sergeant Moore.

He was waiting at an intersection for cart traffic to pass when someone jostled him from behind. He looked up, an angry remark on his lips that died when the fellow next to him spoke. "You're Hanley," he said, with an edge of contempt. "Mike Hickey said to tell you, come by the rail line at Twelfth and Clark tonight. Nine o'clock. He's got something you want. You and him got business to discuss."

Hanley's mouth went dry. *Mam*, he thought. *Kate*. Then, *Why? Because I gave him the slip? For Berwick and his damned client Errol?* "Mike Hickey and I have no *business* that interests me. And you tell him, if he so much as thinks of harming my family, I'll—"

The fellow's snort of laughter cut him off. "You just be there. And bring them papers. He said you'd know which ones. He'll trade. Don't go to your boss or anyone else for help. If you do, Hickey'll hear of it. Do as you're told and no one has to die."

FIFTY-ONE

The rain that had threatened all day began to fall as Hanley set out for the desolate ground by the rail line at Twelfth and Clark. God, was it only Sunday night he'd been there with Rivka and a squad from Lake Street, looking for Aaron Kelmansky? The thought of Rivka squeezed his heart like a vise. Mam, when he'd arrived at their boardinghouse that afternoon half mad with fear for her, was perfectly fine—as was Kate, he learned when he hurried to the house where she worked for a family named Langley. No, Kate told him, no one had come with a message for her, or disturbed her in the slightest. "What's this about, Frank? Is it your murder case?"

"Yes." He gave no details, simply warned her to be extra watchful and hurried away.

His next stop was Market Street, where he found the Kelmansky household in an uproar. Rivka had been missing since early morning—the mulatto boy, Nat, reported that she was about to cook breakfast when he roused himself a little after seven, but he'd seen her leaving hastily with "a fella in blue clothes, looked like a policeman" when he came back from the outhouse. Hanley knew then what Hickey had to "trade," and the knowledge made him sick inside.

Jacob Nathan had set men to scouring the neighborhood for her, some even going to the area around Twelfth and Clark, but the waste ground around the tracks and the defunct switching tower was deserted. Aaron, unwise enough to leave his sickbed and attempt to join the search parties, hadn't made it farther than the bottom of the staircase. "Find her," he'd begged Hanley, pale and exhausted with effort, anger and panic in his eyes. "Lucas Errol, or someone helping him, took her because of you, because he found out somehow that she helped you with your damned investigation. Or it's because of me. Or both of us. I don't know. Just find her and bring her home alive and well. If she's harmed, it's on your head."

"On yours as well," Hanley snapped back, before common decency told him to rein in his temper. "If you'd told me the whole truth sooner, it's a good bet this wouldn't have happened."

She wasn't at the Armory, either. Hanley went there, prepared to tear the place apart until he found her and damn what Mike Hickey might do about it, but she hadn't been thrown in with the women prisoners, and there was no place else for her to be. He couldn't go to Moore, couldn't risk Hickey finding out about it and doing Rivka some harm. Where the devil could the man be keeping her? And why? Surely not for Lucas Errol, even as a favor to his friend Berwick. But what in God's name else explained it? He couldn't puzzle it out now, couldn't muster the focus necessary to think it through. All he wanted was Mike Hickey in front of him, helpless while Hanley pounded him to pieces. *When it's over,* he promised himself, as cold rage and fear beat in the blood at his temples. *When she's safe, I'll bring him down.*

The rest of the day was torture. None of his informants were the slightest use, either ignorant of Rivka's whereabouts or pretending to be because Mike Hickey frightened them more than Hanley did. Around six he took off for the lakeside and spent a fruitless hour searching amid the warehouses and docks for some out-of-the-way corner where Rivka might be held, but found no trace of her.

Now, as nine o'clock approached and a rising wind spattered rain in his face, he hurried toward the appointed meeting place. Ern Prewett's confession—this had to be about Errol, why else would Hickey have wanted that?—was folded and tucked into his coat pocket. He'd no intention of giving it over, but he'd produce it if the bastard demanded to see it. He wasn't used to praying, wasn't even certain he believed in God. But as he crossed Clark and felt the damp soil of the riverbank under his feet, made damper still by the rain, he found the first lines of the Lord's Prayer running through his mind—*Our Father, who art in Heaven, hallowed be Thy name...*

"That's far enough." The voice out of the darkness halted him in his tracks. "If you were fool enough to come armed, don't even think about it. I've a pistol to this pretty girl's head, and even if you hit me with a lucky shot, I'll still pull the trigger."

Hanley gritted his teeth. Standing in the faint spill from the streetlights a few yards away, he felt exposed and vulnerable. "What do you want, Mike?"

"*Captain* to you. Did you bring it?"

"The confession about the stolen guns? Yes."

"Show me."

Slowly, Hanley pulled out the folded papers and held them up. "Now you show me Miss Kelmansky. Unharmed."

Captain Hickey chuckled. "Fair enough." Hanley heard a boot scrape against loose gravel. Ahead, about ten yards away, two indistinct figures stepped out from behind the rundown switch tower into the scant light. One was unmistakably female, bent from the waist up at an awkward angle, held close to Hickey's chest. "Tell the man you're fine, girl," he said. "Tell him I haven't hurt you. Yet."

Rivka spoke next, with shaky bravado. "I am all right."

"And he's to do as I say."

"And you...must *not* do as he says, Aaron told me ev—" Her words vanished in a yelp of pain.

"Try something like that again, I'll break your arm and then shoot you," Hickey growled. "I'm sending someone to take those papers, Francis. Once you give them to him, I'll release the girl."

"Like hell you will." Hanley took a step closer. If he could just get near enough to Hickey to charge him... "I give you this, I'm dead and so is your hostage. What's it to be, Mike—will I die defending her virtue from some unknown, escaped attacker, or will some vanished miscreant murder us both for the money we haven't got in our pockets?"

"I'd rather not kill you, Francis. Unless you make me." Captain Hickey sounded offhand now—he could have been chatting about horses at the racetrack, or how soon they'd next see fine weather. "You're smart and persistent, two qualities I can use. Trouble is, you don't know which side your bread's buttered on. That's where Miss Kelmansky comes in." He paused, and Hanley took another cautious step forward. "I don't know what your interest is in her, though I can guess." That last came in a leering tone that made Hanley want to strangle the man. "But she's been by Lake Street often enough looking for you, and was last winter when you investigated her father's death—and you have a bent toward rescuing innocents. That's inconvenient, Francis. You'll have to give that up once you work for me."

"And why would I do that?" Another step forward. He was close enough now to make out the pistol, its barrel pressed to Rivka's head.

"Stop right there," Hickey snapped. *Damn.* "I'll tell you why," he continued, more casually. "Because your good behavior will be surety for Miss Kelmansky's life. Possibly her brother's life as well—though that'll be up to Mr. Berwick." He nodded toward his left, and Berwick stepped out of the inky shadows. "Get the confession, Clement. That'll take care of your worries about Errol. He won't say anything once he knows he's safe."

Safe... Light dawned in Hanley's brain. Ern Prewett and Lucas Errol had stolen the rifles and transported them to Chicago—but who'd received the stolen goods? "You were the pickup men," Hanley said. "The pair of you. Your friend Berwick damned near got caught when the police raided that barn and found the guns back in '64. Where were you that day, Mike? With the police, pretending you weren't involved up to your neck in the conspiracy?"

"I knew you were smart," Captain Hickey said. Berwick was moving toward Hanley now, grinning with satisfaction. Hanley shoved the papers into his pocket and stepped back.

"Don't play the hero, Francis—"

The rest of what he meant to say was drowned out by Rivka's voice. "*Yitgadal veyitkadash shemei raba bealma divera chirutei...*"

"Shut up!" Captain Hickey shifted his grip to strike her, then gave a yell. Rivka threw herself to one side as the gun went off.

Something struck Hanley's shoulder with the force of a mule kick. He staggered backward, kept his footing, ignored the fierce burn from the bullet and charged. He crashed into Hickey, sending them both sprawling. The pistol flew high and landed somewhere in the dark.

Captain Hickey roared and bucked, then struck a blow to Hanley's injured shoulder that left him dizzied with pain. Hanley held on as hard as he could, but another shove flipped him off Hickey and onto the wet ground. He spat out mud and rainwater, grabbed at the man and pulled him back down. A kick at his midsection made him gasp for air, but he held on and managed to grab Captain Hickey's flailing arm. Where the hell was Berwick? Any second Hanley expected a second assault. His back muscles crawled as he hung onto Hickey's shirt, lashing out with his feet and landing a few solid kicks as payment for the punches that rained down on him. His wounded shoulder burned like fire.

He heard a scream from Rivka, the solid *thunk* of what sounded like wood striking flesh, and a *whuff* as a body hit the ground. A jolt of fear and fury gave him new strength. He bunched Mike Hickey's shirt in his right hand and aimed a wicked left cross at his jaw. The blow connected, sending the bastard flat to the dirt. Hanley staggered upright, searching desperately for the gun. Something glinted in the mud where the ground sloped to the river. Hanley threw himself toward it. Captain Hickey tackled him, clawing at his outstretched hand. He made a fist and struck out across the dirt. Their joined arms knocked the gun down the slope and into the fast-moving water.

Hickey swore and fought free, then staggered to his feet. Hanley pulled himself up and called out, keeping his voice steady with effort, hoping against hope for a reply. "Rivka?"

"Here," she answered. "I am all right. Not so much *him*." The final word carried a hint of triumph, audible beneath the quaver in her voice.

Fierce pride in her flooded through Hanley along with a wave of relief. "It's you and me now, Mike—no hostage, no gun, no strings to pull or judges to bribe. Care to see who wins?"

Incredibly, the man laughed. "I do, Francis. I always do. If you think this is over, you really *are* a fool."

Hanley braced himself, expecting a charge, but Captain Hickey turned and vanished into the darkness. Unsettled, Hanley stared after him. His shoulder throbbed, he could feel spreading wetness down his shirtsleeve, and Rivka was… He turned as she came up beside him, a length of scrap lumber in her hand.

"Are you all right?" she said, before Hanley could muster a word. "Did he hurt you?"

"Not much," he lied, and nodded toward the chunk of wood. "You hit Berwick?"

"As hard as I could. Across the face. He went down. I knocked him out." She sounded dazed, and passed an arm across her forehead as if wiping away sweat. A sudden need to hold her, reassure himself she really was whole and breathing, made him dizzy. Or maybe it was the shoulder wound. No telling how bad it was. He stumbled forward and sank to one knee.

"You *are* hurt!" She grabbed at his shoulders to keep him upright. He cried out at her touch near his injury, then pulled her to him in a rough embrace. "The gunshot," she said, muffled against his uninjured side. "We have to go, we have to get you to a doctor—"

"Never mind it yet." She was right, but so long as he could hold her, he didn't care a damn about anything else.

FIFTY-TWO

Y ou're joking." His shoulder bandaged where the bullet had scored it and his arm in a sling, Hanley sat in the boardinghouse parlor, staring at Sergeant Moore in stark dismay. "Please tell me you're joking. After all that, there's *nothing* we can do?"

Moore looked grimmer than Hanley had ever seen him. "Mike Hickey is damned well connected. They couldn't lay a finger on him for that bail-bond racket he ran during the war, and back then they had a lot more to go on. We have you and Miss Kelmansky. Berwick isn't saying a word, even from his jail cell. She can't name the patrolman who lured her from home, and no one's found a man of his description on the force. She never saw who drove the paddy wagon, and all the known drivers that day swear up and down they never saw a girl being taken. Captain Hickey's got half a dozen men who vouched for his presence at the Armory all day, going over paperwork, inspecting the jail cells, and whatever else he claims he was doing while Miss Kelmansky was being snatched and held."

Hanley clenched a fist against the sofa arm. "They're lying."

"I know that. You know that. Proving it?" Moore shook his head. "Then there's the bad blood between you and Captain Hickey, which makes your word suspect when it comes to him, and—"

"But Rivka." The desperate note in his voice made him cringe. "She can describe Mike Hickey down to the last hair on his miserable head. How would she know that if she hadn't been face to face with him? And where is she supposed to have been all that time? Doesn't that count for anything?"

"Rivka Kelmansky owes you," Moore said gently. "Mike Hickey will claim you persuaded her to lie, told her Lord knows what tale about him and played on her gratitude for solving her father's murder. He'll make a fool of her, and of you as well."

"Lucas Errol, then." He loathed the thought of being beholden to the man, but Errol was the last card he had to play. "He can swear to Hickey and Berwick receiving the stolen guns. Dahlia Ford might testify about the American Knights at her brothel that July—she hates Mike Hickey, she..." He trailed off as he saw Moore shaking his head. "What?"

"Lucas Errol is dead," Moore said. "Knifed in his cell last night. His body was found this morning. No one knows anything about it, of course."

Hanley slumped where he sat, chilled despite the warm spring air wafting through the open windows. "So that's what he meant," he said numbly. *If you think this is over...* "Mike Hickey's off scot free, he can do what he likes to me. To Rivka, to her brother and his family—"

"No," Moore said. "The Kelmanskys are safe. Lucas Errol is dead, Berwick's behind bars, and Mike Hickey doesn't dare go after them. Right now, he can talk his way out of any case we try to make against him. But if he harms the Kelmanskys, and rumors get around as to why, people will wonder. He can't afford that. Likewise if he moves too openly against you. He's a cautious bastard, never moves unless he's sure of the outcome. As things are, he won't risk it. You'll need to watch yourself, but—"

"I'm used to that by now." The words lay bitter on Hanley's tongue. "Stalemate. Does it never end? When do I get to stop watching my back?"

"When you stop fighting them." Moore laid a hand on Hanley's good arm and gave it a little shake. "Which for all our sakes, I hope you never do."

CB

Five days later, with his shoulder on the mend, Hanley made his way to Market Street. He hoped Rivka would be there, not out on some errand or with her students or a friend. He wasn't entirely sure she'd want to see him after everything that had happened, especially that night by the river and the tracks. Often over the past week he'd woken from dreams of her, warm and soft against him. Not thoughts he should be having, maybe not thoughts she'd welcome if she knew of them. Still, when he remembered how she'd stayed in the circle of his arms, he couldn't suppress a glimmer of hope.

Ada answered his knock. "Rivka's out back, planting," she said.

He nodded, suddenly nervous at the prospect of seeing her. "I'd like to talk to Aaron, if he's up to visitors."

"All right. But don't tire him." She stepped back to let him enter.

As he passed her, he recalled his other errand here. "You'll be having another visitor sometime this afternoon," he said. "Will Rushton. Your brother. I told him you're here in the city, where to find you. He asked me to tell you he'd come. I gather you'll have a lot to say to each other."

The sudden fear in her face made him flinch. "You know," she said, her voice low and trembling. "What will you do about it?"

"Nothing," he said, and to his surprise found it was true. "Nothing to hurt him." As to their professional relationship—their friendship, if he was honest—he hadn't decided. The only thing that had truly changed was Hanley's knowledge of what Will had kept hidden from him. Part of him was angry that Will hadn't trusted him, though he knew that was unreasonable. As to the rest—what Will *was*—he still hadn't made sense of what it meant or how he felt about it. "I won't ruin a man I've called a friend. For what?"

"Do you still?" Ada asked. "Call him a friend?"

"I'm thinking on that."

CS

Aaron was sitting up in bed, reading. He looked washed out, but better than the last time Hanley'd seen him, haggard with fear for his sister. He set down the book as Hanley reached him. "Detective," he said, with a look of wary surprise.

Hanley settled in the chair near the bedside. "Lucas Errol won't be making any trouble for you," he said. "Nor will his lawyer. Clement Berwick pleaded guilty to theft of papers relating to the Farnham and Chandler lawsuit. Turns out he was involved with those stolen rifles back in '64, one of two conspirators who got away after the police raid when the guns were found. My sergeant remembers him, and was quite persuasive about the theft charge. He'll do time for it. You and your family should be safe now."

"And Errol? What of him?"

Hanley drew in a breath. "Errol's dead. No one knows much about it, I'm afraid."

Aaron gave him a long look, then nodded. "I suppose I should thank you for saving my sister. Will anything be done about what happened to her? Will her kidnapper be brought to trial?"

Hanley shrugged. He felt uncomfortable lying, even by omission, but the less the man knew, the better—at least for now, while he was still recovering. "Berwick was involved, though we can't prove it. The document theft, we *can* prove. As to anyone else..." He trailed off, an unspoken message to drop the subject that he hoped Aaron would heed. "I'm sorry to tell you, George Schuyler is dead, too." Swiftly and succinctly, he related everything he'd discovered in Alton. "The local police think it was a street crime, and with Lucas Errol gone, there's nothing to pursue in any case. The same goes for your friend Joseph Levin, who died in the night riders' assault."

Aaron stared into space. Hanley wondered what he was seeing. "Joseph had family in New York," Aaron said. "He and an older brother came here before the war to open a clothing store. The brother was stabbed to death for the payroll money in his pocket." He closed the book, and Hanley watched his thin fingers play across its spine. "I'll write them. They'll want to know."

CB

He found Rivka in the yard behind the house, digging a shallow trench with a trowel in a rectangle of freshly turned earth. For a few moments he stood and watched her. She dug with energy, each motion strong and precise. The sun struck auburn highlights from a narrow strip of dark hair where her kerchief had slid back. A dirt smudge decorated one cheek, and her blouse was damp with sweat. Hard at work and oblivious of his presence, she was the most beautiful thing in the world to him.

That realization made him feel as if the ground had dropped from under his feet. She laid down the trowel, raised an arm to wipe her forehead, and saw him.

Caught. He made himself walk over to her, despite the nagging fear of tripping over his own feet. As he drew nearer, he saw a small seed pouch hanging from her slim waist. He nodded toward it. "What are you planting?"

"Carrots." She dug into the pouch and carefully dropped seeds into the row. "The ash leaves are big enough now. It's a good time."

He felt like a fool, looming over her. He leaned over and brushed a hand across the nearby grass. It felt dry. He sat awkwardly beside her, keeping a couple of feet between them. "Aaron looks well. I told him Berwick and Errol will be no trouble anymore." He chose to say nothing of Errol's death, leave that for another time, or for Aaron to tell her. Today, this moment, Hanley didn't want to talk of murder or violence. He had a far different question on his mind, had gone back and forth about it for the past couple of days, ever since Detective Sam McGregor had announced his retirement. Finally, he'd worked up the nerve. The worst she could do was say no.

She stopped sowing and looked up at him. "And the police captain who kidnapped me? What about him?"

He sighed. "That's trickier. He'll leave you alone—I'll see to that— but there's nothing we can prove. He has…connections, and he'll use them to save his own skin."

"I don't understand."

The bewilderment in her voice hurt to hear. How could he begin to explain the reality of pull, that who you knew and what you had on them often mattered more than justice? "I pray God you never do," he said softly.

He felt her gaze on him, but couldn't bring himself to look at her. Condemnation, or even disillusionment, in her eyes would be more than he could bear. He'd been a fool to see her, to think of speaking to her. He should leave things be. *Coward.*

He shifted his weight, ready to get up and leave, when he felt her light touch on his wrist. "It isn't your fault," she said. "I do understand that much."

He dared a glance at her then, and for a moment couldn't look away. Blushing faintly, she moved her hand and returned her attention to the carrots.

New hope flared inside him. "I wondered..." He had no idea how to ask this. He felt awkward in a way he hadn't since he was seventeen. Thank God he was still sitting down, or he'd start pacing, and then he *would* stumble over his own feet. The words he'd practiced went right out of his head. Everything came out in a rush. "Sam MacGregor's retiring. Colleague of mine. Taught me the ropes of police work when I was green as this grass. We're having a ceilidh for him—a dance—this Saturday night. Over on West Monroe. There's a hall right off Desplaines Street, two doors from the corner. Eight o'clock, it starts. Would you come, then, if I asked you?" God, he sounded like a stumble-tongued country boy. He could question a suspect or a witness smooth as butter, yet now he could only fumble and stammer. "I mean, I *am* asking. Will you come?"

She'd gone still, one hand gripping the seed pouch, her attention fixed on the soil as if the answer to some mystery lay there. "No," she said, barely above a whisper. "I can't. I'm sorry."

He'd distressed her. Transgressed, crossed a boundary he wasn't meant to. *It's only a dance, for God's sake,* he thought, but he knew it was more. She knew it too, or guessed. And wasn't happy in the knowledge.

The sunny yard felt too warm, too bright. A puff of wind brought the smell of horse, and the sound of hoofbeats and wagon wheels, from the distant street. He hauled himself up. "Of course. I just thought... never mind. Doesn't matter." He'd gained his feet. He could go anytime. Instead he lingered, hoping for...he didn't know what.

She still wouldn't look at him. He shook his head at his own damned foolishness, turned and hurried away.

FIFTY-THREE

The afternoon was getting on when Will arrived at the little frame house on Market Street. It took as much courage as facing a barrage of Rebel fire for him to knock on the front door, nod a greeting to the young woman who answered it, ask for Ada, and walk into the small front parlor where his sister sat waiting.

He watched her in silence as she rose from the sofa. She'd dressed as if for church or some other special occasion, in a dark blue calico dress with a lace collar that set off the golden brown of her skin. *Did she make the lace herself?* he wondered. Even as a girl, before she was sold away, she'd been good at things like that.

God, what a fool he was. Thinking about lace when Ada stood right in front of him, a look in her eyes as if she hungered to embrace him, and to give him a piece of her mind at the same time. She said not a word, clearly waiting for him to speak. To set the terms of this reunion, just as he had when he'd first found her after the war's end seven years before.

He cleared his throat. "Ada," he said, and suddenly couldn't manage any more.

"Will." She spoke his name as if it felt unfamiliar on her lips. "It's Will now, isn't it? Not Billy. Not for a long time."

"And do you blame me for that?" He heard the ragged note in his voice, but couldn't curb it. "The way things were, the way they *are*...my God, you know it better than I do."

"I don't blame you. Not like I did then, when you first admitted—" She broke off, moved aimlessly away from the sofa. "It doesn't matter. You made your choice years ago."

274

"The Rushtons took me in," he said softly. "Josiah and Abigail. Mother agreed to it. I was thirteen, I'd grown to love this city and my schooling and the future I thought I could grasp. I didn't want to run away to Canada, be a farm boy in yet another new place. A new country, yet. I wanted to stay, to study, to be a doctor. I *am* a doctor. That damned 1850 slave law would've taken that away. Taken everything I wanted, if it weren't for Josiah and Abigail Rushton, and our mother…" His breath caught. "And Ben. Ben Champion was Josiah's clerk then. He helped draw up the papers so they could adopt me."

"As a white boy."

"Yes. To keep me safe from the slave-catchers. There wasn't any other way."

She made no answer, but he had the sense she was turning his words over in her mind. "We got burned out," she said at length. "Aaron and Nat and I. In Virginia, not long after the war ended. Then again in Alton. I'd have given a lot to be safe either time."

Until he breathed again, he hadn't realized he'd stopped. He moved toward her, with a cautious nod at the sofa. "Tell me about Aaron. And Nat, tell me about him. My God, he was so little when I first saw him. He must be nearly a grown man by now."

She managed a smile, her eyes bright with unshed tears. "Oh, Billy. We have such a lot to talk on, you and I."

ꕥ

The next morning found him at the Union Street police station. The jail there had a sour smell, equal parts musty damp, old sweat, and fear. The odor made Will's stomach tighten as he descended the short flight of steps to the half-basement level where the holding cells were. For some they were temporary quarters—where drunks dried out, or doers of petty wrongs who could afford bail waited just long enough for family or friends to arrive with it. The rest lingered here until space opened up at the larger and more permanent Armory Jail, where accused criminals stayed until arraignment and trial. After that, most likely a prison cell…

or the rope. That last thought made Will shudder. He didn't want to be here, wished he could turn around and run back outside. But he kept going, driven by a sense of duty, or pity. He didn't understand it, but he couldn't gainsay it, either.

"Your girl's over there." The guard nodded toward the third cell in the row of five. "They're taking her to the Armory later today. It true she killed a man? With a bayonet?"

"Yes." Will didn't care to say more. He thanked the guard and slipped him a coin for his trouble. The man's retreating footsteps faded as Will approached Dorrie's cell.

She was in the same pale gray dress she'd worn the day of her arrest at Union Park, though now it looked dirty and slept in. Her hair had slipped from some of its pins, and was dull and greasy from lack of washing. She turned at his approach, and for a moment looked blank. Then she drew herself up, proud as a fine lady at a church social. "High time, Billy," she said. "I've been waiting here long enough. You tell them you've come to take me home."

Did she know where she was, let alone what awaited her? Or had she retreated into a world of memory mixed with fantasy? A mad impulse to laugh, or cry, or both, burned in his throat. All those years ago, he'd acted to save her from hanging by the Union army—and now here she was, near certain to hang for murder. Guilt swept through him, sudden and fierce. *I'm sorry, Ben. It's as much my fault as hers you're dead.*

Abruptly, he knew why he'd come. To say goodbye. Not to the Dorrie who'd fought as a bushwhacker, nor yet to Alice Lockwood. To the little girl he still remembered, if she existed anywhere inside the woman who faced him from this dank cell.

"I saw Ada yesterday," he said softly. "You remember her? My sister. Your half sister. She was twelve, last you knew her. Used to watch out for us younger ones."

She blinked. "I don't know who you mean. I want to go home."

He shook his head. "That won't happen."

Bewilderment crossed her face. "Why not?"

"Why not?" Unexpected anger gripped him, his emotions shifting like Lake Michigan surf in a storm. "You can't tell me you don't know. You killed Ben Champion, tried to blackmail me and my Uncle Josiah. What did you think would happen?"

Her eyes narrowed. "Champion deserved it. And you…you and your 'uncle'…he came to Champion's house while I was there. A Saturday, it was. I told the detective it was the day Champion died, but it wasn't. It was earlier. They went outside to talk so I wouldn't hear, but I listened anyway. He begged that man to stop what he was doing, not to publish the war memoir. He'd have done anything to keep your secret." She gripped the bars, white-knuckled. "Even that, you have—and I've lost. Someone to protect you and care for you. A family, a home, a place. You have everything. I have nothing." She fell silent, a look on her face as if she were hearing her own words for the first time. "I have nothing," she repeated—softly, painfully. "Not even my pride. Not in this place." Her eyes met his again, wide and beseeching as a child's. "You see, Billy? You see why I need to go home?"

His anger left him as swiftly as it had come. He felt hollowed out, as if he'd sicked up some illness or poison he hadn't known he was carrying. Later, he might find a name for it. Or not. Right now, it didn't matter.

His gaze drifted to Dorrie's hands, still wrapped around the cell bars. Lightly, he brushed her fingers with his own. Olive-tan and white, a contrast he'd spent the better part of his life trying to forget.

"Goodbye, Dorrie," he murmured, and turned away.

He half expected a last call from her as he left, but none came.

 os

"So," Josiah said.

He and Will sat in the study, the room lit by a single lamp turned low and the fire on the hearth. In its orange glow, Will could just make out the corner of Josiah's desk, the armchair where his uncle sat, the small round table that normally held a decanter of Irish whiskey. The decanter had been moved. In its place was a thick stack of papers bound with string.

Will cradled his whiskey glass and stared into the fire. "It was so...
strange. Seeing Ada, and then Dorrie..." He sipped, savoring the burn
of liquor on his tongue. "Both my kin, though the Whittiers never
acknowledged it. Dorrie and Tom were the daughter and son of the
house, Ada and I were slaves, and that was all there was to it. And yet
everybody knew. Everybody knew, nobody said. That was how things
were. How they had to be, I guess, for the whole rotten system to work
at all."

"But you got out of it," Josiah said. "Even before we fought the war
that kicked slavery to pieces. You got out and built a life for yourself."

"And it cost me. More than I understood at the time. More than
I still understand."

Josiah stared into the fire. "I'd ease that cost if I could."

"I know." The words came out in a whisper. "But as Ada said...I made
my choice long ago." His gaze drifted to the papers. Ben Champion's war
memoir, stolen on the night of his murder and now—finally—in Will's
hands. "I can't be trapped by the past anymore. Or by the fear of it."

He tossed back the rest of his whiskey and stood. Two steps took
him to the table, where he undid the string and grabbed a handful of
paper sheets.

Josiah rose as well and took a few sheets of his own. Together, page
by page, they fed the memoir to the flames.

FIFTY-FOUR

May 11, 1872

The music reached Rivka from down the street—a wild, sweet blending of violin and penny whistle, accordion, and drum. And underneath it all a strange wailing drone, like no sound she'd ever heard. It caught her deep inside, made her think of faraway places and lost dreams. Things never had, yet longed for nonetheless.

Smiling people passed her on the boardwalk—men and women together, old and young and in-between. All in their best clothes, going toward the building up ahead—a large hall built of pine board, two stories tall. Warm light spilled over the boardwalk from a row of glass windows, and from the double doors that opened and shut as people went in. The women wore their hair uncovered, and laughed and joked with the men as well as with each other. Rivka caught the lilt of brogues and scattered phrases of what she guessed was the Irish language. She wondered if Hanley spoke it, or understood a word.

The thought of him made her steps slow. Passersby flowed around her, paying her no more heed than a river to a small rock in its midst. She'd wanted to say yes when he invited her here—wanted it so badly, it frightened her. She couldn't even remember what she'd stammered out after *No.* He had flushed bright red, as if blaming himself for her response. As if, merely by asking her, he had committed some offense.

She'd wanted to explain, but hadn't known how. Putting it into words would make it real, something she could no longer pretend would never happen. Moishe Zalman meant to speak to Aaron about her as soon as Aaron was well enough. He meant to ask for her hand. She knew it from what he'd started to say outside the tailor shop almost two weeks earlier. He was a good man with an excellent living, who wanted to marry her, despite her age and reputation for headstrong eccentricity. Also despite his mother's certain disapproval. What more could a girl ask for?

More, she'd thought that day after leaving the tailor shop. What *more* was, she hadn't fully realized. Not until that terrible night by the railway tracks, and then days later when Hanley asked her to this dance, and she heard in his voice how much it mattered to him.

So now here she was, driven by a mad impulse she would surely later regret. She wanted to see Hanley's world, be with him in it for just a few hours. Find out what it was like. What *he* was like when he was just himself and not a detective on a case. Find out if she was right about the way he'd held her that night, and why he'd asked her here in the first place.

How would he react when he saw her? Anxiety made her stomach tighten. He would think her flighty, unable to stick to a decision. He would turn that same bright red and be unable to look her in the eye. Or maybe he would be glad to see her. Surprised, but glad. She imagined him smiling down at her, eyes warm and bright, and felt her cheeks flush. This was wrong. She shouldn't be here, shouldn't be thinking of him this way. A jolt of defiance made her pick up her pace. She was here now. Why go back to Market Street without at least a glimpse of what she'd come for?

The music briefly rose in volume as the door to the hall opened. Someone was playing a fiddle, lively runs as clear and light as a spring wind. The sound got into her feet, drew her closer to its source. A young couple passed her, the girl Rivka's age, the man scarcely older. The girl's green dress set off her coppery hair. She turned toward her companion, laughing at something he said, and Rivka felt drawn to the sparkle in her eyes.

The fiddle was racing now between low notes and high. The young man went in, but the girl lingered at the door. She caught Rivka's gaze and nodded toward the gaiety within. "Come on, then," she said, with a hint of a lilt. "You'll not want to miss any more of the dancing. They're nearly through the first set."

Rivka nodded shy thanks and followed her inside. The girl gave her a friendly nod, then hurried to catch up with her companion.

The hall was crowded, noisy, hot. People stood in clumps around the edges of the huge room. Others danced in the wide-open middle, trousered legs and skirts flying as they whirled each other in circles and spirals. Men and women danced together, clasping hands, sometimes snaking an arm around each other's waists. The sight was shocking, yet Rivka envied them. They were so free with each other, so easy with smiles and laughter and touch. Over it all rose the music—violin and penny whistle and drum—giving voice to the joy of the moment. Rivka felt it deep inside—the impulse to move, to *be* that fierce, wild gladness.

A group nearby moved aside to make room for a pair of dancers, and Rivka got her first clear glimpse of the musicians. They stood on a dais at the front of the room—the drummer white-haired and bent, the whistle player middle-aged with untidy curling hair and a neat mustache. And Hanley, fiddle on his shoulder, playing with his eyes shut as he coaxed out the sound that made her feet twitch and her heart beat faster.

The tune rose to a crescendo, then struck a final chord and died away. The dancers halted. Applause surged around the room. Voices called out, "Rose of Tralee!" "Molly Malone's Jig!" "No, no, let's have a slow one. Let folk catch their breaths…" Hanley and his fellow musicians grinned at each other and held a quick conference. Then the whistle player sat on a nearby stool, pulled a handkerchief from his pocket and mopped his forehead. The drummer carefully laid down his instrument and left the dais. Hanley, the only one still standing, stepped forward. "There's a thing I'd like to play," he said, pitching his voice to carry over the crowd. He raised the fiddle to his shoulder again and set the bow to the strings.

The slow, sweet tune had a wistful beauty that brought a lump to Rivka's throat. It reminded her of lullabies her mother had sung, songs she knew that held the same blend of sorrow and joy. She let it carry her along, forgetting the crowd of strangers, the over-warm room, her own doubts about what she was doing here. For the moment, there was only the music and the man who made it. He played with his whole body, leaning into the sound as if it held him upright.

Too soon, it ended. Hanley drew out the last note, as if he too wanted to keep it going. In the brief silence just before the hushed applause, he lowered his fiddle and took a bow. "I'll be needing a drink now," he said, as the clapping died away. He went to the back of the dais and gently laid his instrument in an open case, then closed it and stepped onto the dance floor.

She made no decision to move, simply found herself heading toward him. They met in a small clear space, temporarily created by an elderly man escorting his wife toward a laden refreshment table. Hanley looked stunned at the sight of her. "You're here," he said, as if he needed the words in order to believe his eyes. A smile lit his face. "I didn't think you'd come."

"I didn't, either." *What a stupid thing to say,* she thought, but then realized it didn't matter. Nothing mattered except how happy he looked to see her.

"I don't..." He glanced toward the refreshment table. "I don't know what I can offer you. I know you have rules about eating and drinking... do you want anything? There's water, anyway..."

She couldn't help laughing. "Water would be fine." Food and drink were the last things on her mind. She just wanted to keep looking at him, talking with him about things that had nothing to do with murder or danger. "I didn't know you played."

He fetched each of them a cup of water and handed hers over. "Mam traded lessons for shirts and mending when I was younger. The fiddle was my da's." A shadow crossed his face. "It's all I've ever had of him. That and a few hazy memories."

"I'm sorry," she said.

He sipped and gave her a crooked grin. "Don't be. It was years ago."

A thread of music crept through the air—guitar and accordion this time, along with the drum and penny whistle, tuning up. She drank a little, welcoming the coolness as the water slid down her throat, then nodded toward the dais. "Should you be up there?"

He shook his head and downed half his water. "We give each other breaks on sets. This is mine." He listened a moment, then set his cup down and gave her a sidelong look. He sounded almost shy when he spoke. "Would you care to dance?"

She should say no. She couldn't join these free and easy couples, who thought no more of holding hands and pressing close than she might of taking a walk next door. If Tanta Hannah or Onkl Jacob knew of it, they would be scandalized. But they wouldn't know. And what if they did? She was twenty-four, with her own home and her own mind. She could make it up for herself. A brief thought of Moishe unsettled her, but she pushed it away. He wasn't here, and wouldn't know either.

"I'd love to," she said, then faltered. "But I don't know how."

He looked delighted. "I'll show you. Nobody'll care whether you know what you're doing, anyway." He held out a hand and she took it. His callused palm felt warm. Gently, he guided them toward an open space on the dance floor. "Mainly, it's a matter of letting the music do what it wants with you. Let the rhythm take over, and keep hold of me." And then the tune started, and there was no time for anything but the heart-pounding music that got inside her and wouldn't let go; the warmth and strength of Hanley's grip; his smiling face, the hair that kept falling over his smoky blue eyes that never left hers. She wanted to reach out and sweep the hair aside, cup his face in her hands, keep dancing with him forever.

She was sweating and breathless, falling over her own feet and laughing along with him whenever he caught her. At some point amid the whirl she felt her kerchief slide to her shoulders. She didn't pull it back up, didn't care that her head was uncovered in public. All she cared about was the joy of the dance.

FIFTY-FIVE

Hanley never wanted the evening to end. He'd always loved ceilidh dances, but this one had magic in it, all because of her. He still couldn't believe she'd come, couldn't completely shake the feeling this was some kind of dream conjured up because he wanted it so badly. Fey, Mam would have called it. The thought of his mother sobered him, but only for a second. Who he danced with at a ceilidh, and how he felt about it, was his business. A sharper pang caught him as he wondered what Rivka might face from her family and neighbors. An evening at a dance hall, alone with an unmarried man, and a Christian at that. There were chaperones aplenty, of course, but would that be good enough? How much trouble had she let herself in for?

He glanced back at her as he closed his fiddle case. She was leaning against the wall by the refreshment table, chatting with Kate. He'd forgotten they'd met briefly a few months back, when Rivka came to the boardinghouse where he lived with evidence that helped clinch the case against the men who murdered her father. She and Kate looked to be getting on. Rivka seemed relaxed, posture easy and smile bright. He hefted the fiddle case and told himself not to worry. Rivka was a grown woman with her own mind and judgment. If tonight's escapade would put her reputation at stake, surely she wouldn't have chanced it.

"Gerry said he'd walk me home," Kate told him as he came up to them. "So I'll not be needing you, Frank. You can do as you like. Good night, Rivka." With a mischievous grin, she slipped away from them toward her beau, who was heading their way across the floor.

He watched her go, both amused and irritated by her teasing. Then he turned to Rivka. "May I see you home?"

ɔჳ

The horsecar dropped them at the corner. Rivka hadn't said much on the trip, but the glow never left her face. When he offered a hand to help her down, she took it and let her own linger in his. They'd gone most of the block down Market Street before she slipped her hand away.

The streets were near empty now, but Hanley slowed from habit as they approached the intersection. "That song you played," Rivka said, glancing both ways at the curb. "The slow one…just you, all alone. It was beautiful."

"It's an old favorite. I could play it a hundred times and never tire of it." He guided her across the street, a hand at her elbow.

"What was it?" she asked softly.

He debated whether to answer. She would know what it meant if he told her its name, and why he'd played it. He felt balanced on a knife-edge, as if his entire life rested on what reply he gave. If he gave one at all.

They were nearly at her house. The windows were dark, everyone inside presumably asleep. The wind ruffled his hair, toyed with the end of her kerchief. She'd nearly lost it during the dance, but that had been just one more thing to laugh about together. The moonlight brought out every line of her face—the generous mouth, the curve of her cheekbones, her wide-spaced eyes.

He stopped and turned to face her. "'If Ever You Were Mine.'" A brief pause, and then he went on. "I was thinking of you."

She moved then, so quickly he'd no time to respond. A rustle of her skirt, the sweet scent of her breath, soft lips brushing his. Then her footsteps, light and quick, going away toward her front door. And a sense of absence where she'd been, the warmth of her giving way to the cool spring night.

ACKNOWLEDGMENTS

As always, I am indebted to many people in the creation of this book. To my publisher Emily Victorson at Allium Press of Chicago, I owe boundless thanks for editorial comments and questions that were (as usual) dead-on. My writers' group, the Red Herrings, put earlier drafts of this work through the wringer—Libby, Michael, Jerry, David, and Irene, I don't have enough words to say how much I value your collective wisdom. This book rocks because of you.

Thanks also to my husband Steve, and to my best friend ever, Laura Fogelson, for bucking me up when "impostor syndrome" nearly derailed me during major revisions. Steve read the whole third draft and offered intelligent commentary, while reminding me that *yes I can too* write a novel, and talking with Laura helped me remember why I wanted to write this story in the first place. I owe you both copious amounts of homemade cookies and big bottles of wine.

Attorney Joel Androphy, whom I found through online research into the False Claims Act, gave me the rundown on how the act worked.

Finally, I want to thank every reader of the first Hanley-Rivka mystery, *Shall We Not Revenge*—especially the many who have since asked me, "Are Hanley and Rivka getting together?" They aren't there yet, but *For You Were Strangers* brings them closer. And bless each one of you who bought the first book, or asked your local library for it, or recommended it to a friend. Series readers keep a series going, and I hope this one will be around for a while to come.

HISTORICAL NOTE

Although *For You Were Strangers* takes place in 1872, seven years after Lee's surrender at Appomattox, the events of the novel are strongly influenced by the Civil War. What led up to it, stemmed from it, and occurred in its aftermath all prove pivotal in the lives of the major characters, and ultimately shape the novel's outcome.

Chicago during the Civil War was in many ways a contradiction. A Union stronghold and Republican bastion, with an active abolitionist community dating back to 1838, it was also a magnet for "peace Democrats" and other pro-Southern Copperheads, not all of whom were content to vote for Democratic political candidates or write letters to the editor calling for a swift end to "Mr. Lincoln's war." A thriving commercial center even in 1860, Chicago nearly tripled in size during the war years, and its railroads became a vital supply link for the nation, as well as for the Union army. This burgeoning metropolis was also home to Camp Douglas, a stretch of open land outside the city limits where Confederate prisoners of war were detained. Poorly fed and housed, prone to illness from inadequate sanitation, and often desperate over their lot, the prisoners made a ripe target for conspirators who saw in them a potential dagger pointed at the Union's heart.

The Chicago Conspiracy—or the Northwest Conspiracy, as it is better known—appears in current history books as a half-baked attempt by grandiose fools to conquer a city using untrained recruits and a ragged army of sick and hungry POWs, with not enough guns and no planning worth the name. The conspiracy was called off twice before its final, failed launch, mainly because the ringleaders couldn't gather the necessary weapons or manpower by the chosen date. In its day, however, the Chicago Conspiracy was every bit as shocking to the city's residents as any modern-day terrorist plot that never quite happened: José Padilla's alleged "dirty bomb," the American Airlines shoe bomber, and the Christmas Day underwear bomber, to name a few. When the Chicago police burst into "peace Democrat" Charles Walsh's barn in November of 1864 and uncovered a cache of rifles meant to arm the Camp Douglas prisoners, and that same day apprehended several "rough vagabonds and criminals" as they converged on the city, the average Chicagoan read accounts of these events and thanked God that a takeover by the Confederate enemy had been so narrowly averted.

Had the conspiracy succeeded, it might have changed the course of the war. Making the city the capital of a "Northwest Confederacy" would have deprived the Union of Chicago's rail and water transport, a significant strategic blow. It is against this backdrop that Frank Hanley runs the villains Lucas Errol and Clement Berwick to earth. The source of the rifles hidden in Walsh's barn is unknown to history, but offered a perfect vehicle for raising Hanley's ongoing feud with his corrupt superior, Captain Michael Hickey, to a new and deadlier level.

Sources conflict as to whether the Order of American Knights existed, including at least one exposé written just after the end of the Civil War. They are sometimes mentioned as an offshoot of the Sons of Liberty or the Knights of the Golden Circle, who themselves were the more "action-oriented" Copperhead factions. Most Copperheads were Democrats who merely wanted the war to end and couldn't see what all the fuss over slavery was about. Sue for peace, muzzle the abolitionist radicals, and the South would eventually rejoin the Union. Others actively supported Southern independence and worked toward the planter elites' dream of a worldwide slave empire extending from the Confederacy to Cuba and South America. The Sons of Liberty, Knights of the Golden Circle, and Order of American Knights fell into this latter camp, prepared to resort to violence to achieve their aims.

The city's Democratic voters included many of Chicago's Irish, who liked the party's emphasis on "the common man" over the business elites. Clinging to the bottom rungs of the American socio-economic ladder, the Irish saw blacks as direct competitors for jobs and survival. Consequently, racism was deeply embedded in the Irish-American community—though any personal loathing for "the Negro" didn't stop young Irishmen from enlisting in droves to fight for the Union, eager to prove their patriotism to a skeptical adopted country. There were exceptions to the general Irish racism, and I have chosen to make Hanley one. Keenly aware of prejudice against his own group, he has the intelligence and insight to recognize and deplore it against others, though he is not completely free from the baggage of his times.

The picture is more complex for the Jewish community. The largely assimilated Reform Jews contained their share of abolitionists, and strongly supported the Union war effort out of patriotism as well. The Concordia Guards, Aaron Kelmansky's company in *For You Were Strangers*, was raised by the congregation of Kehilath Anshe Ma'ariv, which took up a collection to equip the Guards in 1862. Orthodox Jews were more divided, with some pointing to the Hebrew Scriptures to justify slavery, while others felt uneasy with an American slave system so clearly different from that of the Scriptures in its race-based injustice and brutality. In general, Orthodox Jews preferred to avoid the issue altogether. They had learned hard lessons in Europe about sticking their necks out, and getting involved in a squabble among Christians over slavery was the last thing many of them wanted. Aaron's choice to run off to war happens in this context, and launches him on a journey that takes him farther from home than he ever expected. His return brings up difficult questions—who belongs, who doesn't, and how much risk must one take for a stranger in one's midst?

Kinship and identity are likewise central to Will Rushton's story, and to Dorrie Whittier's. Will has reinvented himself as a white man, but in the end can't escape a reckoning with his past. His having white half siblings was not unusual in antebellum plantation society. More than a few wealthy white slave owners sexually exploited their female slaves and fathered mulatto children. It was, as Will tells Josiah, something everybody knew but nobody talked about. Kin ties ran deep in Southern society, as did an absolute conviction that "the Negro" must be kept down in order for white people to know their own worth. In such a milieu, for whites to admit blood kinship with blacks was literally inconceivable. That Dorrie eventually manages this is an indication of how much her life has turned upside down because of the war, and how desperate she is in its aftermath to reclaim something of what she has lost—family, home, her identity as a privileged white woman. Lacking Will's inner resources, she can't reinvent herself. She can only strike out in anger and destroy.

⋈

The Chicago History Museum was an invaluable source of information on Chicago in the year after the Great Fire, and on the city's vital role in the Civil War. Authors whose works I consulted while researching *For You Were Strangers* are too numerous to mention individually, but a few merit special thanks. Chandra Manning's *What This Cruel War Was Over* provided the novel's thematic heart, especially her depiction of how pathologically deep was the need in antebellum Southern culture for "the Negro" to be a lesser creature so whites could feel worthy. Professor Manning's excellent book relies heavily on primary source material, and should be mandatory reading for anyone who wants to understand the damage racism does to everyone touched by it—including those who benefit from it. Eric Foner's *Forever Free* covers Reconstruction with a wealth of detail and shows both the promise and the tragedy of the too brief era in which another America might have been possible. Tom Campbell's *Fighting Slavery in Chicago*—a lucky find at a downtown Barnes & Noble—gave me an excellent overview of the city's abolitionist history, a fascinating part of Chicago's past.

The Freedmen's Bureau Online (http://freedmensbureau.com/) includes links to Reconstruction-era records of efforts to help freed slaves and protect them against what were termed "outrages" from disaffected whites: assault, arson, and murder, crimes that were all too common in the postwar South.

The historical archive service Footnote.com was a bountiful source of period news articles about Union loyalists in Confederate territory, both men and women, who often took great personal risks to aid Union troops any way they could.

The Chicago Crime Scenes blog (http://chicagocrimescenes.blogspot. com/) provided portraits of famous madams like "Gentle Annie" Stafford and Carrie Watson, and the high- and low-class bordellos that were often the site of all kinds of dirty dealing. Though there is no historical proof that the Chicago Conspiracy was hatched in one of these establishments, it certainly could have been.

Readers interested in exploring the themes and background of this novel can find excellent works in the following bibliography, which includes some, but not all, of the sources I consulted in writing this book.

ⳠⳠ

Budiansky, Stephen. *The Bloody Shirt: Terror After the Civil War.* Viking Adult, 2008.

Campbell, Tom. *Fighting Slavery in Chicago.* Ampersand, Inc., 2009.

Chamberlin, Taylor M. *Between Reb and Yank: A Civil War History of Loudoun County, Virginia.* McFarland, 2011.

Cutler, Irving. *The Jews of Chicago.* University of Illinois Press, 1996.

Edgerton, Douglas. *The Wars of Reconstruction: The Brief, Violent History of America's Most Progressive Era.* Bloomsbury Press, 2014.

Foner, Eric. *Forever Free: The Story of Emancipation and Reconstruction.* Vintage Books, November 2006.

Lankford, Nelson. *Richmond Burning: The Last Days of the Confederate Capital.* Penguin Books, 2003.

Manning, Chandra. *What This Cruel War Was Over: Soldiers, Slavery and the Civil War.* Vintage Books, 2008.

Wert, Jeffry D. *Mosby's Rangers: The True Adventures of the Most Famous Command of the Civil War.* Simon & Schuster, 1990.

Ayer, I. Winslow. *The Great North-Western Conspiracy in All Its Startling Details.* [available online: http://www.authorama.com/north-western-conspiracy-1.html]

Chicagology: http://chicagology.com/

Order of American Knights (from *The Civil War in Missouri* website): http://civilwarmo.org/educators/resources/info-sheets/order-american-knights

GLOSSARY

Alav ha-shalom (Hebrew) May he rest in peace

Bar mitzvah (Hebrew) "Son of the commandment;" refers to the Jewish ceremony commonly held at the thirteenth birthday, when a boy assumes adult religious obligations. In Hanley and Rivka's time, the ceremony was held only for boys. Modern-day Jews celebrate *bat mitzvah* for girls as well.

Baruch Hashem (Hebrew) "Blessed is the Name" ("the Name" meaning God)

Bluecoats Confederate slang term for Union soldiers during the Civil War, based on their blue uniforms

Boxty (Irish Gaelic) A fried mashed-potato cake with onions

Bully boys Thugs, equivalent to contemporary "leg-breakers" or "muscle"

Bunco-steerer Con man, often a card sharp; a bunco-steerer frequently posed as a well-dressed gambler "down on his luck," or an "honest country farmer" new to the big city.

Cabbage-eater Slang term for German-Americans

Ceilidh (Irish Gaelic) A typically Irish celebration involving music and dancing

Cracksman A thief who specializes in picking locks and/or breaking into safes

Fraylin (Yiddish) Miss; similar to the German "Fraulein"

Gabbai (Hebrew) Principal caretaker of the synagogue and organizer of worship services; an important position in the community

Gambling hell Slang term for any establishment principally devoted to games of chance

Gold eagle US gold coin, worth $10 in Hanley and Rivka's time

Goy/goyische (Yiddish) Literally "nation/of the nations;" outsider/ non-Jew

Hashem (Hebrew) Literally "the Name," meaning the name of God (which observant Jews consider too sacred to utter or write)

Jilt Prostitute working with a sneak thief to rob customers

Jilter Sneak thief working with a prostitute to rob customers

Kashruth (Hebrew) Kosher; refers to Jewish dietary laws and food or drink that conforms to them

Kippah (Hebrew) Small skullcap worn by observant Jewish men and boys

Mark Person targeted/duped by a con man, card sharp or bunco-steerer

Mi shebeirach (Hebrew) A prayer for healing

Minyan (Hebrew) A gathering for prayer, daily or weekly, with at least ten Jewish adults who have undergone bar mitzvah; in Hanley and Rivka's time, this would have meant adult men

Panel house Bordello with false interior walls or "panels," that slide back to let thieves rob customers who are otherwise engaged

Rebbe (Yiddish) Rabbi

Shabbos (Yiddish) The Sabbath, which in Judaism falls on Saturday rather than Sunday. The spelling used in this book reflects the Yiddish pronunciation Rivka's community would have used

Shehecheyanu (Hebrew) Prayer of thanksgiving to God for the blessing of life; often recited daily by observant Jews

Shneim asar chodesh (Hebrew) The full year of mourning after a parent dies

Shalom aleichem (Yiddish) Literally "peace be upon you;" used as a greeting

Shul (Hebrew) Literally "school;" refers to a synagogue

Ten-cent/ten-centers Gamblers and bar patrons without much money; equivalent to modern-day "two-bit" or "low-rent"

Two bits/four bits Slang for money; twenty-five cents and fifty cents, respectively

Tsuris (Yiddish) Trouble

ALSO PUBLISHED BY
ALLIUM PRESS OF CHICAGO

Visit our website for more information:
www.alliumpress.com

Shall We Not Revenge
D. M. Pirrone

In the harsh early winter months of 1872, while Chicago is still smoldering from the Great Fire, Irish Catholic detective Frank Hanley is assigned the case of a murdered Orthodox Jewish rabbi. His investigation proves difficult when the neighborhood's Yiddish-speaking residents are reluctant to talk. But when the rabbi's headstrong daughter, Rivka, offers to help Hanley find her father's killer, the detective receives much more than the break he was looking for. Their pursuit of the truth draws Rivka and Hanley closer together and leads them to a relief organization run by the city's wealthy movers and shakers. Along the way, they uncover a web of political corruption, crooked cops, and well-buried ties to two Irish thugs from Hanley's checkered past. Even after he is kicked off the case Hanley refuses to quit. With a personal vendetta to settle for an innocent life lost, he is determined to expose a complicated criminal scheme, not only for his own sake, but for Rivka's as well.

Beautiful Dreamer
Joan Naper

Chicago in 1900 is bursting with opportunity, and Kitty Coakley is determined to make the most of it. The youngest of seven children born to Irish immigrants, she has little interest in becoming simply a housewife. Inspired by her entrepreneurial Aunt Mabel, who runs a millinery boutique at Marshall Field's, Kitty aspires to become an independent, modern woman. After her music teacher dashes her hopes of becoming a professional singer, she refuses to give up her dreams of a career. But when she is courted by not one, but two young men, her resolve is tested. Irish-Catholic Brian is familiar and has the approval of her traditional, working-class family. But wealthy, Protestant Henry, who is a young architect in Daniel Burnham's office, provides an entrée for Kitty into another, more exciting world. Will she sacrifice her ambitions and choose a life with one of these men?

◆

Company Orders
David J. Walker

Even a good man may feel driven to sign on with the devil. Paul Clark is a Catholic priest who's been on the fast track to becoming a bishop. But he suddenly faces a heart-wrenching problem, when choices he made as a young man come roaring back into his life. A mysterious woman, who claims to be with "an agency of the federal government," offers to solve his problem. But there's a price to pay—Father Clark must undertake some very un-priestly actions. An attack in a Chicago alley…a daring escape from a Mexican jail…and a fight to the death in a Guyanese jungle…all these, and more, must be survived in order to protect someone he loves. This priest is about to learn how much easier it is to preach love than to live it.

Set the Night on Fire
Libby Fischer Hellmann

Someone is trying to kill Lila Hilliard. During the Christmas holidays she returns from running errands to find her family home in flames, her father and brother trapped inside. Later, she is attacked by a mysterious man on a motorcycle. . . and the threats don't end there. As Lila desperately tries to piece together who is after her and why, she uncovers information about her father's past in Chicago during the volatile days of the late 1960s . . . information he never shared with her, but now threatens to destroy her. Part thriller, part historical novel, and part love story, *Set the Night on Fire* paints an unforgettable portrait of Chicago during a turbulent time: the riots at the Democratic Convention . . . the struggle for power between the Black Panthers and SDS . . . and a group of young idealists who tried to change the world.

◆

A Bitter Veil
Libby Fischer Hellmann

It all began with a line of Persian poetry . . . Anna and Nouri, both studying in Chicago, fall in love despite their very different backgrounds. Anna, who has never been close to her parents, is more than happy to return with Nouri to his native Iran, to be embraced by his wealthy family. Beginning their married life together in 1978, their world is abruptly turned upside down by the overthrow of the Shah and the rise of the Islamic Republic. Under the Ayatollah Khomeini and the Republican Guard, life becomes increasingly restricted and Anna must learn to exist in a transformed world, where none of the familiar Western rules apply. Random arrests and torture become the norm, women are required to wear hijab, and Anna discovers that she is no longer free to leave the country. As events reach a fevered pitch, Anna realizes that nothing is as she thought, and no one can be trusted. . .not even her husband.

Her Mother's Secret
Barbara Garland Polikoff

Fifteen-year-old Sarah, the daughter of Jewish immigrants, wants nothing more than to become an artist. But as she spreads her wings she must come to terms with the secrets that her family is only beginning to share with her. Replete with historical details that vividly evoke the Chicago of the 1890s, this moving coming-of-age story is set against the backdrop of a vibrant, turbulent city. Sarah moves between two very different worlds—the colorful immigrant neighborhood surrounding Hull House and the sophisticated, elegant World's Columbian Exposition. This novel eloquently captures the struggles of a young girl as she experiences the timeless emotions of friendship, family turmoil, loss…and first love.

A companion guide to *Her Mother's Secret*
is available at www.alliumpress.com. In the guide you will find
photographs of places mentioned in the novel, along with discussion
questions, a list of read-alikes, and resources for further exploration of
Sarah's time and place.

THE EMILY CABOT MYSTERIES
Frances McNamara

Death at the Fair

The 1893 World's Columbian Exposition provides a vibrant backdrop for the first book in the series. Emily Cabot, one of the first women graduate students at the University of Chicago, is eager to prove herself in the emerging field of sociology. While she is busy exploring the Exposition with her family and friends, her colleague, Dr. Stephen Chapman, is accused of murder. Emily sets out to search for the truth behind the crime, but is thwarted by the gamblers, thieves, and corrupt politicians who are ever-present in Chicago. A lynching that occurred in the dead man's past leads Emily to seek the assistance of the black activist Ida B. Wells.

◆

Death at Hull House

After Emily Cabot is expelled from the University of Chicago, she finds work at Hull House, the famous settlement established by Jane Addams. There she quickly becomes involved in the political and social problems of the immigrant community. But, when a man who works for a sweatshop owner is murdered in the Hull House parlor, Emily must determine whether one of her colleagues is responsible, or whether the real reason for the murder is revenge for a past tragedy in her own family. As a smallpox epidemic spreads through the impoverished west side of Chicago, the very existence of the settlement is threatened and Emily finds herself in jeopardy from both the deadly disease and a killer.

◆

Death at Pullman

A model town at war with itself . . . George Pullman created an ideal community for his railroad car workers, complete with every amenity they could want or need. But when hard economic times hit in 1894, lay-offs follow and the workers can no longer pay their rent or buy food at the company store. Starving and desperate, they turn against their once benevolent employer.

Emily Cabot and her friend Dr. Stephen Chapman bring much needed food and medical supplies to the town, hoping they can meet the immediate needs of the workers and keep them from resorting to violence. But when one young worker—suspected of being a spy—is murdered, and a bomb plot comes to light, Emily must race to discover the truth behind a tangled web of family and company alliances.

◆

Death at Woods Hole

Exhausted after the tumult of the Pullman Strike of 1894, Emily Cabot is looking forward to a restful summer visit to Cape Cod. She has plans to collect "beasties" for the Marine Biological Laboratory, alongside other visiting scientists from the University of Chicago. She also hopes to enjoy romantic clambakes with Dr. Stephen Chapman, although they must keep an important secret from their friends. But her summer takes a dramatic turn when she finds a dead man floating in a fish tank. In order to solve his murder she must first deal with dueling scientists, a testy local sheriff, the theft of a fortune, and uncooperative weather.

◆

Death at Chinatown

In the summer of 1896, amateur sleuth Emily Cabot meets two young Chinese women who have recently received medical degrees. She is inspired to make an important decision about her own life when she learns about the difficult choices they have made in order to pursue their careers. When one of the women is accused of poisoning a Chinese herbalist, Emily once again finds herself in the midst of a murder investigation. But, before the case can be solved, she must first settle a serious quarrel with her husband, help quell a political uprising, and overcome threats against her family. Timeless issues, such as restrictions on immigration, the conflict between Western and Eastern medicine, and women's struggle to balance family and work, are woven seamlessly throughout this mystery set in Chicago's original Chinatown.

Bright and Yellow, Hard and Cold
Tim Chapman

The search for elusive goals consumes three men…

McKinney, a forensic scientist, struggles with his deep, personal need to find the truth behind the evidence he investigates, even while the system shuts him out. Can he get justice for a wrongfully accused man while juggling life with a new girlfriend and a precocious teenage daughter?

Delroy gives up the hard-scrabble life on his family's Kentucky farm and ventures to the rough-and-tumble world of 1930s Chicago. Unable to find work, he reluctantly throws his hat in with the bank-robbing gangsters Alvin Karpis and Freddie Barker. Can he provide for his fiery young wife without risking his own life?

Gilbert is obsessed with the search for a cache of gold, hidden for nearly eighty years. As his hunt escalates he finds himself willing to use ever more extreme measures to attain his goal…including kidnapping, torture, and murder. Can he find the one person still left who will lead him to the glittering treasure? And will the trail of corpses he leaves behind include McKinney?

Part contemporary thriller, part historical novel, and part love story, *Bright and Yellow, Hard and Cold* masterfully weaves a tale of conflicted scientific ethics, economic hardship, and criminal frenzy, tempered with the redemption of family love.

Honor Above All
J. Bard-Collins

Pinkerton agent Garrett Lyons arrives in Chicago in 1882, close on the trail of the person who murdered his partner. He encounters a vibrant city that is striving ever upwards, full of plans to construct new buildings that will "scrape the sky." In his quest for the truth Garrett stumbles across a complex plot involving counterfeit government bonds, fierce architectural competition, and painful reminders of his military past. Along the way he seeks the support and companionship of his friends—elegant Charlotte, who runs an upscale poker game for the city's elite, and up-and-coming architect Louis Sullivan. Rich with historical details that bring early 1880s Chicago to life, this novel will appeal equally to mystery fans, history buffs, and architecture enthusiasts.

CPSIA information can be obtained
at www.ICGtesting.com
Printed in the USA
FSOW01n0531090216
16584FS